The
Oracle

ISBN: 979-8-9877835-2-8 (Print)
ISBN: 979-8-9877835-3-5 (epub)

Any references to historical events, real people, or real places are used fictitiously. Names, characters, and places are products of the author's imagination.

Book and cover design: Carol M. Booton

First printing November 2021 Kindle Direct Publishing
Second printing March 2023 IngramSpark

Library of Congress Control Number: 2023903402

Printed on demand by IngramSpark
Published by Crossline Press
Tucson, Arizona, U.S.A.
CrosslinePress.com
info@crosslinepress.com

The
Oracle

Chapter 1

On Monday morning at 9:00 a.m., Pythia set her half-full cup of coffee on her cluttered desk and stood up. She already smelled the methane gas. Her throat itched in anticipation.

"I am going downstairs for a minute," she announced. Her assistant Debra waved a dismissive hand above her half-wall cubicle barricade.

Pythia exited the office into the dingy back hallway that ran the length of the building. She opened a solid metal door, revealing pitted concrete steps descending into darkness. The complex aroma of tar, sulfur, methane, and moldy cardboard assaulted her nose. *That smell.* She inhaled to let the odor settle deep in her lungs. The door swung shut behind her, softened by her backside. Ignoring the nonfunctional light switch, she descended the familiar concrete steps by feel, scuffing her sandals past forty years of dusty client files she stored and ignored.

In ten years, Debra had never ventured into the basement. On her first week on the job, she balked at the top step. "It stinks! What's down there, a gateway to hell?"

The odor was not surprising, given the office was just a block away from the famous La Brea Tar Pits. Every basement in the area reeked of methane gas. Some even had little fountains of tar burbling up through the concrete. On rare occasions, basements exploded.

Pythia visited the office basement almost every Monday. When she needed a boost, she'd sneak away during the week. No one knew those diesel fumes were the sole reason she bought the place in 1973. Pythia didn't explain. No need.

While assistants came and went, the Earth persisted, exhaling its noxious fumes. Some gas burst free to pollute the atmosphere. Some was bottled, pulverized, or smelted into an endless stream of products. The one constant, wherever she lived, whether inhaled from a natural source or sniffed from a metal canister marked *Danger! Do not inhale!* was that smell.

Waving her hand, she found a cord and pulled. Yellow light from a bare 40-watt bulb illuminated a path along the broken floor. She felt around on a shelf for the BIC lighter. After a couple tries, the spark flared. She lit five candles arrayed on a dusty wooden table, shedding weak light on a musty alcove. Every Christmas, someone gave her a candle with some kind of Christian symbol on it, which she accepted with good cheer even though she was not a Christian. These candles tended not to last long but they smelled nice. Her favorite was a pumpkin spice jar from Better Bed & Bath.

She dug in her skirt pocket and pulled out a heart-shaped rock. She polished it with a well-worn handkerchief and placed it among other rocks in a misshapen unglazed clay bowl on the table.

"For you, my Lord, my heart," she whispered, gazing at a framed portrait propped against the concrete wall at the back of the table. Years of dust obscured the image in the painting. She pondered the face, holding her breath, waiting for a connection. Nothing. She tried to remember what he looked like, his curling golden hair, intelligent eyes, and handsome lips. She tried to recall the joy of being his acolyte. Three thousand years, give or take a few centuries, had scraped chasms in her memory.

The candlelight guided her to the tall four-legged stool a few feet from the table. She checked to make sure it sat square over the wide crack in the floor. Wobbles led to painful falls. She hitched up her flowered skirt, settled onto the stool, and tucked her sandals behind the lowest rung. *No way will I be speaking in dactylic hexameters.* She didn't know where the claim to that trait originated. She would be the first to admit she had no facility with poetry. However, sometimes, when her vision was slow in coming, she would raise her arms in the classic Oracle pose she'd seen in old paintings from the nineteenth century. She made sure no one saw her do that, though—it seemed so pretentious.

Clearing her mind, she sucked in a lungful of geothermal fumes. Her stomach lurched and then settled into a familiar clench. Yes, it was still there—the bleached center, the desiccated fount, the weary worn nub of her prescience, somewhere near the shriveled remains of her uterus. *I need to know the future. I cannot stand not knowing.* Head lifted, eyes closed, Apollo's last Oracle hauled in another deep breath, and another. Her head sank onto her chest.

Her consciousness clouded and shredded into tatters. Her last coherent thought was *my assistant thinks I take drugs in the basement.*

A loud scream echoed in a dark cavernous space. Not the basement, somewhere else, a cave? The scream disintegrated into laughter. Light flickered—flames, perhaps lanterns? No, torches, made of dried spruce branches, giving off sweet smoke. Before Pythia could turn, hands grabbed at her clothing, dragging her backwards down stone steps. She kicked and heard giggles. The hands let go. She pulled her hair out of her face, trying to see who chased her. More laughter, echoing off high walls. She dropped to her knees and scrambled away, gathering her . . . peplos? Yes, a long length of coarse fabric restricted her legs. Where was she? *When* was she?

She twisted the fabric and tucked the hem into her leather girdle, peering through thick haze. Where were her comfortable Birkenstocks, her underwire bra, the practical reliable gear of her modern American life? She had forgotten how scratchy, how rough. *When was I ever this slim?* She sat on the tiled steps and waited for her vision to clear. She realized she was not in a cave. Huge marble columns held up a distant ceiling.

Hazy running figures swept past, giggling.

"Come on, lazy donkey!" a familiar voice taunted her.

A wicker basket fell at her feet and spilled red berries across the tiled floor. She reached for one and put it on her tongue. Tart juice burst in her mouth. Ripe currants. She touched the mosaics on the step, marveling at tiny squares of turquoise, viridian, rose, and yellow tile, laid by skilled hands into white mortar. Casting her eyes past the columns, she saw mosaic images of white sheep, green olive trees, pale-skinned gods and goddesses riding chariots across azure skies. Pythia smiled. She knew this place. It was the Temple of Apollo, her home.

"Pythia, come on!" That sweet voice calling across the millennia woke many lifetimes of sorrow.

"Dione," she whispered. "Sister, wait for me. I am coming." She stood, ready to follow the slender figure disappearing behind huge fluted columns.

Torches ensconced along the tiled wall burst into flames, blocking her path. Eerie light flickered around the chamber. Laughter echoed in the distance. Confused, she tried to see past the flames. "Dione!" she cried. "Come back!"

The vision ended before she could take a step. One moment she was backing away from the scorching heat, the next moment she was straddling a wobbly stool in a dark smelly basement. Her chest hitched and heaved as she returned to her body, dragging despair and loneliness with her.

The stench of smoke resolved into a cloying blend of pumpkin spice and black tar, the signature scent of her present.

Sometimes the future unrolled like an old-time movie, flickering, shadowy, filmed by an unknown camera operator at the behest of an unknown director. Characters entered and exited a changing stage. Other times she saw color-drenched snapshots of possibilities, ranged across her mind like a deck of tarot cards and just as ambiguous. She had no control over how the visions appeared or unfurled. Sometimes she was spectator, other times she was participant. Usually, she preferred to be a spectator.

This time, she longed to remain in that sacred space, chasing her sister and their friends across the Temple floor to savor fresh berries, dodging servants in their path before bursting out into heat and light on the hills below Mt. Parnassus.

It was rare for her to revisit the past. Most of her trances sent her forward. *Why am I dreaming of Dione?* Pythia hadn't dreamed of Dione for months, even years.

Images flooded her mind.

She remembered the feel of Dione's hand in hers, pulling her along the dusty trails to the hot springs hidden in secret rock basins. She remembered braiding jasmine and heather into Dione's hair. Memories of Delphi reawakened in her bones. Her sister's face rose in her mind, more clear than usual. Dione's blue-green eyes dominated a beautiful face framed by light-brown hair flowing unbound to her waist. Her lithe figure could always be found leading the cohort of young acolytes, exhorting them to shirk their kitchen duties and run wild on the steep hillsides above the Temple.

Dione was the older sister, the beautiful sister. Before she lost her oracular sense, Pythia's gift had been stronger than Dione's, but she never felt superior. She loved Dione's beauty, strength, and courage. She would give anything to see Dione again.

Pythia sighed. That moment in the Temple happened long ago, one of many similar moments she'd forgotten. Was there a message she could carry forward to her future self? She sorted through the images, searching for meaning. Familiar frustration welled up, flavored with despair that her broken oracular talent had once again left her grasping at nothing.

"Rest easy, my darling sister," she whispered. She smoothed her dusty skirt, marveling at the reliable smoothness and banality of cheap machine-made cotton broadcloth.

She regarded the painting of Apollo. "Do you live, my lord? Or are you withered like an ancient currant berry? Have you mellowed with time or are you still a jealous god?"

Apollo's unreadable eyes regarded her.

It was a remarkable likeness. She found this painting in a thrift store in Oxnard back in the 1980s, some amateur painter's castoff. She wondered how the artist had managed to capture the essence of a myth. His full lips were frozen in paint, one moment from pulling back in a smirk. Yet, in the next moment, his lips could be so generous with praise.

She had worshiped Apollo with childlike faith; after almost three thousand years, that faith was all but dead. She leaned to blow out the candles. The chemical perfumes wafted past, mixing with the vapors emanating from the crack in the floor.

She shook off her melancholy and trudged toward the steps, yanking the cord to turn off the light as she passed. She still grieved the loss of her sister, but she could not bear to think her once-beloved god Apollo might also be gone. She blamed herself. Nothing kills a god quicker than lost faith.

๑

Pythia crossed the hall and entered the office. She paused just inside, inhaling the layered aromas of burned coffee, cheap perfume, printer toner, and body odor. A scratchy song with a heavy beat emanated from behind Debra's barricade. Pythia tolerated Debra's music, along with many other of her assistant's quirks. Music styles came and went, like fashion fads, politicians, celebrities, and assistants. She paid little attention. Modern music could not compare to the simple harps, guitars, and flutes of her childhood.

She surveyed the office, hiding behind the tall four-drawer filing cabinet, which Debra had insisted on painting orange. *When did things become so decrepit?* She noted the shabby square carpet in the waiting area, Debra's solution to disguise the 1970s beige linoleum. Sun-faded visitors' chairs lined the walls in front of the never-used display windows. A wobbly bookshelf in a corner held musty books collected by Debra from thrift stores and yard sales. "These will give us some charm," Debra had said.

Over the years, they had both added little treasures to the shelf—a bronze singing bowl and wooden mallet, an antique picture frame holding a sepia photo of someone's ancestor.

Pythia perused the faded peeling wallpaper. Was it really ten years since they had redecorated? Debra had been so excited about the gold foil accents. Now the whole place reeked of defeat.

Debra made a snorting sound Pythia had come to associate with long-held resentment. "Have a nice nap?" she said from behind her hand, motioning toward Pythia's office with her head. "Your ten o'clock has been waiting fifteen minutes."

Pythia emerged from behind the filing cabinet and peered at Debra over the half-wall. Untidy stacks of unfiled documents flanked the desk space occupied by Debra's massive computer tower and old flat-panel monitor. The flickering screen illuminated Debra's scowl. *It does not take an Oracle to see this whole thing is falling apart.*

"Who might that be?" Pythia asked.

Debra whispered, "It's that S and M freak."

"Ah. Thank you, Ms. Sandhill." Pythia entered her tiny office. "Hello, Ms. Harper." Cindi Harper slouched in the visitor chair, black vinyl spike-heeled boots on the desk, talking on Pythia's phone.

"I'll be there in an hour, and you'd better be waiting," Cindi growled, winking at Pythia.

Pythia sank into her fraying chair and looked at the scuff marks on the soles of Cindi's boots. She pictured those boots grinding into a fat man's groin and winced. Every now and then, her oracular "gift" gave her some images she would rather not have seen.

"You'd better be wearing that dog collar, too, if you know what's good for you."

Cindi made kissing sounds into the phone and slammed down the receiver. She thumped her boots on the floor and rubbed her hands along spandex-covered thighs.

She grinned at Pythia. "You have to show them who is boss, right? Well, you probably wouldn't know. Let me tell you, there is an art to this domination stuff. I'm kind of digging $200 per hour!"

"How is your business plan coming along?" Pythia asked, straightening her phone.

"Great! Look, here's a mockup of our new catalog."

An hour later, Pythia ushered Cindi to the front door.

"Did Ms. Sandhill help you make another appointment?"

Outside on Wilshire, bumper-to-bumper traffic signified the intensification of afternoon rush hour.

"She sure did. That woman is a treasure."

"She certainly is."

Debra had ordered $35 worth of product from Cindi's not-yet-printed catalog. Given Cindi's business history, Pythia wondered if Debra would ever receive her order. *Not my problem.* "Email me if you have any questions about the financial section."

"Thank you, Ms. Apulu. You know, if you ever want to try some of my products, I have some kinky little dildos, might be just your style."

Debra waved something pink and phallic from behind her cubicle wall.

"I'll keep that in mind," Pythia said, nodding. *How could she possibly know my "style"?*

"Well, just because you aren't . . . a spring chicken anymore, pardon me for saying, doesn't mean you can't have some fun once in a while," Cindi grinned. Pythia's gift revealed that Cindi was planning on a tummy tuck in the near future. *Spring chicken, indeed.* Cindi fluffed her halo of bleached hair and bared yellowed teeth at Pythia as she fought with her leopard print bag to see who would make it out the door first. "World domination, here I come!" The door swung closed, jangling the tarnished bell hanging from the ceiling.

Pythia peered between the faded Visa, Discover, and MasterCard stickers and watched the endless flow of traffic as Cindi got into her Volkswagen Beetle. Rush hour seemed to last all day along the Miracle Mile section of Wilshire Blvd. Most of the time she could tune out the sounds of growling engines and honking horns. Later in the evening, when traffic thinned, she would open the windows of her upstairs apartment and revel in the silence. *Is it too early to call it a day?* She felt a familiar twinge behind her left eye. A nap sounded good right now. *Coaching humans is exhausting.*

A rusting hubcap leaned against a parking meter post, like a piece of street art. Without any prompting, the history of the hubcap spooled out in her mind's eye. *It was lost on Monday from Arthur Maler's 1975 Datsun B-210, spinning off his vintage wheel and wobbling to rest against the curb. Some kind stranger—Maury Wilson, to be exact—rescued the hubcap and propped it against the meter, certain that soon its owner would return to retrieve it. And, in fact, Arthur will return next week for lunch at Cheese Louise, see his hubcap, and praise the generosity of the god of his understanding.* Pythia saw all this with oracular clarity, past and present, as if she had seen it in a movie—part of the unpredictable torrent of useless trivia provided by her so-called gift.

Her eyes fell on the office fire extinguisher hanging on the wall near the conference room door. A couple of the fragments from her vision snapped together.

Pythia ripped the extinguisher from the wall and rushed outside. She rapped on Cindi's passenger side window. When Cindi rolled down the window, Pythia thrust the extinguisher onto the passenger seat next to the gargantuan shoulder bag.

"I have a feeling you are going to need this. You know how to work it? Just pull that thing. Okay? All right, be safe." She slapped the roof of the Beetle, producing a hollow thud. Cindi waved. The engine stuttered to life.

Pythia watched as Cindi dove into the stream. Within moments, another driver had swooped in to claim the space.

Reluctant to go back inside, Pythia peered into the windows of the frame shop to the east of her office.

Frank Bristol, the slim red-haired proprietor of I've Been Framed, was hanging some L-square frame samples on the wall while his wife, Helen, helped a woman in lavender pants choose a frame at the long table. He saw Pythia and waved. She waved back.

Turning the other direction, she saw two diners sitting at one of Cheese Louise's two canopied picnic tables, oblivious of the vehicles moving nearby. Louise Romano glided out the door of her café with two menus under her arm and a tray holding two full water glasses. She saw Pythia and nodded her head. Pythia waved.

At the far west end of the block, she saw a handful of fit women in yoga pants carrying yoga mats into Stacy Lander's yoga studio. A class was about to start. Stacy kept inviting Pythia to try a yoga class. Pythia kept declining.

She turned and looked at the façade of her own storefront. Twenty years ago, she had paid a local sign painter to print *Apulu Ltd* in bright red Greek uncials on the stucco wall above the door. The summer sun had beaten the lettering to a pale grayish pink. Was it time for a new sign? Was it time for a new business? *Is my long life finally ending?* She tried to muster some grief and felt only a dusty indifference as she reentered the office. Even the bell sounded exhausted.

"Another one of your feelings?" Debra asked from behind her cubicle wall.

"What? Oh, yes, I guess you could say so," Pythia replied. "How are you coming on the copy for that brochure we talked about?"

"You can see the future, right?"

"Sometimes," Pythia acknowledged.

"Well, look in your crystal ball. Do you see me finishing that brochure?"

Pythia walked to the half-wall and looked over the trailing philodendrons at Debra, who stared at her computer monitor, ignoring Pythia's scrutiny. Debra's pale hair was silvering at her temples. She had a trace of jawline sag. *When had Debra become so cynical? She used to be so . . . What's the word? Optimistic. She used to be eager.* In 2005 Pythia had hired Debra as her assistant straight out of Los Angeles Community College with a freshly minted associate's in business administration. She remembered the day Debra interviewed for the job. She'd worn a short skirt suit she'd made herself from plaid wool, even though it was sweltering outside. Anyone who had the guts to wear wool in summer deserved a job. The young woman had negotiated pay raises every year as she grew into the perfect assistant. Unfortunately, Debra's zeal had evaporated over ten years of boredom and neglect; her enthusiasm peaked around 2010 but she still coerced ridiculous annual raises, which Pythia paid out of guilt.

"How many times do I have to tell you—" Pythia began and then bit her lip, chagrined to find herself falling yet again into Debra's trap.

"I know, I know, you don't have a crystal ball. As your marketing manager, I recommend you get one. I think you'd do better as a fortune-teller than as a coach. People just want to know what's going to happen. They don't want to write a stupid business plan."

"You are right, as usual. Maybe it is time for a makeover."

"Well, let me know what you decide before I do your stupid brochure," Debra said. "Check your calendar, Pythia. You aren't done for the day. You've got Mathison at one and Kahn at two. And that new guy at five. Don't forget to eat something so you don't get a headache."

After two more coaching appointments, Pythia's migraine was in full bloom. She squinted at her desk calendar. She had a two-hour break before her final appointment of the day. She navigated half-blind past Debra's cubicle.

"I am going upstairs."

"Oh, got a migraine? Poor thing," Debra said with no sympathy. "Did you eat any lunch? I warned you."

"Notify me if the place burns down," Pythia growled.

"You bet, Boss."

Pythia trudged along the hallway and up the stairs to the second floor. Familiar pain gnawed behind her eyes. Migraines often followed trips to the basement.

She navigated with squinting eyes past Frank and Helen's apartment door to her own door, which she seldom remembered to lock. She staggered into her living room, sucking in the aromas of sandalwood and currant incense.

A small sitting room occupied the space between the galley kitchen on the left and a tiny bedroom and closet-sized bathroom on the right. Pythia no longer noticed the once-festive red and gold stripe wallpaper, now faded to pinkish gray. She crossed the brown shag rug to the bedroom. Groaning, she sank onto her worn bedspread and pulled a pillow over her head.

When Pythia stirred, an orange sun hung over the smoggy Los Angeles skyline, silhouetting rows of Mexican fan palms.

A moment after she sat up, the speaker on the wall by the bed buzzed twice. Time for her 5:00 p.m. appointment. She hauled herself upright, smoothed her skirt, combed her hair, and headed down to the office.

Debra was leaning back in her chair, looking tired. Her desk was tidy. Her red leather purse sat by the computer. She squinted at Pythia. "You look somewhat better."

"Thank you. And thank you for buzzing me. Am I late?"

"The client just called to say he'll be here in five minutes. I'll give him the paperwork and make sure he's not an axe murderer and then I'm going home."

Pythia went into her office. Her desk looked unusually clean.

"Did she do some filing?" she mused.

"I can hear you."

"Am I going to be asking you to unfile things later?"

"I don't know, are you?"

Pythia sighed.

The bell over the front door jangled.

"Well, hello! You must be Mr. Haven," Debra said in a sultry voice Pythia had not heard before. "I'm Debra Sandhill, Ms. Apulu's colleague. Please come in."

Colleague, indeed. Pythia leaned to the side to peer at the visitor. She saw a lean, tall, dark-skinned man wearing a well-tailored suit and carrying a briefcase. She sat up straight and patted her hair. *What kind of business does he have?* Real estate? Wedding planning? She checked in with her oracular sixth sense. Nothing came clear. The only thing she could see was him dropping off his suit tomorrow at a drycleaner in West Hollywood.

Pythia listened with amusement as Debra flirted. While she waited, she looked around her office, trying to imagine it from a visitor's point of view. The once-blue low-pile carpet was threadbare in places. A couple large framed photos of ancient Greece spruced up the faded beige walls. The oak furniture was heavy and outdated. Behind the desk, a scratched credenza held some business books. All for show. Few visitors would be impressed.

Debra appeared in the office doorway.

"Mr. Haven, I'd like you to meet Ms. Pythia Apulu. Ms. Apulu, this is Mr. Glen Haven."

Pythia held out her hand, trying not to chuckle at Debra's uncharacteristically formal introduction. Debra seemed smitten with the new client.

"Ms. Apulu, I'm very pleased to meet you," said the man in a warm voice with no accent.

"Please call me Pythia," she replied as he took her hand and held it a long moment.

"Please call me Glen," he smiled, showing brilliant straight white teeth. Pythia heard the hallway door slam as Debra left the office, headed for the back parking lot. *I hope she remembered to lock the front door.*

Pythia waved the handsome man to the visitor chair. "Please have a seat, Glen, and tell me how I can help you."

Glen settled onto the chair and put his briefcase on the floor. He raised his eyes to hers, paused a moment, and said, "First, if you don't mind, I'd like to find out about you, if I may?"

Pythia sat down behind her desk.

"Why, certainly, Glen. What would you like to know?"

"You are Greek, are you not?"

"Yes, I emigrated from Greece in the 1970s."

"With your husband?"

"I never married, Glen. I have always been more interested in helping people build thriving businesses." Pythia wished her prescience worked more like a faucet and less like a cloudburst. Not much was coming through. He would be meeting a group of people for dinner, she predicted. How was that foresight useful? Unless he planned to invite her? No, unlikely. She saw her future self in her robe and slippers sitting at her desk upstairs typing a blogpost.

"Right on."

"Would you like to tell me about your business ideas?"

"I'm in property management and real estate development."

"Oh, that sounds interesting. Can you give me more details about what you do?"

"More details?"

"Yes, such as your target audiences, that sort of thing."

Glen laughed. Was that a self-conscious laugh? Something was going on, but her sixth sense wasn't cooperating. She saw him drinking margaritas at El Coyote—no salt. *Apollo save me! How is that helpful?*

"I'd really like to know more about you," Glen said with a disarming smile.

Pythia studied him for a long moment, considering her options. *Could he be an axe murderer after all?* No, not likely. The suit he would be dropping at the dry cleaners tomorrow did not appear to have bloodstains. He looked much too fastidious to be hiding an axe in his elegant briefcase.

"I assure you I am well qualified to advise you on whatever type of business you plan to launch," she said. Pythia arranged her hands on the desk in front of her with her index fingers pointing toward the visitor. Her A.A. sponsor, Lena, had once promised this configuration would ward off bad energy and return it to the sender.

Glen didn't appear to mind reabsorbing his own bad vibes. "Oh, I'm sure you are, please don't think I'm questioning your credentials, Ms. Apulu. I'm so sorry, it's just that, well, you see, I have a silent partner."

Pythia looked around her tiny office, observing the bland wallpaper. "A silent partner?"

"Yes. And this person, my partner, uh, they want me to find out a few things about you before we agree to work together."

"Very well, Glen. What would your partner like to know?"

"First, do you have any family?"

"Not living."

"I'm sorry to hear that. No siblings?"

"A long time ago, I had a sister," Pythia said.

"What happened to her, if you don't mind me asking?"

"She died."

"When was that?"

Pythia stared at the man in the visitor chair. She wanted to say, *three millennia ago, give or take a few centuries; you have no idea how long I have been alone,* but she knew self-pity was a dubious luxury best left to mortals better able to handle it. She thought she was a mortal, just one that for some reason had not yet been allowed to die.

"A long time ago, Glen. I prefer not to remember."

Glen nodded and pulled his briefcase onto his lap. He rummaged inside for a moment and then stopped. He nodded at a large framed photo on a wall of her office. "I've seen those ruins."

She followed his gaze. "Yes, that is one of the Temples of Apollo." She studied the picture of tourists in shorts gawking at a few restored columns and piles of rubble, a forlorn remnant of her god's power.

"At Delphi, I believe." He turned back to Pythia. "Weren't you born near there?"

"Yes, in a small town near the sea," Pythia said. "As I recall, a few ramshackle huts, olive trees, and lots of goats. Not exactly a tourist destination."

"What a beautiful place."

Pythia admired Glen's profile and thought about all the years of her long life she had somehow missed after her illness and exodus from Delphi. Decades had passed during which she was alive but half-aware, going through the motions of living, moving around Greece, from village to village, working in farms and fields, eating with the women, tending the children, feeding the sheep and goats. As time passed, she lost herself in cities. Later, she moved to America and worked for anyone who would accept a somewhat dazed but hard-working woman with a heavy Greek accent.

"You don't have much of an accent anymore."

Pythia stared at him. *Is he a mind reader? Does he know who I am?*

Glen looked stricken. "I'm sorry, did I offend? Please forgive me, I meant to pay you a compliment." He sounded apologetic. Yet he also seemed to radiate satisfaction. Pythia sensed Glen had achieved the purpose of his visit. That worried her a bit. However, she did not sense any violence coming from him.

"Thank you, I appreciate that. Now. I hope I have answered your questions adequately. Please tell me how I can help you, Mr. Haven," Pythia said.

Glen handed her a slick full-color brochure, smiling. On the cover was a rendering of Apollo's Temple at Delphi, a perfect version of the ruins in the photo on her wall. Pythia stared in surprise. Once again, her intermittent prescience had failed to warn her.

"Well, after all my questions, I thought you might guess it has something to do with Greek culture. Take a look at this. My partner and I have a client who wants to build a replica of a Greek temple on some private property above Malibu."

Pythia opened the brochure, mind reeling. *What is happening here? Who is this man and how did he find me?* She studied the brochure. Something about a retreat center, a private members-only club, a small hotel with spa amenities and a four-star restaurant.

"Temple of Apollo Hotel and Conference Center. This is an ambitious project," she said, not looking up.

"Yes, it is impressive."

"How do you think I might be able to help?"

Glen looked again at the photo on the wall.

"From what I've been told, you have an ability to identify problems before they happen. My partner and I raised funds to purchase the property, but we need another round of venture capital in order to break ground. We are hoping you might use your ability to guide us in our search for one or more angel investors."

From what I've been told? Who is talking about me?

Pythia tried to empty her mind, desperate for guidance from the future. She received muddled images that made no sense. She saw a blonde woman standing on a terraced hillside overlooking an azure ocean. Wolves running among black conifers. A silent wave sweeping a swimmer out to sea. Lovers embracing in a cave.

"Mr. Haven, how did you hear about me?"

Glen looked uncomfortable. "I'm sorry, I'm not at liberty to disclose details to you—yet. Not yet! But soon!"

Pythia handed the brochure back to Glen and stood up. Surprised, he held his briefcase closed and stood as well.

"Mr. Haven, I appreciate you taking the time to consult with me. I fear I am not the right person for this project. Please accept my apologies. I wish you the best with your fundraising."

Glen's mouth opened and closed. "All right, I see, certainly, Ms. Apulu." He cast a worried glance at the photograph on the wall. "Please, keep the brochure. Thank you for taking time to see me. I'll convey the news to my partner. Maybe—if you change your mind, you have my number. I'm hopeful you'll see—I really believe this, that our futures are connected."

Pythia frowned.

"In a very good way, I assure you!" Glen added.

He laid the brochure on her desk, snapped his briefcase closed, and reached out to shake her hand. An brief image flashed of a house on a hill with a view of the ocean. A street sign with the words *Oracle Drive*.

Pythia disengaged her hand and led the way to the front door. She unlocked the door and stood back to let him exit. He paused on the threshold as if to say more, and then nodded once and went out onto the sidewalk. She closed and locked the door. They stood staring at each other through the glass. A moment later, Glen walked away.

Pythia waited thirty seconds and went outside. Hands on her hips, she watched him get into the back seat of a white stretch limousine parked in front of Cheese Louise. The windows of the car were opaque black. If other people were in the car, they were anonymous. The car glided into a break in traffic and accelerated west toward the ocean.

After a dinner of store-bought bread, oil, olives, and apples, Pythia opened a window, settled at her kitchen table, and woke up her desktop computer. Something buzzed in the innards of the old machine and then settled into a steady hum. The monitor brightened, already open to her blog page.

She clicked the button to start a new post.

April 6, 2015

In almost three thousand years, I've been through all the layers of grief—starting with denial and ending with resignation. The years have scraped the regret and sorrow from my bones, leaving me skeletal with weariness. I begin to think my adolescent mind dreamed the whole thing, like a childhood infatuation with a handsome soldier who never once looks your way. Crushing blow, to realize you don't even rate a glance. All young girls feel this from time to time, until they outgrow their fantasies and mature into clear-eyed young women who know their duty and obligation.

I thought my duty and obligation was to love my Lord God Apollo and to be loved by him in return. I was taught thus from the day I was consecrated to the Temple at Delphi. My parents sold two of their seven children—Dione and me—to serve in Apollo's Temple. The fear of leaving home was tempered by the presence of my older sister, and after a time, I stopped missing my parents and other siblings, who no doubt forgot about us as soon as we left the yard. More food for fewer mouths.

I took to the rigors of service willingly, being young and pliable. My teachers taught me that Apollo would reward me for my devotion, and indeed, I was well fed and housed in the Temple dormitories, sleeping head-to-toe with a hundred other acolytes, all being trained in service to the god.

I can still conjure up some shame at my naiveté. I believed in Apollo with all my heart, the way a child believes in magic. How could I not? Even though I rarely saw him, the beauty of my god's creation was all around me, in the sunrise, in the ripening grapes, in the green olives, in the lambs I helped raise every spring. Immersed as I was in the world's splendor, it never occurred to me to fear I would someday lose it all. The thought, inconceivable impossibility, never entered my mind. I lived from moment to moment, content to live and breathe in my god's bounty under a boundless blue sky and willingly serve him in his temple. To this service had I been called, and to this service did I devote my best efforts. Long after he deserted me, I continued to worship him. I am ashamed to admit how long I strove—centuries. Even today, I confess, I still have a remnant of hope.

My sister lovingly teased me for my devotion. Dione did not believe in Apollo. She performed her tasks adequately, but reluctantly and perfunctorily, and as soon as she was free to roam, she would disappear until twilight.

Mistress Dora often sent me to find her and bring her home. I searched in the marketplace and found her talking with soldiers by the city wall. I searched in the baths and found her primping with Zaphira. I searched in the Temple gardens and found her not plucking weeds but gossiping with Hester and Lilianna. Sometimes I knew where she was because of our sister connection. Other times, she eluded me, and I had to return to Mistress Dora to admit I had failed in my task. Dione chafed under the yoke of service while I in my ignorance worshiped with blind faith and misplaced loyalty.

Now I fear Dione was right. The god I worshiped was an illusion, a construct created, organized, and implemented by an oligarchy of statesmen who hired cruel teachers to find young female acolytes to train in the ways of servitude toward men. There was never a god Apollo.

Yet if I am not missing a real god, I am missing the idea of him. Why do I miss what I never had? If I had been born with only one hand, would I miss the one I never knew? I miss the potential of him. Not unlike the Christian god, he was a god of sunshine and harvests, courage and wisdom, music and poetry. What is the point of living? Had I the power, I would leave this wretched century that masquerades as civilization to return to the orchards and fields of ancient Greece.

—Yours in exile, Delphina

Pythia had been posting once or twice a week as "Delphina, a three thousand-year-old Oracle" for several years. She had a small following. Most readers visited without leaving comments. However, some commenters praised her "performance art." Some wished her well on her quest to publish her fiction.

Some thought the blog was a joke—half of these readers pretended to be in on the joke; the others expressed annoyance at her audacity. One of her more ardent followers, Class-Act, often wrote something like, "Hey, Delphina, if you hate it here so much, go back to where you came from, you sick liberal Commie spy." Bettina-the-Muse, a frequent visitor, wrote, "You sound so sad. Why do you persist in claiming you are three thousand years old? Admit you are a fraud. Jesus will forgive you."

A recent comment caught her eye. GodsChosen (gender unknown) had invited her to the Church of Apollo. *Is there really such a church?*

She closed the blogging program. She never responded to comments. Mistress Dora taught her never to engage the enemy lest they fill their quivers with your own words and shoot you through the heart.

Chapter 2

The next day, Pythia was in the office before Debra, which didn't often happen. Most days, Debra buzzed Pythia to remind her of her first appointment. Today, Pythia was early. In fact, she had been unable to sleep. Images of Dione burbled up unbidden. Lying in bed, Pythia stared at the dark ceiling, remembering games of hide-and-seek in the scrubby hillside grasses under the blue skies of Delphi. She remembered leaning into the wind, imagining she could smell the ocean that tantalized just beyond her view on clear days.

Spent from restlessness, just after dawn, she trudged downstairs to the office and coaxed the Mr. Coffee machine to life as she watched the sky lighten over the Miracle Mile through the grime on the tall street-facing windows.

In a corner of the waiting area was an ancient portable television meant to entertain clients as they waited for their consultations. She had an impulse to turn it on.

The TV warmed into a glowing yellowish image of four attractive, well-dressed, animated women sitting around an oblong glass-topped table. Three had smooth pale skin and one was a little less pale but just as smooth. An orange neon M lit up the camera side of the table, giving all the women an unhealthy pallor. *That light is probably pink. What fool would put white women under an orange neon light?*

A commercial teaser interrupted the banal chatter to announce an upcoming celebrity guest. The screen showed a close-up of a young vivacious woman with pale twisted locks of hair behind a flashing tagline: *Coming soon! New York celebrity Divina Dee, Psychic to the Stars.*

Anyone claiming to be a psychic was interesting to Pythia. It was no news to her that people just wanted to know their futures. However, humans could still surprise her. Most of those who claimed to read the future were good-natured frauds, but a few were the genuine article. What was Divina Dee?

"She's the real deal!" gushed a dark-skinned woman with puffy black hair, as if in answer to her question.

"She predicted I would win the lottery," squealed a heavy woman in a hot pink jumpsuit. "And I did!" She threw her hands in the air in a *praise God* salute.

"Meet this mysterious psychic who is advising the stars," invited another TV anchor. "Enter to win a chance to meet the psychic and ask her your questions about your future!"

"Rumor has it she is filming a documentary here in the L.A. area," screamed a blonde woman Pythia recognized as one of the speakers sitting at the oblong table. "Go to KWOW dot TV to get the latest news about Divina Dee!"

A teaser for a news show came on showing a video clip of an interview with a blonde-haired woman running for the U.S. presidency, followed by a commercial for a product for gum sensitivity. Pythia mused about humans' desperation to know their fates, as if knowing meant controlling. *Any reader of myths and fairy tales should know you need to be careful what you wish for.* She half-listened to several more commercials for products she would never use. People bought these products based on the manufacturers' promises. Whiter teeth, cleaner toilets, faster cars. It's the same way Americans elect their presidents. That is what marketing is all about, as Debra often reminded her. Is it ethical to make impossible promises in exchange for customers' money? Debra would say yes.

෨

Debra came through the hallway door at 9:00 a.m., lugging her giant satchel, which Pythia knew held a pasta salad, a thermos of tea, several books, a Franklin planner, an entire make-up kit, and sundry other gear necessary for enduring another day at Apulu Ltd.

"Who is this Divina Dee person?" Pythia asked.

"What are you talking about?" Debra said, disappearing into her cubicle. Pythia heard a thump as the satchel found its place on the floor under Debra's desk. Debra reemerged, empty coffee cup in hand, and headed for the small kitchen area in the back of the office. "Hey, thanks for making coffee. I need more hair on my chest." A moment later, she returned. "Now. What's up?"

Pythia waved at the TV, which was showing another commercial for Divina Dee. A pale young woman with long blonde dreadlocks stood on a stage in front of a large audience.

"She's a psychic." Debra sipped her coffee and gazed at the screen. "She has a show on the Psychics Network called Psychic to the Stars. She's quite the celebrity."

"Why does she wear her hair like that?"

"It's a style thing. Dreadlocks. You wouldn't understand. Anyway, other celebrities rave about her."

"Like who? Anyone we know?"

"Since when do we know any celebrities? Oh, wait, you mean, like Ram Leonardo, before he got famous for embezzling funds from the business we helped him start?"

Pythia glared at a hangnail. "Yes, I should have seen that one coming."

Debra looked at her, eyebrows raised. "Are you being serious right now? Because I can't tell."

"I seriously want to know who this Divina Dee is. I have a strange feeling about her."

"Well, luckily, you and Divina Dee aren't the only ones who can predict the future. In anticipation of this discussion, I looked her up online. No, not really. Actually, she's just fascinating. As far as I can tell, she appeared on the celebrity circuit out of nowhere just last year. Her manager is that famous agent from New York. She got Divina Dee on the talk shows. Ellen. Oprah. All the big ones. Now she's the host of her own show. They say her predictions are almost always right."

"Predictions."

"Yep. She predicted Angie Jane and Tad Wheeler would break up."

"Anyone could have seen that coming."

"She predicted that hurricane."

"Which one? We've had so many this year. That is why we call it hurricane season."

"She must have an excellent publicist. She has almost a million TipTap followers."

"What is TipTap?"

Debra stared at her. "You aren't that much older than me, Pythia," she said. "You think email is magic. Hell, you act like TV is a modern invention. It's called TipTap! Welcome to the twenty-first century!"

"You have no idea," Pythia said.

"You'd better get going. You'll miss your witches' meeting."

"We are not witches, Debra, how many times do I have to tell you?"

"As good as," Debra grinned. "Go, I got this covered. I'll work on your social media until you get back."

৯

At 9:30, Pythia unplugged her silver Honda Insight and drove across the city in heavy traffic to the radio station in Westwood. She parked under the building in the vast dark parking structure, always in the same spot so she could find her car again. Below ground her sense of direction deserted her. Even though appearances didn't matter for radio, she checked that her skirt's side seams were straight. The gray calf-length linen skirt was loose and comfortable and complemented her Birkenstocks.

Parking ticket in hand, she ascended the parking elevator to the lobby. She waved to the front desk attendant, Brian, as she switched to the elevator that would take her to the sixth floor.

Feeling inordinately cheerful, she strode along the carpeted hall to the Mystics Roundtable sound booth, pausing to wave through the glass wall at Arnie Solomon, the daytime KROO radio DJ, who was just starting his shift. He smiled and waved back. She liked his gravelly warm voice and the way his eyes crinkled when he smiled. She suspected he hid a dimple under his gray-gold beard—maybe even two.

Pythia was the last to arrive to the sound booth at the end of the corridor. She hurried around the curved table to her place by the wall. In the first seat, Sylvia Benjamin shuffled a deck of Tarot cards, looking like a red-haired goddess in glitter makeup. In the next seat, Mary McMillen, the astrologer, sat with her eyes closed, humming mantras under her breath. Next to Mary, Moon Cloud-River, real name Susan Mooney, rolled a bronze-colored I-Ching coin across her knuckles and drummed the fingernails on her other hand on the Formica.

"Sorry, am I late?" Pythia put her purse on the floor under her chair and adjusted the headphones over her ears. She angled the overhead microphone into place.

"No, plenty of time," smiled Lena Tollefson, the host of the monthly Mystics Roundtable radio show. Lena was an actor but spent evenings and weekends working as a server at the Wild West Arcade, a children's party venue on Pico. Lena also happened to be Pythia's A.A. sponsor. Pythia had been a volunteer Mystic for a few years, at Lena's insistence she "be of service."

The four participants sat around the table, facing Lena who presided from behind the soundboard. Today, Lena wore a green fedora with a dark green wool pantsuit. Her long brown hair was swept up under the hat.

"Do we have a topic for tonight, or are we just going to take questions?" Sylvia asked.

Oh, thank God, pets, Pythia thought with some relief. *Better than romance. It is so much easier to predict the futures of pets than of people.*

"I think our theme tonight will be pets! Surprise!" Lena said, pressing buttons on the board. Pythia heard the show's theme song and opening announcements playing in her headphones. Lena mouthed "three, two, one," and said, "Mystics, are you ready? Hello to our four Mystics, Sylvia the Magnificent, Mistress Mary of the Stars, Conjuror of Coins Moon Cloud-River, and Pythia, our Seer without Peer. I hope you had an excellent month. Welcome, Listeners! Today we are taking your questions about your pets. Looks like we already have our first caller. Lucy is on the line from Burbank. Go ahead, Lucy."

A young child's voice said, "What is my cat Muffin trying to tell me when he stares into my eyes and twitches his tail?"

Lena chuckled. "Okay, Mystics, let's see what we can do to help Lucy."

As the other Mystics competed to answer the question using their various mystical tools and methods, in a single flash of prescience, Pythia already knew everything about Lucy and her cat. A bored, demanding, long-haired child and a restless tomcat in one small room added up to tears before bed.

She let her mind wander. While Sylvia gave Lucy and Muffin a tarot card reading, Pythia reviewed the conversation she'd had last week with Glen Haven, the mysteriously reticent business client. Despite Debra's assurances that he was a great guy, Pythia sensed something off about Glen. *Why was he hiding the identity of his "silent partner"? Why all the personal questions?*

Lena's voice interrupted her reverie. "Let's see what Pythia our Peerless Seer can make of Crowley's lovemaking."

"All cats make noises," Pythia said.

"Crowley's a dog, Pythia," Sylvia said, laughing.

"Oh, sorry," Pythia said. One moment of reflection showed her Crowley's imminent fate. "Say, Bill, is it? Bill, you had better go check that garden gate."

"Garden gate? What are you talking about?" the caller asked, puzzled.

"I would do it now rather than later," Pythia said.

"Bill, if Pythia says jump, we jump," Lena said.

"Uh, okay. Hold on a sec." A thumping sound ensued, followed by yelling and barking in the background.

While the line was open, Pythia regarded her fellow Mystics, who were staring at her. "What?" she said.

Bill returned, breathless. "Oh, my god, lady, you just saved my dog from getting run over by a trash truck! Crowley, you bad boy!"

Lena laughed. "That's Pythia, our Seer without Peer." Pythia winced.

"I can't thank you enough!" Bill said. "Who's a bad boy? Is it you? Crowley, you're such a bad boy!" He hung up the phone.

"How do you do that?" Moon demanded, rolling a coin across her knuckles. The coin went spinning across the table.

Pythia caught it and handed it back to Moon. "Do what?"

"Mystics' mysterious methods are wondrous to behold," Lena intoned into her mic.

A few callers later, the show was over. The Mystics began to pack up their gear.

"Say, Lena, how's your mom doing?" Sylvia asked as she swept her Tarot cards into a silk cloth bag. Pythia knew that the three Mystics had graduated together from Mystics Institute, a school for spiritual advisors. Lena's mother was the owner and president of the Mystics Institute. She was also the main patron supporting the Mystics Roundtable Radio Show.

"Fine," Lena said. "Crazy as ever."

"Give her my regards," Sylvia said. "See you soon!" She exited, leaving behind a glitter cloud on the table and floor around her chair.

Mary turned to Pythia. "Hey, Pythia, why haven't I done your chart for you? When is your birthday?"

"Pythia doesn't want anyone to know how old she really is," Moon said. She packed the coins and yarrow sticks into a velvet-lined carved wooden box and stuffed it in her leather shoulder bag.

Pythia smiled. "Are we all not entitled to some secrets?"

"Pythia is an old soul, anyone can see," Lena said, shutting down the computer. "Anyone want to meet me at the Arcade for lunch? On the house."

"I have a stack of papers to grade," Mary sighed. She taught English comp at a career college when she wasn't giving astrology readings.

"I need to return to the office. Maybe next time," Pythia said.

"I'll go, why not?" Moon said. "I'll meet you there." She turned to Pythia. Her eyes narrowed behind her wireframe glasses. "Wait. Pythia, tell me the truth, did you work that out ahead of time?"

"No, that would be silly." Pythia retrieved her purse from under her chair. "That would be insane."

"Not impossible, though. You have some scam going on, don't you? I want in on it."

"Moon, there is no scam." *Humans are exhausting. I need a nap.*

"I need the money, you don't understand." Pythia caught a brief image of Moon's teenage son Riley. Down payment on braces, $4,500. A handsome kid with crooked teeth and a desperate mother who thought that a perfect smile would be his ticket to Hollywood. *Maybe as a bellhop at the Beverly Hilton.*

Pythia shook off her pessimism. "I do understand," she said. "We want the best for our loved ones. Moon, I have a lucky feeling. Do you ever play the lottery? You know that 7-11 over by that Ethiopian place you like so much, on Fairfax? I heard that is a lucky place."

Moon looked skeptical but, in a moment, Pythia's vision shifted to show Moon winning a modest sum on a lottery ticket. She smiled with satisfaction.

"You had better hurry, though. Maybe skip the Arcade this time."

Pythia watched Moon rush out the door.

"I know what you're doing."

Pythia turned to look at Lena. "What am I doing?"

"It's the power of suggestion, isn't it? Somehow you help people believe something will happen, and then they act as if it will, and then it does."

"That is as good an explanation as any."

"The alternative explanation is that there is a God. And I know you don't believe that!"

Pythia smiled. "Are you going to the meeting tonight?"

Lena nodded. "I'll see you there, but I really don't know why you keep going. I don't think you are an alcoholic."

"Well, I am something," Pythia said. "Not sure what, but something."

❧

Debra accosted Pythia as she came through the front door. Usually, Debra's words were something like, "You're late!" or "Did you forget the toner?"

This time, Debra said, "You aren't going to believe what just happened!"

Pythia's "gift" kicked into gear. She saw the tale laid out before her like a storyboard, frame by frame. Out of respect for Debra, she said, "What happened?"

"You know that weirdo Cindi Harper? She just called to say her car caught fire as she was driving on the 405!"

"Oh, dear. Is she okay?"

"She's okay, but her car is toast."

"I had hoped she would be able to figure out how to use that fire extinguisher."

"That's just it! She did. She used it to put out the other guy's car. She saved his life!"

"That's good." Pythia went into her office.

Debra followed her, vibrating with excitement. "Wait, that's not all. Guess who the guy was!"

Carl Clement.

"Tell me."

"Carl Clement, the producer of Business Barracudas!"

"Well, is that not something," Pythia murmured.

"Wait, you already knew all this, didn't you?" Debra said, frowning. "Did you see it on the news?"

"Yes, I did, I saw it on the news."

"You are such a lousy liar, Pythia. Well, Miss Crystal Ball, Carl Clement is going to invest a million dollars in Cindi's business!"

Pythia laughed. "Now that I did not see coming. Good for them."

"I'm going to post something on FacePlace. We oughta be able to get some mileage out of this. Finally, one of our clients makes it big—legitimately!"

❧

After locking the office, Pythia walked through the building and out the back door to her Honda Insight, which she parked in one of the few spaces marked for tenants behind the office building. She would have preferred to have showered and changed her clothes but the A.A. meeting started at 7:00 p.m. and she disliked being late.

She unplugged the car and motored on autopilot through Beverly Hills, mind meandering in and out of the present and future. The drive to the church on Wilshire near Malcolm in Westwood took about thirty minutes in traffic. Driving time was thinking time. When she'd first learned to drive, the task needed her full attention. Years of practice in Los Angeles had made her an expert. It also helped that she could foresee small fender benders before they happened.

She thought about Glen Haven, the real estate developer. Pythia's oracular gift had so far failed to unravel the riddle of his many personal questions. His visit had left her feeling uneasy, as if something important was hiding just out of sight.

She thought of Moon. In a moment, she saw in her mind Moon sitting next to her son in a pizza restaurant. Across the table from Moon was a dark-skinned woman Pythia had never met. Moon's bright eyes and laughter revealed an aspect of her life she might have preferred to keep hidden. *I will never tell. But why can I not see Glen Haven the way I see Moon? Is it because she is my friend? Apollo, where are you in all of this?*

Pythia thought of Apollo. She pictured his lithe form lounging on the sun-warmed rocks above the hidden springs near Delphi. His golden skin always seemed to glow with inner light, even when clouds obscured the sun. As a child she was content to sit nearby, soaking in the heat and light. *I was where I belonged. I knew the truth in my bones, with a child's unshakeable conviction.*

She found a cramped space to park in the church lot and hustled through the basement door. Someone had forgotten to hang the welcome signs. She didn't need her foresight to know she would spend the next five minutes wandering the basement hallways. Her ability to navigate deserted her in the dark. Basements, caves, underground parking lots ... she lost all sense of direction. She was a creature of the sun. This happened every week if someone forgot to tape up the signs.

She found the meeting room at last and sank onto an empty folding chair near the back wall. She didn't mind missing the opening prayer. She had her own prayers. *Apollo, god of my understanding, are you in a place like this, a pale imitation of the sacred spaces we consecrated to you on the hills of Delphi? Every olive tree, every bubbling spring, every dark ravine singing with the earth's breath—all of it was yours, my Lord God Apollo. Have you forgotten me?*

Almost every seat in the room was occupied. Pythia noted Lena's green felt fedora near the podium. She recognized many people by the backs of their heads. She'd been attending this A.A. meeting for at least ten years and she had yet to speak in front of the group. *They would laugh me out of the church if I told them what I am.* She wasn't an alcoholic. What would they say if she stood at the podium and told them she inhaled geothermal gas to induce a trance? No one would understand; in fact, they might send her to some other anonymous program. Was there a program for inhalers of toxic earth fumes?

Leaders of the group had long since given up inviting her to speak, she'd been silent for so long. *They probably think I am a hopeless drunk,* she thought. Still, she felt at home here. Like her, these alcoholics sought a spiritual solution for their affliction. All higher powers welcome.

She sometimes imagined what it would be like for her god Apollo to enter the room, blazing with golden light and radiating love. No doubt he would find their addiction to alcohol amusing. He might cause all their plastic water bottles to overflow with potent Greek wine. *No, on second thought, better he not come here.*

A tall, beefy man with sandy hair leaned on the lectern. "I can't seem to get past this God thing," he confessed. Heads nodded. "I'm trying to imagine God as good orderly direction, but I don't feel good or orderly, and I'm definitely going in the wrong direction." More head nodding. "My last drink was Sunday, and I feel like I'm jumping out of my skin. Every time my wife walks by, I—well, I won't say what I'm thinking, but it ain't pretty."

He stomped the two steps off the podium to the floor and threw himself into a brown metal folding chair, making it skid on the scratched linoleum.

Applause spattered against the concrete basement walls. Pythia clapped, too. Alcoholics were a supportive bunch, for sure. Four days without drinking was a miracle for an alcoholic. She rarely went a week without huffing gas in the basement. Not quite the same thing, but she could relate.

During the closing prayer, group members held hands. Pythia squinted against the members' psychic energy, transmitted across the clasped hands. She knew three people had cancers of various kinds, one person would soon be heading for a nearby bar, and one person was going to die in a drive-by shooting on Friday. Nothing Pythia did or said was going to change their fates, so she said a prayer to Apollo and wished them well.

People dropped hands. Some hugged. The volume of voices swelled against the cinder block walls. Lena waved from across the room. Pythia nodded back. She smiled at some familiar faces milling past her seat: Blake, Charlotte, and Patty . . . some other people whose names she half knew.

"Hey, Pythia, you want to come out for coffee?" Charlotte asked, moving past.

As usual, Pythia declined. She stood up and waited for the crowd to thin. Out of the corner of her eye, she caught a glimpse of a man with long gray-gold hair and a beard. She leaned sideways but Lena coming toward her blocked her view. Lena pointed a thumb over her shoulder.

"Wasn't that the new DJ?" Lena pointed. She took off her hat, inspected it for fluff, and settled it back on her head. "Have you seen him here before?"

"Perhaps, I did not get a clear look. I could not tell," Pythia said. She walked with Lena into the hallway. The man was gone.

"Pythia, have you ever been to the Renaissance Faire? Sylvia called me. She needs some help at her booth on Sunday the nineteenth. Can you make it?"

Pythia raised her eyebrows and consulted her inner compass. In a moment, she saw herself stuck in traffic on the freeway somewhere near Pasadena, looking for the exit leading to a dirt road leading to a haphazard arrangement of tents and booths set up in an open field.

She sighed. *Not like I had anything planned.*

"You will, won't you?" Lena said with satisfaction, reading Pythia's expression. "You don't want to, but you will. Ha. It's kind of a curse, isn't it, being able to see the future?"

"I keep telling you," Pythia smiled. She followed Lena up the stairs and out the door to the parking lot.

"I know, I know, you don't really predict the future. You are such a bad liar. So, here's the deal. I signed us up to tell fortunes at Sylvia's booth. We have to wear some kind of medieval costume."

"I thought it was the Renaissance."

"What's the difference, some kind of costume. A long skirt or something. A scarf on your head . . . can you figure it out, or do you want me to come up with something?"

Given Lena's fashion sense, Pythia imagined if she let Lena take the initiative, she would end up wearing a muumuu, a tie-dyed apron, and a bustier that pushed her breasts to her chin.

"Certainly, I have something I can wear. What time should I be there?" She waited as Lena unlocked her car door.

"Eight o'clock, if you can. We should get there before it gets too hot. We'll be under a tent the whole time, but it is supposed to be ninety-five."

"I will bring extra water."

"Thanks, Pythia. You are my rock. See you Sunday."

April 7, 2015

Good evening, Blog Readers.

Today I have been pondering the many friendships I have enjoyed over the millennia. People have drifted in and out of my life, or perhaps it was the other way around. I cannot recall anyone wondering why I seem to be forever stuck in middle age. I stay the same; they all move on, to new relationships, new jobs, new cities, and some to illness and death. Friends I cherished, each death a small loss keenly felt but soon forgotten in the passing of the years.

I was able to help a friend with a financial problem today. Well, sort of a friend. Now that I think about it, I do not think she likes me all that much. I am competition. She thinks I am running some kind of scheme. If I thought she would believe me, I would tell her the truth.

People have been skeptical before; I still try to be honest about what I am. They hear my voice, but they do not listen to my words. It is as if I am speaking into the wind. The words bounce back at me and all I see in their eyes is their greed, their desperate need, or their despair. I wish I could help everyone but I am not that kind of power.

My Lord God Apollo could soothe all wounds, if he chose, although he was notoriously fickle about whom he would help. Many sought respite or wealth but were turned away, or worse. I heard a rumor that he turned a lover into a tree, but that is not true. That was his father. They never got along, from what I heard. I never met his father so I cannot say much about that. His mother was a lovely mortal woman.

His stepmother, though, never forgave her husband for his philandering; if that woman lives, I am sure she is as spiteful as ever.

Until my power waned, I predicted the outcome of battles that turned the tide of multiple wars. I predicted famines and earthquakes. Heads of state begged for audiences with me. They laid gifts of gratitude upon the Temple altars and stairs, fine wines, olives, figs, and meat from white oxen, which the priests and priestesses shared among the oracles, acolytes, and servants. Even the lowest slaves ate like kings and queens. The future was as clear to me as a modern movie, unfolding frame by frame in my mind's eye.

Until my illness, I was the most powerful Oracle in Delphi.

Even so, for all my talent, I could never predict Apollo.

—Yours in exile, Delphina

Chapter 3

At 6:30 a.m. on Sunday, Pythia dug in a kitchen drawer for two black linen tablecloths, which she folded and draped, then pinned with safety pins to her bra straps at both shoulders. She added more pins along the arms to create the sleeves of a peplos. A black cotton voile scarf wrapped twice around her waist created a girdle that accentuated her figure and held the peplos modestly in place.

Pythia assessed her reflection in the bedroom mirror. The fabric was thicker than the fine wool voile she wore in the Temple. The scarf around her waist was bulky and wrinkled. *I look like a slightly overweight middle-aged woman wearing a wrinkled tablecloth.* Oh, well. This was better than a Cinderella gown, which is what Lena would have designed for her. She pulled her hair into a bun and draped a thin white linen tablecloth over her head to complete the costume.

She packed a large cloth tote with several plastic bottles of cold water and some cheese, apples, crackers, and figs for lunch, plus a sunhat and a few other things, and went down the back stairs to her car.

Frank was smashing leftover pieces of picture frame glass on the edge of a large metal garbage can. The glass smashing was a weekly ritual. On Monday a large trash truck would collect the glass shards. He stopped when Pythia walked by. "Bless me, Sister, for I have sinned."

"Renaissance Faire," she said, gesturing at her outfit.

"Sounds like fun," he said in a way that let her know he thought it sounded like anything but. He grinned at her and returned to his task.

"Careful with that one, Mr. Bristol!" Pythia stabbed a finger at a piece of glass that was soon going to fall out of the garbage can and make a mess on the concrete.

Frank nudged the glass back into the stack. "It's fine. Thanks, Pythia."

Pythia drove south on La Brea toward the entrance to the Santa Monica Freeway, enjoying the sense of satisfaction she felt after averting a disaster.

Broken glass might be a small calamity, but it could have punctured a tire or harmed a stray cat. She might not be able to foresee the big catastrophes, but she was glad to help in the small ways she could. Since her adolescent illness, the massive tragedies were invisible to her—the earthquakes, hurricanes, and floods. The 1994 Northridge earthquake, for instance, had shocked and frightened her as much as it had everyone else in the L.A. area. She wished she could have seen that coming.

Not that I could have changed anything. We had earthquakes in Greece, and even after burying the dead, people still rebuilt on sand.

The early morning light on the Hollywood Hills reminded her of the sun-kissed hills of Delphi. The air shimmered with misty smog, bathing the mountains in gold. She drove up the ramp to the freeway, enjoying the open vista.

Somewhere to the west was an ocean that could lead her back to the Sea of Corinth if she could follow the waterways across the globe. Somewhere to the east was home, if she could fly on Apollo's sun chariot across the sky. *I miss Delphi. More than that, I miss the sure knowledge that I lived where I belonged and that my service mattered. Los Angeles is a beautiful city in many ways, but it is not home.*

The route to the Santa Fe Dam Recreation Area took her north and then east. She wore sunglasses to block the morning sun, checking her map from time to time, finding the exit onto the 605 north past El Monte and then to the 210 going east. An hour after leaving her office, she arrived at the Faire.

Lena was waiting at the entrance. Pythia smiled to see her friend. Lena wore long double-layered skirt in two shades of mossy green and a loose low-cut white blouse cinched with a wide brown lace-up belt. Instead of her trademark fedora, she had tucked her brown hair in a mesh snood that looked like a cap to keep curlers in place while sleeping.

"There you are! You made it." Lena led Pythia toward the line at the ticket booth. "We have special passes because we're helping Sylvia at her booth. Half price, on me."

The ticket taker was a young man with rings in his ears and nose. "Have a good time at the Faire, Sister," he said to Pythia. She nodded politely. Lena pulled her through the gate.

"You look great, by the way. Very modest. How do you like my outfit?"

"You look quite authentic," Pythia said. "Except for the sneakers."

"Yeah, well. Come on, her booth is back here along this avenue."

As they walked along the dirt road, Pythia admired the colorful tablecloths, flying pennants, and creative costumes. Small groups of musicians practiced on stringed instruments and flutes. Some distance away, knights on horseback jousted in an empty dirt field. Empty bleachers lined the arena, ready for the day's tournament.

The citizens of the Faire took their historical immersion seriously. She saw many costumes that almost looked like the real thing—or what she remembered, anyway—her memories of the Renaissance were hazy. One improvement: These modern-day costumes were no doubt free of lice and fleas.

The air was warming. Her head cloth protected her neck, but Pythia was glad to duck under the awning of Sylvia's booth.

"Lena! Pythia! I'm so glad you're here. Thank you for helping us out today." Sylvia moved close for a hug. She wore a flowing blue gown decorated with little yellow moons and stars and a blue turban over her red curls. "Love your nun outfit, so elegant! Nothing like a fortune-telling nun to get the marks excited."

"Marks?"

"Victims," Lena smirked.

"Customers," Sylvia said. "Here, we've set up little tents for each of us. Look, isn't this cute? Pythia, here you go, this is your tent." She pulled back a dark red velvet curtain hung over a sturdy wooden frame and revealed a small round table covered with a round blue cloth hemmed in gold fringe. Two folding chairs draped in paisley-pattern tablecloths faced each other on either side of the table. "You can put your bag under your chair and hide it with that cloth."

Pythia fastened the sides of the curtain on convenient hooks and entered her domain.

"This will be fun," Lena said. She entered the middle tent and began to set up the paraphernalia of her fortune-telling trade. She leaned around the velvet curtain. "Pythia, I brought everything I had, in case you need something."

"I do not need much, thank you," Pythia said. She pulled an iridescent white gazing ball out of her bag and set it on a black wooden stand in the middle of the table. Pale red and blue reflections swirled on the surface, reflecting the tents.

"Ooh, pretty," Lena said. "You can't actually see into that thing, can you?"

"Oh, for heaven's sake, Lena," Pythia laughed.

"Doug—oh, sorry, the fabulous Douglas Goodfellow—will collect the money and usher the people into our tents," Sylvia said, waving toward a slender man wearing a bright yellow waistcoat and purple bloomer style knee-length pants over gray hose.

"Very handsome. Although, I do not think peasants were allowed to wear purple," Pythia smiled.

Sylvia laughed. "Don't call my husband a peasant, at least, not to his face. He's the one paying us at the end of the day."

"How long are these readings, Sylvia?" Lena asked.

"We aim for fifteen minutes." Sylvia began to wrap a colorful silk turban around her head, covering her red hair. "And you keep the tips!"

"I see you have little clocks in each tent! How thoughtful." Lena clapped her hands.

Sylvia tucked the ends of the turban and pulled a shiny gold compact out of her pocket. Pythia stepped back—she didn't need her foresight to know what was about to happen. "They can choose an astrology reading with me, a palm reading with Lena, or a crystal ball reading with Pythia. Something for everyone." Sylvia began patting glitter on her face and arms.

"Don't get that stuff on me!" Lena followed Pythia to a safe distance.

Sylvia laughed and pretended to blow glitter toward them.

Trumpets blared, making further conversation impossible. Pythia turned at the sound of horse hooves plodding on dirt. Around the corner of the avenue marched a row of four heralds blowing on gleaming trumpets. Name-brand sneakers flashed beneath their flowing gauze robes. Behind them two knights in silvery gray armor rode on slow farm horses. Their visors were open so Pythia could see one knight was a woman. They carried lances draped with gold and green pennants and shields painted with a rampant lioness. Behind the knights came a horse-drawn wagon holding a silk-draped canopy decorated with the same symbol, under which sat a buxom woman wearing layers of gold- and sequins-encrusted velvet robes. The costumed workers in the booths rushed to wave and shout as she rode by with her retinue.

"That's the Queen of the Faire," Sylvia shouted over the trumpets. "Huzzah, Your Majesty!" She waved both hands at the Queen, who was looking in another direction.

"She must be baking in that gown," Lena said to Pythia.

Pythia nodded, knowing that soon the so-called Queen would be prone in the infirmary tent, recovering from heat exhaustion. "She will be okay," she said, "But we will have a new Queen by this afternoon."

Lena smiled. "It's getting warm, so I bet you are right."

Sylvia's husband opened the gate to the first customers of the morning. The three Mystics went into their tents and were soon swamped with customers.

Giving customers enough to make them happy but not enough to frighten them required some care. Fortune-telling could have a dark side. Pretending to see things in the crystal gazing ball helped Pythia focus on happy outcomes: A lost ring soon to be found under a couch cushion, a letter of acceptance to a prestigious college coming soon in the mail, an impending marriage proposal.

Sylvia was having good luck with her clients as well. "Your mom would be so proud of us!"

Lena rolled her eyes at Pythia. Pythia knew Lena had some issues with her mother.

By late afternoon, dark stains radiated above and below Pythia's cloth girdle, which she tightened every so often to keep her peplos in place. During lulls in the stream of customers, she fanned her face with her white head cloth and cooled her neck with a dripping water bottle grabbed from a cooler of ice.

"This is brutal," Lena gasped from the booth next door. Pythia knew without looking that Lena and Sylvia were likewise drenched with sweat.

The worthy Douglas Goodfellow sprawled in a lawn chair under a dusty market umbrella with a wet cloth over his head.

"Most of the customers are probably in the big tent," Sylvia said. "It's got AC. Hardly anyone comes out when it's over one hundred. Too bad." She raised her voice. "Honey? Do you think we should lower our rates when the temperature goes over a hundred?"

Sylvia chuckled as Douglas waved his hand.

Pythia closed her eyes and leaned back, relishing the contrast between the hot dry air and the cold wet bottle. *I smell olive trees.* She sank into a partial trance—an easy slide after a morning of practice. Images rolled through her mind like molasses: Weaving among olive trees, cypress, and scrub heather, dodging butterflies, catching juniper berries as she passed low branches. Running through sweet wheat grass at summer's end, following the dusty trails to the hidden springs. Lying boneless on warm rocks with her sister in the shade of the craggy spires above Apollo's temple. Her mind roamed free, untethered to the present, with no inkling of what was about to happen.

April 19, 2015

It is late. I feel very old and powerless tonight. I failed to predict a tragedy today, and now a child is in the hospital, hooked to machines that keep her precariously attached to her life.

I was helping some friends at an outdoor event. It appears a horse got loose from its master. In my experience, horses often get loose; it is the nature of some horses to seek their freedom. Someone was not watching the child, someone provoked the horse, I am not certain what happened. I am ashamed to admit, I was sleeping on the job.

It was so hot. We were taking a break. I was resting my eyes. I should have seen it coming. I blame myself. I deeply regret that I was unable to prevent the collision of the horse and child. I know the child will survive, but she will walk with a limp, and worse, she will fear horses for the rest of her life. The horse will be sold to a cruel master, another senseless outcome. The horse was not at fault; fate dictated a small girl ended up in its path.

At the height of my power, I could foresee the fates of armies, predict hurricanes and tornados, feel the movement of the plates deep in the earth. Why could I not have predicted the fate of one child?

—Yours in exile, Delphina

∽

The incident was on the local news channel when Pythia entered the office Monday morning. Debra stood in front of the television in the waiting area, watching video footage of frantic people trying to soothe and corral a rearing horse.

Debra turned a stricken face to Pythia. "You were there!"

"Yes, I was," Pythia said. "It was terrible."

"They said the little girl is in critical condition."

"She will live."

They watched the video unfold in slow motion. Sharp hooves threw gouts of dust into the air.

Debra pointed at the TV. "Hey, isn't that—that looks like Divina Dee!"

"What?"

"Behind that jester guy. I'm almost positive that is Divina Dee. Dressed like Snow White, looks like. Standing in front of that evil-looking witch queen lady, see? That older gal dressed in black."

The video sped up to normal speed. Members of the crowd tried to rescue the child crumpled in the dirt. The horse's flailing legs kept people from getting close enough to drag the child to safety. Pythia felt ill watching a scene she had witnessed in person the day before. The video failed to capture the heat, the dust, the screaming horse, the frantic people.

Now Pythia saw the two women milling on the edge of the crowd. "I did not see them in all the commotion."

The woman in black was pointing what looked like a wand at the horse. *That cannot be.*

"That's Glen!" Debra shouted, pointing at the screen.

Pythia saw someone who resembled Glen Haven move across the frame near the camera's position. *It is almost as if he is intentionally blocking the camera.* A moment later, the video ended, and the TV showed the news anchor standing at the entrance to the Renaissance Faire parking lot, talking at the camera.

Debra and Pythia stared at each other. Pythia could read Debra's expression. *She is wondering, is Glen a good guy or a bad guy?*

"I do not know," Pythia said, shaking her head.

"That sure looks like him."

"I think you are correct, Ms. Sandhill," Pythia said. "And I think you are right to question his motives."

"I kind of liked him," Debra said. "Cute as hell."

Pythia went into her office and stared at the photo of Apollo's temple. *Apollo, my Lord, my God, what is happening here?*

Around lunch time, Lena called Pythia's direct office line.

"How are you doing?" Lena asked. "Are you okay?"

Pythia sighed and stopped doodling on her notepad. "I keep seeing that child lying in the dirt."

"I know. Me, too. It was awful."

"She will live."

"I'm glad to hear that," Lena said. "What kind of Higher Power allows such a terrible thing to happen to a small child?"

"Gods do not disclose their motives to humans." She gazed at the photo of Apollo's ruined temple.

"In the program, they say we should seek to know and do God's will, but how do we know what that is?"

"I know not, Lena. You are the sponsor. Do they not teach you that in sponsor school?"

"Ha, funny," Lena said.

"How do you find the will to carry on, Lena? What keeps you coming back?"

"Back to the program? Or do you mean, what gets me out of bed in the morning?"

"Either one."

"Oh, boy. Let me put on my sponsor hat. Well, anytime I start to wobble, I remember what it felt like when I was still drinking, when I couldn't keep a job and had to declare bankruptcy, when I was homeless because I couldn't pay the rent, and my parents disowned me. If I need proof that I'm powerless over alcohol, all I have to do is remember. If I go out, my life will very quickly become completely and totally unmanageable. And in short order, I will be dead."

"I envy you your clarity," Pythia said.

What about me? I keep trudging forward, but why? What am I supposed to be doing? I thought I knew my God's will for me, but I fear whatever knowledge I had is long since lost in time. As am I.

"Clarity, I don't know. Maybe some. Life is definitely better sober, considering the alternative is death. But that doesn't mean I wake up every day and thank God for letting me live." Lena laughed a little. "What about you, Pythia? What keeps you coming back? You aren't even an alcoholic."

"Lena, my life has been long and complicated," Pythia said.

"Ha, spoken like a true alcoholic!"

"You mean, self-centered and fearful?" Pythia laughed. "Yes, you are correct. I am sure if I put my mind to it, I would make an excellent alcoholic."

"Well, don't go out, Pythia, it would kill me. Plus, it would reflect poorly on my reputation as a sponsor."

"I treasure our friendship, too, Lena," Pythia said, responding to Lena's unspoken thought.

"Hey, don't get soggy on me, Pythia. I'm the actor!" Lena sniffed a little and said, "Well, thanks. Me, too. Maybe just being present for our friends is enough of a life purpose, maybe we don't need to get bogged down in the deep questions."

"The old-timers in A.A. say service is the answer. What can we do to help the family of the child who was injured?" Pythia asked.

"Great question. I'll ask Sylvia. Maybe the Faire has set up a fund."

�৯

On Tuesday morning, Debra called to say she would be spending the morning at the optometrist, getting her eyes checked. Pythia knew that after the appointment, Debra would also shop for new eyeglasses, lingerie, and sandals at the Beverly Center and meet a friend for lunch at El Coyote. Pythia didn't mind paying Debra sick pay for hours spent shopping. She relished the peaceful silence of the office when she was alone.

First, she checked the calendar on Debra's desk and saw bookings for two clients. One was a returning client who painted pet portraits and the other was a new client who hoped to get some guidance on becoming a holistic wellness advisor. Nothing she couldn't handle.

Next, she checked the news for updates and was glad to learn the child injured at the Faire would be released from the hospital tomorrow. She pondered the identity of the woman who had seemed to be pointing a wand-like object toward the rampaging horse. Could it have been some sort of electrical device?

The artist wasn't due until eleven. *I should not do this, but I feel compelled.* Pythia locked the front door of the office, hung a sign that indicated she would be right back, and went downstairs. She brought some rags, spray cleaner, and extra candles.

Without Debra there to make her feel guilty, she lit more candles than usual and set about dusting the table and altar in the alcove. She emptied the pebbles and coins from the clay dish into her skirt pocket, where they rattled and dragged one side of her skirt toward the floor.

Why do I keep bringing him offerings? Does he know? Does he care?

She lifted the heavy painting from the shelf. Apollo's visage was obscured by dust. Chagrined, she dabbed at the grime with a rag. *I am sorry, my Beloved.*

Gradually, the face she knew so well emerged. Bright eyes, golden curls, perfect chiseled lips. She gazed at the face, hoping to feel a connection, a stirring, something to show she was not alone. Nothing.

Sighing, she burnished the wood frame to bring back some of the gloss and replaced the painting on the shelf. The brightened tones glowed in the candlelight.

"Help me understand what happened, my Lord. Lend me your wisdom so I can see the truth. Apollo, I do not ask for myself. Please help me help the child."

Clambering onto the stool, she settled the legs over the crack in the floor. She inhaled until her lungs were full and aching with the stench of tar and sulfur, raised her hands into the air in the classic Oracle pose, and plunged into the dark space that opened in her mind.

Pythia tried to steer her oracular sense toward useful insights but as her mind descended into darkness, her conscious control fled. Since her adolescent illness, her ability to guide her trances was erratic or nonexistent. She was at the mercy of unseen forces. Often, nothing she saw made sense.

Her eyes opened. She seemed to be standing on a dirt path cutting through a wide grass pasture. Behind her was a mountainside of tall fir trees. Off to the west she saw the last of the day's light dimming. No structures were apparent, no signs of people. Cold air seeped around her sandal-clad feet. A frigid breeze ruffled her hair. She turned to look over her shoulder and saw a bank of storm clouds coming on fast. A heavy rain began, transforming the dirt at her feet to mud. Soon she was drenched and shivering.

"Apollo!" she cried, wrapping her arms around her waist. "Apollo, where are you?"

Lightning arced down from the sky and smashed into the ground a few yards from where she stood. She squatted to present less of a target. *Dang it, there goes my skirt.*

She wondered what this vision might have to do with the accident. *This is ridiculous. I can't sit here in the mud. Apollo, give me a sign!*

Nothing happened except the rain intensified. Wiping rain from her eyes, she started walking on the path, headed downhill away from the forest. Her wet skirt was soon clinging to her thighs. As she rounded a curve, lightning revealed the wide dark mouth of a tunnel, a hundred yards away. The rough road headed straight for the tunnel. She grimaced. *Or is it a cave? I have seen these stories. They never end well.*

"What would you have me do, my Lord? I am too old to be running around on slippery hillsides in the rain!"

Thunder crashed overhead, obscuring the sound of approaching horse hooves. Almost too late she sensed rather than saw the impending danger. She fell into the grass on the verge as a huge black horse thundered past, kicking up great clots of mud from the road. On the back of the horse clung a tall figure in a hooded black cape.

"Hey!" Pythia shouted but her voice was lost in the wind and rain. *What fairy tale is this? There are so many dark caves, countless black horses with mysterious riders. Why is it the only way out is always through some dark tunnel?*

After some minutes of trudging, Pythia gained the opening of the tunnel. It was barely tall enough for a vehicle. Or a horse and rider. *Not impressed.*

Inside, flames flickered. Someone was tending a campfire set not far from the opening, right in the middle of the road.

"I am coming in," Pythia warned, voice echoing. "My name is Pythia, and I was once an Oracle to the god Apollo."

"Is that so?" said a loud hoarse voice. "Well, la di da. What are you now, wretched little Oracle?"

Pythia entered the tunnel, stubbing her toe on uneven pavement. "Dang it," she muttered.

She flung her hair out of her eyes and sought her questioner. She saw a tall figure wearing a long black cape seated on a large rock, one of several arranged in a rough circle. The person, presumably the rider, seemed to be tending the flames.

"Who are you?" Pythia demanded.

The person dropped a couple branches onto the fire with one hand. Long gray hair fell to the side, revealing a wrinkled face, gender indeterminate.

"Sit here by the fire, Oracle, and warm yourself."

Pythia shrugged. *What can happen in a vision? I may die but I will awaken in my basement. It has happened before.*

She seated herself on a rock furthest from this strange character and started wringing water from her skirt. "You know me. Tell me what I came here to learn."

The figure leaned forward and pointed a gnarled finger. "You want to fix something that has already happened."

"A child was injured."

"You think someone provoked the horse." *How could she know this?* Pythia realized her mind had conjured a classic fairy tale villain, the ubiquitous witch, black robes, long stringy hair. *Is this the best I can do, after all these years? Have I so little imagination?*

"Was it you? Were you there at the Faire?"

"And if I were?"

"Did you do something to upset that horse?"

"And if I did?"

"Who are you?" Pythia demanded again.

The witch pointed at Pythia. This time, the gnarled hand held a black wand.

The witch leaned forward and reached toward the fire. The flames grew to twice their size. A hank of white fire attached itself to the end of the wand.

"You don't get to ask me questions, you insignificant worm!" cried the witch as she lobbed the fireball straight at Pythia. "Crawl back to your pathetic god!"

Pythia had time to think *Really? Who is this lunatic?* before she fell out of the vision back into the basement.

Pythia was glad to note her clothes were dry. Nevertheless, she checked her clothing for smoldering embers, just in case. She sighed and got to her feet.

She paused in front of the portrait, perplexed. *Did you happen to notice, Apollo—not that you would care, given your current silent treatment—that witch was wearing what I believe was some rather expensive designer footwear?* As usual, no answers were forthcoming from the portrait, so she blew out the candles and went upstairs to the office with a migraine blooming behind her eyes.

April 21, 2015

As I have shared before, I was one of many Greek children ordained to serve in Apollo's temple. My mother had ten children. She did not want to let us go—Dione was her favorite of her daughters—but my father was not a wealthy farmer. We struggled to grow barley and millet to feed our five goats and ourselves. Feeding so many mouths was difficult. Selling us to the temple gave us all a better chance to survive.

Now, after doing some reading, I realize he could have sold us into prostitution. My life would no doubt have been much shorter and more painful. Had that been my fate, I would never have known the love of my God Apollo.

Dione and I had no say in the matter. One morning before dawn, Mother gave us each two barley cakes and bade us goodbye. Was she sad? I do not recall. I was five years old; Dione was eight. Father lifted us onto a donkey and led the way up a long dusty mountain trail. I dozed with my cheek against Dione's back, smelling her distinct scent of dirt, sweat, sea salt, and lavender, rocking to the jerky gait of the donkey as it labored.

I was hungry and thirsty when we reached the temple at Delphi near mid-day. Dione and I dismounted, muscles stiff, and stood in the yard by the quivering donkey.

My home by the azure sea, miles away, was already fading in my mind, hidden in pale mist far below Mt. Parnassus. The sun ruled here in Delphi. The heat and light energized me. I felt as if I could gather the burning orb into my arms.

I had never seen anything so magnificent as the city of Delphi. Stone columns rose in the air, holding up roofs that seemed as high as the clouds. Sunlight reflected on marble facings. People moved with purpose across smooth cobbles, carrying lemons and huge heads of lettuce in wicker baskets, leading animals, herding wayward shouting children.

I examined the faces. Except for a few irate youngsters and some scowling slaves, people appeared content.

Father conducted the transaction with a woman priestess. In exchange for two daughters, he received baskets of high-quality wheat and oats, bronze tools, and fishing implements. These he loaded into the donkey's saddle bags. He ordered us to obey the priests and priestesses. Dione explored the nearby hillside while I bade farewell to the donkey.

Father patted my head once as he watered the donkey at a stone basin fed by a carved fish spouting spring water. The priestess called Dione down from the hillside and ushered us into the temple. When I last saw Father, he was giving the patient donkey a handful of oats. I dawdled, waiting for a wave that never came. I presume our father reached our village some-time before nightfall, if the donkey did not put a foot wrong and send them both tumbling into a ravine. I never saw my home or family again.

I was too excited and overwhelmed to be afraid at first. Later, when Mistress Dora showed us the dormitory, I began to cry. The straw mattresses smelled like weeds and old hay. I was not the only child crying. Selling poor children into temple service was common in ancient Greece. We all missed our families, our pets, and our simple pastoral or pelagic homes.

The air smelled different on the mountain. Parts of Delphi were not far below the snowline. It was cold at night, and the wool blankets were scratchy. The food was different too, meat rather than fish. For a few days Dione tried to console me, but she was busy learning how to navigate our new environment. She was a strategic thinker. Right away she saw the potential in her new position.

Dione and I were chosen to train as Oracles, along with a dozen or so other young girls and boys. Dione wanted to be the best Oracle, but she was not inclined to study. I, on the other hand, loved to study and found I had a knack for telling the future. Dione was not adept at *seeing* but she was an expert in human behavior long before that was a field of study. What she lacked in oracular art she made up in manipulation and appearances. She was soon the temple favorite among our cohort.

Until I came into my power, I gained some cachet simply by being Dione's sister. As my power increased, though, we grew apart. Dione began spending her time with the older acolytes. I saw her rarely, usually from afar, as she led her friends across the plaza or lounged with them in the herb garden, pretending to be working. She said I was still a baby, and perhaps I was.

In other news, the smell of methane in the basement was stronger than usual this week. I remember the year Kress Dress for Less exploded. I failed to predict that event. Fortunately, no one died. I cannot guarantee I will have a premonition if such a thing were to happen again. I hope we are not in for another episode. For now, Blog Readers, for the next few weeks, if you are visiting the Los Angeles area, I recommend you stay away from the vicinity of Wilshire and Fairfax.

—Yours in exile, Delphina

ॐ

"I hate artists."

Pythia paused at Debra's desk and looked at her. "Why do you hate artists, Ms. Sandhill?"

"Because they pretend like they want to turn their art into a business, and then when you help them start doing it, they head for the hills like it's the zombie apocalypse."

Pythia smiled at the image. "To whom do you refer, in particular?"

"That idiot Renee Fletchall. I asked her how she was doing on her business plan, you know, just making conversation, and she started crying."

"Oh, dear."

"I'm just warning you now, in case she gives us a bad review on Groodle."

Pythia continued on toward her office.

"By the way, Pythia, I really need a new computer. This thing is ancient. It's not powerful enough anymore to handle the newer programs. I'm starting to run out of memory."

Pythia sighed. *So are we all.* "You are right, Ms. Sandhill. Give me some estimates of what you need, and I will see what I can do."

Pythia sat down at her desk and stared at the photo of Apollo's Temple.

A polite tapping on the door jamb interrupted Pythia's reverie.

Stacy Landers, one of her tenants, leaned partway into the office. "Hi, Ms. Apulu. Do you have a minute?"

"Certainly, Miss Landers. Please have a seat." Stacy perched on the edge of the visitor chair. Her neon orange tank top and black yoga pants left little to the imagination.

"Call me Stacy, would you? I keep telling you, Miss Landers sounds like a kindergarten teacher."

"All right, Stacy. And you may call me Pythia. How may I help you today?"

Pythia didn't need her gift of insight to know what Stacy was going to ask but she waited for Stacy to explain the problem in her own words.

"Well, plain and simple, I need more clients."

"I see. What types of marketing tactics are you using now?"

"Uh, none, really. I'm mostly word of mouth. I ran an ad in the local newspaper, that didn't do anything. What else, let's see, I have a website."

"Very good. One moment. I am going to ponder your situation and see what comes to mind."

Pythia closed her eyes and let her mind roam. She didn't mind looking silly in front of Stacy. All her tenants knew she was a bit eccentric. They'd often seen her descending into the basement but were too polite to ask what she did down there.

Debra no doubt had told them she was doing drugs. *I am their landlord, what can they say?*

Pythia relaxed and let images come. She saw animals: Horses, chickens, tame rabbits running in a cage . . . the types of animals she used to help care for at Delphi. Even powerful Oracles had chores. Young acolytes helped in the gardens and in the pastures, tending crops and feeding livestock.

For some reason, Pythia kept seeing one type of farm animal in particular.

She opened her eyes. "I think I have a solution," she said. "Goats."

"Goats?" Stacy echoed, shaking her head, making her blonde curls flutter.

"Yes. I picture people doing yoga poses with little goats."

"You mean, the goats jump on their . . . ? I don't know. Are you sure? That sounds crazy, Pythia."

"Nevertheless," Pythia said firmly. "It will soon be on Good Morning America." *Next year.* "I hear it is just catching on in Oregon. If you offer goat yoga now, you will be ahead of the curve in Los Angeles."

"Are you serious?" Stacy started giggling, displaying chipmunk teeth.

"Stacy, you could put them in little pajama jackets!" Debra stood grinning in the doorway.

"Where do I find goats?"

Pythia pointed to Debra. "Ms. Sandhill will help you with that. I suggest you write up a marketing plan, detailing the strategy and the costs associated with implementation."

April 22, 2015

Long ago I accepted that I was just another Pythia in a long line of Oracles named Pythia, going back at least to 1400 BC. I considered it an honor. Dione, on the other hand, thought it was absurd. One day we were sitting on our favorite shaded rock outcropping overlooking the amphitheater where some second-rate actors were rehearsing a performance on the distant stage.

"Why should we give up our names to serve this god?" she demanded. "It is like we have no identity."

"We are called to serve with all our being," Pythia said. "That means even giving up our given names."

"We were born on a poor farm by the sea. Do you remember? Our mother, our father? The goats and the stink? I cannot forget. I will never forget your name," she said. She pulled up a handful of wild daisies that had managed to grow in a crack in the rock and began plucking the petals, letting them flutter over the edge of the crag.

"What was my name, Sister?" I asked. I was not intending to start an argument. I had truly forgotten. At the time, I was about ten, and she was about thirteen, a grown woman. I had been a working Oracle in the temple for at least four years, ascending the ranks to the top. I was no longer a child.

"Your name is . . . " She stopped and frowned. "Your name was something like . . . Sofia, Saffia. Selena? Why can I not remember?"

"Serving Apollo has changed us," I observed.

"I do not want to be changed," Dione said. "I want to be myself, forever."

As usual, I said the wrong thing. "I am content to serve."

"Yes, we all know you are the Pythia," she said in a bitter tone. "You are the strongest Oracle in generations, so the priests say. Your foretelling is sought after by kings and princes. La di da."

She had a right to be jealous. I was arrogant. However, I was only ten, Blog Readers, therefore not fully mature. I admit, I was proud of my exalted rank in the temple. Humility did not come until later, after I lost my powers and position.

"What does that mean, those words, la di da?"

"An old lady in the laundry says it sometimes. It means be careful, your arrogance and pride are making you a fool."

"Sarcasm does not become you," I said.

Dione snorted. "Serving Apollo has turned your brain into goat mash."

Several days later, I met Dione on our favorite rock. I gasped when I saw her face. A painful red welt blemished her right cheek near her lower eyelid.

"Sister, what happened to you?"

"Nothing. I fell." She pulled away from me.

"That looks like a burn," I said. "Did someone hurt you?"

"Mind your own business, Pythia. You are a meddlesome brat."

"You should tell Mistress Dora," I said.

"I am fine. Leave me alone."

I let her be. Before long, her cheek healed, leaving an H-shaped scar. She was still beautiful to me, and I thought no more about it. I never did learn what happened to her.

Blog Readers, the reason I write about this memory is this: In one of my recent visions, I heard someone use this term, *la di da*. I looked for the phrase in the dictionary and discovered the term is modern. It is not possible that Dione knew this term when we were children in ancient Greece, not unless someone is traveling through time.

As far as I know, the only ones able to travel through time are the gods and goddesses of Mt. Olympus. Since my childhood illness, I cannot see the future clearly, no matter how much methane I inhale.

I fear something bad is on the horizon.

—Yours in exile, Delphina

Chapter 4

"I'm thinking of giving up acting." Lena walked with her head down, looking at her sneakers, even though the hiking trail above Malibu was rock-free and the view was spectacular.

Pythia could tell something had happened to Lena. While she waited for Lena to share, Pythia inhaled the scents of heather and wild grass and imagined she hiked the hills of Mt. Parnassus. Far below was the blue Pacific Ocean—not the ocean she was used to seeing, but a soothing sight nevertheless, stretching to the horizon where it blended with a fog bank. The mid-morning sun was hot on the back of her neck. She was glad she wore her wide-brimmed straw hat.

"I'm not getting the right kind of parts," Lena said. She wore a multicolored sundress made of tie-dyed cotton that she'd purchased at a flea market in Pasadena. Pythia had been with her that day, another hot day in the California sun.

Pythia hand brushed against Lena's arm. An image of a short fat man with grabby hands flashed into her mind.

"Ah," she said. "Your agent is not doing his job."

"I've been praying for his sorry-ass soul," Lena said.

"I love this place," Pythia said. She looked out over the landscape and pretended the town of Delphi was around the next bend. She and Lena hiked this trail frequently, if the weather wasn't too hot. They enjoyed hiking Bronson Canyon in Griffith Park as well.

"Does it remind you of Greece?"

"I was born near the ocean but grew up on a mountain, in terrain similar to this."

"Pythia, do you think I should quit?"

A sudden intuition made Pythia stop and look back along the trail. A man was visible below them, headed in their direction. A little shiver ran up her spine. *What is this? Is this something I should fear? Apollo, everything is so hazy, why can I not see?*

Lena stopped walking as well. The man was just fifty feet behind and closing fast. With relief and confusion, Pythia recognized Glen Haven. She waited, seeing an interaction could not be avoided.

"Oh, good heavens. Fancy running into you here! Hello, Ms. Apulu!" Glen's surprise seemed feigned, but she detected no malicious intent. His dark face glistened with sweat. He wore a blue baseball cap with an embroidered insignia that appeared to be a stylized H. *For Haven, probably. He seems like the type.* He wore a tight blue t-shirt and long athletic pants that showed off his fit form.

"Greetings, Mr. Haven. How are you? Lena, this is Mr. Glen Haven, the gentleman I met with last week about the property development project. Mr. Haven, this is my friend Lena Tollefson."

"Oh, the actor?"

Lena smiled with pleasure. "Why, yes, Mr. Haven, I've had a few parts in some things," she said.

"Please, call me Glen," Glen said, extending his hand.

Lena shook his hand. "Do you hike this trail often, Glen?"

"Actually, it's my first time. I'm staying not too far from here, in the Palisades. I was told this was a great hike. Thought I'd check it out. The view is fantastic."

"Lovely day for it," Lena said.

Glen put a hand on Pythia's arm.

"Say, Ms. Apulu, have you had a chance to reconsider my request?"

Pythia stepped back from Glen and extended her right hand. He responded without thinking, as she had hoped. As they clasped hands, she stared into his eyes, digging deep for something, anything, to tell her what was going on. His hand was warm. His handshake was firm. Small beads of sweat dotted his forehead. She smelled a pleasant mix of sweat, after-shave, and something herbal, like lavender, but not so pleasant. *Who are you? What is your story?*

She cocked her head to one side, delving, listening.

Glen tried to disengage his hand, but Pythia held on. She sensed something around the edges of his aura preventing any insight from reaching her oracular sense. *You have something on you, something—*

"What are you doing?" Glen said, tugging.

"I am considering your request," Pythia answered.

She let go of his hand. "My answer is still no. Good to see you today, Mr. Haven. Enjoy your hike." She turned away.

"Wait! Up there on that hill, that's the land we've purchased for our retreat center and resort hotel," Glen said, pointing. "We won't destroy the environment! We've hired an award-winning architect. We have promised to donate substantial funding to the Friends of Malibu Hills."

"That is commendable, Mr. Haven. I wish you all the best."

Pythia settled her sunhat more firmly on her head and continued up the hill with Lena. After a minute, she looked back and saw that Glen Haven had turned around and started descending the trail.

"What the hell was that all about?" Lena said.

"I am not sure."

"He's the one you said came to your office and pressured you into getting involved in his project?"

"Yes, the one with the so-called silent partner." Pythia inhaled the clean scent of the ocean. Her heart settled back into a rhythm. She focused on imagining she was hiking the trails at Delphi, reveling in the motion of her muscles pro-pelling her along the dusty track.

"Sounds fishy to me. Cute dude, though. Damn. Hey, slow down a little."

"I think my assistant has first claim on him."

"Huh. Well, what about you and that DJ?"

Pythia looked at her friend in surprise. "Arnie?"

"Yeah. I've seen how you smile at him."

Pythia smiled.

"Yeah, like that. That smile," Lena laughed, nudging Pythia's shoulder with her own. Pythia laughed, too.

"Acting makes you happy, Lena. As long as it still makes you happy, no, you should not give it up."

"Maybe a new agent would help."

Pythia caught a glimpse in her mind of a cheerful woman with pink and green hair and a nose ring. Tattoos peeked out from an open-necked suit jacket.

"Her name is Milly. Molly? Something like that, starts with an M."

Lena laughed. "I think I know the one! Thanks, Pythia. I'll give her a call when I get back to the Arcade."

"Cindi Harper wants you to review her new website," Debra said as Pythia came into the office on Monday morning. "I've seen it. It's pretty great. I've ordered more stuff."

"How did the . . . shopping basket, is that what you call it? How well did that part work?" Pythia said, pausing at Debra's counter. Debra sometimes wore her brown hair loose around her shoulders; today, she wore a ponytail clipped with a white plastic bow.

"Shopping cart. I'd say it worked pretty good. It sucked fifty bucks out of my bank account with no problem."

"Let's see if she is able to ship the products in a reasonable amount of time."

"Hey, you know that guy, Glen Haven?"

Pythia nodded. "Did he call?"

"He called and left a voice mail message. Something about apologizing for something he said? Did you meet him over the weekend or something?" The tone of Debra's voice accused Pythia of something nefarious. *And perhaps a bit of jealousy?*

"Lena and I were hiking in Malibu and ran into him on the trail. He tried again to involve me in his property development project."

"And you said no, again," Debra grinned. "What's with you, Pythia? That guy is hot."

Pythia continued on into her office cubicle. She put her purse in a desk drawer. "I am going downstairs for a minute."

"Every Monday like clockwork. What do you do down there, Pythia?"

"I sit and think."

"In that smelly basement? You must be crazy."

"Some would say you are correct, Ms. Sandhill."

Pythia opened the hallway door and trudged the well-worn carpet to the basement door. *She thinks I am doing drugs. She is not wrong.*

After a few moments of inhaling the gas from the crack in the floor, Pythia wafted down a gentle slide into her center. *The boundary between waking and sleeping is thin even in real life. Waking and sleeping, life and death, it is all the same.*

She opened her eyes to a familiar sight of the village of Delphi bathed in moonlight. The city was dark. She could see no torches. The streets were empty of people and animals. She could hear no sound but her sandals scuffing along the cobbles. *It must be near daylight. Everyone is still asleep, even the wrens and sparrows. All the torches and watch fires have gone out. Even the wind in the olive trees is silent.*

She walked up the steps into Apollo's temple, footsteps echoing off the stone walls and marble columns. The darkness was near absolute. She stubbed her toe on some obstacle on the floor. She reached down. *A block of stone, in the walkway? Was there an earthquake?*

She drifted along the colonnade with one hand on the wall, listening for signs of life. Even in the dark, her feet found the way to the supplicants' hall. Moonlight flooded through a jagged hole in the roof. *I see the cracks in the floor but I smell nothing. What is that pile of sticks in the corner? Is that my stool?*

A soft sniffing sound made her turn. In the pale moonlight, Pythia saw a child huddled against the wall.

"Are you hurt?" Pythia asked.

The child's eyes glinted with fear. "Who are you? Are you a spirit?"

"Perhaps, in a manner of speaking. My name is Pythia."

"My name is also Pythia," the child said.

Pythia examined the girl. Her arms were bone thin and covered with sores. Her feet were bare. Even in the dark, Pythia could see her tunic was filthy. *She needs a bath and a good meal.*

"Where are your servants, young Pythia?"

"They ran away when the earth shook. The walls and ceiling fell down. The air from the earth stopped coming. The Oracles' power is gone. I have been left behind."

"Where is Apollo?" Pythia asked in dismay.

"Dead." The child's voice quavered with unshed tears.

"Apollo is a god. He cannot die. Perhaps he has returned to Mt. Olympus."

"To eat ambrosia and nectar?" the child whispered. "Without me?"

Pythia held out her hand to the child. "Come, we must leave this place."

The instant they clasped hands, the child dissolved. Pythia was left holding empty air.

"Apollo, do not leave me," she whispered in despair.

Pythia found her way back to the moonlit street. She stood in the center of the avenue and looked around. *What am I here to learn, my Lord? Show me.* Upon closer inspection, she saw many buildings had tumbled into piles of blocks and columns, pummeled by the shifting of the earth. *Mt. Parnassus wakes from time to time to let us know it still has the power to destroy what humans so arrogantly build.*

Pythia heard a swelling sound in the distance. *Is that thunder?* Her twenty-first century ears recognized the sounds of traffic approaching. She saw nothing but the sound made her leap out of the street to hug an adjacent wall. *I do not see the cars, but I can hear them.* A horn honked. A truck engine swept past, followed by the unmistakable stutter of a motorcycle engine. A dog barked and then began to howl. She looked all around but could see nothing, not even a breeze moving leaves on the trees.

This is my vision. Who is guiding this vision if not me? Pythia raised her hands in the air in the classic pose of the Oracle and stepped back into the street. She held her pose as the whine of a large grinding engine got louder. Tires screeched on pavement. A warning horn began to blast. *I cannot see them, but I fear they can see me.* The next moment, the impact of something large, heavy, and metal sent her flying out of her body and back into the office basement.

She caught her breath, feeling her skull begin to tighten with an impending migraine. *If this were real life, I would surely be dead.*

§

"You really know how to whip them into shape," Stacy said as she entered Pythia's office cubicle.

"What do you mean?" Pythia asked, setting down her pen.

"I just saw Renee out in the lobby. She was crying. I asked her what was wrong and she said she didn't understand how you could expect her to make a spreadsheet. Her being an artist and what not."

Pythia hid her smile and waved Stacy to the visitor's chair. "How can I help you today, Ms. Landers?"

"I found four goats!"

"Excellent. Have you started offering classes with them?"

"They are so cute, Pythia. You should come take a class. They jump on your back and go around your legs."

"That sounds like fun."

"They come dressed in little jackets. The goat owner brings them in a cute little van with their portraits painted on the sides. These guys are celebrities."

Pythia smiled. "How are your customer reacting to the goats?"

"They love them!" Stacy laughed. "Guess what! Channel 6 News is coming next week to do a segment."

"That is wonderful. Be sure to take lots of photographs and videos. You can use them in your marketing materials."

"I've been doing some videos. I started a YourTurn channel, with Debra's help," Stacy said. "I've already got 10,000 views!"

"That sounds good," Pythia said.

"I can't thank you enough for all your help, and for the break on the rent for the past few months. I think very soon I will be able to pay you all the back rent."

"Please do not worry about it, Ms. Landers." Pythia's insight was sending her some signals she could not interpret. *What is this? I see a shaggy dog wearing sunglasses. A small car going over a cliff into the ocean. A pear tree bending and breaking in the wind. Four black goats in polka-dot pajamas running past the Bob's Big Boy mascot.* "By the way, did you get a dog?"

"No, why?"

"Just a feeling. I am sensing trouble with a dog."

"No, no dogs. Just baby goats! I'll let you know when the news segment airs. Goat yoga is going to be a thing!"

&

"Tonight as our speaker we have Nathan from Phoenix, Arizona," George said, peering over his half-glasses at the audience assembled in the church basement room. "I heard Nathan was visiting the area and asked him to speak. Please welcome Nathan."

The group applauded as a heavy man bounded up the two steps to the podium, making the platform rattle. He wore a purple polo shirt tucked into brown pleated slacks. A narrow belt supported his pants across the wide expanse of his stomach.

"Hello everyone, my name is Nathan, and I am an alcoholic."

"Hi, Nathan," the group mumbled.

"I'm visiting L.A. for a dance convention. All they do at these conventions is dance and drink. Happy hour is nonstop. It's always time for cocktails. I don't know how they do it, drink and then dance. Thank God there are so many A.A. meetings in L.A. I've been going to a meeting twice a day. Seriously, without meetings, I'd be dead. I'm a blackout drunk. I used to go on a bender and wake up in rehab with no recollection of what I did, who I met, how much money I spent, or who I had sex with."

Several audience members nodded in agreement.

"I kept promising my friends and family I would stop drinking. I didn't stop. I couldn't stop, but they didn't know that, and neither did I. My parents couldn't bear to see me destroying myself. One by one, they all turned away from me. I was too sick to realize they were heartsick with grief. I blamed them for abandoning me. I carried the resentments for many years."

Nathan scanned the audience. Pythia met his eyes. *I do not understand this story. My so-called family expected me to inhale methane gas so I could fulfill my function.*

"I've been sober for twenty-three years. I still feel the urge to drink, especially when other people are drinking and getting away with it." He shook his head. "I know I have a disease. I'm like a guy who gets a thrill out of jumping off buildings. I start with garages and treehouses, and break an arm or a leg. It hurts, and I promise to stop. When I get out of the hospital, I head straight for a five-story condo. I know it's going to kill me but I can't stay away from the edge. That is the disease of alcoholism for me."

More heads nodded.

"I met a man in rehab who was just as sick as I was. He said something that stuck with me. He said, 'How can we assume we will be alive tomorrow just because we are alive today?'" At the time, I didn't understand what he meant. I thought he was just being obtuse. After I had time to think about it, I think he was asking how is it possible to have faith in the face of un-certainty."

Nathan laughed. "I think he was also deep into his persona as the very special worm around which the universe revolves!"

The audience chuckled. Nobody minded that his story seemed rehearsed.

"The trick that works for me," Nathan said, "is that I've stopped fighting with the idea of a higher power. I just assume something exists. My life is more serene and less angry if I just decide to surrender. I don't know what God is, or even if there is a God. I just act as if there is, and then I get busy living. Maybe the sun won't come up tomorrow. That is not in my control. All I can do is make sure I do my best to make this day a day filled with kindness and compassion toward others.

Whatever God is, God is good. I came to A.A. looking for a miracle cure and found a spiritual awakening."

At the end of the meeting, the group held hands and recited a prayer. Pythia steeled herself for the onslaught of images that always came through the shared connection. Tonight she saw Nathan dancing on a stage in front of thousands. *Convention, indeed.* Despite his bulk, he could bend and twist as gracefully as any ballet dancer she had ever seen. Nathan's creative interpretation of music by a modern composer received a standing ovation. Pythia felt his elation, and through that elation, for a few moments, she felt a connection to someone else's higher power.

May 2, 2015

I have always been interested in people. Unlike my sister, I was a helpful child, mostly. I found satisfaction in serving supplicants who came to the temple seeking wisdom and guidance. I did my best, until I fell ill.

After my illness, my oracular powers failed to return. Mistress Dora nursed me back to physical health but my attempts at predicting the future were no better than those of a novice. Even when fully engulfed in the fumes rising from the cracks in the earth, I could help only with the small things, and even then my predictions were often incorrect. Accordingly, I was demoted to a junior position. Sometimes, the cook consulted me on matters of cuisine, which I believe she did out of pity. It was infuriating to see other Oracles take my place on the ornate stool in the temple.

I do not remember much from the time of my illness. When I regained consciousness, I immediately called for Dione. Mistress Dora told me my sister had been sent to another temple in the northeastern part of Greece. I was aghast. Daphne, the servant who tended me after Namia disappeared, told me Dione had left of her own accord and was glad to be rid of me. No one had the courage to tell me the truth. On reflection, I do not think anyone actually knew the truth. Dione always had her own agenda, even when we were young.

I admit, I spent a lot of time in the garden, moping under the arbors and praying to my Lord God Apollo to restore my powers or send me to Dione's temple, preferably both. I felt anger and resentment that he was not fulfilling my demands. What good was he? He had failed to keep me safe, and then he had sent away the only family I had. I was alone because of Apollo. Fickle, cruel god!

I refused to believe my sister had abandoned me. Only Apollo would have had the power to send her away, so that must have been what happened. Another reason to hate him. I begged my caregivers to let me find her, but each time I was refused. That was the beginning of my loss of faith.

In addition to losing my faith, I lost my sense of reason. People could see I was increasingly distraught. I admit, I had tantrums. My peers began to avoid me. Eventually I was deemed unfit for service and asked to leave the temple of Apollo. Once I got over my shock, I was glad. If Apollo and his minions had not cast me out of the temple, I would have left on my own.

When I was about fifteen, I was assigned to help a goat-herder and his wife in a village a mile or so outside Delphi. They were a kind couple, but I did not last long in their service. I gathered my strength and hoarded my supplies, and one night under a full moon, I started walking across Greece, seeking my sister.

I never found her.

I looked in every small village but could not sense our sister connection, hard as I tried. I even searched for the village of our childhood. I discovered the village had vanished into the sea, and with it all trace of our history. Eventually I came to accept that Dione had died.

I moved with Greek migrants as they moved around the Continent. By the time I emigrated to the United States, I was more or less fully present in my body, but my oracular powers had not healed. I had occasional flashes of prescience but could offer little of any real value to anyone. I worked like any mortal, and when I had the funds, I sailed across the ocean in a steamer in the late 1880s with hordes of Greek men and a few courageous women seeking a new life in America.

I blended in. I learned useful skills. I created a new persona and lived on the periphery of the Greek communities coalescing in the U.S.

For some years, I worked in a textile mill. Later, I helped a man and his wife open a Greek restaurant. In the 1930s, I moved from the east coast to the Midwest, Chicago, to be precise. There was not much geothermal activity in Chicago. I carried a vial of gasoline and sniffed it like the addict I was.

In the 1950s, I migrated west to Los Angeles. I found the climate to my liking, not to mention all the geothermal activity in the area, and I have grown to love the landscape for its resemblance to my homeland.

Blog Readers, you no doubt have realized my feelings about my Lord God Apollo have softened with time. I walked many miles and had many years to contemplate my situation. Twenty-five centuries is a long time to remain angry. Eventually even stubborn Oracles have to surrender. We cannot do everything on our own. Sometimes we need the help of something greater than ourselves. Or at least the illusion of something greater.

I knew Apollo when he was young. Older than I by millennia, certainly, but still, as gods go, a young god still in the process of forming and learning. He could be fickle. I saw him be cruel at times. Sending Dione away was cruel. I never saw her again. I can only assume she died. If she lived, I am sure she would have searched for me, as I searched for her. No, she must have died long ago.

Apollo's second cruelty was casting me out of his temple simply because I was no longer fit for purpose. Cruel heartless god, I called him. I had served him faithfully until my illness. I was more faithful than Dione. I was the most powerful Oracle in all of the Mediterranean. Kings and queens, rulers of every state and nation, came to hear my foretelling. Everything I did was in honor of my Lord God Apollo.

Those days are long past. Now I am old and tired, and I am certainly less angry. A long time ago, I forgave my Lord Apollo. Dione is gone, Apollo is gone, but I am still alive, for reasons unknown to me. My prayer is that Apollo still lives. If Apollo still lives, somewhere, perhaps the years have given him wisdom and compassion.

Some of you have asked me, did I ever marry? The answer is no. I believe my position as a former Oracle of Delphi gave me an aura that protected me from the interests of men. Or women. I do not judge. Perhaps it was my air of grief and despair, I do not know. Impossible as it may seem, in all those centuries, I was neither courted nor assaulted. That is all I am going to say on that topic.

Why am I writing this story? You probably think I would do better as a fortune-teller at the county fair. I have been told time and again, people just want to know what is going to happen—to them. They do not care about me or anyone else.

Self-centered Americans are a bundle of contradictions. They want to believe in magic but when they see it, they refuse to believe what they are seeing. They claim to be compassionate and caring, yet when asked to give of themselves, so many balk. When told that life is uncertain and they can never truly know the future, they pretend they can manage and control life anyway, as if they are gods. Even the gods on Mt. Olympus could not control all things.

Where are they now, the omniscient gods of my youth? Forgotten. Mere footnotes in history textbooks. No one knows or cares.

—Yours in exile, Delphina

The next evening, Pythia glanced at the blog comments. The usual commenters expressed opinions ranging from sympathy to scorn. Bettina-the-Muse wrote, "You need to get a life, Delphina. Stop making everything about you." Razzle-dazzle wrote, "Imagination is a powerful tool to heal our psychic trauma. Since 2013, I have counseled many artists and writers to help them overcome their creative resistance and find their voices. Please check out my YourTurn videos."

GodsChosen wrote, "Come to the Church of Apollo and find peace."

Pythia shut down the computer.

Chapter 5

The television in the waiting area was on when Pythia entered the office.

"Pythia!" Debra said, rising from her chair. "I've got an idea on how we can build up your business."

She beckoned Pythia into the waiting area and turned up the volume.

"We missed the first few minutes because you were late, but here, this is that show that nutjob Cindi Harper was telling us about."

"Carl Clement's show."

"Right! Business Barracudas!"

"What is your suggestion?"

"Watch."

Pythia sat next to Debra in a client chair and watched Carl Clement, an enormous black man in a shiny gray suit, and two white men half his size, sit on a stage, and gaze skeptically at two women pitching some kind of plastic apron.

"They listen to pitches and then decide if they are going to invest."

"What is your thought, that we should pitch our business?"

"No! I think you should become a Barracuda!"

Pythia frowned at the television. One of the women was weeping into her apron sample. Carl Clement had just called her *honey* and told her to get back to the kitchen.

"I suppose I have had some experience making entrepreneurs cry," she said.

Debra grinned. "I think you should send in your application and résumé to Carl Clement."

"My résumé."

"Yeah. You have one, right?"

Pythia looked at Debra, at a loss for words. *My so-called résumé would require a hundred pages.*

"I suppose I could gather some information, if you could collate it into some sort of format. It has been a number of years since I had to think about my professional curriculum vitae."

"Right, whatever. Get me what you've got and I'll massage it into a masterpiece!"

Pythia tried to imagine herself sitting on the panel of men, listening to product pitches from misguided visionaries. As the woman wept into her product sample, her partner was pointing and yelling at the men, calling them sexist relics from a dying patriarchy.

Debra seemed hopeful for the first time in a while. "Don't you just love it? That could be you!" She leaped up and headed for her desk. "Time to get busy turning you into a TV star!"

Pythia watched the show until the end, in the interest of research into her new role as a Barracuda. She couldn't often see her future but glimpses flashed into her awareness from time to time. Even without her gift, it wasn't hard to guess that being a Business Barracuda was not going to be part of her future career. *Not sure what I have could be called a career.*

It was not lost on her that Debra had said "your business," not "our business." *I sense something is ending. That can only mean something new is starting. Change is inevitable. We ask for change, we pray for change, but we forget change comes with costs. By the time we realize that, it is too late.*

Pythia let her mind wander. The sunlight coming through the unwashed windows turned the peeling wallpaper a rich gold, lending the place an air of decadent nostalgia. Commercials came and went for products and services that meant little to her. Celebrities and silly animated cartoons promoted car insurance, reverse mortgages, dripping beef burgers, and carbonated beverages. *I cannot believe people pay money for bottled water that they could get almost free from their taps. Marketing truly is a monstrous machine.*

"Join us every day for Psychic to the Stars, the show where all your questions about the future are answered!"

Pythia opened her eyes and sat up. "Divina Dee has a daily show?"

"She's on every day, like a soap opera," Debra confirmed. "Isn't that crazy?"

§

Pythia arrived in plenty of time for the May episode of the Mystics Roundtable. She waved to Brian in the lobby and headed for the elevator. She noticed a wall of green plants near a shimmering fountain. "Has that always been there?" she asked Brian, pointing.

"Long as I've been here, 'bout eight years," he grinned.

"It is so pretty." She smiled as she got on the elevator, even though she was the only occupant. *Why am I so happy? Business is terrible. My assistant is restless, probably leaving. My connection with Apollo is in tatters. In spite of all that, I almost feel like . . . singing! Well, humming. What is happening? Maybe my luck is changing for the better.*

She waved at Arnie as she passed by his DJ booth. He waved back, smiling, and gave her a thumbs-up for some reason. She felt her heart lift.

Sylvia, Moon, and Mary were in their customary places.

"Am I late? I am so sorry," Pythia said.

"No, Lena's late," Moon said.

"I'm not late!" Lena said as she burst into the sound booth followed by an older woman with bouffant white hair trailing onto her shoulders. She wore a long baggy dark blue dress printed with tiny yellow moons and stars. A huge loosely woven shawl made of burnished bronze threads outlined thin shoulders. A fist-size amber brooch pinned on her chest held the shawl in place. To complete the ensemble, she carried an enormous bronze straw tote bag over one shoulder. Pythia noted gold sandals on tiny well-manicured feet. *She looks like a professional Mystic.*

"Hey, you all know my mother. Well, Pythia, you don't. Mom, this is Pythia Apulu, our Seer. Pythia, this is my mother, Madeline Frances Barrington, whom we know as Madame B."

"How do you do, Pythia? That's an unusual name. Are you foreign?"

"Mom, I need to start the show. Pythia, sorry, can you—?"

Arnie popped his head around the door. "I noticed you have a visitor," he said and produced a folding chair.

"Oh, thank you, Arnie," Lena said with relief. "Over there." She pointed to a corner. "Pythia, I'm so sorry."

"This is fine, Lena," Pythia said as Lena's mother took Pythia's seat and Pythia sat on the folding chair in the corner. She smiled at Arnie, who waved and retreated out of the sound booth.

"It's like a clown car," joked Sylvia. "Hi, Madame B. We haven't seen you here since our first show."

Lena shushed them with her hands and started the introduction to the show. After the opening, she played a short pre-recorded announcement. While her mic was off, she said, "The topic for today is—"

"Love," announced her mother. "Let's talk about love today."

Lena rolled her eyes and shrugged. "That okay with everyone else? I'll introduce my mother and the topic and then we'll take the first caller. Ready?" Lena adjusted some switches on the panel in front of her and leaned into the microphone hanging in front of her mouth.

"Welcome to the Mystics Roundtable. Hello to our four Mystics, Sylvia the Magnificent, Mistress Mary of the Stars, Conjuror of Coins Moon Cloud-River, and Pythia, our Seer without Peer. I hope you had an excellent month. We are honored to have a special guest with us today, Madame B, the president and head Mystic of the Mystics Institute, the organization that underwrites this program. Today we are taking your questions about love. Fantastic. Looks like we already have our first caller." Lena pressed some buttons. "We have Judy on the line. Judy, do you have a question about love for the Mystics today?"

Pythia watched from the corner, content to listen.

"Yes, hi, I'm Judy Weiss, calling in from Panorama City? I have a question? Can you tell me if I'm really in love? Uh, thanks? I'll take my answer off the air?"

"Thanks, Judy. You didn't mention your birthday, so let's have Moon do a I-Ching reading for you with her special coins." Lena looked at Moon.

Moon cast a nervous glance at Madame B before pulling three coins from a small black velvet bag. She set them on the narrow table in front of her.

Lena said, "Moon has a little velvet sack to hold her coins. Moon, will you tell us what you are doing?"

"Sure, Lena. First, I take a breath to center myself in Judy's question. Next, I take my three coins in my hand and breathe the question into them."

Before Lena could speak, Madame B unfolded her arms, reached a manicured hand to her mic, pulled it to her lips, and asked, "What coins are you using today, Moon?"

"Madame B, today I've chosen three American pennies, all minted in 1980. I keep these pennies in a special little velvet bag so they don't get contaminated with energy from other coins I might have with me. So, now I'm going to throw the three pennies six times."

Pythia couldn't see the coin tosses but she could hear the pennies rattling against something wooden.

"I throw the coins into a wooden box so they don't go all over the place," Moon said into her microphone as the coins clattered. "After each toss, I write down the value of the coin. Heads get a value of three. Tails get a value of two."

"Is this going to involve math? I hate math!" Sylvia interjected, and everyone laughed except Madame B.

"Don't worry, Sylvia. There's a bit of addition involved in this process, but I think you will be able to handle it," Moon said. "When you do six throws, you will get four possible outcomes. Three tails, three heads, two heads and one tail, or two tails and one head. Are you with me?"

"Sort of!" Sylvia said, grimacing sidewise at Mary.

"Each one of those four outcomes represents a certain state of yin or yang," Moon said. "I'm writing down the outcome after each throw, and I'm assigning a yin or yang to each throw, and I'm drawing a line on a piece of paper. We call the line 'changing or unchanging' and 'broken or unbroken.'"

"She's drawn six lines on her paper," Lena said, glancing warily at her mother, who had refolded her arms tightly under the shawl, showing thin shoulders and a flat chest. Lena twitched her jacket away from her own ample chest.

"Now I can use the I-Ching book to determine how to interpret the hexagram I've drawn on the paper. The I-Ching book is an ancient text explaining the meanings of the 64 hexagrams."

"Moon, if someone wanted to do a coin reading at home, could they get this book?"

"Certainly, Lena. The book is available at most libraries, and you can access it online. Companies also make special calculators that will give you the meaning of the hexagrams."

"What answer can you give Judy today? Is she in love or not?" Lena asked.

"Judy's hexagram is 44. I've consulted my I-Ching Book of Changes," Moon said. "This hexagram represents heaven above, wind below. In other words, temptation!"

Lena laughed into the microphone. "So . . . ?"

"My interpretation is that Judy is not actually in love, that rather, she is tempted by the presence of someone near her who has power and influence."

"Thanks, Moon," Lena said. "Judy, the I-Ching does not tell us what to do. It's a tool to help us understand and make meaning of the events in our lives. It is not a therapist or a dictator! We hope that helps you gain some clarity. Let's take a short break for some station announcements, and then we'll have our next caller."

The red light over the soundboard went off. Lena sagged back in her seat and grimaced at Pythia.

"Very nice," Madame B said to Moon, patting her on the arm. *They were students at her school. No wonder they are so nervous.*

Madame B turned to say something to Lena, but Lena raised her finger to head off her comment. "Sorry, we don't have time. Three, two . . . and now we have our next caller, Billy. Billy, welcome to the Mystics Roundtable. Where are you calling from and what is your question about love today?"

With no responsibilities, Pythia let her mind drift. Most callers asked typical questions—Will I get married? When will I find the right person? Will we be in love forever? Pythia didn't try to discern the answers. Love is not an event, it's a state of mind. Like faith. It's not something that happens to you, it's a condition you choose. *Not that I would know. Have I ever loved anyone but my Lord God Apollo? Yes, I loved my sister.*

Madame B had grown increasingly agitated as the discussion progressed. She snorted when a caller mentioned having found her true love. Lena glared at her, and Madame B scowled back.

Finally Lena took a deep breath and said, "Madame B, would you like to make a comment about true love?"

"Why, yes, Lena, I would, thank you for asking," Madame B said, grabbing the microphone.

Pythia caught short bright flashes: a long white lace-covered gown in a zippered dress bag thrown on an unmade bed, a yellow bowl smashed into pieces on a red tile floor, torn flowers in a plastic-lined trash can. *Not happy images, I would say. Images of lost love. A woman scorned, perhaps. Lena never mentions her father.*

"For all of you who believe in true love, I have a terrible truth for you. I, Madame B, see all and know all, and I know that there is no such thing as true love."

Lena shrank in her seat, head down, fingers resting on her forehead. Moon looked alarmed. Pythia saw Sylvia making the universal sign for *stop talking* by slicing her finger across her throat. Madame B ignored all the warning gestures and raised the volume, spearing Lena with her glare.

"A belief in true love is simply a crutch that allows us to limp through our lives without showing up for our responsibilities. Chasing true love is a distraction, like a feather in front of a cat. The chase gives us the illusion of forward movement, but there is no destination. True love is not a place you arrive at, like a honeymoon cottage in Fiji. True love does not exist, except as a figment of your tired, desperate, grasping imagination. You need an excuse to avoid being present in your sad humdrum mundane life—seeking true love is that excuse. You are welcome to it, but know that you are wasting your life energy on a fruitless quest for something that does not exist."

Madame B sat back in her chair and crossed her arms over her chest. She bared her teeth at Lena. "That is all. Carry on."

9

"Do you want to talk about it?" Pythia and Lena stood together in the parking lot after the A.A. meeting. It was another lovely spring evening. The pink and purple sky was mellowing into a balmy twilight. Pythia leaned against her car, enjoying the warm air on her bare arms.

"Oh, that woman," Lena said, leaning her elbows on the hood of the Insight and putting her forehead in her hands. "She is in such denial."

"Yes?" Pythia said in a neutral voice.

"I mean, she's such a nihilist. She believes in nothing, absolutely nothing. It drives her crazy that I go to A.A."

"She does not support your recovery?"

"I wasn't expecting her today. She didn't give me any warning, she just shows up and barges into my show. Like she owns the place. She's such a control freak."

Pythia remained silent.

Lena chuckled. "Well, I guess she does own the show." She threw her head back and gazed into the deepening blue sky. "I need to do some Step work around my mother, clearly. She's still got her hooks in me. You'd think after all this time."

Pythia nodded and touched her friend's arm. "The threads of family tapestries are tightly woven. Time does not relax the threads."

May 5, 2015

I listen to businesspeople complaining all day. That is my job. I use my gift as best as I can to give them good business advice. It is more like being a sponsor, if you are familiar with that concept. I cajole them into writing business plans and creating strategies for their little ventures. I encourage them to think long-term—to imagine their enterprises in fifty years, a hundred years. They stare at me like I have an extra head, like Hydra.

I have an assistant who is supposed to handle my marketing, including this new thing called social media, but she does not seem to like the job much anymore. She used to be a sweet girl. I do not know what to do. I am not adept at navigating this modern technological world. I was just getting used to telephones and yellow pages. You would think I would be able to anticipate some of these modern inventions. Blog Readers, I am sad to report that my oracular gift has not healed with time. I did not foresee the advent of computers, let alone this thing called social media.

My assistant's half-hearted attempts at marketing have failed to bring us new clients. Most people care only about getting the lowest price. They use the World Wide Web to compare prices among business coaches. My rates are already lower than other rates in this area. That is never a good business strategy.

I heard a rant today about the nonexistence of true love that could have been spoken by my sister, substituting "love" for "god." Is it true that my search for my Lord God Apollo serves to distract me from my humdrum life? Maybe I am wasting my life energy on a fruitless search for meaning. Should I resign myself to a small morose life, I, who used to be the most powerful Oracle in Greece? After almost three thousand years, I am tired. Maybe I should retire to a cave, if any still exist that are not made over into tourist attractions. This modern world was not meant for ancients such as I, especially ones severed for all time from the love and sustenance of their gods. I could look for other gods, as my friends in the program do, but no higher power could replace my Lord God Apollo.

Some of you have asked why I do not make predictions here in this blog. The truth is, I "see" very little anymore. I failed to predict the Northridge earthquake, and I completely missed the Malibu fires of 1994. However, I can help with small things.

For example, Rhymer, tomorrow you will wonder where you put your keys (they are in the freezer). SillySally44, please be forewarned that in a couple days the clutch on your 2001 Ford Escort will malfunction. The good news, the clutch cable will break just as you pull up and park in front of your house. You are welcome. Randall-in-Tucson, I am sorry for your impending loss.

—Yours in exile, Delphina

༄

Wednesday morning started like any other morning. Pythia doodled on her calendar, wondering when the overcast skies would clear. Debra was working on the proposal to Business Barracudas. Two clients were scheduled for the afternoon. Pythia made a couple trips to the coffeemaker, feeling restless.

"Stop checking up on me," Debra complained as Pythia walked by the second time.

"Forgive me, Ms. Sandhill. I am feeling strangely unsettled this morning."

"Well, go do something. I'm working."

Pythia returned to her desk with a full cup of tepid coffee. Before she could take a sip, a loud crash shook the building.

"What was that?" Debra hustled out of her cubicle, heading toward the front door. Pythia was close behind. They burst onto the sidewalk, nearly colliding with Frank and Helen.

"Did you hear that?" Debra said.

"Sounded like a bad one," Frank said.

Everyone looked west toward the intersection, where a crowd of people were beginning to converge at the end of their block.

"Something happened at the corner," Debra said.

"There's Louise," Helen said, pointing.

Pythia scoured her mind, trying to get her vision sense to activate and tell her what had happened. The others started walking quickly toward the corner. Louise beckoned them to hurry. Frank started running.

"I don't want to see any blood," Helen said, hanging back.

"Stay here, Mrs. Bristol, and mind the shops," Pythia said. "I am sure someone has called the authorities by now."

"I hear sirens," Helen said.

Pythia followed Debra and Frank toward the accident at the corner. As she got closer, she could see a beat-up Toyota Tercel had run up on the sidewalk and crashed into the front window of Stacy's yoga studio. Window glass shards littered the sidewalk. Pythia crunched gingerly across broken glass to peer into the back window of the car. She saw a white and tan collie sitting in the driver's seat, watching with great interest as a goat wearing a red plaid jacket galloped across the median and disappeared into the business park beyond.

A young blonde woman was standing nearby, clutching a rolled yoga mat to her chest.

"I only left him for a minute," she wailed.

"What the hell?" said Debra.

Frank edged through the doorway into the space that used to be Stacy's yoga studio. Pythia waited with a sinking feeling in her stomach as Frank knelt over something on the floor. He stood up, met her eyes, and shrugged. She didn't need her sixth sense to know that Stacy had met her end.

A red paramedic truck pulled up halfway onto the sidewalk, taking up two empty parking spaces, lights flashing, siren blaring. The siren cut off. Two men in uniform leaped out and came toward the scene. One carried a bag. "Coming through!"

Pythia backed away and leaned against the wall of her building, thinking about the ephemeral nature of life, the always-near specter of death. No matter how many times she'd seen death, no matter that she knew for most people, death was inevitable, the death of someone she knew always shocked her. She hadn't known Stacy well, but coaching her had been pleasurable. She had admired the young woman's plucky entrepreneurial spirit.

Two police cars arrived from the east and parked, blocking the corner in all directions. Four officers emerged. Two began to set up orange traffic cones to direct vehicles to merge into one lane. One officer started waving gawking drivers past the mess. The side street was soon blocked with more cones. One officer, a heavy-set woman with a tight Afro, began to string up some yellow tape between a parking sign and a telephone pole to clear out the crowd.

Looking pale and shaken, Debra came over to Pythia. Frank joined them. They leaned against the warming stucco and watched the officers move the crowd back into the side street. The marine layer began ebbing to the west, revealing blue sky.

"She didn't know what hit her."

"Ugh, Frank, gross," Debra said.

"Really, no kidding. She was in a downward dog, perfectly balanced. Not a drop of blood on her. She looked like she was meditating."

Debra huffed a breath and then snickered. "You're kidding. Downward dog?"

The paramedics walked back to their ambulance, removing their gloves. They appeared to be smiling. Pythia heard one technician say, "You don't see that every day."

The other paramedic said, "Looks to me like she went out happy."

The ambulance left. The crowd waited impatiently on the other side of the caution tape.

"What are they waiting for?" Pythia asked Frank.

"The coroner."

The police put the owner of the car into the back of a police car with the collie. She hugged the dog and wailed loudly into its fur.

"Shut up," someone in the crowd complained.

A tall man poured some water into a plastic dish and handed it to her through the car window. She stared at the dish. "Give the dog some water, lady."

"I killed my yoga teacher!" she wept. "Wait, no, I don't mean that! It was my dog. Oh, Timmy, how could you?"

"I don't think I'm going to be able to get much work done today," Debra said. "Maybe we should take the day off."

"We have clients today," Pythia said.

"Only two. You want me to call and reschedule?"

"No, thank you, Ms. Sandhill. We really need the income."

"I hope you have insurance, Pythia," Frank said. "You need to call someone to come board up this window."

Pythia looked at Debra.

"Don't look at me!" Debra said. "I'm sick. I'm going home." She stomped away. Frank and Pythia watched Helen stop her before she could enter the office.

"I'd better go tell Helen the news," Frank said, shoving off from the wall. "You want me to call the window guys?"

"Thank you, Mr. Bristol, very kind of you, no need. I will take care of it."

Frank left Pythia alone by the wall. She watched as the coroner's van arrived. Two people wearing hazmat suits exited the van and entered the studio, dragging a gurney between them. Within a few minutes, what was left of Stacy was placed in a white body bag and loaded into the van. The crowd began to disperse.

A flatbed tow truck arrived, lights flashing, pulling in as the coroner's van pulled away. One large man took his time getting out of the cab. He pulled on heavy gloves as he surveyed the crashed car. In a half hour, he had attached chains to the back axle and yanked the demolished car onto the back of the truck. Soon the truck and car disappeared west on Wilshire.

Finally, one police car remained. Pythia made eye contact with an officer and waited. A pale clean-shaven officer sauntered toward her.

"Hello, Miss. You seem to be here for the duration of this event. Did you see what happened?"

"No, sir, I am sorry, I did not. I am the owner of this office building, and Miss Landers was my tenant."

"Did you know the perpetrator?"

"Did I know the . . . the dog?"

"Yeah, or the owner of the dog?"

Pythia shook her head and tried not to smile. "Officer, I am sorry, I have no information on the woman or her dog. She was one of Miss Lander's yoga clients."

"It's a first for me, I have to say. A dog driving a car. Oh, by the way, I've called Glass Docs to board up the window."

"Thank you, that is very kind."

"You'll get the bill," he said. He handed Pythia a card. "When you submit your insurance claim, please call this number to get the police report."

"Oh, by the way, Officer, four young goats got loose and ran across the street."

"Goats?"

"Yes. From the yoga studio."

"Why would there be goats in the yoga studio?"

"Miss Landers was famous for her goat yoga classes. She will be greatly missed."

May 6, 2015

Human lives are filled with tragedies. It is the nature of human existence. No one escapes from the reality of life. What can I tell you that you do not already know but refuse to accept?

Some folks go years without attending a single funeral and then in the space of a few months, they lose everything and everyone they hold dear. Cancer, car crashes, house fires, heart attacks, drug overdoses, strokes—even pedestrians, nonsmokers, and vegans are not safe. No one is safe from death.

People try to bury their heads in statistics in a superstitious attempt to deflect fate. In 800 BCE, I had a fifty percent likelihood of dying before age thirty. Here in 2015, I have a zero percent likelihood of living three thousand years. Statistics are impersonal, like a thundercloud dumping rain on a community in the next county. Who cares if it is happening to someone else, until the windstorm rolls over your house and drops a tree on you.

In the end, life happens to everyone. Everybody dies.

Except me, for some reason.

—Yours in exile, Delphina

Chapter 6

"Our finances are wrecked, Pythia," Debra said. First thing Monday morning, Debra entered Pythia's office with a clipboard in her hand and sat in the visitor chair. "What are you going to do about it?"

Pythia looked down at her desk. When the newsprint clipping of Stacy's obituary had appeared in the LA. Times, she'd cut it out and tucked it under the desk calendar, a constant reminder of her failure. *What could I have done? Sometimes I see impending death. What good does it do to know when or how death is coming? There is no way to stop it.*

Debra's irate words echoed her general feeling of malaise. For the past few days a sense of dissatisfaction had pervaded the building. Her neighbors Louise, Frank, and Helen seemed to be avoiding her. She heard them moving about in the upstairs hallway outside their apartments but when she opened her door to say hello, they somehow vanished. *Do they blame me for Stacy's death? Maybe they should. If I had not recommended goat yoga, perhaps the dog would not have driven the car through the window. And if the gods had not created the earth . . .*

Pythia knew her thoughts were scattered. She wasn't sleeping well. Stacy's death had intensified a growing melancholy. Even before the accident, her dreams had been disjointed and chaotic. Twice she had dreamed of an assault in the Temple of Apollo. She was beginning to believe she might have witnessed such an event as a child. In the dream, the temple seemed much larger than she remembered, but it could be that she herself was smaller by comparison—seeing the incident from a child's point of view. None of the images made sense to her.

Even if I had seen Stacy's fate, even if I had told her she would soon die, it would have changed nothing. I can see the future—sometimes—but I am powerless to change it. And what a cruel thing it would have been. Get your affairs in order, your end is coming soon? Not the words of a friend.

Last night she'd awakened calling her sister's name. She tasted smoke and bitter berries. A stab of guilt shot through her as she realized she had prayed for her sister to save her. *Apollo, forgive me. Am I lost, am I frozen in time because I failed to remember my master, my Lord God Apollo?*

The malaise was affecting her coaching business. Even before this terrible week, new clients had stopped calling. Old clients cancelled appointments with no explanation. Her bank account balance had dropped to alarming levels.

"Pythia! Wake up, this is serious."

Pythia gazed at her assistant. "I seem to recall you saying that your creative social media campaigns on, what was it— Ticky Tacky?—were going to bring in new business."

"Oh, sure, blame me. You obviously know nothing about marketing."

Pythia sighed. "You are correct. I am sorry, Ms. Sandhill. Please forgive me." Debra stomped to her cubicle. Her desk chair groaned as she flung herself into it. Pythia heard the clipboard clatter.

Pythia got up and headed for the door to the hallway.

"Oh, now you are going downstairs? When the going gets tough, the not-so-tough do drugs, is that it? You'd never make it as a Barracuda with that attitude."

Pythia stopped, considering her options. None seemed terribly appealing. *What should I say? I do not do drugs? She would not believe me. She has a story about me but it is really her story. She is sad and scared. She is also not wrong. I am an addict.* Pythia looked over the half-wall at Debra with compassion, noting Debra's fatigue.

Debra looked away. "Sorry. I'm on edge. What with the money and all."

"No apology necessary," Pythia said, knowing Debra was thinking of Stacy. "I miss her, too. No, it is I who should be apologizing to you. Please do not worry, Ms. Sandhill. Your future will be abundantly satisfying."

"Huh. So you say." Debra scowled, then looked at Pythia sidelong. "Abundant *and* satisfying? Or just extremely satisfying but not terribly abundant?"

Pythia smiled, and in that moment, she saw Debra's path.

"Ms. Sandhill, it has been an honor and a privilege."

"Wait, what? You're not firing me, are you?"

"No, you are firing me. Soon, if I am not mistaken."

"No, I would never quit on you, Pythia. You gave me my start, right out of college. I owe you."

Pythia shook her head. "By the way, I ordered you a new computer. It is coming tomorrow. I think you will be able to use it for a while before you go."

"Pythia, I hate it when you go all mysterious on me." Debra scowled, and then grinned at Pythia. "New computer, huh? Is it a Mac?"

After Stacy's death, Debra stopped playing her portable radio. Instead, she listened to music on her new computer, using headphones plugged into a port in the side. To fill the silence, Pythia started turning on the little television in the client waiting area when she came down in the morning.

Most days, the TV stayed on all day, providing muted sounds and voices she found comforting. When Debra was out running errands and taking longer and longer lunches, Pythia sat in a client chair and watched whatever was on the screen, which increasingly was tuned to daily talk shows and daytime programming. Most mornings, she watched the morning news shows to catch up on current events, especially happenings around L.A.

Every day at 11:00 a.m., she tuned in to see Psychic to the Stars, Divina Dee's entertainment talk show. Sometimes Debra joined her.

The format of the show was consistent: Divina Dee invited studio audience members to present questions about their futures, which she would answer, ostensibly using her psychic powers. Guest stars made appearances to help out. Viewers submitted home videos of their questions and outcomes, which appeared on a huge screen behind the stage. Divina Dee dispensed life, love, and career advice with a brilliant infectious grin.

In the show's energetic introduction, a prerecorded clip showed Divina Dee laughing and proclaiming "I don't read minds. I read futures. I just happen to know what is going to happen—to you, to your loved ones, to everyone."

Today, the bubbly star of the show bounced onto the stage as a small studio audience applauded and whistled. Divina Dee wore her trademark tight jeans and loose gauzy shirt over a hot pink tank top. Her outfit for the day included bright white sneakers. Her blonde dreadlocks were pulled up and over to the side, where they hung in hanks down one cheek. She'd woven tiny feathers and leaves into her hair.

"She looks like a pirate," Debra said. "She's amazing."

Pythia frowned. "Why, because she looks like a pirate?"

"Well, yeah, and because she knows what's going to happen."

"She helped me regain my sense of self," a man said, his face ten feet tall on the screen behind the stage. The studio audience clapped in appreciation. "I was down and out, had a drinking problem, lost my house, and she gave me hope."

Another video showed a young woman holding a squirming toddler on her lap. "Divina Dee told me my baby had a serious illness. If she hadn't responded to my question, my Brandon might not be here today."

Members of the audience wiped away tears.

"My mission is to help wherever I can," Divina Dee said into the microphone she carried in her hand. "After the break, we'll take some questions from our audience."

Pythia and Debra pondered a commercial for a new kind of organic dog food, followed by a commercial for a skin cream product to help women appear younger. *Why is it so terrible to grow old?*

"Do you think she is really able to predict the future?" Pythia asked.

"I don't know. Does it matter? People think she can. She's got some great marketing strategy going on, that's all I can say. It's all about perception." Debra stood up briskly. "Which is why I need to get busy making you seem like a perfect coach for Business Barracudas."

"Even if I am not."

Debra grinned. "Welcome to the dark side of marketing, Pythia."

Pythia shook her head. "I do not have a good feeling about this. I fear something bad is going to happen."

"Oh, lighten up, Pythia. Most of the time, you have to admit, your half-assed sixth sense is just plain wrong. You aren't Divina Dee, after all. Stop living in fear."

May 11, 2015

Humans have lived near the La Brea Tar Pits for ten thousand years, using the asphalt to waterproof canoes and baskets. By those standards, I am a newcomer. Moreover, I am not interested in the asphalt but in the toxic vapors that emanate from below ground. Like all the Greek Oracles, I enter trance after breathing the earth's gases. Thus, over my long life, I have usually sought to live near areas of geothermal activity.

In Los Angeles, the oilfields have lifted gas close to the surface. Methane lurks in subterranean pockets and occasionally starts spontaneous fires in basements and sewer pipes. Perfect for an Oracle. Usually I can see these fires before they become a problem in the area. I am happy to make a preemptive call to the fire department.

You might wonder how I found this building. After I moved to the west coast of the United States, I hired a real estate agent and told him to find an affordable commercial property somewhere near the La Brea Tar Pits. I did not care if the building had some cosmetic problems or even structural flaws in the foundation. Poor Mr. M thought I was insane, but I had cash, lots of it, so he faithfully searched until he found this block along Wilshire Blvd., the heart line of the city. Upon inspecting the premises, Mr. M smelled methane in the basement and warned me I was making a mistake.

I made sure he did not object when the sellers' agents failed to disclose the methane leaks in the basement. I signed the papers on a sunny day. We all went away happy. The sellers celebrated, thinking they had fooled me, the stupid foreign female buyer. I should add, they went bankrupt several years later when another buyer sued them for failure to disclose structural flaws in a building's foundation. Not my problem. My agent, the faithful Mr. M, was thrilled at the commission. He retired to Hawaii and left a sizable fortune to his many children. And I considered myself blessed to have found my Los Angeles home.

When the developers built the property in 1965, they included three apartments above the offices to generate extra income. I live in one, and the proprietors of the two largest shops on the street below live in the other two. Even though we do not socialize much, I enjoy our little community. In the interests of maintaining their privacy, I will not disclose their names or the location of our shops. Suffice it to say, if you drive along Wilshire Blvd. near the Tar Pits, you will probably recognize my office. Please call first to make an appointment if you would like personalized business coaching.

—Yours in exile, Delphina

"Do you think she's for real?" Debra asked, lounging comfortably on a visitor chair. She placed a mug of steaming coffee on a fake wood side table. A commercial break had interrupted Psychic to the Stars.

"It seems unlikely," Pythia said. She balanced her coffee cup on the arm of her chair.

"Why? You seem to have some psychic powers, or so you claim. Why couldn't she?"

"She could, I suppose. Anything is possible. And I have never claimed to have psychic powers."

"Well, you go to that witches' meeting every month."

Pythia smiled. "You mean the Mystics Roundtable."

"Right. A bunch of witches."

"Have you ever listened to the show?"

"Well, no. But I've seen the webpage on the radio station's website. A tarot card reader—"

"Ms. Sandhill, the phone is ringing."

"I'll let it go to voicemail. Look," Debra said, pointing at the TV. "She just told that old guy he was going to marry his childhood sweetheart!"

"That is nice. Is it not?"

"Not with his current wife sitting right next to him!"

They watched the show in silence for a few minutes. At the next commercial break, Debra got up to check the messages.

"Another hang up," she announced.

"Something about this Divina Dee person bothers me," Pythia said.

"She's certainly popular. I've seen her videos on YourTurn. She's got over a million subscribers. That's insane."

"Maybe we should do a video," Pythia said. "Instead of that Barracuda thing."

Debra started laughing. "Oh, poor Pythia. The twentieth century is so confusing, isn't it?"

"You have no idea," Pythia sighed. "And this is the twenty-first century, last time I checked, which I do daily."

"I know! I've seen you."

A close up on Divina Dee showed her moving gracefully among the audience members, who sat on bleacher-style seats arranged at the back of a small sound stage. Divina Dee's age could be anywhere between twenty and forty. She always wore tight jeans and flowing white linen shirts over brightly colored tank tops. She never wore heels, only white sneakers or ballet slippers. She moved with mesmerizing energy, shuffling her long blonde dreadlocks off her face with charming flicks of her head as she interacted with people in the seats.

Pythia knew she shouldn't be watching a show about predicting people's futures. After failing to predict Stacy's death, Pythia felt useless. *What is the purpose of being an Oracle if I cannot use my gift to help people?*

"What's on your mind?" Divina thrust a microphone in front of a thin black woman.

"I want to know if my son will graduate high school," the woman said in a dignified voice.

Divina paused and raised her arms into the air in her trademark pose. Pythia recognized the pose as one she'd seen in paintings and lithographs from earlier centuries. *I have used that pose myself.* The audience hushed, waiting. After a few seconds, Divina did a little dance and said, "Yes! I'm happy to predict that Jason will graduate with honors!"

The audience erupted in applause and whistles. The woman sat down, smiling.

"That's such a crock," Debra said. "Who would believe that was real? I bet if we checked that lady out, we'd find she didn't even have a son."

The bell jangled as the front door opened. Pythia stood up and turned off the television set. She turned to greet the visitor, a short middle-aged woman with skin the color of mildly roasted coffee beans. She wore a clingy black dress Pythia guessed might be nylon printed in large pink peonies and white gardenias. She clutched a black faux leather bag that matched low-heeled Payless shoes.

"Hello, how can I help you?"

"Hi, is it okay that I don't have an appointment? I wanted to talk to someone about a business problem I'm having. I can come back if this is a bad time."

"Please come in. My name is Pythia Apulu." Pythia led the way to her office. She pointed at the visitor chair just inside the door. "May I ask your name?"

"Bernice Brown."

"Please have a seat, Ms. Brown. I will get some paperwork and be right with you." Debra had a clipboard ready to go. Pythia took it into her office and sat behind her desk, leaving the door open.

"Would you please fill out the top few lines of this form?" Pythia asked, handing Bernice a pen. Pythia waited in silence while Bernice complied. "Thank you, Ms. Brown. Now, please tell me about your business problem."

Bernice opened up her bag and pulled out an expensive laptop. She set it on the corner of Pythia's desk. "You got Wi-Fi in here?"

"Of course." Pythia gave her the passcode and after a few tries, Bernice managed to log on to the internet and pull up a webpage.

"This is my website," she said. "I make organic haircare and skincare products."

"That is impressive," Pythia said. Bernice scrolled through her website. "What kind of results are you seeing? Sales, page views, that sort of thing."

As Bernice talked, Pythia began to get some glimpses of a busy household. She saw dirty dishes soaking in greasy water in a stained stainless steel sink. She saw a wooden rack layered with drying baby clothes sitting on the living room rug and baby toys scattered underfoot.

"I can't seem to get any traffic to my website, even after I spent $200 on FacePlace ads. I don't know what I'm doing wrong."

"Is this you, modeling this head wrap?" Pythia asked, pointing to an image of a tired gray-faced woman gazing hopelessly into the camera.

"Yeah. I can't afford professional pictures. Buying photos is expensive. I spent almost all my money developing my line of products and getting the packaging made. I didn't set aside much for marketing."

"It is very common for business people to build a website and then wait in vain for people to discover it," Pythia said.

"What do I need to do, Ms. Apulu?"

"Have you conducted some simple market research to learn how customers are connecting with your products?"

"Yeah, I got it all right here. I did a survey." Bernice read some survey responses off the screen.

"Excellent," Pythia said. "I suggest you listen to how they talk about their haircare problem and then use their words in your marketing messages."

"Yes, but how do I do that?"

"You listen to their words and then use their words in your social media posts, for example. And on your website."

"Sorry, I'm not a writer, Ms. Apulu. I don't get what you are saying."

Pythia sat back and rested her brain for a moment. She could see some paths opening up for Bernice. She could see other paths closing off.

She leaned forward and pointed at the website on the laptop. "This business idea was not yours, was it?"

Bernice frowned. "No, not at first. It was my sister's idea."

"You do not actually want to do this business, do you? You would rather . . . finish your hair design certificate and rent a booth at your cousin's salon."

Bernice slammed her laptop closed. "Now you just creeping me out, lady."

"Ms. Brown, life is too short not to do what you love. If you cannot figure out how to turn your customers' words into a social media post, then you do not really want to. You need to follow your heart while you still have time."

"What do you mean, while I still have time?" Bernice whispered, looking stricken.

"You know what I mean. But you will beat the cancer. You have a long life ahead of you, Ms. Brown. Do not waste it on someone else's dream. Even if she is your older sister."

Pythia watched as Bernice stood at the counter in front of Debra's cubicle and wrote a check for $30.00 with shaking hands. Pythia knew the check would bounce, but she didn't care. In about forty-five minutes, Bernice would tell her sister and husband that they could carry on the business without her. She was going back to cosmetology school.

On Tuesday, when Pythia arrived for the June meeting of the Mystics Roundtable, Lena was the only member there. Pythia's sponsor hunched behind the sound board, looking depressed. Pythia tried to access her second sight but got only a few disjointed images of Lena wearing a cowboy hat and sitting on a plastic folding chair in a dingy breakroom. *She must be working tonight.*

"What's wrong, my friend?" Pythia asked, sitting in her usual seat by the wall. "Is your mother returning today?"

Lena heaved a long noisy sigh. "Today for some reason, as I was driving past Clancy's, I felt like stopping."

Pythia knew Lena used to be a bartender at Clancy's in West Hollywood. Another image came clear. Pythia said with conviction, "You will not drink today."

Lena looked at Pythia with relief.

"Most of the time when I'm serving drinks at the Arcade, I'm fine. Every now and then, though, I get—"

At that moment, Sylvia entered with her usual cloud of glitter and perfume. "Greetings, dear ones! Have you seen? My latest Instafame post got three hundred likes!" She flopped into her seat and dug in her bag for her cards. "Look at these, I hired an artist to design my own deck! I'm selling them on Wertsy."

Mary came into the room, dragging a bulging briefcase. "Ugh, grades are due tomorrow. Oh, hey, those are cool." She held up a card from Sylvia's deck. The sun. A comforting memory of Apollo, the sun god, flitted through Pythia's mind.

"It's almost time to start," Lena said. "I wonder where Moon is."

Pythia's insight kicked in at the mention of Moon's name. *Something has happened. Something to do with Moon's son.*

"I think Moon is going to be late," Pythia said.

"I hope she's okay," Mary said.

Lena started the show. "The topic for the month is a big one. We are going to be talking about death."

Pythia wasn't surprised, given recent events. *Should have seen that coming.* Despite the bleak topic, the Mystics seemed willing, if not exactly cheerful. *Probably because Madame B is absent.*

The first caller was a young man with an accent Pythia could not place. "My name is Orlando, and I'm calling from Oxnard. Can you tell, when will I die?" he asked in a cocky voice, clearly assuming the answer was *never.*

"When is your birthday, Orlando?" Mary asked, spreading open her star charts.

Lena and Pythia looked at each other. Lena shrugged.

Mary proceeded to do an extensive reading for the young man. He learned his life expectancy was approximately eighty-seven years old, that he would have ten children, and die a wealthy man.

"Remember, we Mystics don't know everything!" Lena said. "We provide our best guesses in the spirit of entertainment and education!"

"That's all right!" Orlando said. "Wow. Ten kids!"

"Enjoy your Ferrari," Pythia said just before Orlando hung up the phone. Lena grinned.

The next caller was an older man. "I'm Bill, and I'm calling from Encino. I'm purty sure I don't have a lot of years left," he said. "I want to know, will my wife Sheila be okay?"

Sylvia did a quick shuffle of the Major Arcana tarot cards. "Well, Bill, it's possible. The cards seem to be showing that some of the people closest to you will live a long time."

"She don't know how to balance a checkbook. I don't know how she's gonna take care of herself." Bill sounded sad.

Pythia hummed and sank into her center to see if anything came clear. She saw some images of a man she assumed was Bill. Then she saw another man. *Wait, is that the same man? Which one is Bill?* Pythia leaned up to her microphone and pressed the button. "Bill, do you have a brother?"

"Yep. His name is Fred. I'm William, he's Wilfred. You can't hardly tell us apart. We used to fool Sheila all the time when we was young."

"Well, Bill, I think you can die happy knowing your wife will be okay, even if she outlives you."

There was a moment of dead air while Bill processed the prospect of his wife and his twin brother. "That son of a gun," he said. "I'm gonna kill them both."

Bill hung up the phone.

"Oops," said Lena into her microphone. "Bill, if you are still listening, please don't do anything rash."

"Yeah, please don't murder anyone," Sylvia laughed.

"Very bad for your karma," Mary agreed.

"Whew. Let's take another caller," Lena said, pushing the button.

The next caller was an older woman with a shaky voice. "I'm Marge, calling from Venice, California. I've wondered for a while now, what is the purpose of death?"

"The purpose of death?" Lena echoed.

"Yes. I want to know, why do we have to die? Why aren't we allowed to just keep on going?"

Mary pulled out her star charts. "When is your birthday, Marge?"

"July 28, 1929."

"Let me see. Leo, huh. Well, I can understand why you might not be ready to give up the ghost. Leos are famously outgoing. You must have tons of friends."

"All dead now. I'm the last one. But I'm still not ready to go."

"What about the idea that we need to make room for new generations?" Lena asked.

"What, like my children? Worthless parasites. I had five of them, and not one gave me a grandchild. Why should I make room for the likes of them?"

Sylvia pulled out the Death card and held it up for the Mystics to see. *Death looks a little like Apollo.* "In the tarot, the Death card might not mean literal death. It could mean that your life is about to go through a change of some kind."

"Already happened! My worthless children put me in assisted living. Like all I'm good for now is playing Bingo all day. There's no men left, they're all dead. This place is the pits. I'd like to jump in my car and drive to Mexico but they took away my keys."

"Why do you want to keep on living, if it is so terrible?" Mary asked. "I mean, maybe death isn't so bad."

"I'm afraid to die," Marge admitted. "I made my friends swear they would come back and tell me what it's like on the other side. Betty promised she would come back and give me the scoop, but I haven't heard anything from her yet, and she stroked out weeks ago. I thought for sure Thelma would make it back, send me a letter or something. She croaked just last week. But nothing. I get nothing. What is over there?"

"Uncertainty can be difficult for all of us," Pythia said.

"Uncertainty is a hallmark of the human condition," Lena agreed. "Nobody knows what is going to happen next."

"Well, I know one thing. Growing old sucks," Marge said. "If you can, don't do it." She hung up the phone.

After a couple final callers who wanted to more about the tarot Death card, Lena wrapped the show and signed off. The four Mystics packed up their gear and exited the sound booth. As they entered the hallway, they saw Moon sitting on a bench. Moon leaped to her feet.

"I was waiting, didn't want to interrupt. Good show? Sorry I missed it. My son, my brilliant insane son, got busted last night for dealing drugs at his senior prom." She burst into tears.

Lena, Mary, and Sylvia rallied around Moon, making noises and patting her shoulder.

Pythia looked across the hall. Arnie Solomon was in his DJ booth, queuing up a record. He set the needle on the spinning disk and sat back in his comfy chair, toe tapping. As if he felt eyes on him, he swiveled around and saw Pythia. He smiled and waved. She waved back.

Something about the old bearded hippie made her smile. She wondered what song he was playing. To her amazement, he held up an album cover she didn't recognize. She squinted at it through the glass. She saw a close-up of a man's face. *Looks like a country western singer.* In the corner, she could make out the words *Johnny Cash Live at Folsom Prison.*

"Ah," Pythia said. The other Mystics turned to look at her. "Oh, my apologies. Moon, do not worry. He will have to spend a night in jail, but in the end, I predict home confinement with an ankle monitor."

Moon threw her arms around Pythia. "Oh, thank God, thank God."

Pythia disengaged herself. Moon led the way along the hall, prancing toward the elevator.

Pythia glanced back at Arnie, who gave her a thumbs-up. *It seems I did something right.* She waved and followed her friends.

Pythia arrived on time for the A.A. meeting, thanks to the kind soul who posted the signs in the basement maze of halls and rooms. She found a chair in the back row, nodding to Charlotte and Patty, who nodded back.

Lena sat in her usual front row seat. Her straw panama was easy to spot. She turned in her seat, caught sight of Pythia, and leaped to her feet. She hurried up the aisle.

"Pythia, hi. Hey, want to do some service? I need you to help me out at the Arcade on Saturday the twenty-second. We need a fortune-teller. Anna can't make it that night. I thought you might enjoy thinking of something else for a while."

"Certainly, Lena, I would be happy to help out."

"Thanks, Pythia, I'll call you with the details!" Lena hustled back to her seat.

After the opening prayer, readings, and introductions, George, the group secretary, introduced the speaker as "Sinnadd," peering over his half-glasses at the group. He nodded as a short slender woman ambled to the front. George stepped back to his seat. The woman stood at the lectern, looking composed. Pythia admired her tastefully patterned navy knee-length dress and low-heeled shoes. She wore a tan fedora similar to the style Lena favored.

"My name is Sinead, and I'm an alcoholic." She pronounced her name "Shinn-ade." Pythia recognized an Irish accent.

She waited politely while the group sought to understand. The responses unfolded a few at a time. Some members said "Hi, Sinn-add." Some said "Hi, Shinn-addy." Some said "Hi, Shiner." One or two said "Hi, Shiny." A couple said "Hi, Nader." The last person to speak shouted, "Hi, Neighbor," and everyone laughed, including the speaker.

Sinead waited for the group to quiet down. "I may not look it now," she said, "but I was a low-bottom drunk."

She told of coming close to death three times, the first when she was fourteen. She'd been abused much of her life, she mentioned in a matter-of-fact voice, which had led her to escape into alcohol. "First, me brother. Then me uncle. As soon as I turned eighteen, I got married to escape me family, but I married a violent abusive alcoholic who used to black me eye and take me money. Luckily, I outlasted him. He died in a drunken stupor, fell off a bridge, actually, and me, well, I'm still here."

Heads nodded.

"I'm still here, and I'm still an alcoholic," she added.

Pythia noticed a man off to the side who resembled Arnie Solomon, the DJ at the radio station. She was almost certain the man was Arnie. Not many old men wore long beards in the twenty-first century. His gray hair was abundant for someone that old. She noted a dent around his head, probably from a baseball cap. As she listened to the speaker, she found herself relaxing. The Irish accent soothed her ears. Seeing Arnie gave her a good feeling for some reason. Knowing Lena was in the room made her feel safe. She closed her eyes.

"In thirty years in this program, I've learned a few things. Number one, this is a spiritual program. It's not about the booze, I hate to tell ya. Even after I stopped drinkin', I was still a drunk. I had to get down to causes and conditions and become willing to have my shortcomings removed. Number two, to maintain my sobriety, I have to go to any lengths to recover. For me, that means service. I drove down from San Francisco because George invited me. Carrying the message of recovery to other alcoholics is how I ensure I have the best chance of staying sober meself."

After the meeting, Pythia stayed seated near the back door and watched the members mingle and talk. She lost sight of Arnie, saw Lena talking with Sinead, saw Arnie again as he was exiting through the front door into the hallway. She was content to observe the fellowship among members. *I am a part of this group if I say I am. I am not sure I am ready to say I am. But something about this program feeds my soul. Maybe because everyone who comes here is a seeker.*

Lena came over, leading Sinead.

"Sinead, this is my friend, Pythia. Pythia has a touch of the second sight herself."

"Is that so?" Sinead said, sizing Pythia up.

"Oh, not really," Pythia said. "Lena is reliably clairvoyant. Have you heard of the Mystics Roundtable?"

"Yes!" Sinead said. "I love that show. Wait, you are *that* Lena? I promise to keep your anonymity, but I have to tell ya, you are quite famous in San Francisco."

"No!" said Lena, pleased.

Pythia edged past them and out the door, leaving the pair talking about the radio show. *My service for the evening.*

In the parking lot, Pythia found a yellow heart-shaped sticky note on her windshield, tucked under a wiper. She plucked it free and turned it over but the note was blank. She pasted the heart on the edge of her rearview mirror and noticed it from time to time as she drove home.

❧

On Sunday morning, Pythia motored her Honda Insight past a row of storefronts on Washington Boulevard in Culver City. A neon sign over a shiny gold door proclaimed she had reached her destination: The Church of Apollo.

An arrow pointed along a narrow driveway toward parking in the rear. Consulting her future sense, she found no signs of impending danger, so she inched her car along the driveway and found a spot to park in a small back lot adjacent to an alley. Fuchsia bougainvillea heaped the chain link fence on two sides of the lot, which held five other cars. There was room for two more. *Not a big congregation, it seems.*

Pythia went up three wooden steps and entered the building through a flimsy metal door. Across the shallow lobby, she saw a tiny foyer and the front door leading out to Washington Blvd. To the right, the lobby opened into a large sanctuary carved out of the building's interior. Light slanted in from western-facing skylights, illuminating a handful of people scattered sparsely among perhaps forty folding chairs arranged in rows with a central aisle. The chairs faced a stage at the far end of the room.

She paused in the doorway.

"Welcome to the Church of Apollo."

Pythia turned. A man with pale skin and a short brown beard smiled at her. He was a nondescript man she might never have noticed, except for his attire. He wore a long robe made of shiny gold lamé fabric, belted below his slightly protruding belly with what appeared to be gold braid and tassels. Black military style boots peeked from under his robe.

"Hello, thank you," Pythia said. The scent of gardenias swept past her. "Am I in time for the service?"

"Yes, we'll be starting in about ten minutes. Please have a seat." The man put his hands inside voluminous gold sleeves, as if warding off a handshake. "By the way, I'm Rodney Blass. You might know me as God's Chosen."

At the mention of the name, Pythia squinted, peering into his future. She saw him eating steak later. Steak with Tater Tots, sitting on a shabby couch with an older woman in front of a big-screen television. Apparently, Rodney and his mother were fans of professional wrestling. Not helpful. She came back to the present and noticed he was waiting for a response. "I am sorry? Did you say . . . ?"

"I invited you here."

"You did?"

"Welcome, Delphina. I hope you find what you seek. Perhaps we can talk after the service?"

Pythia thinned her lips, not sure how to respond, but Rodney had already turned away, heading toward a side door.

Pythia moved into the sanctuary and found a seat near the wall. She sat with her purse on her lap. *Should I feel disturbed that he knew me?* She wanted to feel nervous, but the golden light coming through the skylights was distracting.

She closed her eyes. What was she fighting? *I came here because I was curious, that is true. I am seeking relief from overwhelming sadness. I have a hope that I might find a connection to my beloved Apollo. Who cares that Apollo's church is a decrepit storefront in Culver City? Gods are everywhere they want to be. Apollo could be here if he so desired.*

She opened her eyes and looked around. There was certainly enough gold to appeal to a greedy god. Gold lamé curtains hung on both sides of the stage. Shiny gold metallic tiles covered the ceiling. An enormous white marble statue of Apollo dominated the stage, the centerpiece of the sanctuary. A gold sequined loincloth covered his groin. She smiled. Apollo had never been modest.

An older man in loose faded blue jeans and a yellow windbreaker entered and sat in a chair to her left. She looked more closely. He sported a familiar long gray-gold beard. *I think that is Arnie from the radio station.* The scent of gardenias drifted past again, and she inhaled deeply. Something inside her belly unclenched.

Arnie turned and waved at her. She waved back, pleased. *I keep running into him. What does that mean?* Before she could move to a closer seat, the sound of flutes and harps filled the space. She and Arnie exchanged rueful smiles. She settled back in her seat and let her mind drift. She did not try to anticipate the future. She pretended to be a normal person, waiting to see what would happen next.

The music swelled toward the ceiling. A few stragglers hurried to take seats. A fake wood-paneled door at the rear of the stage opened. Rodney emerged, still wearing his golden robe, and closed the door behind him with measured movements. Pythia couldn't help but smile. *Does he know how silly he looks?*

Rodney stood in front of the marble statue and raised both hands in a salutation, showing hairy arms. "Welcome, Lord Apollo, enter and be with us today. We are here for you."

The music faded as Rodney moved to the lectern. He raised his hands in a benediction.

"We know there are many gods and goddesses, but for us, Apollo reigns supreme above all others. God of truth, logic, and reason, we come before you to acknowledge your all-encompassing strength, love, and healing light. Behold the Lord God Apollo!"

Rodney clapped his hands twice. A boom of thunder accompanied a bright flash of light. Pythia winced. Some people sitting nearby cried out, whether in ecstasy or fear, she couldn't tell.

"Let our hearts be open to messages from our Lord God Apollo," Rodney intoned in a deep voice. "Apollo, be welcome in your house!"

Pythia smelled gardenias and a subtle hint of lavender. She looked around and saw an air freshener unit plugged into a nearby wall socket. Clearly, this was not a prosperous church. *Apollo, if he lives, is unlikely to be fooled by gold sequins and air freshener. However, Apollo used to favor all those who worshiped his godhood, even if they had no gold to offer on the altar.* A young Apollo might have been attracted to such obvious pandering simply out of recognition that a god who was not worshiped was a god soon forgotten.

"Today we will ponder the origins of Apollo's temple at Delphi," Rodney said. He unfolded some sheets of paper that looked like a printout from Wisdopedia. He grasped the sides of the lectern and perused the mostly empty folding chairs. "Long ago," he intoned, "Apollo sought a fitting location for his temple. He heard that Delphi on Mt. Parnassus was a good place. However, he had some bad information from an evil nymph. The mountain had a previous occupant, namely, a monstrous snake named Python."

Ancient history, Pythia thought, settling back in her chair. She closed her eyes. She knew the story. When Pythia was a child, Apollo's priests told the tale for the acolytes who served in his temple.

Creatures often misjudged Apollo. They assumed he was a lazy god who lounged around drinking wine and playing music in the shade of the cypress trees. *Big mistake.*

Pythia sighed. *Apollo, do you care now what others think of you?*

The famous story seemed to expand from year to year as the priests tried to outdo each other, until the Python was as big as a mountain and Apollo's sword was made of lightning. Some of the newer acolytes teased Pythia for being named after the Python, until they learned she was the most powerful Oracle at Delphi. After that, they avoided her.

Apollo laughed when he heard the priests embellish the stories. He did nothing to correct the priests' exaggerations. He had no remorse. After he slew the snake, he went back to Telphousa, shoved her off a cliff, and buried her under a stack of boulders. *Poor Telphousa was not really evil. The nymph was just trying to protect her spring from hordes of tourists.*

Nor did he care about Pythia's discomfort at being teased. When she knelt at the altar to grumble about her peers, she heard a resonant voice say, "My Oracle, do your duty to me, your god and master." Chastened, Pythia vowed to focus on her chores and not complain.

When she told Dione about being teased, her sister had shrugged. They were resting in the shade on a flat sun-warmed rock above the amphitheater. One of many sacred springs burbled nearby, trickling into a stone channel leading to a basin below. "Apollo cares nothing for anyone but himself," Dione said with disdain.

"For shame, my sister. Have a care. Apollo is here, and he hears."

"To you, Apollo is everywhere. To me, he is nowhere. These stories are merely tall tales based on old men's yearnings to bed young Oracles."

Pythia was aghast.

Dione laughed and extended her bare toes into the sun to admire her shapely feet. "The whole episode is foolish. I think he really preferred Delphi over the spring in Boeotia. He did not actually want that silly nymph's spring, he just wanted to make trouble. Your beloved god is a troublemaker."

Pythia remembered praying to Apollo to forgive her sister. Were her prayers answered? She couldn't remember. That day was long past. She missed her sister, but years had dulled the pain, the way deep wounds eventually scab over, leaving a timeless scar.

As Rodney droned on, Pythia mulled over the project proposed by Glen Haven. Building a replica of Apollo's temple on a hill above Malibu was ambitious, perhaps foolhardy. She cast into the future with her oracular sense, looking for some insight into Glen Haven, his project, and his mysterious silent partner. Nothing came clear but she felt at peace. The scent of lavender was soothing, even if it came from an air freshener.

With her eyes closed, she let her mind range further. She thanked Stacy's spirit for being part of her journey. She imagined basking in the sun on the hills above Delphi, attempting yoga poses under Stacy's patient tutelage. *I cannot change the past but I can be here in the present.* She sent mental well wishes to the child injured at the Faire. She ruminated on Lena's challenges with the demanding Madame B. She contemplated Moon's anxiety over her son's drug habit. She let herself drift. *Who is the woman in black? More will be revealed.*

Pythia came awake with a jolt when a loud clap of thunder echoed in the sanctuary. She straightened in her seat. Other worshippers were blinking and staring at the stage. The marble statue of Apollo was glowing as if a light illuminated the inside. Rodney was staring at the statue with shock and confusion, which quickly turned into elation.

"Apollo is with us now!" he cried, raising his arms to the statue. Some worshippers murmured and raised their hands in the air. A soft breeze lifted Pythia's hair for a moment and caressed her neck. She looked up at the twirling ceiling fans. She scanned the room and was disappointed to discover Arnie the DJ had left sometime during the sermon.

After the service, Pythia noticed Rodney wave at her. He hustled down the steps from the stage, lifting the hem of his gold robe.

"Wasn't that something? What did you think? Apollo was here!"

Pythia paused to let him catch up and then continued walking toward the foyer. "That was something, all right." The transformation between the Rodney she'd met earlier and this new enthusiastic Rodney made her smile.

"I guess this is nothing new to you, right? Oracle of Delphi and all. You've probably seen Apollo a million times."

"Are you the proprietor of this . . . church, as well as its pastor?" Pythia asked.

"Yeah. What do you think? Is it too much? You know what I mean, too much Hollywood glitz? It's so hard to find the balance, you know what I mean?"

Pythia smiled. "I imagine Apollo would love this place."

Rodney looked grateful and relieved. "I wasn't sure. I mean, he's the god of gold, so I thought, well, okay, right? Oh, my, that was so exciting! This really is the best day ever. Wait 'til I tell my mother! Do you think Apollo was really here today?"

"I cannot say, Rodney, but with gods, I believe anything is possible."

"Please come back again soon, if you can. As Apollo's favorite Oracle, you are always welcome here."

Pythia opened the back door and felt sunshine on her face. "Why do you think I am Apollo's favorite Oracle?"

"Don't worry—Delphina. Your secret is safe with me." Rodney grinned and held out his hand. She took his warm damp hand in hers.

Images flashed through her mind. She saw him driving a dusty green 1978 Buick Regal to an apartment building on Detroit Street, chortling when he found a parking space in front. She saw him carrying macaroni and cheese on a micro-waveable plate to his elderly white-haired mother sitting in a recliner in front of a blaring television. She saw him placing an offering of a unique pink crystal at a gold-painted altar set up in his bedroom under a faded curtain. *Rodney needs something to believe in.*

"If Apollo is anywhere in this city, this is the place he would be," Pythia said.

Rodney beamed. Pythia released his hand and went outside to her car. Rodney waved good-bye from the back steps, sun-light bouncing off his shiny gold robe.

June 7, 2015

Dione and I explored every ravine, boulder, and scarp at Delphi. Before she decided my youthful presence was damaging her reputation among her peers, we spent many happy hours traipsing the hills above and below the village. We knew every tunnel and cave. We visited gardens to steal figs and napped among the heather, lulled by the buzz of lazy bees. Frigid meltwater from Mt. Parnassus flowed through channels in the rock, bubbling up in humid grottoes and gathering in shaded basins. We followed each stream to its source. Like mountain goats, we sipped on crystal clear spring water and rested on cool rocks in canyons hidden from the sun.

My childhood was peaceful and idyllic, but like most children, I never knew what I had until I lost it. I thought those lovely summer days would last forever. Dione was both family and friend. Serving Apollo gave me a life purpose. Without Delphi, no matter my oracular power, I would have died just another child of just another poor farmer or fisherman. I do not know if Apollo called me to his service thereby prompting my father's trip up the mountain, or if my service at Delphi was the outcome of a series of random events and circumstances. Who can know? In any case, I bloomed at Delphi. The mixture of talent and environment created me, the most powerful Oracle in the ancient world. However, my potential would have remained unfulfilled if not for the blessing of the god Apollo.

I was Apollo's most devoted acolyte. I cannot conjure that feeling of devotion now. I only know that I once felt intense devotion. It is similar to the feeling you might have on a hot day, when you are outdoors and shade is a mirage. A wall of heat envelopes you. You forget what cold felt like, you aren't sure if you will ever feel cold again. You know that you once felt cold, and you hope to feel cold again, but right now, the memory of cold is all you have, and it is a pale substitute for the actual thing you are missing. I know I once felt devotion. Now I am unable to invoke anything but despair and grief.

I once asked Dione about her devotion to Apollo.

We were sitting in the shade of an olive tree on a flat boulder overlooking the stadium. At the far end of the concourse, stable hands led two plodding horses in a wide circle. Dione plucked flowers to put in her hair.

"Are we not fortunate to serve the god Apollo?" I said, reveling in the warm rock at my back.

"I serve Apollo only by chance," Dione said. "I did not choose to serve."

"I have grown to love Apollo," I said.

"I know you have, silly little sheep. That is all you ever talk about, your shiny golden god."

"How can you serve if you feel nothing?" I asked. I was young, Blog Readers, that is my only excuse for my arrogance.

"Why do you keep asking me about Apollo?" my sister said. I had succeeded in annoying her, something I did often. "He is your god, not mine."

"If you do not worship Apollo, whom do you worship?" We both knew there were many gods and goddesses. "Perhaps Artemis is more to your liking?"

"I have been approached by many deities. I am not without talent, my sister." She tossed her sun-bleached hair. "You are so enamored with your own lofty perch, you see nothing else."

"I am not!" I said in anger, not asking the more important question of which gods had approached her.

Dione threw a handful of flower petals at me. "Someday I will be where you are, my sister."

"Is that a prophecy?" I asked, laughing. "Are we breathing earth fumes right now?"

Dione was not amused. "Be forewarned, little sheep. Power, like spring water, flows to the receptacle made ready to receive it. Besides, why must I worship any god? Gods and goddesses are fallible creatures, prone to stupidity just like men. I see none worthy of my praise."

"Have a care, Sister," I whispered. I expected lightning to strike from above for her audacity.

Dione laid back on the rock and put her arm over her eyes. "You have a care, Sister. I know my path."

Blog Readers, my heart seems destined to break again and again. A friend died recently. Her death seems to have precipitated buried memories of Delphi, of Apollo, and of my sister. My sister's words have emerged from my memory and set me pondering. Something is coming, Blog Readers. It is as if a freight train is coming at me in a dark tunnel. I cannot see it but I feel the weight of it and the pressure of it as it flies toward me on the track.

—Yours in exile, Delphina

Chapter 7

"Ms. Apulu, I am hoping you can help me." The sandy-haired man perched on the edge of the visitor chair and set his grimy backpack on the floor.

"I hope so, too, Mr. Collins," Pythia said. "Would you like to tell me about your business idea?"

"It might be easier to show you. Can you access a Your-Turn video on your computer?"

"Certainly." Pythia pulled up the YourTurn website and found the client's video. She clicked the Play button. A two-minute video showed someone's hands and lips playing a flute-like instrument she'd never seen before. Pythia could tell it was the client's lips, although his entire face never appeared in the camera's range. The flute produced a melodic tune in a high-pitched warble when the user pressed buttons, turned dials, and covered holes along the front of the flute. The instrument appeared to be plugged into an electronic device that allowed it to play through computer speakers.

"I invented this instrument a few years ago," the man said proudly. "I have more."

"This is an interesting product, Mr. Collins."

"Please, call me Dwayne."

"Very well. Dwayne, what is your vision for this product? Would you like to manufacture and sell it?"

"I want you to help me find someone who can take on all the business aspects of the business venture, so I can keep inventing."

"I see." Pythia checked in with her internal compass. Not much was coming clear.

"I really want to hand this whole thing over to someone else. They can manage it as they please, take care of manufacturing and marketing and sales and all that stuff. I'm terrible at that sort of thing."

"What have you done so far to attract or locate such a person?"

"I sent a few emails. I posted something on Rerverbit. Nobody has responded."

"Are you ready to do some networking?" Pythia asked.

"Well, no, not really. I'm a very private person. I really hate being on the internet. It took me two years to work up my nerve to post this one video."

Pythia started to receive images of Dwayne sitting in a dark studio littered with electronics components. Dirty dishes and empty fast food containers covered the table in a filthy kitchen. She saw dirty white socks and wrinkled boxers in a pile on his unmade bed. She saw him trimming his own hair with tiny scissors, peering into a streaked mirror and ignoring the back of his head.

"How much time are you willing to devote to doing some outreach to potential prospects?"

"None. I was hoping you would do that for me."

"Dwayne, I am not a publicist."

"Well, but . . . can't you . . . "

"Dwayne, in the coaching relationship, the entrepreneur does the actual work. I can help you set goals, identify tasks, and help you be accountable. I can give you feedback on your publicity messages. I can propose plans of action. However, you must do the work yourself, or else consider hiring a publicist to help you."

"I'm on a fixed income."

"Dwayne, perhaps you can prepare a list of benefits, reasons why someone would want to take on this project."

"Aren't they obvious?"

"Perhaps to you, but pretend I am a potential investor in your business. Why should I invest?"

"But just look at my invention. It speaks for itself!"

"Dwayne, products don't actually speak for themselves. We have to use the right messages to help them find their audiences. Even then, there are no guarantees a product will find its market. You can do it, but it will take time and persistence. Are you willing to do this work over the long haul?"

"No. No, I just want to make my inventions." Dwayne picked up his backpack and stood up. "My apologies, Ms. Apulu. I thought you were the right person for this job. I thought you would want in on the ground floor. It appears I was wrong. What do I owe you?"

"No charge, Mr. Collins. Good luck to you." *Ground floor, indeed. The land has not even been cleared.*

Pythia showed Dwayne to the door and watched him walk to the bus stop on the corner.

"Wow. What was *his* story?" Debra asked.

"A lost soul, I think," Pythia said.

"Right. Another damn artist. Pythia, artists don't appreciate you. You need a higher caliber of clientele, like chiropractors or naturopaths. Those guys have money and they know how to spend it."

On Friday morning, Pythia paused by Debra's cubicle and said, "I am going downstairs."

Debra waved her hand above the wall of her cubicle, and then stood up in surprise. "Hey, it's Friday! Not your drug day!"

"Nevertheless."

"Rough week, I guess. Rough month. I get it. By the way, Pythia, I need a long lunch today. I have an appointment."

"Thank you, Ms. Sandhill. Please lock the door if I'm not here."

"We don't have any appointments on the calendar today, so I thought . . .

"Of course, I understand."

"I'll be back before 2:00, I'm sure." *Does she sound guilty?*

"Please take all the time you need, Ms. Sandhill. Career decisions should not be made hastily."

"Well, okay," Debra said.

"How is your new computer system working?"

"Oh, Pythia, it's great. Thank you."

"Good. I am glad. And thank you. For everything."

Pythia knew that Debra was finalizing her new job details this afternoon. She couldn't discern Debra's new employer, but the job appeared to be something glamorous and exciting—or at least, Debra thought so. *Definitely more interesting than anything my little coaching business could offer.*

The stench in the basement seemed especially strong today. Pythia noticed some new patches of black tar on the concrete floor. A few more cracks had emerged, extending from the floor up the wall on the side near the steps. Small earth tremors happened with regular frequency, hardly noticeable, prompting new fissures in the building's foundation. *Sooner or later, this will all come tumbling down.*

Pythia slipped into a trance the moment she settled onto the stool. With no transition, she found herself flung into the tunnel where she'd met the witch. The campfire contained cold ashes, the fire long dead. The air smelled like sulfur and heavy gas, as if the tunnel had once been a thoroughfare for diesel trucks. She could see no light in the depths.

Is this Delphi? Caves riddled the mountains around the mountain village. Pythia had explored many caves with Dione, reveling in the cool air, enjoying the respite from the heat. Some had springs, others were filled with the noxious fumes the acolytes had come to associate with being Oracles of the temple. *Perhaps this is the Corycian Cave. Where am I? When am I?*

Pythia did not want to explore the depths of this cave. *I am not going to risk my neck wandering around in the dark. Show me what I need to see.* She seated herself on one of the rocks by the dead campfire and waited. The odor of sulfur intensified. Pythia again felt herself slipping into a trance. *A trance within a trance? How is this possible? Whose dream is this?*

For a few moments, Pythia could not feel her body but she could tell she was still seated on something. Warmth crept back into her hands. Even before she opened her eyes, she felt her legs encased in heavy linen. A peplos, she guessed.

Under her robe, against her skin, something nestled against her breasts, some sort of warm feathered creature—a bird? Her hands stroked some kind of bird, perhaps a chicken. *Why would I be holding a chicken?* She'd tended chickens and geese as a child at Delphi, part of the duties of an acolyte. *Am I back in the chicken yard? Why is it so dark? Shoo!*

She discovered she could not make her hands let go of the chicken. No, not a chicken—but some kind of bird. She felt soft feathers as the bird began to struggle. It seemed to somehow grow larger. She tried to set it free from her garment. Strong wings buffeted her stomach. She cried out in fear.

To her shock, the bird seemed to be growing hands. She was no longer clutching the bird—now the bird was clutching her, running hard hands along her sides, pinning her arms as she tried to break free.

In few moments, the bird had transformed into a large warm naked human man, dwarfing her in huge arms, clasping her tightly as she struggled.

"What is this? Who are you?" she cried.

"You cannot refuse me," a voice whispered in her ear. She recognized that rough voice.

"I will not give in," Pythia gasped, but she was no longer Pythia. She was a strong powerful woman—in fact, no less than a queen! Yet against this man she had no power.

All the strength drained from her limbs as he broke her wide open and violated her in the cold ashes on the floor of the cave. Afterward she wept and he held her and whispered that she was the most beautiful woman in all creation and she would be his wife and queen forever.

In her shame, she acquiesced to his offer of marriage, but in her heart, she vowed to fight him with all the breath in her bruised and broken body.

The trance within a trance faded. Pythia was slow to regain her senses. *Whose rape did I just relive?* She felt she should know the answer but a mental veil seemed to blur her perceptions.

She climbed off the stool in the basement and felt pain between her legs. She made her way slowly upstairs. Rarely had the physical effects of her visions followed her back into the present. *Someone else's shame and grief.* Yet remnants of shame and grief lingered. And a burning desire for revenge.

She sank into her office chair and stared at the photo of Apollo's ruined temple. *What in Hades is going on?*

The afternoon passed in a fog. Debra returned at 3:30 p.m., throwing her bag in her cubicle. A moment later, she stuck her head in Pythia's office. *She got the job.*

"Sorry I'm so late. I got hung up in traffic. Whoa, you look like crap. Migraine?"

"Something like that," Pythia said, putting her head in her hands. Debra waited in the doorway, looking less confident than usual.

"I understand," Pythia said, waving her hand.

"Wait, I haven't even . . ."

"Two weeks is more than enough."

"Stop doing that! Jeez! You should have your own TV show!"

"We will have a farewell party for you on Friday the twenty-sixth, if that is all right. I will take care of everything."

"Well, thanks, Pythia, that's super nice of you. You going to be okay? I feel bad leaving you like this."

Pythia waved a hand to dismiss Debra's concern. "Please, do not worry. This has been coming for a very long time."

June 12, 2015

Psychics and seers are everywhere. In centuries past, we were not always easy to spot, depending on the mode and fashion of the time. During some parts of my long life, to be named a witch or warlock was a death sentence. Sometimes shamans were revered while prophetesses were reviled. It was usually safe to be a midwife but not safe to be any sort of mystic.

It is understandable that society would tend not to welcome those with "special powers." The ordinary person does not want to be thought of as ordinary. Most humans are not content to be ordinary; we want to be special, even though the laws of statistics dictate that few people are. In fact, most of us are quite average, tucked neatly under the bell-shaped curve. However, we balk at that label. We want to be special, unique outliers, preferably on the positive end of the scale.

For Oracles, the so-called positive end of the scale refers to the strength and accuracy of our visions. Just as people have different physical strengths, so do Oracles have different oracular strengths. I am not bragging when I say that for the few years I was Oracle at Delphi, my power was well above average.

However, there were many Oracles at Delphi. Some were in training, learning the art, and several junior Oracles were available to step in when I was occupied or indisposed. In that capacity, Dione occasionally filled in. She was not in high demand. Her visions tended to be less accurate. Supplicants complained that she often spoke with such ambiguity, they did not know if they should go to war or sue for peace.

"I do not care what they think," Dione told me once when we were picking figs in the temple orchard. Her basket was half-full; she ate more figs than she plucked. The sun was filtered through the leaves, but the heat was heavy. We stayed in the shade as much as we could, sharing water from a heavy gourd, and picking and eating figs and talking.

"Mistress Dora trained us to be clear and precise," I said, with my usual conceit.

"I like to see them scowl as they try to discern my message," Dione smirked. "It is funny to see them pretend they understand the vision, when I've twisted the words into knots. They cannot afford to appear ignorant. The dolts. I just want the jewels they bring."

"Sister, who was that woman I saw you with in the kitchen garden? The one in the black robes."

"You could see her?" Dione asked in wary surprise.

"She had a haze around her, but she was visible."

Dione shrugged. "She is no one you know." She inspected a fig and flicked away a bug. "Forget you saw her."

"I could see she was a beauty," I said, "But there was something strange about her, a shimmering aura. Who is she? Is she a goddess?"

"A goddess? No, certainly not, what would a goddess be doing here at the temple of your beloved Apollo?"

By Dione's barbed response I knew that the woman was indeed a goddess. Like any annoying younger sister, I could not resist teasing.

"What would Apollo think to know a goddess was secretly visiting his temple?"

Dione turned on me with her fists clenched. "You'd better not tell anyone, you little goat. You will ruin everything."

I stared at her in confusion. "Ruin what, my sister?"

In answer, she picked up her basket of figs and moved under the next tree.

All these centuries later, I still do not know what became of my sister. I do not know what she was talking about. Knowing what I know about gods and goddesses, I suspect that black-robed goddess was the cause of my sister's death. When it comes to humans and gods, humans rarely win, and few survive. So far, my trances have shown me only a disjointed mélange of images that do more to confuse than to clarify. I may never know what became of Dione. I miss her every day. I am ashamed to admit, I miss her more than I miss my Lord God Apollo. Apollo was a busy god—he rarely had time for me, so I was used to his absence. Dione, though, was my beloved sister. Now that she is back in my mind, I feel her absence constantly.

—Yours in sadness, Delphina

Chapter 8

"You can set up in that booth over there, Pythia, in the little alcove, while I set out these candles."

Lena lugged a heavy shopping bag around the dim dining room of the Wild West Arcade. At each table and booth, she placed a battery-operated candle and switched it on. Soon flickering "candles" illuminated the room in a soft glow. Lena added one fake candle to a shelf in Pythia's alcove. "There, now you'll be able to see what you are doing. Isn't that pretty? Look how it reflects in your crystal ball."

Pythia had to admit, the atmosphere was charming. She sat on a plush chair at a small velvet-covered round table with her crystal gazing ball in front of her. She felt a little self-conscious in the gypsy-style skirt and shawl Lena had given her in the employee break room. She reminded herself she was helping Lena of her own free will. *I am not a victim, I am a volunteer.* She tried to keep her mind in the present.

With her eyes squinted, the candles almost looked real.

"Those almost look real," she told Lena, who smiled.

"Thanks for helping me tonight. I think you will have fun." Lena straightened a tablecloth. "After the dinner rush, this room will be the sanctuary for stressed out parents. They can rest in here while their kids play on the machines. I'll turn on some soothing New Age music. You'll still be able to hear the video games in the arcade, but the acoustics in here are surprisingly quiet."

"Is there anything I should watch out for?"

"You are the psychic! Just be your usual kind self," Lena said. "You ready? I'm going to open the doors. In about an hour, I'll turn on the light above your table so people know they can visit you."

Pythia tried not to think about the last time she served as a fortune-teller. That was in April at the Renaissance Faire, helping Sylvia. Memories of the runaway horse and injured child came up but she pushed them aside. She remembered seeing Glen Haven and the mysterious woman in black on the news the next day. With a start, she realized the woman in black resembled the witch of her vision. How many women wore black and wielded a wand?

"Oh, my goodness," she said, and then customers came streaming into the room and she forgot about the woman in black. Soon every table and booth was occupied by chattering parents and children. Pythia sat in the dark alcove, sipped on a big glass of ice tea, and watched Lena and another server take food orders and serve pizza and ice cream. Before long, children migrated in hordes to the video games and pinball machines in the arcade while worn-out parents lingered over coffee and dessert.

A bell rang and a neon light over Pythia's booth lit up: *Fortune-teller is open.* Pythia pulled her shawl over her head, stashed her ice tea on a nearby shelf, and made ready to welcome her first clients of the evening.

A man and a woman slid into the opposite side of the booth. They were both slender, dressed in jeans and t-shirts, and had long blonde hair. The man had a blonde mustache. Other than the facial hair, they looked like twins.

"Do you, like, read palms, or something?" the man said.

The woman slapped his arm. "No, silly, look, she's got a crystal ball."

"Kind of small, isn't it?"

Pythia smiled. "I assure you, it is adequate for the task."

"So, this is free, right?"

Pythia nodded at the man. "Yes, it is included in your admission." Because she could see that this visit to the Arcade had pretty much tapped out his wallet, she added, "All my tips are covered by the Wild West Arcade. We want you to enjoy your visit without worries. Do you have a question for me?"

The woman pointed to the crystal ball. "Can you really see our future in that thing?"

"I can see some things, not everything," Pythia said. "Gazing is more of an art than a science."

"Well, I don't have a specific question," the woman said, shrugging a little. "Honey, do you have a question for the gypsy lady?"

"Nah, not really. You wanna go get more ice cream?"

"Wait," Pythia said. "Before you go, let me give you a message from your, let us say, from your ancestors. Your oldest son wants to be a dentist. Let him. He will provide for you in your old age. Your middle son wants to be an artist but is afraid you will not approve. He will never make money as an artist, but he will also never be happy if he becomes an accountant, so good luck with that."

Both parents gaped at her. "Uh, what?" said the man.

"One more thing. Your youngest son might be gay, and right now he is getting his hair stuck in a pinball machine. Wait, I misspoke. He is gay, no doubt about it, and you should probably go help him now. I hope you brought some scissors? If not, I am sure one of the servers will be able to assist."

"Jesus Christ!" the woman cried, scrambling out of the booth and running for the exit. "Tony, come on! Bennie, Bennie? Baby?"

"Holy shit," the man said. "Gay?"

Pythia sat back in her seat and stared into the crystal ball.

Her mind drifted back to the question that nagged her: Who was the woman in black? She closed her eyes and sought some insight. As usual, nothing clear emerged. The witch costume was clearly a disguise, and not a very good one. *I think I should recognize her but for some reason, I cannot see past the fog.* It's the same feeling she had when she was hiking with Lena and they met Glen Haven on the trails above the ocean. It's almost as if something were blocking her perception.

"Hello?"

Pythia opened her eyes and found a slender teenaged girl sitting in the seat opposite.

"Hello, how may I be of service?" Pythia smiled.

"I need to know my future," the girl said, tucking her brown hair behind her ears. Glasses perched on a sharp nose.

"Is something specific troubling you? Are you worried about your love life?"

"No, I don't care about that. It's my career. I want to be a writer but my father thinks I should do something safer, like be a lawyer or a doctor."

"What is your name?"

"Martha." The girl put her hands on the table.

"Martha, it is true it is not safe to be a writer."

"But that's all I ever wanted to be," the girl said, dropping her chin on one hand. She stared into the crystal ball. "I wish I could make that thing give me the future I want."

Pythia leaned forward. "You can. Put your hands here, like this." She placed her hands on either side of the crystal for a second to demonstrate. "Good. Now keep them there. I am going to try something. Do not be afraid." She placed her hands over Martha's hands. "Close your eyes, and I will do the same."

Pythia felt energy flow through Martha's hands into her own. With that boost, she was able to see. After a few seconds, she removed her hands.

Martha sat back and tucked her hands in her lap. "Whoa. What just happened?"

"What did you see?"

Martha stared at Pythia in awe. "I saw myself typing on the coolest keyboard ever."

"What else?"

"I was in a beautiful office. Outside the window was a blue swimming pool. My desk was huge. There was a white couch. There were palm trees all around a yard of flowers. I saw the ocean in the distance, down a hill. It sort of looked like Venice or Santa Monica."

"I think it might have been Santa Barbara," Pythia said.

"You saw it too?"

Pythia smiled. "Lawyers can be writers, doctors can be writers. Writers can be anything, many things, more than one thing, any time they want. Yes, it is not safe to be a writer. Writers can change the world. Yes, it can be hard sometimes, but if that is what you truly want, please do not give up. The world needs your voice."

Martha beamed, revealing a mouthful of braces. "Thank you!" She slid out of the booth and went back to a table where her parents were eating chocolate cake. Pythia couldn't hear their conversation but she could see that everyone was smiling.

Lena took a break and came over to sit in Pythia's booth.

"Let me turn off your light," she said, reaching over to flick a switch. They sat in the dim light of the fake candle. "Oh, my aching feet."

"Have you had any luck with the new agent?" Pythia asked.

Lena sighed. "I'm too old. I'm too fat. I'm too this, I'm too that. Hey, that rhymed. Anyway, nobody wants me. I can't get parts in commercials anymore. Thank God I have some residuals and this job, otherwise I would be homeless."

"You can always stay with me," Pythia said.

"Oh, thanks. You are a good friend. Say, I don't know how you are going to feel about this, but I saw your former assistant, what's her name, Debra, at my agent's office."

"Oh?" Pythia said.

"Is your spidey sense telling you something right now?"

Pythia chuckled. "No, Lena. My insight does not appear on demand, much to my dismay. Most days, I am as anxious and uncertain as anyone else."

"Your insight, as you call it, should have warned you that Debra defected to the enemy!"

"What do you mean?"

"My new agent represents none other than Divina Dee!"

The pieces clicked into place. "And Ms. Sandhill is Divina Dee's new assistant."

"She was embarrassed to see me. I wasn't sure how to play it. Should I pretend I don't know her? Give her a big sloppy kiss? You know, it's so hard being famous. I didn't know what to do, but turns out I didn't have to do anything. Divina Dee came in and everyone in the agency went bonkers, I mean, absolutely crazy ass looney tunes bonkers."

"Well," Pythia said, at a loss for words.

"Don't you think it's odd that your assistant went to work for the Psychic to the Stars girl?"

"Well, not really, no. She has always been enamored with Divina Dee."

"But aren't you afraid Debra will spill all your trade secrets?"

Pythia laughed. *Trade secrets, indeed. A crack in the floor and old wobbly stool.* "Lena, I am a business coach, not a psychic."

"You can't deny that you have a certain knack for telling the future."

"I do not deny it, no. But anyone can have a knack if they just pay attention."

"I'd better get back to work. Those kids over there are about to pull the tablecloth onto the—dammit! Why didn't you use your spidey sense to warn me?" Lena grinned. She grabbed a broom and dustpan from a hidden closet and went to clean up the mess. When she returned the broom to the closet, she said, "Oh, I forgot to mention, you got a rave review from a young lady named Martha. Her parents insisted on leaving you a tip."

"Thank you. Lena, may I ask you for a favor?"

Lena looked at Pythia in surprise. "Of course, always. You need some time off from the Roundtable? Want me to set you up on a blind date? Need to borrow my Rolls Royce for the weekend? Name it, you got it!"

"As my sponsor, would you be willing to work the Steps with me?"

Lena raised her hands and chortled at the ceiling. "Oh, my God, I thought you'd never ask!"

June 15, 2015

In other news, this week I asked my friend L to help me work through a dilemma I am calling my lack of faith problem, for want of a better term. Maybe as we go along, I will think of something more apt to call it. For now, I have decided that the reason why I am feeling despair and discontent is that I have lost my faith.

Some of you might be familiar with a set of suggestions called the Twelve Steps. These twelve suggestions came out of the Alcoholics Anonymous program. And before you leave me disdainful comments about my drinking habits, I will tell you, I am not an alcoholic. However, I am an addict of some kind. My compulsion seems to be related to my oracular talent. That is all I will disclose at this point. You might be able to guess more. I ask that you keep your guesses to yourself out of respect for A.A.'s tradition of anonymity.

In still other news, I came across an article in a scientific journal several months ago. A group of researchers traveled to Delphi and explored some of the caves there to measure the components of the fumes emanating from fissures in the earth. Their instruments confirmed what people in the region have known for millennia—the gases issuing from the earth have the potential to cause hallucinations. I do not think it matters at this point. Make of it what you will. I have been gone from Delphi for a very long time. I just thought the article was interesting.

My sponsor suggested I attend an A.A. meeting that focuses specifically on the Twelve Steps. Accordingly, I sought out some options using an old listing I found in a drawer. The only group that meets at a (relatively) convenient time and place is in Marina del Rey on Mondays at 7:30 a.m. That would not be my preferred time and place, but I have been told we need to go to any lengths to recover. Even if we are not sure exactly what we want to recover from. I will let you know what I learn.

—Yours in recovery, Delphina

Pythia placed cards in her tenant's mailboxes, inviting them to attend Debra's farewell party. She asked Debra to help her send email invitations to their best coaching clients.

"I agree, it would be weird if I sent out the invitations to my own farewell party," Debra laughed. She stood over Pythia's shoulder and instructed her on the buttons to click. "Oh, there's Stacy on the list. Dammit, I keep forgetting to remove her from my address book."

"No matter," Pythia said. "I too see Stacy's name in my e-mail system."

Debra sighed. "If they get email in heaven, Stacy will see it and know we haven't forgotten her."

"By the way, Ms. Sandhill, please do not feel you must hide your new employer's identity. I am very happy for you. And no, I did not see that in my crystal ball. Lena told me she saw you at her agent's office."

Debra looked chagrined. "Yeah, I didn't exactly handle that well. I figured you'd find out."

"You have nothing to hide, Ms. Sandhill. This is the career boost you have been waiting for."

"I'm sorry about not finishing the Business Barracuda's proposal. If you want, I can still . . ."

Pythia waved her hand. "Please, do not. I would make a terrible Barracuda."

Debra laughed with relief. "Yes, you would. I don't know what I was thinking."

"You were trying to help."

Debra picked at the door jamb. "Pythia, will you be okay?"

Pythia looked at the photo on the wall. "That used to be my home," she said.

Debra frowned. "That ruin? That's in Greece, right?"

"Yes, the Temple of Apollo at Delphi."

"What, your parents were, like, tour guides or something?"

Pythia smiled. "Something like that."

"Why are you telling me this?"

"I sense that at your new job, you will be involved with Glen Haven's project."

Debra flushed pink. "We've only been out once!"

"I am not judging you, Ms. Sandhill. I am warning you. Please be cautious. I want you to be safe and happy, if such a blessed intersection exists." Pythia folded her hands in prayer for a moment. "By the way, I ordered a chocolate cake. I will pick it up Thursday night after we close."

"I can pick it up," Debra protested.

"No, please. I would like your final week at work to be a relaxing cessation of duties. I want you to remember your time here with fondness, if that is possible."

"It's time to lock the front door." Debra preceded Pythia into the front lobby area and reversed the open sign. "Remember when I interviewed for the job?"

"Yes. You were wearing a charming outfit you made yourself."

"That's right! I forgot! It was wool. I was sweating like a wrestler in that thing. I almost slid off the chair."

"We had high hopes," Pythia said, looking around.

"Hey, don't get morose, Pythia. It's not over yet."

"Thank you, Ms. Sandhill, for your loyalty and efforts over these past ten years. This business would have failed a long time ago if not for you."

Debra and Pythia stood side by side and surveyed the dingy room.

"I always meant to ask you, are you nuts, what the hell were you thinking?"

Pythia frowned at Debra. "About what?"

"That wallpaper! Nineteen seventy is calling and they want it back!"

Pythia had to laugh. "I will miss you, Ms. Sandhill. More than you will ever know."

On Friday of the following week, Debra and Pythia closed the office early and began to decorate. After sweeping the linoleum floor and vacuuming the faded rug with the ancient Kirby, they tackled the seating problem. The office had quite a few somewhat shabby client chairs stashed around the place, but Debra thought they needed more.

"I invited everyone," Debra said. "All our clients, past and present. All my friends. FacePlace followers. Everyone!"

Pythia asked her tenants for folding chairs. Frank and Helen offered a dozen or more they used for giving do-it-yourself matting and framing demonstrations. Each chair bore the I've Been Framed logo on the back of the seat. Debra arranged the chairs against the walls in the main lobby area. She put some of the shabbier client chairs outside on the sidewalk in groups of four facing each other with a sturdy cardboard box between them to serve as a table.

"The overflow can sit outside," she said. "Once the sun starts going down, it won't be so bad."

Pythia had ordered dozens of helium balloons from Ralph's. Most were plain silver Mylar, but many were imprinted with the words *Farewell* and *Good luck*.

"These are so pretty!" Debra said. She attached the balloons in bouquets behind the chairs to fill in blank corners, where they bobbed in the breeze stirred up by several portable fans, also borrowed for the evening.

Pythia enlisted catering help from Louise, owner of Cheese Louise.

"I'll cater everything but the cake," Louise said. "You can store it in my big refrigerator, but buy it at Costmart!"

Cheese Louise donated a long folding table, complete with festive silver tablecloth. Debra set up the table outside Pythia's office cubicle. Louise trundled the sheet cake along the sidewalk on a rolling cart and set it in the middle of the table as the centerpiece.

"The table looks perfect," Debra said, clapping her hands. Two large flower arrangements adorned each end of the table, set toward the back to leave room for the food. Before the guests arrived, Louise placed stacks of tiny plates close at hand next to platters of one-inch pizza squares speared with toothpicks. Green and white paper napkins were stacked in convenient locations, sporting the festive Italianesque red, green, and white Cheese Louise logo.

"I'll bring a chest of ice," Louise promised. "We'll serve drinks like they do on airplanes. It will take up two square feet of floor space. Well, three, counting the server. "

Debra placed her radio on the half-wall of her cubicle and turned on some jazzy background music. "I think the office is ready. Now for my personal transformation!"

Twenty minutes later, Debra emerged from the restroom in a tight long-sleeved dress covered in black sequins. It was cut high in the front but low to her waist in the back, exposing her tanned skin. "No swimsuit lines," she said to Pythia, twirling with a grin. "I've been tanning every other day for two weeks for this!"

Pythia went upstairs to change as well. She combed her hair and put on a simple short-sleeved white linen shift and flat-soled jute sandals. *I do not want to embarrass my employee on her final day. Apollo knows she has been embarrassed by me enough over the years. This is her day to celebrate.*

When she reentered the office, guests had started to arrive.

Pythia greeted Lena at the door. Lena gave her a hug and said, "We knew this day would come."

A parade of current and past clients arrived. Cindi Harper brought her big bag and began handing out samples from her new line of adult pleasure products. Debra hurried to give Cindi a hug and press a drink into her hand. Renee Fletchall, the artist, appeared with a tall thin man with pasty skin and a tangle of silver facial piercings. She hugged Debra but avoided Pythia.

The room filled with people. Louise and one of her staff stood by the table serving drinks from a chrome cart. Pythia sat in a corner and let the pleasant white noise of voices wash over her. Her mind drifted back to the problem of the woman in black. *Who is this modern-day witch?* No answers appeared.

"You need to say something," Lena said in Pythia's ear, jolting her out of her reverie.

Lena turned off the music. She edged over to the bookshelf and tapped with the wooden stick on the bronze singing bowl, sending out a rich chime. She tapped two or three more times, gradually gaining attention from the guests. When the room was quiet, Pythia stepped to the middle of the lobby area and raised her hand to acknowledge Debra.

"Thank you, everyone, for coming this evening to be part of a sad but happy celebration and farewell to honor Debra Sandhill, who has served as my assistant for the past ten years."

"Hear, hear!" Cindi hooted, raising her glass.

"Those of you who have worked with Ms. Sandhill know that this office would have closed long ago without her expertise, skills, and determination."

"Aw, that's sweet," said a woman in the corner.

"It is the truth. Ms. Sandhill has developed the unique ability to organize a business that defies easy organization. She made this business a success."

"Way to go, Debra!"

"Along the way, she has done her best to bring me into the twenty-first century," Pythia added.

"No easy task!" Debra said, laughing.

Looking around the room at the smiling faces, Pythia noticed Glen Haven standing near the back of the crowd, clapping and smiling. Debra saw him as well and maneuvered between guests to stand next to Glen, who put his arm around her.

The crowd was in a dancing mood. Pythia raised her voice. "Finally, let me wish Ms. Sandhill every success and joy as she moves on to her next opportunity to shine. I am certain that her path will be satisfying, rich, and purposeful. I envy her next employer. I predict great things for our Ms. Sandhill, and I am honored to have been part of her amazing life and career."

Pythia smiled at her former assistant, who was dabbing under her eyes with a napkin.

"Ms. Sandhill, would you like to say a few words?"

"Oh, Pythia!" Debra wiped her nose and stuffed the napkin in a sleeve. She hurried to Pythia and gave her a big hug. Pythia accepted the hug without pulling away. *Is this our first embrace? What kind of deceitful liar am I, to say I will miss her and wish her all the best and yet still treat her like a stranger?*

As Pythia had feared, touching Debra opened up a floodgate of insight from all directions. Holding her breath against the roaring in her ears, Pythia disengaged and stepped aside for Debra to take the center.

As Debra talked, Pythia held onto a wall and rode the wave of images. *The widower standing by the food table will eat pancakes for dinner when he gets home to an empty house. That woman with the false eyelashes and long platinum wig is enduring cancer treatments but she will survive and write a bestseller next year that will eventually become a movie that will win an Academy Award.* She saw a flash of Apollo's temple on a hill overlooking the Pacific Ocean—Glen Haven's project, no doubt. She caught a glimpse of people swimming in a blue pool. *That couple will divorce before Christmas. That man will die in a surfing accident—oh, Apollo, bit by a shark. That woman will accidentally forget her baby in the backseat of her car but will remember just in time to save the baby from heat stroke. Apollo, save me, grant me release. What is the point of this power if I can't save anyone from the pain of existing? We might as well all be dead.*

"Pythia, are you okay?" Lena's familiar voice cut through the torrent of images and brought her back to her senses. She grabbed her friend's hand. "Whoa, panic attack," Lena said. "Take a breath. Let's say a quick prayer."

"Let's dance!" Debra shouted and turned up the music.

As Lena mumbled A.A.'s serenity prayer under her breath, Pythia fought to stay in her body. The familiar smells of asphalt and tar permeated the aromas of cake, pizza, wine, and soda. *And something else, something I do not recognize but that makes me want to hide under a table. Apollo, what is happening?*

"There's a midnight meeting over on Sawtelle," Lena said in her ear. "Hang tight. You can do this."

A few minutes before midnight, Lena led Pythia along a dim walkway at a West L.A. middle school. The evening air smelled of jasmine and roses. They entered a brightly lit classroom that smelled of paper and crayons. *Safe odors, familiar scents.* Chairs were arranged in a circle. Now that she was away from the office, Pythia felt better. She recognized a few faces from her other A.A. meeting. She sank onto a chair. She inhaled the innocent aromas of crayons, flowers, aftershave, and body odor and started to relax.

Partway through the speaker's share, the door opened to admit an older woman wearing a pink ballet tutu and chunky roller skates. Her long gray hair was pulled up in a messy ponytail. She floundered into the center of the circle and struck a pose with her hand in the air. She had applied shocking pink lipstick with a heavy hand, framing white teeth too perfect to be real.

"Hi, I'm Crazy Polly and I'm an alcoholic. So sorry to be late." She performed a pirouette and fell onto the folding chair with a clang. She cackled and sucked her upper denture back into place. Some members rolled their eyes. Most tried to ignore the interruption.

Without much effort, Pythia could see the woman's painful past and glorious future. Her three children had disowned her long ago, even though she no longer drank—and even though she never gave up on them. Her mental disorder propelled her into periods of frenzied creativity, during which she painted canvases that would be auctioned for millions of dollars after her death. *She will last another thirty years, happily painting until the end when she drops dead of a heart attack. Her children will squander their inheritances but her paintings will be treasured for as long as there are museums full of art lovers.*

When Lena dropped her off at the office, Pythia climbed the back stairs to the second floor apartments feeling weary but at peace. She thought about opening up a blogpost but her bed beckoned.

What I would write, Blog Readers, is this: Not everyone is fortunate enough to leave a remarkable legacy. In fact, most people do not. But that does not mean our lives were wasted. We can still make a difference, if only for the few people around us. We do not all have to be stars.

Chapter 9

Pythia spent an hour Saturday morning cleaning up the office. Empty plastic cups and bent paper plates covered tables, shelves, and chairs. Napkins littered the floor. Fortunately, Debra had taken all the helium balloons with her as souvenirs. However, the office was a mess. Visitor chairs needed to be brushed for crumbs and returned to their proper places. Borrowed chairs and dishes had to be cleaned and returned to the lenders.

Pythia worked in silence, filling up several large black plastic trash bags and sweeping up all the detritus left behind when people party in the twenty-first century.

At 9:00 a.m., Frank and Helen opened the front door of their shop. Pythia helped Frank fold and stack the chairs on a storage platform, which he wheeled into the back room where he framed customers' art. Pythia thanked Helen for the loan of their chairs.

"What now, Pythia?" Frank asked. "You gonna get another one?"

Helen said, "My sister's stepdaughter might be looking for something."

Frank chortled. "Tiffany, you mean? The crackhead?"

Helen smacked his arm. "She's not a crackhead, Frank."

"Yeah, just a little drug problem is all."

Pythia was in no position to judge anyone else's drug habits. "I do not think I am going to look for a replacement just yet."

"By the way, Pythia, Fourth of July is coming up next month. July first is the start of our annual summer frame sale.

Debra's party gave us the idea. We were talking to Louise about having some sort of street fair out front here. What do you think?"

"I think that is a wonderful idea, Mr. Bristol. Let me know what I can do to help." Pythia's insight showed her festive images of customers milling about in front of her shop.

"Well, in that case . . ." Helen began. Pythia caught a quick mental snapshot of frames stacked against the wall inside her office waiting room.

"Please consider using my foyer and waiting room for your event," Pythia said. "In fact, why not use the entire sidewalk?"

Helen beamed and went into the shop to get ready for the day. Pythia walked along the block to Cheese Louise and waved at Louise through the front window.

"Are you going to go it alone?" Louise asked as they walked back to Pythia's office. "Debra will be hard to replace."

They lugged the folding table along the sidewalk and into the restaurant where they handed it off to the sous chef to drag into the storeroom.

Pythia wiped her hands on a paper napkin. "Truthfully, I do not have enough clients right now to support an office person. Business has been declining for a while."

Louise leaned on her deli counter. "Maybe you'd be better off renting out that space. Maybe to an accountant or someone like that." *Not to a competitor.*

"I would not rent to anyone who might compete with you," Pythia reassured her. "However, I fear the entire building needs renovating." Pythia looked at the faded facade.

"Well, give me plenty of notice if you decide to do something drastic!" Louise said. "I'll need time to plan."

"Of course, Ms. Romano. I will consult all the tenants before making any decisions."

"Don't worry, Pythia. Whatever happens, we'll be okay. By the way, I was talking to Frank and Helen. Independence Day is next month. We want to do some sort of street event on the sidewalk. Frank's having his frame sale, and I think I would like to offer some Italian desserts. If it is hot. Or coffee if it isn't. What do you think?"

"That sounds like fun," Pythia said, smiling. "How can I help?"

"Maybe we can use your foyer and front office for shade?"

"Certainly. And more room to display frames, perhaps. I can move the furniture into the hallway. I suggest you talk with Mr. and Mrs. Bristol and let me know your plan as the holiday weekend approaches."

June 27, 2015

Change is surprisingly difficult to accept, even though we know it is inevitable. I have heard people say the only constant is change. Why, then, do we get so upset when something changes? It defies logic.

Some changes we welcome. I have always liked the change of seasons. I could count on spring following winter and summer giving way to autumn. Those changes were predictable and expected. Whenever the seasons failed to perform according to expectations, regional rulers would send emissaries to plead for insight from the Oracle at Delphi.

After my illness, another Pythia took over the crucial task of reassuring the ambassadors and supplicants (after they had paid their proper tributes of gold, jewels, oats, barley, and beef) that the seasons would resume their necessary order. Winter would pass. The rains would come. The harvest would feed the people. The people would grow strong. Or not. Sometimes starving kingdoms fell, usually to soldiers sent by other kings to capture land and slaves in their king's name. The mixing of peoples made Greece a lively place for centuries.

I mentioned in a recent blog post that a friend had died. It was not from gun violence, as seems to be so prevalent in American culture these days; it was just a fluke traffic accident, an odd case involving a dog driving a car. Change happens in an instant sometimes.

You would imagine I could have predicted and perhaps prevented my friend's death. I am deeply ashamed that I, once the most powerful Oracle in Greece, failed to do my job. I would have done my best to somehow prevent it. I do not have the power to change fate, but I do sometimes have insight that can help others change their behaviors and achieve positive outcomes.

Death is death, though. Knowing when or how it comes does not make it any less fatal.

A less fatal failure of my talent occurred this week, yet another example of an event I could not foresee or forestall. My assistant found a job better suited to her skills and ambitions. I always knew she would—career ambition is the norm for modern American women in their thirties. I did not need my oracular ability to know that day would eventually arrive. Now I know who her new employer will be. I believe she will be happy there for a time. I wish her all the best.

—Yours in exile, Delphina

On Sunday, Pythia found a closed sign on the back door of the Church of Apollo. A hand-lettered sign announced that the church was closed for the rest of the summer. The pastor was seeking spiritual guidance. Rodney had signed his name at the bottom. Pythia put her hand on the sign and caught a flash of Rodney hiking on a dusty trail overlooking a green valley. *That looks like Delphi! Would that I were there.*

"Hello, Pythia."

Pythia turned to see Arnie Solomon standing at the bottom of the steps with his hands in his jeans pockets.

"Arnie?" she smiled, holding out her hand, even though she was on the porch. "I have seen you so many times from afar, I feel like we have already met!"

"How you doing today?" He reached up and clasped her hand with two big warm hands. She felt energy flow into her center. He released her hand, leaving her dizzy. To hide her surprise, she grabbed the stair railing and smiled down at him.

She waved at the sign. "It appears the Church of Apollo has gone on a spiritual retreat."

"Oh, too bad. I was hoping to see that statue light up again."

Pythia laughed, feeling inordinately happy. Arnie stepped back, and she joined him on ground level. He wasn't that much taller than she. *What amazing blue eyes!*

"I'm guessing our young minister is vacationing in Delphi," Arnie said with a twinkle.

"I wish him all the best! Now that we are here, would you like to grab a coffee somewhere?" Pythia said. *What did I just say? My lord Apollo!*

"I'd be delighted! There's a little Greek café just down the block, if that would suit? We could actually walk there. I think our cars will be safe here, don't you?" He waved at her Honda Insight, next to which was parked a somewhat scratched and dented yellow-orange Chevy pickup.

"Orange!" Pythia exclaimed. "Oh, I am sorry—"

"I like to think of it as gold," Arnie laughed. "Makes me feel like King Midas."

They walked side by side without speaking along the narrow driveway out to the sidewalk. Arnie pointed toward the west, and Pythia followed his lead.

On Washington Boulevard, they walked past an alterations shop, closed on Sunday, idle machines and spools of thread visible through the dusty front window. Next was an insurance agent's office, windows covered in foot-high lettering warning of the dangers of being uninsured. The third storefront was empty, possibly for a long time, judging by the dust and cobwebs in the display area. The fourth storefront was an eatery called Corinth Café.

Arnie opened an old-fashioned wooden screen door and ushered Pythia into a cool light-filled space with a cobalt blue concrete floor. White walls edged in royal blue borders gave the rustic space some Greek charm. White lace tablecloths and blue placements decorated a dozen small round tables.

"Ya!" A tall heavy man came toward them, arms open. "Welcome back, Mr. Solomon!"

"Hello, Niko. Pythia, this is Niko Nicoli, the proprietor of this establishment. Niko, this is my friend, Pythia. We were hoping for a bit of coffee. You still open?"

"For you, always, morning or night! Please, sit here, Miss Pythia. I will bring fresh coffee and ice water."

Pythia sat on a straight-backed wooden chair in front of a royal blue paper placemat that aligned perfectly with the one in front of Arnie. The white linen tablecloth was trimmed with a delicate lace border. She did a double take. "I think this is real Greek lace!"

Pythia and Arnie chatted about Greek lace and Greek coffee and discovered a shared interest in all things Greek. In about ten minutes, Niko brought a tray holding two glasses of ice water, two small blue coffee cups, and a steaming copper briki. First, he placed the two glasses of water on the table. Next, he set the coffee cups in blue saucers on the blue placemats. Finally, he deftly poured rich thick black coffee into each cup, being sure to leave a robust head of crema. He stood back to admire his work.

Arnie grinned at Pythia. "Niko is the real deal."

"I see that," she said, smiling at Niko and then at Arnie. *Apollo, save me! I could lose myself in those blue eyes.*

Arnie lifted his cup and took a long slow slurp. "Delicious, as usual!"

Niko bowed and departed with his tray.

"Tell me, Arnie. How did you end up working as a DJ at the radio station?"

Arnie sat back in his chair. "I've always loved music. When I was young, I used to play some classical stringed instruments. However, I found that I enjoyed listening to others' music more than I enjoyed playing music myself. Truthfully, I wasn't all that good. So I became a patron of musicians wherever I found them. One acquaintance told me about the part-time gig as a DJ. I thought, why not? Sounded like fun."

"What kind of music do you enjoy?"

"Just about everything. I feel like I've seen the evolution of music from its classical beginnings to the many genres we have today. I love rock music from the 1960s. I've even grown to appreciate rap and hip hop. I am really partial to country. Not sure I am all that fond of new age stuff, but I support creativity in all its myriad forms. Music is an expression of life."

"Beautifully said." Pythia sipped her coffee, not as loudly as Arnie had, but still maintaining proper Greek coffee-drinking etiquette. She knew Niko was listening.

"How about you, Pythia, what music do you prefer?"

Pythia pondered. "I grew up with plain classical music. Lutes, guitars, flutes. I still like that style, but honestly, I don't listen to music often. What I really enjoy is hiking outdoors, especially on the trails above the ocean."

"Oh, like Malibu, that area?"

"Yes. It reminds me of my childhood."

Arnie gazed at her over his cup of coffee. "You've lived in L.A. a few years, right? It's quite a town, don't you think? Lots of history. Do you remember Ship's?"

Pythia laughed. "Ship's Restaurant? There were several, as I recall. My favorite one was at Wilshire and Westwood."

Arnie nodded. "Always open, never closed."

"Do you remember the Brown Derby?"

"Yeah, the one on Wilshire, shaped like a hat? That was something. I drive part-time for a limousine company so I get to see lots of Hollywood landmarks."

"I do not dine out much. However, I do enjoy visiting the Art Museum."

"The one by the Tar Pits?"

"Yes, that's just a block from my office."

After a long companionable silence during which they both appreciated their coffee, Arnie said, "What inspired you to attend a service at the Church of Apollo?"

Pythia set her cup down in the saucer and looked at her hands. "I do not know, really. I read a comment on a blogpost. The commenter mentioned the Church. I had never heard of it, well, not like this, as the Church of Apollo. I was curious, I suppose."

"I heard about it in much the same way," Arnie said. "Found a reference to it on the Internet, thought I'd check it out."

"That day I saw you there, that was my first time."

"Yeah? Mine, too. What did you think?"

Pythia smiled. "I thought Rodney was a kind man with a desire to find a connection to something greater than himself. How he decided to worship Apollo, I do not know. I certainly had to admire his preparations—and decorations!"

Arnie laughed. "Yes, all that gold was impressive."

"This is going to sound odd, but Rodney knew me." Pythia said. "Not my name, but my internet name. That puzzles me."

"What do they say, God works in mysterious ways?" Arnie said.

"Could that be it? I have never been able to relate to the Christian god." Pythia stared at the bit of foam left on top of her coffee. The brew had cooled to a rich sweet syrup.

"Neither have I. In this modern era, we don't hear much about any god but the Christian god, at least in this country. So, whenever I hear a reference to Greek mythological figures, I am interested. I mean, I am not necessarily looking for god, with a capital G, I don't think. But aren't we all on some sort of spiritual journey?"

Pythia nodded. "I have done my own seeking over the years."

"Have you found what you sought?"

Pythia shook her head. "No, I am sad to say. But that does not mean it does not exist. I have not given up."

Arnie smiled. "I'm glad to hear it. Neither have I. If it is any consolation, we aren't alone. Most people are looking for something to believe in."

"What is your interest in Apollo, as an entity to be worshiped, if I may ask?" Pythia said. When Arnie hesitated, she added, "Please forgive me, I do not mean to pry."

"Oh, no, I don't mind," Arnie said with steepled fingers. "I've always had a personal connection to Greek mythology. When I was a kid, everyone around me talked about this god or that goddess. It seemed normal to me, the drama of Mt. Olympus. My entire family was enamored with the idea of a pantheon of gods."

"That is fascinating," Pythia said. "I confess, my knowledge is limited. I have had a personal interest in only one specific figure from Greek mythology. That happens to be Apollo."

"You must know quite a bit about him, then."

"I thought I did. Now, I am not so sure."

"May I ask, is your interest more historical in nature or more metaphysical in nature?"

Pythia looked into Arnie's blue eyes and saw only interest and compassion. "This is going to sound insane, I fear. I will be candid. I am looking for Apollo, the actual god Apollo," she said. *Why did I say that? He is a stranger. A nice stranger, but why would I admit such a thing?* She laughed a little and waved her hand to dismiss her words. "Please forget I said that. I am feeling sad. A friend died recently, and my assistant left for a new employment opportunity. I am sorry to be so morose."

"Please don't apologize. Grief is a powerful force with its own path and pace."

"Thank you for understanding." Pythia took a sip of ice water and smiled with relief at Arnie. They sat for a minute in silence.

Arnie cleared his throat. "About Apollo, you said you were searching for him. What makes you think he exists to be found?"

Pythia stared into her cup and shook her head. "Faith." She shrugged her shoulders and smiled. Arnie returned her smile.

Arnie paid for the two coffees. Niko wished them a pleasant rest of their day. They walked back to the parking lot, where their cars remained unmolested.

"Thank you for the coffee, Arnie. I enjoyed our visit very much. Although, if I remember correctly, it was I who invited you. Therefore, according to modern custom, I should have been the one to pay."

Arnie laughed. "Next time, Pythia."

She got into her Honda, feeling pleased. *Next time!* He got into his Chevy pickup and started up the engine, which caught with a roar. A song she didn't recognize came blasting through the pickup's open window. Arnie started bouncing his head in time to the music.

"It's a classic by The Clash," he yelled. "It's called 'Should I stay or should I go?'" He played air guitar for a moment, grinned at Pythia, and then backed his car out of the parking spot. "See you again soon, my friend."

Pythia watched him drive away, feeling lighter in spirit than she had in a long time. She started up her Honda Insight, which merely hummed. For the first time in a long time, she turned on the radio. A song with a catchy beat was playing, something about walking on sunshine. Pythia found herself tapping her fingers with the beat on the steering wheel.

～

On Tuesday evening, Pythia arrived early to the A.A. meeting to find the chairs in the room arranged in a circle, rather than in the usual classroom-style layout. As she stood contemplating the new configuration, Charlotte and Patty entered the room behind her.

"What the fuck!" shouted Patty, pushing past Pythia. "What is this bullshit?" She stomped around the outer edge of the circle.

Charlotte shook her head. "This is so weird."

"This is utter bullshit!" Patty yelled, waving her arms.

George, the group secretary arrived, carrying the meeting notebook. "Hello, ladies. Sorry I'm a bit late."

"What is this fucked up shit?" Patty screeched.

"What, the chairs, you mean?" George said in mild surprise. "It's always like this when I get here. There's an Al-Anon meeting here in the afternoon. They like their chairs set up in a circle. I happen to prefer rows, so I try to get here early to move the chairs around. I'm glad you're here. You want to help me?"

Under George's guidance, Patty, Charlotte, and Pythia soon rearranged the chairs, making sure the rows and aisles were properly aligned. Once they were done, Patty sank into her usual seat and put her head in her hands. Pythia sat in her preferred seat in the back row. Charlotte sat next to George.

Soon other members arrived and began filling the chairs. Lena entered through the front door, wearing a lacy cream-colored beret, for a change. She waved at Pythia.

At 7:00 p.m., George stood up and moved in front of the lectern. He opened the notebook and waited for the conversations to slow and stop. When it was quiet, he said, "Welcome everyone to the Tuesday Night Westwood Meeting of Alcoholics Anonymous. My name is George and I'm an alcoholic and your secretary for this evening's meeting."

"Hi, George!" the group responded enthusiastically. After some opening readings came the part Pythia dreaded and often tried to miss. *Is this why I tend to get lost in the basement trying to find this room? Oh, my Lord Apollo, save me from my madness.*

"Now it's time for introductions," George said. He pointed to the person sitting in the first seat in the first row, which happened to be Patty.

I'm Patty, I'm an addict," she mumbled. George pointed to the next person. Going row by row around the room, one by one, people introduced themselves, most as alcoholics. Lena's voice was audible and clear—"My name is Lena, and I'm an alcoholic." Not proud, just matter-of-fact. Other voices were strained, or quiet, or raspy.

When it was Pythia's turn, she said what she always said: "I am Pythia, and I do not know what I am," which was as close to the truth as she could bring herself to say in this group. However, her introduction often earned her rolled eyes and snorts, mainly from long-timers who'd seen and heard it all and had no patience for dissembling. *A.A.s are strict about their recovery. But I do not want to lie. Someday I may have to tell the whole truth. Apollo, I don't know if I can be that honest. The prospect terrifies me.*

"Our topic tonight is Step One," George said.

Pythia forced herself to pay attention to the reading and the shares that followed. *Lena is going to ask me about this later.*

Patty was the first person to ascend to the lectern to share, a rare occurrence. She stood in front of the group, twisted her uncombed hair in one finger, and picked at the lectern.

"Hi, I'm Patty, and I'm still an addict."

The group murmured, "Hi, Patty."

"When we came into the room tonight, the chairs were out of order."

Some members mumbled a protest.

"I freaked out," Patty admitted.

"Right on," a man said.

"I had an idea about how the chairs were s'posed to be arranged, and I came freakin *unglued* when they weren't the way I wanted them to be!"

The group chuckled and heads bobbed.

Patty started to smile. "Then George came in and said, 'They always like this, 'cause of some other group,' and come to find out, he been fixin' the chairs this whole time!"

Now the group roared and applauded.

"I'm not a real smart person. Drugs and booze have wrecked my brain. I do know this: My brain is trying to kill me. This thing in me that keeps me coming back to this group is the flip side of the thing that wants me dead. They is a war in my head. Something as simple as chairs in the wrong order and I'll be at the bar by 8:30 and overdosed by 9:00. No joke, people. Powerlessness, I don't want it, but it's mine. Step One. I need to own it and claim it."

Patty sat down in her seat to hearty applause.

After the meeting ended, Lena and Pythia went out to the parking lot together. The evening was warm. Pythia smelled jasmine nearby.

"I didn't see your friend tonight," Lena said, leaning against Pythia's car.

"Who, Arnie?"

"He seems like a nice old guy. Would you have coffee with him again, if he asked?"

"Of course. I like him very much."

"What are you powerless over, Pythia, if it isn't alcohol?" Lena asked. "Is it relationships? Food? Sex? Money? Meth? What?"

Pythia sighed. "Lena, I have told you several times before. You refuse to believe me."

Lena frowned. "You mean . . . the gas thing?"

Pythia nodded.

"Pythia, we've been friends a long time. You have to tell me the truth."

"I treasure our friendship, Lena. I would not want to lose you as a friend. The truth about me is not easy to handle."

"Well, whatever your drug of choice, right now, you sound like a garden-variety self-obsessed alcoholic." Lena leaned over and kissed Pythia's cheek. "I love you anyway, you crazy addict. You want to go get some frozen yogurt?"

June 30, 2015

Blog Readers, I believe I owe you an apology. Some of you have pointed out my tendency to be self-centered. Self-obsessed, some of you have said. I have not wanted to pay attention. Last Sunday, I met a new friend in Culver City for Greek coffee. I am astonished at how much I enjoyed this simple social event. Talking with a friend about Greek mythology while sipping perfect Greek coffee from delightful blue cups . . . the sheer joy of the experience has shown me I have been too focused on my own life and problems.

Therefore, I admit you may be correct, and I appreciate you bringing it to my attention. I have been focused solely on my own grief and homesickness for so long, I lost my joy of people. For example, I see now that I failed to appreciate my assistant when she was here. No wonder I lost her to a rival. She deserved to be nurtured, and I failed to provide that nurturing.

Maybe I need to stop moping. Even if Apollo is sleeping, or resting, or missing, that does not mean I have to spend all my time grieving. Yes, I have had some losses in my life—my sister, my home, my oracular talent, and hardest loss of all, my faith in my Lord God Apollo. Still, I persist. As long as I am living, I can help others in my own small way. If Apollo lives, he will appear in his own time. I never could force my Lord God Apollo to do my bidding. That is probably a good thing. What kind of god would he be if he yielded to the demands of a self-centered fearful powerless former Oracle?

I am learning to accept that I am powerless. It is a new concept for someone who used to know everything. It is not always necessary to know what is going to happen next. Most humans live their lives in that state. It has been difficult to accept that I am no better—no, my apologies, that is not the way to say it. I mean, it is enough to be alive. Living life means having emotions.

I will always miss my beloved sister. I will always regret that I could not foresee the death of my friend or the falling of the Twin Towers or the riots and earthquakes and other disasters that repeatedly befuddle and confound us. I need to remember that life is a privilege, not a guarantee, and I need to earn my happiness.

I await your comments with remorse and chagrin, but mostly gratitude.

—Yours in exile, Delphina

Chapter 10

The office without Debra was eerily empty and silent. *I did not appreciate her. I took her for granted.* Pythia sat in her office, missing small sounds. Debra's cough. The squeak of Debra's chair. Her snort when Pythia made some observation Debra thought was inane. *She had dreams and ambitions. I was an obstacle.*

Pythia felt a sudden urge to write a blogpost, but it passed quickly and left her feeling at loose ends. *I could go upstairs. I could go to bed. I could die on the floor here in my office. No one would miss me. Except perhaps for my tenants, when it is time for the party.*

The thought of preparing for the July Fourth party seemed overwhelming. Moving furniture, dusting . . . it would have been so much easier with Debra's help. Debra would have handled it with ease. Debra handled every situation with ease.

Pythia checked the appointment book. The day's schedule was clear—not a single client name on the page. The empty office felt intolerable. *There is no reason to be here.*

Pythia put on a straw hat, threw her cell phone in her purse, and went out the front door, locking it behind her. She walked briskly past Cheese Louise, trying to give the impression she had a destination. She imagined Louise looking at her with pity. *That's foolish. Nobody cares about me. I am just a poorly dressed middle-aged woman walking along the street toward the park.*

Pythia slowed as she walked by the dark windows of Stacy's former yoga studio. The window had been replaced and the wall patched and painted. However, Stacy's hand-lettered name was still on the door, competing with a large red and white for-rent sign. Pythia peered through the door. A dusty yoga mat lay on the floor. A calendar on the wall showed the last day the studio was open, the day Stacy died, killed by a dog driving a Toyota Tercel. *Why could I not have seen that coming? What good is an Oracle if the future is as impenetrable as a dark pool of tar?* Pythia took a deep breath and caught a whiff of tar on the breeze. She resumed walking toward the smell. *No more self-pity. No more self-obsession. Life comes at everyone. I am not special. Not anymore.*

Pythia rarely visited the park around the La Brea Tar Pits. She preferred to avoid the wandering tourists and crying school children who stared in distress at the sculpture of the baby wooly mammoth leaning toward its mother, who was mired in the sticky tar lake. *Fake. All drama for the tourists. This entire city is just a massive façade built to entertain gullible customers. Why did I ever think I could find a home here? Wait, stop. No more self-pity.*

Pythia found an empty bench facing away from the lake, tilted her face toward the sun, and closed her eyes. The sun was warm. She was glad for the hat. Her loose linen jacket shaded her arms. She tried to let her limbs loosen and relax into the bench. Sunshine always helped. *Where is my insight? I am blind. Why can I not see what is coming?*

A sudden sharp pang sliced through her gut. She rubbed her stomach and leaned forward, trying to ease the ache. Instead of receding, the pain intensified. *What is happening? My stomach is on fire all of a sudden, as if I ate something poisonous.*

The familiar stench of noxious fumes was in the air. Her head felt fizzy. She knew better than to fight it. *Maybe I will feel better after this is over.* She settled on the bench with her purse clutched on her lap and inhaled deeply, trying to ignore the pain in her stomach, letting her mind sink into the black hole in her center.

Dizziness rolled over her.

She felt herself falling and realized she was in warm water. She opened her eyes and saw turquoise tiled floors below and golden light above. She kicked for the surface and gasped air into her lungs. She recognized her favorite bathing pool at Apollo's temple.

She was naked. Tepid water swirled around her legs, erotic but uncomfortable. She paddled toward the edge of the pool. *This is not my place any longer. Why am I here?* The air was moist and scented with rosemary and sage. A robed servant hurried along the pool deck, carrying an armload of linen towels, disappearing into the darkness between columns.

"Look at the dolphin," a voice teased, echoing in the large tile-walled chamber. Pythia clung shivering to the edge of the pool, searching for the owner of that voice. The tiled panoramas on the walls were as bright as she remembered. High above, a few openings to the outside let in filtered light and fresh air. The space between columns held shadows.

"Where are you?" Pythia called. Her voice bounced around the tiled walls and back.

"Right where you left me," the unseen speaker said, giggling. "Where are *you*?"

"Dione, I cannot see you."

"You are not looking hard enough, little Oracle."

Pythia pushed wet hair out of her eyes. The shadows around the pool were impenetrable. She scanned for a towel or a wrap, peering into the dark, trying to find her sister.

"I will tell Apollo," she threatened.

Laughter echoed off the walls. "Apollo is dead."

"For shame, Dione. Why would you say that?"

"It is true, Pythia. Your god has abandoned you, and now you are lost in time."

"That cannot be!" cried Pythia, searching for the steps that would lead her out of the pool. Had the steps crumbled? Why could she not find them? The water dragged at her legs. Darkness engulfed the colorful tiles. The pool seemed deeper than she remembered. "Apollo lives still!" Pythia yelled into the shadows.

Laughter followed her as she was sucked under, flailing.

She inhaled a lungful of water just as the vision ended. Leaning over her knees, she spat into the grass. Gasping, she sat up. The park bench was just as hard as before, the sky just as filmy with the famous L.A. smog. Her breath hitched in her chest. She was surprised to find her cheeks wet. She hadn't wept in a long time. *What is happening to me?*

She looked around to see if anyone had noticed her uncouth behavior.

Across the lake, beyond a chain link fence, a small crowd of people stood around in a group, too far to notice her on the bench. Large photo reflectors had been erected on tripods. *Shooting a commercial, probably, or a music video.* Spectators had gathered to view the filming, but they seemed to be tourists. Locals would not stop for something as boring, commonplace, and annoying as a photo or film shoot.

Lively music wafted across the lake. Some dancers of indeterminate sex began to writhe in rhythm on a platform.

She had no interest in going closer. Pythia held her belly and watched from the bench, still breathing hard. She closed her eyes. The vision had left her with the beginning of a migraine.

Instead of feeling better after giving in to the trance, she felt worse. A frisson of anxiety intensified in her stomach. The sun, the unexpected smell of pomegranates, the music, the headache . . . Something—someone—was on the way, coming closer. Her stomach clenched and she leaned forward with a small cry, squeezing her eyes shut, feeling as if her blood were on fire. Her heart froze between beats. *Apollo, I am dying.*

When she opened her eyes, someone was sitting next to her on the bench, someone she recognized from the television screen. She saw smooth tanned skin, blue-green eyes, a chiseled nose, full lips, and long honey-colored dreadlocks, twisted with pink ribbons and tiny pomegranate flowers. Divina Dee smiled and revealed flawless white teeth.

Her skin was perfect, too, except for one tiny H-shaped mark on her right cheek near her lower eyelid. Few would have noticed that tiny imperfection. Anyone who noticed it would think nothing of it, just a flaw that made the entire face more lovely. A beautiful exotic creature, smelling of lavender, heather, bay leaves and some other unidentifiable perfumes, not all pleasant to Pythia's nose.

Pythia felt her mouth gape open and closed, like a fish dragged up on a beach. She could not breathe through what felt like concrete in her chest. Her heart shuddered, stopped, and thudded back to life. A gray cloud swallowed her.

As her eyesight faded to black, she heard a voice she had not heard in almost three thousand years say, "Hiya, Sis."

ဢ

Pythia woke slowly, feeling disconnected from her body. *Am I in bed dreaming? Was I in a car crash? Am I dead? Where is my Lord Apollo, here at the end of my life?*

Her hearing returned first. An unfamiliar male voice said, "Is she diabetic?"

"Not that I know of. Pythia, are you diabetic?"

Pythia found she was able to roll her head from side to side. "Unh," she said. *What is happening? Why can I not think?*

"History of epilepsy? Heart problems?"

Pythia opened her eyes.

A man in a uniform crouched on her left. Feeling rushed back into her body. She realized she was lying on grass. The man held her wrist in his hand. His hand was warm. She shivered. Dione—no, Divina—knelt on her right. A large group of people stood watching.

Pythia gazed at her sister. "What did you do?" Her tongue felt heavy in her mouth.

"What did she say?" the park attendant asked Divina.

"She wants to know what happened. Pythia, you fainted and fell off the bench. Come on, can you stand up?

"Do you know this woman?" Pythia waited for Divina to answer and then realized the attendant was talking to her.

"Yes, yes, I know her." Her mumble set off a wave of vertigo. She made motions to sit up.

"You should wait for the EMTs, Miss. You might have hit your head."

Pythia shook her head. "No, no, I am all right. Please, just help me sit up. I will be fine. I am sorry to cause you trouble."

The circle of curious bystanders parted to admit Glen Haven and her former assistant, Debra. They both crouched awkwardly on the grass, staring at Pythia with concern.

Divina was smiling at the bystanders. Pythia realized the crowd was paying more attention to Divina than they were to her, the woman in distress. *Welcome to Los Angeles.*

"Pythia, are you okay?" Debra sounded anxious, perhaps a little guilty.

"Help me up," Pythia said. Glen and Debra got their hands under her arms and dragged her upright.

"Ms. Dee, can I have your autograph?" a young man in the crowd shouted.

Divina laughed, a delighted giggle. She grinned at Pythia. "You go with Glen and Debra to the car. I've got my guys." She waggled her fingers at two burly white men in black jeans and black t-shirts standing nearby. "I'll meet you over there in five minutes." Divina shook back her famous dreadlocks and let herself be surrounded by fans.

Pythia gawked at the scene.

Debra kept hold of her arm. "What happened, Pythia?"

"Come on, Ms. Apulu." Glen put his hand on Pythia's back. "The car is just over here. Can you walk? Here, let me help you."

Pythia leaned on Glen's arm, inhaling his warm scent. The grass beneath her Birkenstocks seemed exceptionally green, practically vibrating. They walked slowly along a path and across a grassy berm toward a small parking area.

"Why is the light so bright?" she complained, flapping a hand at the sky.

"Is it bright?" Glen said. "I thought the smog was bad today."

"She's on drugs." Debra said. "God, Pythia, I always knew you were a drug addict."

"I am not taking drugs, Ms. Sandhill." *Nothing but the usual noxious gases emanating from cracks in the earth.*

Glen intervened. "Come on, let's get you into the car. We have some water and some protein bars. Maybe you have low blood sugar."

"Yeah, when did you last eat, Pythia?"

"I thought you two were dating," Pythia said, sensing they were no longer a couple.

Glen coughed. Debra let go of Pythia's arm and brushed some grass off the knees of her slacks.

"Here we are," Glen said. Pythia saw an older man in a white uniform and white cap standing next to a long white car. As they approached, he snapped to attention, and she recognized Arnie Solomon.

"Hey, Arnie, you remember Ms. Apulu? She had a fainting episode and needs to rest for a minute. Ms. Apulu, this is Arnie Solomon, our part-time driver."

"Sure, I know Pythia," Arnie said, opening the door to the back seat. "We're old friends. She's one of the Mystics. Are you okay?"

Pythia stood face-to-face with Arnie for a moment, lost in his blue eyes. She swayed on her feet. *I feel like sobbing. What is wrong with me?*

Arnie took her arm with care. "Here, come in out of the sun."

Soon Pythia was seated on a plush white leather seat with a bottle of sparkling water and a variety of packaged snacks in the sag of her skirt. Debra sat on her right. Arnie and Glen sat across from her in the rear-facing seats, staring at her. The well-insulated car muted sounds of traffic. She sipped some water, inhaled the aromas of leather and air freshener, and imagined she smelled lavender blooming in the sun. She leaned her head back against the plush headrest and closed her eyes.

She thought she might have dozed off for a few minutes. Consciousness felt fragile. She opened her eyes when the rear door opened. Divina slung herself into the back row of seats, next to Debra. One of the bodyguards folded himself into the back row. The other bodyguard got in the passenger seat next to the driver's seat and started scrolling through his phone.

"Whew!" Divina, fanning her face. "That was fun." She grabbed a bottle of water from a hidden refrigerator and guzzled half of it. She eyed Pythia sidelong. "How are you feeling, Pythia?"

Pythia's insight lurched. She foresaw multiple paths opening in front of her, an incline of possibilities beckoning, all leading to uncertainty. She opened her mouth to speak.

"Ah, ah, ah, don't do that," Divina warned with a grin. "I know what you are doing. You still have it, don't you?"

Pythia closed her mouth. The multiple paths disappeared.

"Wait, Ms. Dee, how do you know Pythia?" Debra asked Divina.

"Everyone who is anyone knows our Pythia," Divina answered, turning sideways to gaze at Pythia.

"What the hell?" Debra frowned at Divina, then at Pythia. Pythia felt some sympathy for her former assistant.

Casting backward, Pythia realized the interminable centuries of sadness had brought her here to this moment, where suddenly everything seemed to fall into place. The circle felt complete. She saw only one possible future. She looked at Arnie and found him smiling. For no reason, she felt her heart lift a little. *Whatever is to come, I have found my beloved Dione. At last, my heart is whole.*

"Hey, I hate to interrupt," Arnie said. "You guys ready to go? We've gotta be at the interview at five."

Glen rubbed his hands together. "Right. Traffic will be bad. Let's get going. We can drop Ms. Apulu off along the way."

"It's only two blocks, she can walk," Debra said. "If she's not too high."

"She's had a shock," Glen said. "We can give her a ride."

"It will only take a minute," Arnie said.

Arnie exited through the passenger door and opened the driver's door. The car beeped melodiously as he backed out of the parking space. Soon they were motoring in slow traffic on Wilshire Blvd.

A tinny speaker buzzed near her head. Pythia recognized Arnie's voice. "Pythia, I'm going to have to drop you off on this side by the crosswalk. This car is a beast to turn around. Are you going to be okay to cross the street?"

"Of course. Thank you so much for the ride, Arnie," Pythia said, feeling a surge of energy.

"I'll see you next week at the station," Arnie said. "Have fun this weekend."

"What's happening this weekend?" Debra asked Pythia.

"Our July Fourth thing, he means," said Divina.

"But we don't even know where . . ."

"It's a secret," Divina said with a finger on her lips. Debra settled back in her seat, looking confused.

Pythia floated above it all.

When Arnie pulled up to the curb, Pythia turned to Glen. "Mr. Haven, thank you for your kind assistance. Ms. Sandhill, you, too. Good to see you again. I appreciate your concern."

Debra narrowed her eyes. "Get some help, Pythia."

Pythia turned to Divina and forgot to wonder how Arnie knew about her weekend plans. She gazed at her sister and held out her hand.

After a moment, Divina leaned forward and took it. Pythia's heart soared with joy. For the first time in years, her smile felt genuine. She gazed into Divina's eyes and saw her sister Dione. *Same eyes, same grin. Apollo be praised, Dione lives!*

"My darling sister," Pythia said. "Welcome to L.A."

As she exited the limousine, Pythia heard Debra screech, "What! Pythia is your *sister?*"

Chapter 11

Walking on air, Pythia waved at Arnie as he maneuvered the limousine away from the curb. She glided across Wilshire without mishap, found her key, and opened the front door of the office. Bubbling with joy, she surveyed the space with new eyes. *It is just furniture and wallpaper, rugs and popcorn ceilings, nothing that cannot be updated, rejuvenated, renewed. Dione is alive!*

Pythia locked the front door, hung the closed sign, and locked the hallway office door behind her. In her apartment, she dialed Lena on her landline, a vintage tangle-corded tan Trimline phone she'd had since it was new.

When Lena answered, Pythia said, "Something happened today."

"Pythia? Uh oh. Tell me you didn't."

"Didn't what?"

"Lose your sobriety! Oh, no, Pythia, what happened?"

"I did not drink, Lena. Do you have a few minutes to talk?"

"Yes. Mom is here taking a nap, like she doesn't have a perfectly good bed at her apartment. Tell me what happened? You don't sound drunk."

"I am not drunk, Lena," Pythia said. "Listen. Remember I told you I had a sister who died?"

"Yes, so sad."

"Lena, I was mistaken. She is alive. I found her today. Well, actually, she found me."

Lena was silent for a long moment. "Your sister? The one you thought was dead?"

"Yes. My sister, Dione. She lives."

"Oh, my God, that's bizarre! But fantastic! Bizarrely fantastic!" Lena gasped. "It is fantastic, isn't it?"

Pythia dragged the long phone cord into the bedroom. Kicking off her shoes, she sank onto the bed and stared at the ceiling. "It certainly is bizarre."

"Tell me what happened."

Pythia told Lena about fainting in the park. "They were shooting some sort of music video or something. People were there to see Divina Dee. You know who Divina Dee is?"

"Who doesn't know Divina Dee, the famous psychic to the stars?" Lena laughed. "She's so hot."

Pythia sighed. "Well, Divina Dee is my sister."

Lena gasped and then screamed into the phone. "Divina Dee is your *sister*?"

Pythia nodded and held the phone away from her ear.

"Holy shit, holy shit!" Lena shouted.

"Lena, calm down."

"Okay, okay, sorry. I'm calm. So . . . what are you going to do now?"

"I do not know. We left it open-ended."

"Open-ended! This is your sister! Divina Dee! Do you know where she's staying?"

"No, somewhere in L.A., I do not know where. I guess I could call Debra and find out."

"Debra, pah. That traitor. Oh, sorry. I know you liked her."

"She was there today, too. And that man, Glen Haven." Pythia smacked her forehead. "Now it makes sense. Divina Dee is Glen's silent partner. That is why he asked me all those questions about Greece and my family . . . that swine! He knew the whole time that Divina Dee was my sister, Dione. Now I see it."

"That slimeball. He played you. Damn, it's a good thing you didn't take him on as a client. Wasn't he dating your assistant? Oh, my God, the plot thickens."

Pythia smiled, remembering the frosty interaction she'd seen today between Glen and Debra. "I think that relationship has ended."

"Well, the real question is, do you want to see your sister again?"

"Of course I do. Yes. I think she knows what happened to us when we were children. I have some questions. I would like to know why she vanished, why she did not seek for me."

"Oh, okay. Get some information, that's good. And then what? Just, like, let her go off back to New York? Would you go with her?"

Pythia tried to imagine leaving Los Angeles, the palm trees, the ocean, the mountains that reminded her of home. Her friends, her recovery life, her business . . . could she leave it all behind? She'd seen New York, although she had to admit it was a long time ago. *About a hundred fifty years.*

"I do not know what she wants, Lena," Pythia said. "Why did she find me now? I think she has known all this time where I was. For almost three thousand years, I have grieved her death every day. I wept an ocean of tears. Could she have known where I was? How could she let me suffer?"

"I love how in touch you are with your former lives. Well, something sounds fishy to me, Pythia. But, hell, it's Divina Dee!"

"I have to pray."

"Good idea. Always a good option. Do you want me to pray with you?"

"No, I am going to do my usual ritual."

"Which is?"

"I am going to go downstairs to the basement and inhale some geothermal fumes emanating from a crack in the floor."

Lena snorted. "You are so funny. You should write a blog."

Pythia rolled her eyes but only because Lena couldn't see her.

"Hold on a second. Mom, sorry, yes, that was me yelling. Pythia had some good news. I was helping her celebrate. Sorry I woke you."

Pythia heard Madame B say, "I'm hungry."

"I'll fix you a sandwich in just a minute. Go sit at the table. Oh, hey, Pythia, now that your sister has returned, good news, now you'll be able to make a proper amends for your Ninth Step."

Pythia rolled onto her back on the bed. "Thanks, Lena. You are a good friend. I will see you at the meeting." She hung up and put a pillow over her head.

On Saturday morning, Pythia was up early with her tenants, hanging balloons, decorating the doorways with glittery fringe, and leaning Frank's largest picture frames against the building under the windows. Shoppers began to arrive.

Pythia sipped iced tea from a plastic cup and watched Louise serve gelato while Frank and Helen sold picture frames. Some visitors were intent on shopping for frames—Frank's sale gimmick was buy one, get one for a penny—too good to miss. A few people fought over frames in anxious yet restrained tones. Children chased each other around the adults, licking spoons full of ice cream while their parents chatted and shopped. Pythia let herself sink into the commotion, enjoying the energy of the crowd.

Soon the morning sun grew oppressive. Pythia moved indoors to her office cubicle with her iced tea. She gazed at the photo of Apollo's ruined temple. *All is right with the world. Praise Apollo. My sister lives! Then why do I feel so unsettled?*

At 11:00 a.m., a special edition of Psychic to the Stars came on the TV. Pythia turned up the volume with an anxious knot growing in her stomach.

"Happy Fourth of July! I'm Divina Dee, Psychic to the Stars. Welcome to a very special live edition of my show. I'm going to be roaming the city of Los Angeles, looking for guests with questions about their futures. This is live! Where will I be? Only I know the answer to that question. Stay tuned. If you see a neighborhood that looks familiar, go outside! I might be on your doorstep!"

Pythia's stomach lurched. *I have a bad feeling.*

The scene cut to Divina standing next to a white limousine. The image on the television was small, but Pythia recognized Debra and Glen milling around behind Divina. Debra wore a gray tailored pants suit. Glen was outfitted in a black polo shirt and what appeared to be khaki pants. Arnie stood by the driver's door, looking dapper in a white jacket and chauffeur's cap. In the background was a tall woman dressed in black. *Wait, is that—?*

Another fast cut showed Divina getting inside the limousine. Debra and Glen were already in the back, and Arnie was in the driver's seat. Divina grinned into the camera. "Let's go!"

She looks like my sister. Is she really? Why did I not recognize her sooner? What strange magic is at work here?

The next scene showed the limousine pulling up outside a row of shops where some kind of street fair seemed to be in progress. A television truck had pulled up and blocked off several parking spaces. The camera panned across, showing cars slowing for pedestrians who were crossing the street, running right at the camera with big smiles on their faces, hands waving.

A quick cut to the interior of the limousine showed a close up of Divina's excited face as she shouted with glee, "Here they come!" Pythia began to taste pomegranates at the back of her throat.

Somehow another camera showed the limousine stopping in the street as it was mobbed by pedestrians, laughing and calling "Divina! Divina Dee! Over here! Miss Dee, over here!" *How are they filming this chaos? Where are all these cameras? Wait a minute, that street looks familiar . . .*

Pythia's musing was interrupted by a knock on her office door. Frank stuck his head in and said, "Sorry to bother you, Pythia. You aren't going to believe this."

Two burly men muscled Frank aside, quickly scanned the office, and stepped back to admit Divina Dee.

Pythia stood up. *Apollo, save me, why did I not see this coming? Look how beautiful and young she is. How is it possible she looks barely twenty?*

"Hiya, Sis!" Divina said. "Can I come in? Is this the nerve center? The inner sanctum where the magic happens? Okay if I bring in a camera?" She turned and motioned to someone behind her.

A short slender woman with a shaved head edged in past the crowd with a chunky video camera on her shoulder. Pythia saw a long thin black braid hanging down her back to her waist, emerging from the crown of her bare scalp. The woman leaned against the wall under the photo of Apollo's temple, aiming the camera at Divina.

Divina said to no one, "Are we live?" She turned to Pythia. "We're on a commercial break."

Pythia realized Divina had a device in her ear. She was listening to someone giving her information. The camera operator appeared to wear a similar earpiece.

Divina grinned at Pythia. "I'm going back outside to interview a couple people for the show. You want to come watch? No? Okay. Then afterward, maybe is there a quiet place—bigger than this—that we can hang out and chat? Just you, me, and a few of my staff?"

"Yes, of course, my sister," Pythia said. "My apartment is upstairs."

"Debra!" Divina shouted into the main office. "Go upstairs with Pythia, would you? See if you can do any staging with what you can find." Divina looked at Pythia. "Chop, chop," she said, motioning with her head toward the exit.

"Of course, my sister."

Divina moved out of the doorway, making room for Pythia to exit her office. As she passed Divina, she stopped and stared into her eyes. They were the same height, although Pythia appeared older and heavier. Divina's blue-green eyes sparkled. Pythia smelled lavender, pomegranates, and something else she could not identify. The H-shaped mark was clearly visible under her right eyelid.

"Whoops, gotta go, Sis," Divina said, touching her ear. "I'll see you upstairs in a few minutes."

Pythia found Debra already in the hallway moving toward the stairs.

"Hi, Pythia. Are you feeling better? That was so weird, huh, you fainting? I can't believe Divina is your sister! Why didn't you ever tell me?"

Pythia followed Debra and two lanky young men up the stairway to the second floor.

"These are our PAs," Debra said. "Ralph and Sid."

"Hello." Pythia led them to her apartment. The door was unlocked. She opened the door and stood back to let them enter.

Debra took charge, moving from the kitchen through the sitting room to the bedroom, quickly examining the entire apartment. "This is it? Huh. I thought it would be bigger."

Pythia realized she'd never invited Debra to her apartment, even though it was right upstairs. Even though Debra had been her assistant, her only employee, for ten years. *What does that say about me as an employer? As a friend?*

Debra turned to the two staffers. "Hey, remember those chairs in the hallway downstairs? Go grab a couple, quick."

Pythia sank down on her couch. Debra snapped her fingers. "Don't sit yet. Help me move the couch over here. We need to make a space for Delores."

"Delores?"

"The camera."

Pythia helped Debra move the couch into the preferred position, exposing an impressive amount of dust, a few coins, a pencil, desiccated tissues, some toothpicks, a key, and a matchbook.

Debra looked at the carpet and then at Pythia. "Man," she said. Then she bent over and picked up the matchbook. "Tiny Naylor's?" she said in disbelief. "Holy crap, Pythia. This is, like, a collector's item." She put it in her pocket.

The two staffers returned lugging visitor chairs. Debra pointed. "Put them both over there in that corner."

Debra stopped moving and appeared to be listening. She looked at Pythia and pointed at her ear.

Pythia nodded. Everyone apparently had devices in their ears to allow them to hear each other. She pointed at the chair and raised her eyebrows. Debra shook her head and pointed at the couch. Pythia sat down on the couch.

Thirty minutes later, when Pythia, Debra, and the two PAs had run out of things to say and were sitting in awkward silence, the bodyguards strolled through the open door, followed by Divina, Glen Haven, and another bodyguard. Delores brought up the rear with the camera on her shoulder. Pythia stood up to greet the new guests.

"Whew, that was fun," Divina said, glowing. Debra handed her a bottle of water from her shoulder bag. "Delores, where do you want us?"

"I thought on the couch?" Debra said, pointing.

"That'll work," Delores said in a gruff voice. She sat cross-legged on the floor opposite the couch and fiddled with the camera.

Glen and Debra perched on the visitor chairs, crammed in one corner. Ralph and Sid leaned against a wall. The three bodyguards milled around the kitchen, bumping shoulders.

"Pythia, sit here," Divina said, slapping the couch cushion next to her as she sat down. Pythia sat, mind reeling. *My brain seems to have failed. What is happening? Apollo, save me. I am lost.*

A soft tapping came at the door. Arnie Solomon stuck his head around the door jamb. "Is this the place? I guess it must be! Holy Zeus!"

"Arnie, do we have room for you?" Glen said, shaking his head.

"Oh, yes, I think so," Arnie said. "I'll just stretch out on the floor over here by the window and snooze while you guys do your thing."

Pythia watched in amazement as Arnie settled onto the carpet of her sitting room. He stretched out with his chauffeur's cap on his stomach, locked his hands behind his head, winked at her, and closed his eyes. Pythia couldn't help but smile. Her stomach started to settle. *I am glad he is here. I think he is an ally, perhaps even a friend.*

When she turned to Divina, she was surprised to see her sister looking a bit unsettled. "What's the matter, Sister?" she whispered.

Her sister looked around the room and shook her head, as if she had lost her train of thought. She looked with surprise at the water bottle in her hand. Then she pulled herself together, grinned, and with her usual aplomb said, "I can't believe you live like this, my sister. We need to get you a home makeover!" Divina turned to her crew. "Okay, let's make some magic."

※

After the interview with Divina Dee, it had taken some time to return her apartment to its former configuration. When she was finally alone, Pythia called Lena and left a message. It was late when Lena called back.

"Sorry I missed you. I was working. Busy night. Fourth of July, fireworks, screaming kids, the usual," Lena said, sounding tired. "I think I know what you are calling about, though."

"You do?"

"I was going to call you after it aired but I had to go to work. You obviously didn't see it, considering it was live. Maybe you can watch a replay of it on YourTurn."

"What did I miss?" Pythia sat on the edge of her bed and stared at her scuffed slippers.

"Your sister is a genius," Lena said. "Cute as a bug, too. Looks like she's about twelve. You told me she was the older one. Well, never mind. Wow, her show was amazing."

"Oh, dear. May I ask . . . ?"

"Don't worry, your part was really short, you were hardly in it, you mostly talked about how hard it is to live with uncertainty. You sounded very mature."

"She invited me to lunch at her house."

"That's great! I suppose it's some huge mansion in Bel Air? Fancy hotel in Beverly Hills?"

"She is renting something in the Pacific Palisades, she said. On Oracle Drive."

"Ha, what are the odds, right? So what did you tell her, did you say yes?"

"I said I have work."

"What did she say?"

"That she knows I have no clients."

Lena chuckled. "Harsh. But true, right?"

"What she actually said was, 'Your coaching business is pathetic. Why don't you let me help you?'" Pythia grimaced and flopped on her back. *Then she said, Come up to my place. We can sit on the patio overlooking the ocean. The view looks like the Sea of*

Corinth. The air smells like Delphi. We can talk about your future.
"Should I let her help me?"

"This feels like in invitation to Step Three to me," Lena said. "Surrender."

"What am I surrendering to, Lena?"

"To God's will," Lena said. "Whatever you conceive of God to be."

"I should be happy."

"Yes, you should! Divina Dee is your sister! I still can't believe it."

"I am happy," Pythia said. "Or I will be, I believe, once I get used to the idea."

"Well, go have lunch with her, that's my suggestion. It's bound to be strange after so many years apart. Bring some flowers or something. Be brave. Surrender to the experience"

"All right. I will accept her lunch invitation."

"But keep your eyes open." Lena said. "She's family."

Chapter 12

On Tuesday morning at 9:30 a.m., Pythia turned the open sign to closed. *Not that anyone would notice. I have not had a client in weeks.* A layer of dust covered all the surfaces in the waiting area. She took a moment to wipe off the television, even though she had stopped watching Psychic to the Stars.

Pythia pondered the future as she drove to the radio station for the July episode of the Mystics Roundtable. Traffic was slow on Wilshire through Beverly Hills. Her mind wandered. *So many people, always in a hurry. Do I belong here anymore? Should I go to New York and become part of Divina's entourage? Maybe I will see Arnie today.*

Pythia pulled toward the curb to let an ambulance speed past. *Apollo be with them.*

She arrived at the radio station and parked in the underground lot with plenty of time to spare. In the lobby, Brian waved as she headed for the elevator. She felt her mood lifting in anticipation of seeing Arnie. She hummed a little as she went up to the sixth floor.

Pythia paused outside the DJ sound booth, smiling, and stopped short, shocked to see someone else sitting in Arnie's chair. A bald man, ruddy faced and clean-shaven, placed a record on the turntable. He saw Pythia watching and nodded with a polite thinning of his lips. Pythia tried to see beyond the booth into the station office but shelves of records and CDs blocked her view. *Where is Arnie?*

Lena and Sylvia were in the Mystics sound booth arranging their headsets and microphones when Pythia entered.

"Did you see Arnie?" Pythia asked Lena.

"No, there's another DJ in there."

"Arnie is cute but he's old enough to be your father!" Sylvia laughed, unwrapping the silk scarf that protected her tarot cards.

"Oh, you might be surprised!" Lena said. "That beard is deceptive."

Moon bounded through the doorway. She tossed her bag of gear under the table in front of her chair. "Pythia, you were right! Ankle monitor at home!"

"I am so glad for you, Moon. And for Riley," Pythia said.

"Where's Mary?" Sylvia asked, looking at the clock. It was almost show time.

"She's grading papers," Lena said. "She told me she would get here as soon as she could. Meanwhile, I have a great topic for today's show: Time!"

"Whoa," said Moon, nodding.

"Oh, I hope Mary makes it," Sylvia said. "She will hate to miss this."

Lena sat in her chair at the soundboard. "You guys ready?"

She leaned into the mic and opened the show with the intro and announcements. "Our show today is about time," she said. "Do you have a question about time? Call our hotline at 213-555-MYST and we'll put our Mystics to work." She peered at the computer screen and pressed a button on the board. "Our first caller is Dave. Hi, Dave, where are you calling from?"

"Hi, girls, love your show. Calling in from Anaheim, just had to ask, since I am known for running late all the time, is there any way I can be two places at once?"

"Wow, that's a great question, Dave," Lena said. "Mystics, what can we do to answer Dave's question? Sylvia, you want to tackle this one?"

"Sure, Lena. Dave, if we assume we are all living along one timeline, then unless you clone yourself, you cannot be in two different places at the same point in time on this timeline.

However!" Sylvia added as she shuffled her cards. "We can do a tarot card reading on the problem of procrastination, if you like."

"Uh, no, I don't actually want to change," Dave said. "I just want to be working out at the gym while my alter ego is lifting boxes at work. I guess it's not really a problem of time. I just hate my job."

Pythia leaned up to the microphone. "Dave, if I may? Check yesterday's classifieds in the online section of the *Times*. I think there is a job for which you are particularly well suited."

"It's not in waste management, is it? People see my muscles and think that's all I'm good for." Dave sounded frustrated.

"No, Dave. It is a trainer job at a very reputable gym. Talk to Randall. I think you have an excellent chance of being hired."

"Okay, wow. Thanks!" Dave hung up.

Moon looked at Pythia and shook her head in wonder. "Pythia, our Seer Without Peer, does it again."

"We have another caller on the line. Go ahead, Cynthia."

A child voice came over their headphones. "I want to know if I can make time go faster sometimes, like when I'm in school."

"And then slow it down when you are doing something fun?" Moon said.

"Right!" said Cynthia. "I hate school."

"What do you like to do?" Moon asked.

"I like to read. I go outside in the backyard. I have a fort and lots of books. I read all the time, until my mom says time for dinner."

"Why don't you like school?" Moon asked.

"Because the other kids make fun of me. They call me a bookworm." Cynthia sounded sad.

"I'm sorry to hear that," Moon said. "Reading is the best thing ever."

Sylvia leaned into her mic. "I was a bookworm, too. I would have gone off the deep end if I didn't read. I used to get in trouble in class for reading when I wasn't supposed to."

"Me, too!" said Cynthia.

"Reading is like time travel," Lena said. "It takes us to places and times we can't even imagine. We can meet new people and learn new things."

Moon said, "Cynthia, I'm sorry we can't slow down or speed up time. That would be a great superpower to have. Time moves at the same pace for everyone. It's hard when we are young, but it gets better, we promise."

"Okay, thanks," said Cynthia in a brighter voice.

An older woman's voice came on the line. "Hi, I'm Cynthia's mother. Thank you for your kind words. She's been struggling."

Pythia leaned into her microphone. "You might be relieved to know that Cynthia will be a gifted young writer. You will be proud of her accomplishments. She will live a long, creative, satisfying life."

"Oh, thank you! Will I have grandchildren, or is that too much to ask for?"

Pythia chuckled. "I believe Cynthia and her partner will adopt two boys from Ethiopia. Yours will be an unorthodox family but your lives will be filled with love."

"Oh, my goodness!" the woman said, voice quavering. She hung up the phone. The Mystics looked at each other and grinned.

"Let's take another caller," Lena said. "We have Marge on the line. Go ahead, Marge."

A woman's raspy voice came over the headphones. "Yeah, hello girls, I talked to you last month."

"Oh, yes, I remember," Lena said. "Do you have a question about time?"

"Well, not really. I wanted to let you know, I heard back from Thelma."

"Thelma?"

"Yeah, my friend who died? She was a real firecracker. She choked at lunch a couple months ago. They pounded on her chest while the accordion guy was playing. Then they took her out in a body bag. She was my only friend in this hellhole. Remember I said I wanted to know what was on the other side? Well, I got a letter from her!"

"Oh, my," said Lena. "What did she say?"

Marge cackled. "She said I should make peace with my kids while I still have time. She wrote it before she died, obviously, right? I guess it got stuck in the mail slot in the activities room. She said I didn't have a lot of time left and I should use it wisely."

"She sounds like a good friend," Lena said.

"Yeah. Yeah, she was. Just wanted to let you know, I don't feel so scared anymore about death. That's all. The daycare bus is here to take us to Bingo. You girls take care. Bye now."

After several more callers, Lena wrapped the show. When the red on-air light went dark, the Mystics took off their headphones and started packing up their gear.

"Good show. I wonder what happened to Mary?" Sylvia said. "Pythia, your second sight tell you anything?"

Pythia stopped and concentrated. After a moment, an image came through. She smiled. "Mary is trapped in a space-time warp."

"What?" Sylvia said in alarm.

"She is stuck in traffic on the 405."

The Mystics exited into the hallway. Pythia was disappointed to see the other DJ still occupied Arnie's chair. Lena looked at her and shrugged, frowning. *May the Lord Apollo bless my new friend, Arnie Solomon.*

July 7, 2015

Blog Readers, as you know, I have been alone for a very long time. That means I have forgotten what it is like to have family. You all have family, most likely. Maybe you still have your parents. Maybe you have siblings, people who know you. You know them. You grew up together. You share some common experiences, perhaps. You might not like some of their characteristics, but you give them the benefit of the doubt, because they are family.

I do not how to tell you this. A strange, miraculous, impossible event has occurred. I have written before about my beloved sister, Dione, whom I thought long dead in Delphi. It seems my illness compromised my memory as well as my talent. Praise Apollo! My sister lives across time as I do. This week, Dione found me. I find myself at a loss. Is this the miracle I hope it is? I will find out. She has invited me to lunch.

You might be wondering, is she an impostor? Although I do not feel the sister connection we had as children, I believe she is my sister. No one could impersonate Dione. She is one of a kind. It seems that after so many years of being alone, I now have family.

Last week she came to my apartment. In my defense, I was not expecting guests. I was a little embarrassed when we moved the couch. However, that is not important. You remember my assistant who recently left me for a better position? She is now working for my sister!

If that is not evidence that unseen hands are at work manipulating fate, what is? I have learned to fear those unseen hands. I await your comments.

—Equally elated and confused, Delphina

§

On Wednesday at 10:00 a.m., Pythia drove her dusty Honda Insight west on Sunset Boulevard and then up into the winding hills of Pacific Palisades, puttering slowly past multimillion dollar homes and gated mansions. After some backtracking and map checking, she pulled up in front of a black iron gate. Blooming pink bougainvillea climbed both sides, meeting at the top.

The number on the gate matched what she'd written on the map. *This is the place.* One side of the gate was open, so she drove through the gap under pink flowers and parked between two cars much larger and newer than hers.

The front of the house, from what she could see, was flat and modern. Judging by the other houses in the area, she guessed the lower floors of the house extended down a hillside into a lush ravine.

She smoothed her striped cotton skirt and checked that her pale tan linen blouse was buttoned correctly. Usually she wore a wide-brimmed straw hat when out of doors but today she had opted to go bare-headed. She tended to leave hats and umbrellas behind.

She left her straw bag on the floor of her car, grabbed the cellophane-wrapped bouquet of mixed flowers, and shut the door. She smelled jasmine in the air. *Deep breath. I am powerless over what others think of me. I know I look like the poor sister. It matters not. Step Three. Apollo grant me grace to accept what comes.*

A wide walkway made of huge concrete squares led from the parking area over a burbling koi pond to the front door. The door was burnished copper, twice as wide and tall as a normal door. As Pythia reached out to touch the warm copper door, it opened.

An unfamiliar woman blocked her way. The woman posed in an ankle-length beige linen peplos, long sun-bleached hair draped over one shoulder. She grasped the edge of the door in one hand, showing off a shapely tan bare arm, and waved a joint in the other. Pythia noted the woman's sandals were modern, expensive replicas of ancient Greek sandals.

The woman sucked on the joint, gazing at Pythia without moving. "You're the sister. I saw you on TV."

"Yes, I am Pythia Apulu. I am pleased to meet you . . ."

"Tina." The woman blew smoke, stood back, and waved Pythia into a tall open foyer lit by a skylight. "Dee Dee is out by the pool. Straight through there. Stop in the kitchen and grab something to drink. There's all kinds of stuff in the fridge. We got beer and wine, hard stuff too, if you are into that. And this, if you partake."

"Thank you, that is very kind. May I ask why you are dressed like that?"

"Like a Greek?" The woman laughed and blew smoke out her nostrils. "Because Dee Dee is a Greek goddess. Give me those, I'll find a vase."

Goddess, indeed. Pythia handed the flowers to the woman and moved through the living area. There were vases of fresh flowers everywhere. Through open glass doors she saw a pool and some people sitting in chaise lounge chairs in the shade of large beige cloth umbrellas. Pythia paused to admire a pitted marble statue of a half-naked naiad holding a tipping urn. *That might actually be authentic.*

In the kitchen she marveled at the light from three huge skylights. The refrigerator was almost as big as her office cubicle. She opened one huge door and saw glass bottles of water imported from a spring in Greece, or so the labels claimed. She chose one bottle and carried it through the patio doors onto the deck by the pool.

"Pythia, my sister!"

Dione called a greeting without getting up from her chaise. She was wearing a bright pink one-piece swimsuit under a gauzy white sundress. Her feet were bare, displaying pink toenail polish. Her twisted locks of hair were tucked up in a pink scarf.

One of the people lounging in the shade was Glen Haven. He rose to his feet, chocolate skin glistening with sweat. His eyes were hidden behind dark sunglasses. He waved. "Hello, Ms. Apulu. How are you feeling these days? No more fainting episodes, I hope?"

"Thank you, Mr. Haven, I am well. How are you today?"

"Very well, thank you. Gorgeous day. Please, call me Glen. What did you think of the live show on the Fourth?" Before Pythia could answer, Dione raised her voice and pointed at Pythia.

"Hey, everyone, this is my sister, Pythia." She sat forward and pointed. "That's Danny and Carmen Esperanza."

Two people spread-eagled boneless in the shade raised lazy fingers in the air in her direction. Both had long wavy dark hair pulled up in loose buns. The man seemed a bit younger than the woman. He wore a gaudy print shirt and white shorts, showing off shapely smooth tan legs. His wife wore a pareo made of the same fabric, slung low around her hips, exposing a gaunt, tanned abdomen. Bulging breasts strained to break free from a tiny print bikini top.

"I am pleased to meet you," Pythia said. Glen remained standing beside his chair, tapping a bare foot on the concrete.

Divina laughed and turned to the couple. "She has no idea who you are. I told you she wouldn't. She's lived under a rock for the past three thousand years."

"That's okay, darling," Carmen Esperanza said in a sultry voice. "It's nice to be anonymous for a change."

"Don't lie, my love. You hate being anonymous," Danny Esperanza said. *I think Danny might be a woman.*

"Pythia, pssst, preferred pronoun *they*," Divina said. "Next in line we have Clementine Sands, recently back from a trip to Cannes, where she won best in something. Or her dog did, not sure, what was it, Clemmie?"

"Oh, you," chuckled a white-blonde woman with the palest skin Pythia had ever seen. The woman raised over-sized dark glasses, revealing pink eyes. "Extraordinary that Divina Dee has a sister," she said. "Older or younger?"

"Both!" Divina said, and her guests laughed. "Sit, Pythia," Divina said, waving at an empty chaise next to her. "Is that all you are drinking? Do you drink anymore, Sister? I seem to recall you used to like pomegranate wine. Come on, sit down so Glen can stop having to prove he's a gentleman."

For a moment, Pythia tasted something bitter on the back of her tongue. A quick pain stabbed through her gut but passed before she had time to respond to the pain. *What was that memory? It's just out of my reach. If I could just—*

"Ah, ah, ah, there you go again," cautioned Divina, waving a finger. "None of that magic stuff, won't work here. Sorry." She paused. "Tell me, Pythia, why do you keep rejecting my proposal?"

Pythia sank onto the chaise. "Proposal?" Pythia echoed. *Why does my brain feel so fogged?*

"Yeah, you've figured out that Glen's silent partner is me, so what gives? We could use another Oracle on the team."

"My darling sister, please forgive me. You refer to your property development scheme. Of course I will help. You had only to ask."

Divina clapped her hands. "That's the spirit. Glen, tell her what she's won."

Glen chuckled. "Maybe I should show her the you-know-what."

"Oh, great idea. Go downstairs to our office, Pythia, and prepare to be amazed. Grab a swimsuit, too, while you are down there."

Glen stood up and beckoned Pythia toward the house. She left her bottle on a small round table and followed. In the living area, he pointed to a plush carpeted staircase in the corner. Pythia descended ahead of Glen into a large open daylight basement.

A carpeted office area wrapped around a wall of windows that looked out on a ravine of green foliage and colorful flowers. At one edge of the room were two sturdy folding tables holding a large diorama. As she approached, Pythia saw skillfully crafted miniatures representing buildings clustered around a large white three-layer box. Pythia recognized the façade as a replica of Apollo's Temple.

"The largest building is the hotel and conference center," Glen said, standing next to Pythia as she surveyed the massive display. "These outbuildings are bungalows and small group residences. Here's another meeting space with rooms of different sizes." Glen pointed. "Look, there are hiking trails everywhere. We plan to leave fifty trees intact and plant a hundred new trees. Here's a garden, big enough for weddings."

"It's impressive," Pythia said. "Where is the parking area?"

"Pythia!" Pythia turned to see Debra emerging from an outside patio, wearing a stylish designer jacket over creased trousers. "What did you think of that live show? Crazy, huh?"

"Hello, Ms. Sandhill, how are you?"

"Oh, Pythia, can't you start calling me Debra?"

"Ms. Apulu, if you are going to be our new partner, you'll have to get used to our informal ways," said Glen.

"Every day is casual Friday around here," Debra confirmed.

Pythia noticed Debra's hair was a lighter shade of blonde, with no gray anywhere. *She colored her hair. Of course. What woman would not, if she were aspiring to move up in the world?*

"Very well. Debra. Glen. Thank you." She turned back to the diorama. "Please tell me more about your strategies to minimize the impact of the development on the environment."

Pythia listened to Glen and Debra chatter about the plans and let her mind roam. She wasn't feeling well. The queasiness she'd felt earlier with Divina had intensified. Something here in this space was fogging her brain. A chill made her skin crawl. *I have felt this before. Right before I fainted in the park. My Lord God Apollo, protect me, I beg you.*

"What do you think, Pythia. Do you like it?" Debra seemed eager for Pythia's approval.

Pythia took a deep breath and coughed on purpose, just a little more than necessary. Covering her mouth with one hand, she grabbed Debra's hand with the other as she bent over, pretending to struggle to clear her lungs.

"Are you okay?" Glen said. "Let me get you some water."

"Here, Pythia, sit here." Debra guided Pythia to a black ergonomic office chair that probably cost $2,000. Pythia kept her hand in Debra's and started to get some glimpses. Images of a woman. A tall slender extraordinarily beautiful woman dressed in a black mermaid style dress and designer spike-heeled shoes.

Debra shook her hand free, frowning. Glen handed Pythia a glass of water. She sipped and pretended to catch her breath.

"Thank you. I am very impressed with your plans. I have just one question," she said. "Who else is on the team?"

After a long silence, Glen said, "What makes you ask that?"

"Please take off your sunglasses, Glen," Pythia commanded and tried to hide her surprise when he complied. He looked chagrined and anxious.

"Ms. Dee said not to tell you," Debra said, smoothing her creased trousers and looking away. "She wanted it to be a surprise. We aren't allowed to say."

Pythia scrutinized their faces, first Glen and then Debra. They both seemed embarrassed and ashamed. That part was authentic. She knew that neither one actually knew the answer to Pythia's question. *They think they know but they know nothing. I do not either. But I am certain I will find out in due time.*

"Sister, hurry up, come on!" Divina's voice preceded her exuberant entrance into the basement room. "Isn't this fabulous? Look at the view! All that lushness and life. Did you find a swimsuit?"

"No, I—" Pythia began. She stood up and pressed a hand against her stomach, trying to gain her composure. "I need to know some things, my sister."

"Okay, okay," Divina said. "I understand. Of course, my sister. Come upstairs and let's talk."

Divina led Pythia up the stairs to a sitting area on the far side of the living room. A couch and two stuffed chairs faced a smooth white marble fireplace that looked as if it had never been used. Divina shoved some throw pillows onto the floor and sprawled at one end of the couch. Pythia sat at the other end and tried to look calm. *Can she tell I am afraid? Apollo protect me.*

She took a deep breath. "Sister, what is going on?"

"Well, I didn't want to tell you. I didn't want you to be upset." Divina put her bare feet on the low coffee table and admired her pink toenails.

"Tell me what, my sister?" *Will she tell me the truth? Who else is involved in this venture? Why are Glen and Debra so uncomfortable?*

"The truth is, I'm going to be a guest judge on Business Barracudas!"

Pythia stared at her sister. "What—?"

Divina took off the pink scarf and shook her hair out onto her shoulders. "Debra told me you wanted to be a Barracuda. I didn't want you to find out this way. I'm so sorry."

"But—" *Oh, my Lord Apollo, my brain is stammering, my tongue is frozen. What is happening? Why is nothing making sense?*

Tina approached, still wearing the peplos. "Dee Dee, the luncheon is ready." She waved her hand toward the patio.

"Thank you, Tina." Divina grabbed Pythia's hand and hauled her to her feet. "I know disappointment is hard, my sister. Come outside. My chef makes a killer hummus. Just the right amount of garlic."

Divina pushed Pythia ahead of her through the patio door toward a long table loaded with food. Debra and Glen were filling plates with pita bread, gyros, hummus, and salad. Clementine and the Esperanzas were already seated, nibbling from plates. Soon Pythia was seated on the edge of the chaise with a plate of food balanced on her knees. *How is this happening? It is as if I am no longer in my body.*

Divina sat on the edge of the next chaise. She placed a plate of food and a glass of something on the side table. Pythia smelled retsina.

Pythia took a deep breath. *Now or never.* "My sister, I must ask you something," she said, setting her untouched plate aside. "What do you remember from our childhood?"

"Well, now." Divina gazed past the pool into the trees. "Why do you ask this, Pythia?"

"Something happened to me, my sister."

"Yeah?" said Divina. "What makes you say that?"

"I remember very little."

"I, too, remember very little," Divina said, nodding her head. "It was so long ago."

"Do you remember that I was ill?" Pythia asked, looking into her sister's eyes.

Divina looked away. "No, I told you, I don't remember."

"Still, something happened to me, and when I came back to myself, you were gone. I thought you were dead, my sister. I sought you far and wide. I was out of my mind with grief."

Divina took a long sip of her drink and would not meet Pythia's eyes. Then she clapped her hands. "But I am here now, my sister. Alive and well, as you can see. We should celebrate!" She turned toward Debra, who was eating at a nearby patio table. "How about some music!"

July 21, 2015

These past few weeks, my weary brain feels like it has run a marathon in wooden clogs. I am confounded by this perplexing new whirlwind in my life. Yes, Blog Readers, I refer to my sister, Dione.

Her long life has given her deep knowledge about many useful things, including business strategy, which she has kindly offered to share with me. All my years of business coaching seem to be worthless in the modern era.

"You need to think like a consumer," she told me.

"I thought I was," I protested. She laughed at me.

"You should come back to New York with me," she said. "I will introduce you to some players in the tech industry."

"What use would they have for someone like me?"

"You can still predict the future, can't you?"

At those words, I felt like weeping. I held back my grief, not wanting to attract more attention. We were sitting in a Mexican restaurant in Santa Monica. People noticed her but were politely restraining themselves from asking for her autograph. She is somewhat famous; I will not say for what—suffice it to say (as you might have guessed), she is in the entertainment industry.

A couple young women interrupted our conversation to ask for self-photos with her, and I had to move out of the frame, but other than that, we were left alone.

The food was quite good. I have always enjoyed *chile rellenos*. The chef presented them with a skilled eye and a minimum of oil. Dione ordered a tostada, and barely picked at it, which might explain why she is half my size.

I was sad when she asked me if I could still predict the future. "Do you not know? I lost my talent after my childhood illness."

She shook her head and tried to look concerned, but I knew by her face that she did know. My sister was always a liar. My failed ability was not news to her. "That's terrible," she said. "I'm so sorry."

Because I know my sister's face better than I know my own (or I thought I did), I believe she was not sorry. She was actually glad. I do not understand why, but I intend to find out.

My sponsor L thinks Dione might simply be jealous of me. My memories are cloudy. I cannot think of why she might harbor jealousy toward me, unless it was because for a short time, I—her younger sister—was the most powerful Oracle in Greece.

Those days are long past. We are both here in the twenty-first century. For some reason, she seems to be glad that my business is failing. I am unable to discern a motive for her satisfaction, except that perhaps she thinks my failure will drive me to become more involved in her real estate projects.

"If you want to succeed, you need to master social media," she admonished me, as if I were a recalcitrant child. I tried to explain but she refused to hear my excuses. Perhaps she is correct. I admit I have a mental resistance to learning new technology. I had my assistant for that. And now Dione has my assistant. What a world.

Truly, I can make sense of nothing. My fear of the unknown future is causing me great anxiety. I assume this is how mortals always feel. I apologize if I sound insensitive. Please forgive me. This fear gnaws at my sanity. I can hardly think.

—Yours in exile, Delphina

Chapter 13

On Thursday, Pythia turned on her office computer for the first time in several days and found an email in her inbox from Debra.

> *Hi, Pythia,*
> *I hope you are well. Divina Dee would like to invite you to visit the Malibu site to get your thoughts. We are planning to meet Saturday at 10 a.m. at the gravel parking area off Miller Road. For your convenience, we can have the limo pick you up at 9:30.*
> *See you there.*
> *Debra Sandhill,*
> *Assistant to Divina Dee, Psychic to the Stars*

Pythia replied.

> *Dear Debra,*
> *Please thank Divina Dee for the invitation. My friend Lena and I will be hiking in the area that morning. We will meet you at the parking area at 10:00 a.m. Therefore, there is no need to send the car. I look forward to seeing the site.*
> *Sincerely,*
> *Pythia Apulu*

Pythia wrote the date on her pristine desk calendar. Her calendar seemed to be the only thing not muddled these days. *It is simple to keep track of things when you have no appointments.*

On Monday, Pythia had made her usual trek to the basement in the hope of gaining some insight into the upheavals wrought by Divina Dee and company. She sat on the stool for several long minutes inhaling deeply of the noxious gas before she was able to let go. Entering a trance state had lately become more difficult. *The return of my darling sister has brought me great joy but destroyed my routines. Hard to believe that my simple, morose life has been upended by happiness.*

Pythia opened her eyes and found herself gazing up at the façade of her home, the stone blocks of Apollo's temple. She put her hand on a column, warm from the sun, and reacquainted herself with the familiar veining in the marble. She let her gaze follow thin gray veins wrapping the columns, like she used to do as a child.

However, all around her, off to the sides, details were obscured by haze or fog. The veins were indistinct. Her sight had telescoped to a narrow aperture, blocking her peripheral vision. She sensed people and animals moving nearby—she heard people talking, goats bleating, wooden cart wheels creaking, sandals scuffing on the cobblestones—but could see only blurry shapes. The sounds were familiar to her, though. She took a deep breath, savoring the smells of Delphi. *It is wonderful to be home.*

She lifted her linen peplos so she wouldn't trip and started to hurry up the steps into the temple. However, to her surprise, she launched into the air. The ground receded as she felt herself caught by an invisible wind, wafting her between two huge columns into a bright, airy cavernous space. She blinked into the wind, desperate to clear her blurry eyes before she crashed into something.

Gradually her vision cleared. *This is not Apollo's temple. This looks like a hotel lobby.*

One of her sandals brushed the shiny marble floor before a gust of wind carried her upward, taking her past groupings of brown leather couches, chairs, and ten-foot palms in giant copper urns. Full-grown trees emerged from openings in the floor, stretching toward light coming through a distant glass ceiling five stories above. People in business suits sat on the couches, staring in shock as she floated overhead.

She grabbed onto a tree branch and hung ten feet above the marble floor. *This is ridiculous. Who thought flying would be so difficult? Would it help to flap my arms?*

She saw clumps of mountain grass growing from cracks in the marble walls, filling the space with the welcome scent of Delphi. *Has gravity forgotten only me? What would happen if I let go?*

Four black goats milled just below her feet, browsing the grass, herded by a young acolyte in a brown linen tunic tied at the waist with a roughly braided rope. Pythia felt a goat's horn poke her leg as it nibbled on her sandal. She kicked. The goat bleated and dodged away. The herder admonished her in ancient Greek.

"What in Hades is going on here?" Pythia said, but no sound came from her lips. "Wait, stop!" *I can hear them, but they cannot hear me.* The goat herder kept her little herd moving across the floor and soon disappeared into a dark area beyond a marble colonnade.

Pythia ducked as two fluffy white Polish chickens swooped down from a balcony to peck at seeds scattered on a rug that looked like closely mowed green grass.

The lobby wind continued to blow. A great gust broke her grip on the branch. Gravity seemed to be on hiatus. Pythia couldn't get her toes to touch the floor, no matter how she stretched. She drifted toward the check-in desk. *Good, now I can find out what is going on.* A young woman in a long white peplos belted with a beaded girdle gaped at her.

"What is this place?" Pythia asked her, but again, her voice had no sound. The young desk clerk frowned and shook her head. "Help me get down!" Pythia entreated, reaching toward the clerk. The wind pushed Pythia further into the lobby. "Wait! Stop, you can't—" the clerk shouted and put out a hand too late to catch Pythia's robe.

A white bull chased a black cow through the lobby, hooves clattering on the marble, scattering squawking chickens. She smelled farm odors long forgotten. People moved out of the way of the large animals, but no one seemed to think their presence was odd. The wind of their passing sent Pythia bobbing like a balloon.

"Hey, stop!" A bellhop tried to grab the hem of her peplos. She reached her hand at him, hoping he could bring her down to earth, but the wind pulled her away.

She floated like a cork in an invisible stream of air, bobbing past an impressive array of marble columns toward a wide doorway. *A ballroom, perhaps?* She grabbed onto a column to slow her pace but the suction of the wide doorway tore her fingers free and sent her roiling and bobbing into the massive airspace beyond. *Good thing there is a ceiling on this room, else I would be headed for the moon.*

She ascended on warm air currents and wound up bumping her head among rafters, air ducts, light fixtures, and sprinkler heads. She grabbed a metal support beam and rested.

Now that she was clinging to something solid, falling seemed like a real possibility. She found a narrow place to sit. Her feet dangled as she tried to manage her queasy stomach. Conscious of the increasing pull of gravity, she caught her breath and surveyed the layout below.

The room was set for a large banquet. Twenty large round tables occupied the room, ranged around three sides of a wooden dance floor and a stage. Place settings of black plates, crystal glassware, and silver cutlery decorated each table. Large arrangements of black and white flowers marked the centers.

As if waiting for her arrival, a floor-to-ceiling curtain made of light-absorbing black velvet split in the middle and flew apart to reveal an dimly lit stage. Spotlights illuminated two boulder-sized square-backed copper thrones, set twenty feet apart facing each other.

One throne was occupied by a huge bearded man with absurdly large muscles and alabaster skin. He leaned his chin on one hand, one tree-trunk leg thrown out in front, toe tapping the stage. If his toe had not been tapping, Pythia would have thought he was carved of marble, so smooth and white was his skin. His inhumanly brilliant skin glowed under the white spotlights hanging from the stage ceiling. *He would be twelve feet tall if he stood up.*

The man—not really a man, more like a god—gazed at the empty throne opposite. *I have seen that look on the faces of bored children just before they pluck the grasshopper's wings. Apollo protect me! I know who this is, and I do not belong here.*

After several long minutes, Zeus appeared to sigh. He lifted a stick from the floor beside him and pointed it at the other throne.

No, not a stick, a branch. . . No, not a branch, Apollo save me, a lightning bolt—an actual hissing, glowing lightning bolt.

Zeus pointed his weapon.

The lightning bolt sizzled and spat, sending energy at the empty throne, which in short order was no longer empty. The hazy figure of a woman shimmered into view.

The woman solidified.

Pythia could see she possessed an ethereal beauty, even though at the moment she seemed to be screaming. Frozen in motion, she had been immobilized leaning forward, caught in a moment of fury. Her gloved hands clutched the arms of the throne. Her black dress glittered with black jewels from neck to hem. One long leg extended from a thigh-high slit in the dress, displaying a stylish knee-high black leather boot. Long black hair floated in a halo around her head like Medusa's snakes, divided by a white streak running front to back. Her face was dark with rage, locked in a rictus of hatred.

Pythia noticed the woman seemed to have a few cobwebs festooning her hair, and some unravelings at one sleeve, as if she'd been held in stasis for a very long time. *Who is this woman? Does he pull her out of nowhere from time to time, just to torment her, and to let a few more spiders spin their webs in her dress? She clearly cares about her appearance. When she wakes up, all hell is going to break loose.*

Zeus gazed at the woman. He didn't seem angry. If anything, he seemed sad, perhaps regretful. *I am witnessing something private. Zeus was a well-known philanderer. Is this one of his many mistresses? Or could this be his wife, Hera? She reminds me of someone, but I cannot think who.*

Pythia felt a shift in the energy of the room. Zeus raised his head and sniffed the air, frowning, as if sensing an observer. Pythia gripped the rafter, holding her breath, trying not to make a sound, praying to Apollo that Zeus, the mightiest of the Olympians, would not sense her presence in this vision. *Apollo, let me be an invisible fly on the wall!*

Prayers inside of visions often went unanswered. At that moment, one of her Birkenstocks slipped off her foot and fell fifty feet to land on a banquet table, knocking over a crystal wine glass and sending forks and knives clattering to the floor. She moaned soundlessly. She knew what was coming but could do nothing to stop it.

Zeus sprang to his feet. Pythia clung to the metal beam, limbs frozen. The thunder of his sandals on the stage echoed throughout the hall. He scanned the rafters. In a moment, his eyes met hers. A tingle of terror shot up her spine. *Apollo, save me!* The lightning bolt moved. She had no time to react. A bolt of electricity shattered her brain into a million pieces.

What was left of her plummeted toward a banquet table. Before she hit, she was thrown out of the vision back onto the stool in the basement. She gasped and clutched her chest to make sure her heart was still beating.

After she caught her breath, Pythia descended from the stool and stood in front of Apollo's portrait, still shaken. "My Lord, it is clear, all is not right on Mt. Olympus. Any suggestions would be appreciated."

∾

On Saturday, Pythia placed a plastic cooler of ice cubes in the trunk of her Honda Insight and stocked it with a dozen small plastic bottles of water. She tossed in some protein bars. She was dressed in her preferred hiking gear: loose beige linen trousers, a long cream-colored linen tunic, and her widest-brimmed straw hat, tied under her chin to keep it from blowing off in the ocean breeze. She slung a cloth bag over her shoulder to carry her phone, handkerchief, sunblock, lip balm, and wallet. After checking the laces on her sneakers, she added a few more things to her bag, just to be safe—*because you never know. Although Oracles are supposed to know.*

She unplugged the car and drove over to Lena's apartment in West L.A.

Lena greeted her at the door with a glum expression. "Guess who's here."

Pythia didn't have to guess, nor did she need her second sight to know that Lena's mother was visiting. Only her mother could produce that amount of anxiety in her friend. She looked over Lena's shoulder and saw Madame B in a neon pink track suit sitting on Lena's sofa, strapping on bright white walking shoes.

"She wants to come walking with us," Lena said. "I told her no, that we had some work to do, but she keeps saying she is meant to come along. I can't reason with her."

Pythia cast her senses into the unknown to see if she could get a hint of what was coming. She caught a flash of Madame B striding along the trails in the sunshine. "It appears as though she is correct. I cannot discern a reason, but my senses seem to indicate that she is going hiking with us. Or with someone, anyway. That is all right, Lena, my friend. I have room in my car. I will keep you safe."

Lena smiled. "It's not like she bites."

"Mothers may bite," Pythia said, and added, "But only in that special way between mothers and daughters. So I have been told."

"I'm sorry, Pythia. Your mom . . . ?"

"No matter. I do not remember her at all." *But now I fear I have a sister who bites.*

Lena stood aside to let Pythia enter her apartment. Pythia had been there before. Lena lived alone in a modest one-bedroom in a building built in the 1980s. The living room was cream except for some beige pillows on the sofa. Madame B sitting on the sofa was a wild splash of pink.

Lena's mother rose gracefully to her feet. The track suit revealed how slender she was. Her bouffant hair made her head appear too large for her thin frame. *Is she ill?* Pythia put the thought aside. *Time enough for that later.*

"Hello, Pythia. Nice to see you again," said Madame B, extending her right hand with the palm facing downward. *As if she expects me to kiss it.* Pythia grasped Madame B's hand with care and turned it into a proper handshake.

"I am pleased to see you again, as well, Madame B."

"Indeed. Very kind of you to offer to drive."

Lena rolled her eyes. "Come on, Mom. Let's go. Got all your gear? Check one more time. Okay? Pythia, lead the way." Lena ushered her mother out the door and locked it behind them.

Pythia pulled the passenger seat forward so Madame B could climb into the tiny back seat. Madame B waited with her knees almost under her chin until Lena was seated in the passenger seat to say, "This is quite cozy, isn't it?"

"Would you like me to move the seat forward a little?" Lena asked.

"No, no, I'm fine," Madame B said. "Stay where you are."

Pythia always drove with heightened awareness whenever she had passengers, wanting to be safe. Today, she listened but did not speak as Madame B discussed the terrain, the sky, and the behavior of other drivers. Lena responded to her mother's critical comments with restrained annoyance. The tension was palpable. Pythia kept her focus on the road.

Everyone was relieved when they arrived at the trailhead parking area. Pythia found a space and parked the car. She and Lena got out and stretched. Lena nodded to a hiking couple they saw often on the trail.

Madame B crawled out of the back seat on her own, ignoring Lena's helping hand. "You know those people?" she said, frowning and straightening her jacket.

"We see them sometimes," Lena said.

"What's that big truck doing there?" Madame B said, pointing at a diesel truck and fifty-foot trailer pulled in at an angle, blocking a good portion of the parking area.

"Candlelight Transport," Lena read. As they stood looking at the enormous truck, two more box trucks pulled in. "Oh, it's a movie production, I bet. Look, there's the honey wagon. Yeah, it's a film shoot, maybe a music video."

"It stinks, whatever it is," Madame B said. "Smells like manure."

"It's probably that porta potty over there. Hey, look on the bright side, we might see some movie stars."

"I forgot my water bottle," Madame B said.

Lena sighed. "I asked you if you had all your stuff."

Pythia intervened. "Do not worry, I have plenty of water for all of us." She opened the cooler in the trunk and handed out cold bottles of water. She put several in her shoulder bag. She handed out protein bars as well.

"I don't know this brand," Madame B said.

"I think you will find it is both low carb and low sugar," Pythia reassured her. Lena turned her back and pretended to tie her shoe. *Trying to avoid committing matricide.*

Madame B looked around. "Which way do we go?"

"Up!" Lena pointed, and off they went.

The blend of sun, heather, and ocean air worked its magic. Soon tensions eased. The view was magnificent. Pythia let her mind roam as her feet navigated the trail. The shock of being pulverized by Zeus had faded over the past couple days, and this hike was helping put things in perspective. *I survived Zeus' lightning bolt. Apollo would have been proud. He never got along with his father.*

"What is this secret work you girls have to do over here?" Madame B asked.

"It's not secret. Pythia is involved in a hotel development project. They are starting to clear land just over that ridge."

Madame B stopped walking. "You mean the Temple of Apollo Hotel project?"

"You've heard of it?" Lena asked in surprise. "It's barely started."

"You know I'm a member of Friends of Malibu Hills! We are dead set against any development in the hills above Malibu."

"Oh, dear," Pythia and Lena said at the same time. They kept walking up the trail, and Madame B trotted behind.

"I was up here yesterday, as a matter of fact," Madame B said.

"What? How did you get up here?" Lena asked. "What were you doing?"

"Dorothy and I drove in from Miller Road, like any sane person. We were joining the protests."

Pythia said, "Protests?" *Oh, my Lord God Apollo, why did I not see this coming?*

Just over the next rise was a cleared area for the future site of the Temple of Apollo Hotel and Conference Center. With some misgivings starting to flutter in her stomach, Pythia led Lena and Madame B along a side trail to a large gravel parking area, where more box trucks and cars were parked.

"More of the film crew," Lena said. "I know that guy." She pointed. They were too far away for anyone to recognize her. "There's the director." *She enjoys showing her mother that she is part of the movie production world, even if she rarely gets work.*

"Do you see Debra and Glen?" Pythia said, holding her hat brim to block the sun.

"There are quite a few cars up here," Lena said. "They would be in Arnie's limo, right?"

A truck pulled out of the parking area, revealing the familiar white limousine.

"There they are," Lena pointed.

As the truck left, a passenger van pulled up near the limousine and disgorged a handful of people. They appeared to be older folks dressed in pith helmets and sunhats and collars turned up to protect their necks from the sun. They retrieved placards attached to sticks from the back of the van and surrounded the limousine, waving their hand-lettered signs and chanting slogans.

"Who are all those people?" asked Lena.

"Ha!" shouted Madame B in triumph. "Those are the Friends of Malibu Hills!"

Pythia started walking toward the limousine. Lena shook her head and followed with her mother.

The limo's two front doors opened. A bodyguard stood up from the passenger side door and yelled at the protesters. The protesters ignored him. Arnie Solomon in his white chauffeur's uniform got out of the driver's side and stood by the open door, leaning on the car, grinning. He saw Pythia approaching and waved. She waved back.

The protesters milled around the back end of the car. They couldn't see inside through the tinted windows but they yelled and shook their fists anyway. They tapped on the back windows and took self-photos of themselves shouting and waving their signs.

Madame B trotted toward the group.

"Mom, come back here!" Lena shouted and scampered after her.

Pythia strolled over to Arnie. "Hello, we meet again."

"Lovely day, isn't it?" Arnie chuckled. "Sorry I missed you at the radio station. I'll tell you about it later."

"Nice to see you again, Arnie. It is a lovely day. However, I feel I should warn you, something is coming," Pythia said.

Arnie nodded. "I can't see things the way you do, but I can sense some instability. Should we move?"

Pythia stood next to him in the lee of the car's open door. "No, I think this is the right place to be." Pythia turned her face toward the sky and closed her eyes. *I feel as if I am standing on an island in a storm. Is that thunder? Here it comes.*

A moment later, a herd of black cows burst over the crest of the hill.

"Whoa," said Arnie. "Are those cows?"

Hooves thundered as the cows flattened small bushes and grass.

"I believe so," Pythia replied. "Yes, about thirty cows, I would say."

The creatures fanned out across the parking area, flowing between vehicles, startling people back into their cars.

"What the fu—!" The bodyguard jumped back inside and slammed the door. He pressed a shocked face to the window.

"I don't see any bulls among them," Arnie observed. "Still, they look pretty determined. Hold on! Here they come!"

The cows sped toward the car, heads down, legs churning. Pythia didn't think she and Arnie were in real danger but she was glad when Arnie grabbed her hand. She found herself laughing as snorting cows plunged past without giving them a glance.

As the noise mounted, the protesters at the back of the limo looked around in confusion. When they saw they were in the path of a stampede, they shrieked and scrambled to cower behind the limo. A couple slowpokes ended up sitting in the gravel. The cows swept past, bumping among the vehicles in the parking area and fanning out into the brush, leaving a spinning cloud of dust and a few stunned people cowering on the hoods of their cars.

The protesters picked up their fallen comrades and their trampled signs and trudged to their passenger van. Madame B went with them.

Lena stood at the rear of the limo, covered in dust, and watched with her hands on her hips as the driver helped Madame B into the van. Her pink tracksuit was visible through the window. She waved at Lena. In a few minutes, the protesters were gone.

All the doors of the limousine opened at once. Debra, Glen, Divina, and four bodyguards piled out and stood staring after the protesters' van.

"Wow, that was crazy," Debra said.

"I wasn't expecting those cows," Glen said.

"I must admit, she never fails to impress," Divina said. "Oh, hello, Pythia."

August 2, 2015

My friend L and I often hike in the hills above Malibu. The terrain there reminds me of Delphi. Lavender and sweet peas grow wild along the trails. Stunning views of the Pacific Ocean appear at intervals as you ascend the path. If you hike in the area, you know what I mean. It is spectacular. You may have seen us yesterday if you were up there enjoying the beautiful scenery.

Besides reaping the usual physical and mental benefits of hiking, we were to meet my sister and her entourage at a parking area near the hiking trail to discuss a project Dione's company is developing. Coincidentally, a film production company was just over a nearby hill, shooting a scene requiring a small herd of cattle. Perhaps you can see where this is going.

I received an inside view of the process of movie making. With my friend L to explain the nuances, I learned what happens when an animal wrangler with minimal experience tries to manipulate a herd of cows using what I believe is called an ATV. Some herds are used to being herded by wranglers on horseback—cowboys, in other words, and yes, I understand there are cowgirls, too. Apparently this herd was used to seeing people on horses. The noise of the ATV sent these cows stampeding.

I grew up around livestock. At Delphi, my sister and I often traipsed through fields containing cows, goats, and sheep grazing on sweet grass. Most villagers in the area preferred goats, considering the rocky hilly terrain. Cows tended to stumble into ravines. In any case, cows do not frighten me. Second, my stuttering ability to sense the future indicated to me that we were in no danger. I felt I could trust that intuition, and indeed, we came to no harm.

What did concern me, however, was the observation my sister made after the herd had gone by: She said, "She never fails to impress." To whom did she refer, Blog Readers? No one in the party could have served as the subject of that sentence.

I am starting to sense an undercurrent, a subplot, a story lurking under the surface of the new life I am experiencing since my sister's return. Small clues start to add up to a larger mystery. You might be wondering why I do not use my oracular powers to discern the truth. I confess, I have tried. After my illness, my powers do not flow on command. Visions come as they will, and when they do, they are ambiguous, as dreams often are. I have grown to accept the limits of my ability.

Since the return of Dione, however, the visions I receive are muted, twisted, obscured in a way I have not seen before—I am "seeing" more than ever but understanding virtually nothing. I used to see the thread connecting a series of images. Now I see a million snapshots, a billion threads, but no connections. It is as if half my brain has been torn from my skull.

In other news, after the dust had settled, my sister invited me to participate in a public event that will be broadcast on television. I will not tell you what it is, out of respect for my sister's privacy. Suffice it to say, she thinks I need a makeover. I am not certain what that entails, if she means my physical persona, my business, my life, or all three. It is not until Christmas. I have not decided if I will accept her invitation.

—Worried in exile, Delphina

On the first Tuesday in August, Pythia sat on the bench outside the Mystics sound booth, reluctant to enter. Pythia knew already the topic Lena had chosen.

Lena was inside getting ready for the show. Pythia watched Arnie spinning records in his DJ booth. He turned and saw her. Arnie's blue eyes twinkled. She smiled and for some reason felt better. *So what if it is a topic I'd rather avoid. Life is full of topics like that. It does not mean we stop living.*

She realized she had come to think of Arnie as a friend. During the adventure with the cows, they had shared laughter. When she reviewed the day on the Malibu hills, the part she remembered with joy was the time she spent with Lena and Arnie. The obligatory time spent reviewing the site with Divina, Debra, and Glen weighed lightly because her friends were with her.

Still, one more mystery nagged at her memory.

After Pythia had walked around the site with Divina and her crew and looked at the blueprints, Divina had asked, "What do you think, Pythia? Is this project going to work?"

Pythia didn't know how to answer. *I have told her my gift is broken, and I know she knows it is true. Yet she persists.*

"My sister, I see nothing anymore with certainty," Pythia had said. "You need to tell me what you want."

Divina studied her a long moment. "Success," she said. "I want success. Money. Fame. Power. Pretty much what anyone wants." She laughed and waved a hand as if to brush away a fly.

"We have investors," Glen said. "It would be helpful if we could assure them of a decent return on investment."

Debra nodded. "Some rather important people are counting on us."

Pythia had sighed. She turned and saw Arnie standing nearby. Lena rested against the limo, basking in the sun. In spite of her concern, Pythia had smiled at her sister with love.

"The future is always unclear," Pythia had said. "For me, for a time in my distant past, it was less unclear. But now I seem to be more or less as gifted as anyone else, and perhaps less so than you, my dear sister. I would turn the question back to you. What does your second sight tell you about your project?"

Sitting outside the sound booth, Pythia remembered her sister's reaction. Divina had turned and scowled into the back window of the limousine. *As if someone were there.*

Before Pythia could look through the still-open car door, Divina grabbed her arm and pulled her away. "Listen, Pythia, we have a lot riding on this project."

"I understand, my sister. Please accept my apology," Pythia had said. "As far as I am able to tell at this time, your project will be a success."

Everyone had smiled.

Divina got back into the car to escape the sun. Debra and Glen led Pythia and Lena around the site, pointing out invisible landmarks. Fifteen minutes later, Lena and Pythia were hiking back down the trail to Pythia's car.

They hiked in near silence. However, something kept bothering Pythia, and when they reached the trailhead, she finally found the right question. "Lena, did you see anyone else in the car?"

"You mean besides the bodyguards? I didn't see anyone, but now that you ask, I remember seeing a pair of black heels on the white carpet. I noticed them, A, because they seemed out of place, and, B, because they were Jimmy Choos. Gorgeous strappy things, probably cost $2,000. Yum!"

"But no one was wearing them."

"No, they were just sitting there on the carpet. I assumed maybe Divina Dee was going to a party or something later.

Although come to think of it, they looked like size tens, maybe bigger. Way too big for your tiny sister. Or for Debra."

My sister does not wear shoes with heels. This then is the question that puzzles me: Who else was in that car? Someone with a penchant for designer footwear...

Pythia returned to the present as Sylvia, Moon, and Mary arrived together. They were comparing the Renaissance Faire to the County Fair. Pythia let their energy carry her inside. She settled into her chair and arranged her headphones and mic.

Lena opened the show with the usual introduction. "Today's topic has been on my mind lately, and I'm curious to find out if our Mystics can shed light on it, for me and for you. Our topic for today's show is family. That's right. Family. Love them or hate them, what questions do you have about your family, or the concept of family in general, that the Mystics might be able to answer? Give us a call. Looks like we already have our first caller. Howard, welcome, you are on the air."

A man's voice came through their headphones. "Hi, Mystics. I'm calling in from Glendale. I enjoy your show every month. I've never called in before. This is a great topic. My parents died when I was quite young, and I was an only child. They were only children themselves, so I have no aunts or uncles, no cousins."

"Go on, Howard," Lena encouraged.

"Well, I'm almost seventy, and I'm used to not having any family. I have a few good friends so I'm not alone at holidays and whatnot."

"That's good," Lena said.

"And then I had my DNA test done."

"Those things are always so illuminating," Lena said.

"I found out I'm part Scandinavian," said Sylvia. "Never suspected."

Lena laughed. "For those of you who don't know, Sylvia is a natural redhead. So, Howard, what did you find out?"

"I found out my father had another family."

"What!" Lena said.

"That dirty dog," Sylvia said. "Oh, sorry, Howard."

"No, you are right. He was a dirty dog, apparently. But now, because of his philandering, I have family. He had four children with another woman, so that means I have four half-siblings. And they have children of their own, which means I have half-nieces and half-nephews and whatnot."

"Wow, what an amazing story," Lena said. "Howard, is there anything you would like to ask the Mystics?"

"Well, one of my half-brothers lives in Burbank. He sent me an email but I haven't responded yet and whatnot because I'm not sure how they will feel when they find out their beloved father and grandfather had another wife and child stashed away in Glendale. I guess I would like to know, if I reach out to them, will they accept me as family?"

"Mystics, can we help Howard?"

The Mystics got busy with their various tools. Pythia exchanged smiles with Lena. She didn't need a crystal ball to know the answer. However, she enjoyed watching her fellow Mystics apply their craft to discern what they also knew. *The bonds of family are undeniable, much as we might wish to deny them.*

"Howard, according to your star chart, you will be surrounded with family and love until the end of your timeline, which goes a good long ways into the future." Mary pointed to the chart, holding it up to her microphone. "My answer is that this family will welcome you as one of their own."

"Howard, I concur," said Moon. "The I-Ching coins show me Hexagram 37, which is the symbol for family. Faith and loyalty will be nurtured."

"Whatever that means!" Sylvia laughed. "Howard, I concur with my fellow Mystics. I drew one tarot card to show me your future. The Four of Wands, which tells me you will soon be immersed in family—by Hanukkah, I'd say. Masel tov!"

Lena said, "Sounds like good news to me, Howard. What do you think?"

"The Seer hasn't spoken yet," Howard observed.

Pythia honed in on Howard's voice and followed it down into whatever dark grotto held the dregs of her oracular gift, hoping for some images that might shed some light. She put a finger in the air next to her forehead—that sometimes helped.

"Howard, I see only a little. I see a tree. It has deep roots and the branches reach into the sky. You are one of a thousand nodes on one branch of that tree. I do not know if that tree is just your family or the entire human species. I am sorry. But one thing I can say for certain—you are part of a very large family. In fact, Howard, I suspect your father had one or two more families. I am seeing . . . Eagle Rock? Yes, Eagle Rock and Pasadena. You are definitely no longer alone."

Howard stammered a shocked thank you and hung up. The Mystics stared at Pythia, wide-eyed.

She grinned. "What? It stands to reason."

"Our Seer without Peer does it again," laughed Lena.

August 7, 2015

I was a terrible sister.

In my defense, I was just a child. However, now I see why Dione might have been annoyed with me. I was so arrogant. All I could see was my own conviction that I knew best. After all, I was the most powerful Oracle in Delphi, perhaps in the entire ancient world. So everyone said, and I believed them when they heaped praise upon me and gave me gifts. I must have been insufferably priggish. No wonder Dione preferred the company of others.

Before I became a powerful Oracle, I worshiped Dione. I believed she could do no wrong. Nothing Mistress Dora said about her could take the tarnish from my sister's glorious crown.

That changed after I came into my full power. My head began to swell as the accolades poured into the temple. I confess, I started to believe I was a superior being. Gradually, Dione became inferior.

I am sad to say, I judged her and found her wanting, even when I was not with her. Even though I loved her, to my prideful mind, I took a perverse pleasure in proclaiming her faults. She was uncouth and rebellious. She shirked her chores. She never helped muck out the goat shed. She did not collect eggs or herbs or feed the pigs. She ran with a wild pack of acolytes and soon was their leader. I overheard Mistress Dora complaining to a priest that Dione had singlehandedly ruined an entire cohort of young Oracles.

I was so judgmental. Under the guise of helping her, I chastised her at every opportunity, warning her that she would be punished if she continued her wild behavior. She just laughed at me. She would say, "What punishment could be worse than serving your wretched god Apollo?"

After a while, she avoided me. Who could blame her? Being constantly criticized eventually grows wearisome.

In truth, I think I was envious. She was everything I was not—courageous, intelligent, spirited, independent, and free. Popular, too—She had a coterie of friends who supported her and always had her back. I had no friends. Instead, I had the temporary grace of teachers and priests, who praised me as long as I performed to their standards and then tossed me aside the moment my gift faltered.

The loss of my gift was the beginning of my freedom, but by that time, Dione was gone, and I had lost my mind.

Before my illness, I thought if she would follow the rules, she would be safe. If she would learn to conform, no harm would come to her. The temple would be her safe haven, as it was mine. I believed that with all my heart and soul, because for me, it was the truth—until it was not. Then the temple became a reminder of all that I had lost.

Now, through some miracle I do not understand, I have a chance to make amends to my sister.

In the program, we talk about a "living amends." When the moment seems appropriate, I will apologize to my sister for treating her so poorly when we were children in Apollo's temple.

In the meantime, I am doing my best to acquiesce graciously and willingly to all her requests. If she wants me to have a makeover, I will comply. If she wants me to color my hair and powder my face, so be it. I will have a hard time maneuvering in shoes with heels, but if she says that is what I must do to succeed, I will make my best attempt.

In other news, Blog Readers, I am shocked and confused to report that, according to my bank, someone has stolen my identity. I am not sure what this means, but I know it is not good. I find it remarkable that one's identity is a tangible substance that can be stolen. Why would anyone want to be me? This is truly an unprecedented time.

—Yours in humility, Delphina

Chapter 14

At the end of August, Pythia closed Apulu Ltd.

Since Debra's exit and Dione's return, Pythia had been spending less and less time in the office. Clients were no longer booking appointments for business advice. People weren't walking in the door seeking help. The office phone had stopped ringing. Even telemarketers had ceased to call. *Debra took the last bit of energy with her.* Without Debra's enthusiasm, Apulu Ltd had collapsed like a week-old party balloon.

Pythia drew the twenty-year-old drapes that since the last redecorating spree had never been closed. Quite a few holes and desiccated spider husks appeared when she yanked the moldering fabric out of the corners to cover windows she no longer planned to wash. The stripes had faded from the ancient damask, leaving a tired pinkish-gray. Pythia turned the *Sorry, we are closed* sign permanently facing outward and pulled the shade on the front door.

She cleaned the kitchen area, emptied the cupboards, unplugged the refrigerator, and took out the trash. All the other office furniture she left where it was, including Debra's ergonomic chair. Debra's new computer found space in a closet. A thick layer of dust had begun to settle over everything the moment Debra left. It would take a lot of dusting and scrubbing and painting to breathe life back into this space.

She flicked the switch on the fluorescent lights. The office was plunged into a dusky twilight. She locked the hallway door behind her and abandoned the office, retreating upstairs to her apartment with the portable television.

August 25, 2015

My former assistant once told me she hated artists because they did not want to do any work. She was referring specifically to artists who balked at taking actions related to turning their art into a business. I felt obligated to defend our artist clients, but I have to admit, there might be some truth to her complaint.

Artists are like Oracles in some ways. They present visions of an alternate reality. They cannot help it; it is their calling. Oracles predict. Artists create.

The friction sparks when artists are called upon to shift their perceptions of their art. Instead of perceiving their art as a unique and precious miracle of creation, we ask them to think of their art as a product, even a commodity. This shift is difficult for most artists, and for some, it is impossible.

In my coaching practice, we asked all our coaching clients to prepare a business plan. It is a standard approach. For artists, I did not expect anything elaborate. So many artists hate to write.

I am sad to report, after preparing their business plans, a sizeable group of artist clients called to say they had decided not to try to turn their art into a business after all, that it was simply anathema to their creative process. Much as they wanted to earn money with their art, it was less distasteful to get a job serving bagels at the local café. They anticipated that turning their art into a product they would have to promote would kill their muse. Perhaps they were correct. It is a rare artist who makes money with her art while she is still alive.

However, in my experience, luck, hard work, and persistence are much more important than talent. My friend L, who is an actor, is a living example of persistence. Luck favors those who aim high, begin low, climb slowly, and do not give up.

That is the last bit of coaching wisdom I will offer. Do with it as you will.

—Yours in exile, Delphina

On Tuesday before the September Mystics show, Pythia met Lena for breakfast at the Farmers Market on Fairfax, a popular tourist destination with ample parking. It was early; the tourist buses had not yet arrived. They found a quiet outdoor table in the breezeway under a white umbrella. The air was hazy with a cool marine layer, not quite fog. They both wore cardigans. Lena had traded her straw panama for a brown wool fedora. Pythia wore a scarf of gray wool challis.

"How is the bank doing on figuring out the identity theft problem?" Lena asked as they sipped coffee and waited for their food.

"It is taking a while to get things unfrozen," Pythia said.

"If you need anything, let me know," Lena said.

"Thank you." Pythia knew Lena did not have resources to share but she appreciated the offer.

"How are you feeling about closing your office?" Lena asked. A server in a white apron swooped under the umbrella, set two plates of scrambled eggs and toast on their table, and disappeared. "You want my toast? I'm trying to cut back on the carbs."

"Since my sister returned, everything is so strange and confusing. I cannot seem to catch my breath."

"My old sponsor told me confusion is a state of grace."

"I used to pray that I would find my sister. I thought then I would be content. I was certain, if only I could find her, my life would be perfect. And now she has returned. Why is my life not perfect? Why am I not content?"

"I don't have the answer, Pythia. All I can say is, I relate. Guess what! My crazy mother was diagnosed with dementia last week. Turns out she really is crazy!"

Pythia stared at Lena in dismay.

"I thought if she would just be the mother I wanted her to be, then my life would be perfect. If she would just . . . I don't know, approve of me, tell me she understood why I wanted to be an actor, then I could be happy. And now, I find out she really is crazy, it's not just me making it up, and she will only get crazier."

"I am very sorry to hear this, my friend," Pythia said.

"There will be no approval coming from Madame B," Lena said.

"She may yet surprise you."

"Argh! We're powerless over family! Eat your toast. We need to get to the radio station."

ঃ

Arnie was waiting in the lobby as Pythia exited the elevator from the parking garage.

"Hello, Arnie. Are you leaving?" she said.

"No, I'm waiting for you. I have something to give you." Arnie dug into the pocket on his flowered Hawaiian shirt and handed her what looked and felt like a lump of metal.

"What is it?" she asked, peering at the thing in her palm as they walked across the building lobby to the other elevators.

"It's something you should carry with you for the next month or so."

She stared at him. "Why?"

Three other people were already in the elevator. Pythia and Arnie shuffled inside and rode upward in silence. Pythia cupped her fingers over the object, hiding it from view as she examined it. It looked a bit like a prehistoric amulet or talisman, crudely fashioned in vaguely human shape, sex and age indeterminate.

"What is this thing?" Pythia asked when they reached the door to the radio station.

Arnie shrugged. "I'm not exactly sure. Bronze, I think. That's where I was last month. I was off tracking down a friend to see if he would let me borrow this thing for a while. He told me it can ward off evil spirits. Took me a while to convince him you need it." They both looked at the clock. "Time to go. Just wear it on you, Pythia, please? Put it on a chain or something. See, there's a little hole there. Don't take it off until . . . well, you'll know when it is time."

Pythia hurried into the Mystics sound booth. The other Mystics were all set up. Lena had started the opening. She smiled with relief when Pythia entered and took her seat.

"Our topic today is money! Yes, money, that thing we all wish we had more of. What questions do you have for our Mystics about money? Call our phone line now."

Pythia put the amulet in her purse and then, remembering Arnie's instruction to wear it, took it out and put it into her skirt pocket. To make sure she didn't lose it, she rummaged for a safety pin in her purse and pinned the pocket closed.

"The phone lines are blinking," Lena said. "Let's take our first caller. Go ahead, Suzanne, you are on the air."

"Hi, Mystics. I'm an artist. I want to know, is it true that if I do what I love, money will follow? I'll take my answer off the air."

"Wait, before you go, when is your birthday?" Mary said.

"December 31, 1999."

"Wow, an auspicious date," Mary said. "The eve of Y2K, when some people thought the world was going to end. Okay, let me pull up your chart."

Moon began tossing I-Ching coins in her wooden tray. Sylvia laid out a spread of tarot cards.

"I wonder if Suzanne isn't really asking a general question that all artists struggle with," Lena mused. "It's sort of a myth, isn't it, that if we focus on pursuing our dreams, that money will somehow appear to support us? While the Mystics are applying their craft to answer Suzanne's question, I'll just mention that as an actor, I've pretty much accepted the reality that if I do what I love, which is acting, then I will probably starve—unless I have a day job." *She sounds discouraged.* "Okay, enough about me. Looks like our Mystics have an answer for Suzanne."

Mary leaned into her microphone. "Suzanne, I'm sorry to say, things don't look good for you in the money part of your chart. You've got creativity out the wazoo, but not much wealth. Sorry!"

"I'm seeing something not quite as discouraging," Moon said, holding up the paper with the results of the coin throws. I got the Hexagram 41, which refers to decrease of something, maybe wealth, maybe something else. The thing to remember is even without a lot of money, you can still make great art."

"That's true," Sylvia said. She held up a tarot card. "I drew one card for you, Suzanne. It's the upright Five of Pentacles. This card represents a state of lack and limitation. At first glance, it would seem the answer to your question is no, money will not follow. However, when we focus on what we lack, we sabotage our ability to create."

"Too true," Mary said.

"So, if I'm understanding you, you are saying we should focus on what we have, not on what we don't have," Lena said, tapping irritated fingers on the console.

"That's right," Sylvia said. "Over time, our mindset shifts from lack to abundance. Eventually our external circumstances catch up to our internal reality."

"Hmm. Sounds appropriately mystical to me. Pythia, do you have any insight for Suzanne?"

Pythia had been feeling a surge of clarity since putting the amulet in her pocket. Images were flowing without effort, more than she'd felt in months. She leaned into the microphone and pressed the button.

"Suzanne, in a few years there will be these things called nonfungible tokens."

"Nonfungus what?" laughed Sylvia. "Sounds dangerous."

"You will make millions. In the meantime, while you are waiting, Suzanne, get a job. Any job! You can't make great art if you can't pay the rent."

"The Wild West Arcade is hiring, in case you are interested in the service industry," Lena said. "Nothing like hard work and low pay to build character. But enough about me! Let's take our next caller. We have Bradley on the line from Santa Monica. Bradley, what is your question about money?"

"Hi, Mystics. I was wondering, can I sell my soul for money, and how much do you think I could get for it?" Bradley sounded like a young man with a sinus problem.

"Whoa, Bradley, can I ask why you want to sell your soul?" Lena sounded impressed. *Perhaps a little envious?*

"Well, I'm a little short this month. I already sold my car. I was making a list of what I have left, you know, my assets? All I have left is my microwave and my bong, and those are non-negotiable. I stole a little weed from my friend and sold it, but I'm still short. Plus I smoked most of it. I read somewhere that some dude sold his soul online, so I thought I'd ask you guys."

"You mean, like to the devil or something?" Mary asked, awed.

"I dunno, I guess. I don't really care who buys it, but I'd like to try to get at least ten grand for it."

"Don't you have a job, Bradley?"

"Well, I did, but I got fired for bad customer service. Plus I stole some stuff. What can I say?"

"Can't you find another job?"

"I don't really wanna work," Bradley admitted. "Working for some dumb company is stupid. It seems easier to sell my soul."

"I don't know," Lena said. "I can't say I have much experience with this sort of thing."

"Come on, there's gotta be some fool who will pay me something for it, right? I mean, there's a sucker born every minute, right?"

Lena looked at the Mystics. "What do you think, Mystics? Got any advice for Bradley?"

Moon mouthed "idiot" at Lena and twirled a forefinger around her temple.

Sylvia said, "When is your birthday, Bradley? I can calculate your soul card."

Bradley rattled off a date. Sylvia started doing some calculations. In a moment, she said, "Bradley, believe it or not, your soul card is the Fool, reversed."

"What does that mean?" Bradley said. "It's good, right? The opposite of being a fool?"

The usually competent Mystics were floundering.

Pythia grabbed her microphone. "Bradley, what makes you so sure you have a soul?"

The Mystics gaped at her. Lena winced and waved her hands in a *slow-down* motion.

"But, but, everyone has a soul," Bradley sputtered.

"We do not actually know that, do we? However, Bradley, if you had one, I would say you have already sold it."

"Whoa, you bitches are—"

Lena quickly stabbed a button and glared at Pythia. "Apologies to our listening audience," she said. "And to Bradley, I'm so sorry. We weren't trying to upset you. And let me take this moment to remind everyone of our disclaimer. We are not spiritual advisors or psychics or witches. We offer suggestions in the spirit of entertainment, fun, and education. We don't have any particular religious affiliation or position about God, the Devil, heaven, hell, or the existence of souls. Got it? Now, let's see who our next caller is. Hi, Jordan, welcome to the Mystics Roundtable. Do you have a question about money?"

On Monday, Pythia didn't bother getting dressed. She checked her email wearing her bathrobe. In the afternoon, she found a message in her inbox from Debra.

> *Hi, Pythia,*
> *I hope you are well. We would like to invite you to the Palisades house to watch Divina Dee on Business Barracudas this Sunday September 13 at 7 pm. Refreshments will be served.*
> *Best,*
> *Debra Sandhill,*
> *Assistant to Divina Dee, Psychic to the Stars*

Pythia replied.

> *Dear Debra,*
> *Please thank Divina Dee for the invitation. I am delighted to accept.*
> *Sincerely,*
> *Pythia Apulu*

∾

Pythia had accepted the invitation with misgivings. The moment she stepped out of her car at the Palisades house, she knew her intuition had been correct. As she approached the house, every blade exploding from humps of ornamental grass came into sharp focus in the slanting rays of the evening sun. The koi bunched together to stare at her as she crossed the concrete slab bridges over the pond. She touched her chest where the amulet hung warm against her skin under her dress. During her previous visit, she had been fog-bound. Now she could see, and she was afraid.

Since she had been wearing the amulet, her oracular ability had reawakened. Small premonitions percolated like tar bubbling in her basement. Nothing much made sense, but her oracular insight was sending vague, unsettling warnings. The general feeling in her stomach was dread.

Accordingly, this afternoon she had dressed with care. She strung the amulet on a sturdy leather cord so it hung under her clothes against her skin at the top of her stomach, a place of power. The metal immediately grew warm. It seemed to pulse in time with her heartbeat.

She had chosen to wear a pale brown linen A-line dress. The loose mid-calf length dress was lined in wispy off-white China silk. She covered the dress with her favorite wrap, a long beige linen jacket that hung loosely even when buttoned. Flat sandals seemed the best choice for the day. *In case I have to run.*

She wore her straw hat on the long drive to the Palisades but planned to lock her hat in the car along with her handbag. *Travel light, hands free, unencumbered.*

Many cars were parked near the house when she arrived. She found a parking spot just inside the gate. She put her car key in her dress pocket, shut the car, and contemplated the façade of the house.

From the front walkway, Pythia could see the huge copper door was open. She nodded to the fish and threaded her fingers through the grasses and lavender stems as she passed, releasing wild scents into the air. *Apollo bless this place. May we all find peace.* Pythia approached with caution. After one last glance at the dark blue sky, she entered the dark foyer.

At first, she thought she was alone. Then she heard sounds coming from the living room and stepped through the foyer in that direction. She caught a glimpse of someone retreating into the kitchen.

"Welcome, my sister!" Divina lounged on the living room couch, looking at ease in pink yoga pants and a long white linen tunic. She propped her bare feet on the coffee table. A glass of something clear rested on a cork coaster near her manicured toes. "Please have a seat." She waved to the cushion next to her.

"Greetings, my sister," Pythia said, choosing a chair on the other side of the table. "Thank you for inviting me to view your success."

"I heard you closed your office," Divina said, looking concerned. "I'm so sorry. Are you okay?"

"I am fine, thank you."

"I heard you are having some banking difficulty?" *Who is telling her these things?*

"Yes, it is true. My identity was stolen last month."

Divina raised her eyebrows. "That sounds like a feat, to steal the identity of the world's most powerful Oracle."

"Please," Pythia said.

Divina looked uncomfortable for a moment. She took a sip of her drink. "Tell me how you know your identity has been stolen. I ask out of curiosity—if it happened to you, perhaps it could happen to me. And perhaps I can do something to help."

"Someone opened several credit cards in my name. Over the past month, I have received emails of bills from stores I have never visited. Establishments on Rodeo Drive, for example. Two thousand dollars were spent at a store called Forever 21. Someone enjoyed two $500 facials at a place claiming to be a day spa in Beverly Hills. Ten thousand dollars were spent on an entire pallet of anti-aging cream from a company called Oil of Olive or something like that."

"Wow, someone doesn't want to grow old," Divina said.

"These bills were forwarded to me by an anonymous sender. The bank is investigating. Meanwhile my accounts are frozen. In light of these troubles, it seemed best to close my business at this time."

"Do you need some cash, my sister? I would be happy to lend you some to tide you over."

Pythia could see paths opening before her, but she knew better than to speak of them. Divina had demonstrated an uncanny ability to know when Pythia was accessing her gift to discern the future. The amulet was warm against her skin. *This charm seems to be working. I must remember to tell Arnie. If I survive.*

"Thank you, my sister. If you would like to help, perhaps you could locate a computer expert who would be able to discover the perpetrators. I fear my situation is a low priority with my bank."

"Certainly, I could do that! Debra!"

Debra appeared in the doorway as if she had been listening and waiting to be called. "Yes, Ms. Dee?"

"Please help Pythia find out who stole her identity."

Debra's eyes opened wide. She looked from Divina to Pythia and back to Divina with a small frown line between her eyebrows. "Of course, Ms. Dee, I'll get right on that. After the show, that is. Right?"

"Of course, after the show." Divina dismissed Debra with her hand. Debra disappeared into the kitchen.

"You haven't seen our fabulous viewing room, yet, have you, Pythia?"

Pythia shook her head.

"Come on downstairs. This is going to blow your mind."

Divina grabbed her drink and led Pythia down the stairs past the diorama of the Temple of Apollo Hotel and Conference Center and around a corner to an open area flanked by windows on one side and a bar made of dark marble on the other. A six-foot tall cooler behind the bar displayed racks of beverages. A popcorn maker stood unused next to a cupboard of wine glasses. The ravine outside the windows was lush and green.

"Grab something," Divina said, opening the cooler door. "It's almost seven."

Pythia found a bottle of something she hoped was water. "Thank you."

"Check this out! It's a private movie theater!" Divina said. "The guy who owns this place is a movie producer."

Divina pulled open a heavy black door and ushered Pythia into the back aisle of a twenty-seat auditorium built into the center of the house. Deep burgundy carpeting covered the walls. On both sides of the room, half-lit wall sconces illuminated steps leading down past five rows of plush recliners toward the front, where floor-to-ceiling velvet drapes framed a white screen. The screen was blank. The seats were full of people. Despite the low lighting, Pythia recognized Glen, Debra, Clementine, Tina, and the Esperanzas. Several others were strangers to her.

"Hello, Pythia," Glen called, waving from the second row. She waved.

"My devoted entourage," Divina said. *Devoted, indeed. More like brainwashed.*

Images appeared on the white screen. Two dogs chased each other around a kitchen. Pythia realized it was a commercial for a dog food product. Another commercial came on, showing a gray-haired couple smiling at a cellphone.

"Something about you smells funny," Divina said. Pythia felt the amulet pulse against her skin. She put her hand on her stomach. "Come on, it's starting," Divina said. "Sit here."

The lights in the theater dimmed and then faded entirely. The screen was the only illumination. Pythia felt her way to the second seat in the back row and sank into the puffy chair. Divina sat next to her and put her drink on a long narrow table in front of the seats. Pythia put her beverage in one of the cup holders between the seats. She looked over her shoulder and saw light emanating from a hole in the back wall. A projector threw the image across the room onto the screen in front. The volume increased until Pythia could feel the bass vibrating in her stomach.

Another commercial followed, this one for a familiar brand of face cream. *I paid $10,000 for someone to receive a small truckload of that product.* Sound swelled. The announcer promised younger-looking healthier-looking skin after one month or your money back.

The opening segment of Business Barracudas began. The audience in the viewing room applauded along with the studio audience on the screen. The Esperanzas howled like wolves as the projectionist cranked up the volume. Divina laughed.

The show began with Carl Clement introducing his fellow Barracudas. Carl, a former football star, faced the camera with confidence, wearing a designer suit tailored to streamline his bulk. He displayed perfect white teeth in an infectious grin. His dark head was bald and shiny as a crystal gazing ball. Pythia had seen him on television before, but not paid much attention, until Cindi Harper saved his life with Pythia's fire extinguisher.

Two Barracudas were already seated in chairs on the stage. Both men had burnished bronze skin.

"Spray on tans," Divina whispered to Pythia.

Thomas Spazov was in his sixties, a handsome grizzled man with dimples and a lopsided grin. He wore designer blue jeans, trendy sneakers, and a red baseball cap with a fish on it, presumably a barracuda. He lounged back in his chair with steepled fingers. The man to his left, Hamilton Clyde, was a slightly heavier, younger clone of Thomas.

The studio audience whistled and applauded for both men. They seemed to be well-loved regulars on the show.

"And finally, our lovely guest Barracuda, Ms. Divina Dee, Psychic to the Stars! Ms. Dee, come on out here and take this seat."

The camera tracked Divina as she entered the set from an opening in the back. She looked young and limber in tight jeans and a long loose gauzy white shirt. Her blonde dreadlocks bumped around her face as she hopped across the set and sat in the seat next to Carl. The studio audience applauded. *That was supposed to be me sitting on that stage. A cold day in Hades.*

"Woo, looking good!" said someone in the front row of the viewing room. Pythia saw several arms waving in appreciation, making shadows on the screen. She glanced at Divina, who gave her a sidelong smirk.

"Watch this," Divina said. "This will crack you up."

The first contestant, a young man with a shiny black six-inch Mohawk, sauntered onto the stage wearing a yellow pleated cotton skirt and a bulky turquoise jacket that appeared to contain some sort of stiff metal contraption.

"My name is Xavier, preferred pronoun *they*, and I'm a fashion designer."

The studio audience hooted, and the audience in Divina Dee's movie theater laughed and clapped.

Xavier twirled in a graceful pirouette to display the outfit. Their Mohawk held solid.

"What you got there, Hoover?" Carl said.

"The name is Xavier, and I have designed the ultimate in loungewear," Xavier said. "It's a jacket that turns into a chair."

"Whaaaaaat?" said Thomas in a high voice.

"Whaaat?" echoed Hamilton in a higher voice.

"Say what, now?" Carl said.

"Please allow me to demonstrate." Xavier removed their jacket as they twirled, and through some quick sleight of hand, revealed a lawn chair, into which they flopped, raising their hands and exposing a bare chest covered in tattoos. "Ta-dahh."

"Whoa, now," Carl said, sitting forward, hands on his meaty thighs. "Ain't that a trip? Barracudas, what you think about this crazy thing? Hoover got himself a coat that turns into a chair you can really sit in. This gonna fly? Thomas, you go first."

Thomas gave a thumbs-down. "I'm out."

Hamilton also gave a thumbs-down. "Stupid," he said.

"Ms. Dee, what about you? This idea gonna fly?"

The Divina Dee on the screen gazed into the camera. She raised her hands into the air in the classic Oracle pose. The audience fell silent. Then she grinned.

"I think you have something here, Xavier," she said. "The idea needs some work, but I give it a thumbs-up." The studio audience yelled and clapped.

Pythia noticed Divina was emulating the thumbs-up sign and mouthing the words with the image of herself on the screen.

Xavier sashayed off stage, dragging the lawn chair.

A commercial for a large pickup truck came on the big screen, showing a shiny truck bashing through a stream, shoving aside rocks, crushing rare plants, and terrorizing endangered forest creatures while trying to reach a pristine campground hidden in a fragile ecosystem.

"It's very strange to watch myself and remember what I was thinking when this was recorded," Divina said. She leaned forward to take a sip from her glass. Pythia opened the bottle in the cup holder and discovered she'd selected ginger ale instead of water. She set it aside.

They sat through three more commercials in silence.

The show resumed. Divina said, "Now the real fun begins."

September 13, 2015

Greetings, Blog Readers.

My sister is dragging me headfirst into the twenty-first century, it seems. For reasons I cannot divulge to you at this time, Dione invited me to watch a television show at her rented house in the Palisades. As part of my living amends to her, I accepted her invitation. It was a lovely evening. I would have preferred to be hiking with my friend L, but I did not begrudge the time with Dione. Every day, I am astounded that she lives, that she found me, that we are spending time together again, like family.

Almost like family. Perhaps like a modern twenty-first century family whose two surviving members are almost three thousand years old. She has teased me for not adapting to the modern era. Her lifestyle is somewhat different from mine. As far as I can tell, she is quite wealthy, while I am currently working with the bank to regain access to my accounts after my identity was stolen. In any case, I am doing my utmost to be the good sister I was not when we were children. I owe her.

My sister has a viewing room in her rental house. If you have friends in the movie industry, you know what that is. We watched the television show with some of her friends and staff. It is a show you may have heard of—Business Barracudas. The show got off to a slow start. Even though I was not feeling well, I enjoyed sitting with my sister, watching her enjoy watching the show. Sometimes we have to appreciate the moments as they happen.

The first contestant came and went quickly. You can watch the replay if you want to see the coat that turns into a chair. The second contestant on the show is the one I want to write about.

The contestant presented a perfume made from several ingredients, some of which might be illegal in the State of California. I am certainly no expert on the nuances of perfumery. As far as I could see, the perfume bottle looked like any other expensive perfume bottle. About palm-size, made of translucent green glass. I do not wear modern perfume myself, preferring to enjoy nature's aromas in their original forms. I love the scents of heather, lavender, rosemary, jasmine, and honeysuckle because they remind me of Delphi. However, one scent I cannot stand is pomegranates. I do not know why.

The entrepreneur on stage was a young Muslim woman named Kali, originally from India and now living in Orange County. She was quite well dressed in a lovely turquoise silk sari and hijab, and she wore quite a bit of gold jewelry—bracelets, earrings, and a huge gold necklace—which the host of the show, Carl Clement, commented on. He also wears a lot of gold, chains mostly. I suspect he was envious.

Kali stood before the panel of Barracudas and claimed if applied at bedtime, her perfume would improve users' sex lives. "You'll have sweet dreams of love and passion," she said. "Just a little bit behind the ears or on the wrists, and you are on your way to heaven."

"What's in that stuff?" Carl asked.

"I cannot tell you, because it is a secret. However, we use the same perfume maker who makes Glivenchy's Immovable."

"Oh, yeah, I've heard of that junk," one of the judges said.

"Our perfume is called 'Your Rapture,'" Kali said. "Because everyone has a different idea of heaven. Right? 'Your Rapture,' it's personalized."

All four Barracuda judges seemed interested, so Kali popped open a bottle and let them smell it for themselves. Carl seemed impressed. The other Barracudas nodded with appreciation. Kali turned back to Carl, and then we heard a thump.

Television is a frustrating medium. By the looks on everyone's faces, something odd had just happened. However, it took a moment for the camera operator to aim the camera down so we could see that the judge named Hamilton had fallen out of his chair and landed face down on the floor.

The other Barracudas seemed paralyzed, eyes and mouths round with shock. A few audience members began to applaud and then trailed off into silence. After a short glimpse of that disturbing scene, the Barracudas went to a commercial break.

Dione's camera operator turned the volume down a bit while we waited. And waited. It was quite a long commercial break. It seemed the show might not resume. My sister assured me it would, so we waited and talked. She had inside knowledge of what had happened, so she started to fill me in on what the home-viewing audience was missing.

The show returned before she could finish the story. The volume increased to its former deafening level. Carl stood in front of the camera and made an announcement.

"Hamilton had a medical emergency," he said in a solemn voice. "Before you get upset, he's not dead! He's okay. The paramedics fixed him up and he's on his way to the hospital right now. We were assured that he's going to be fine." He asked the three remaining Barracudas, "What do you say, shall we keep going?"

"The show must go on," the judge named Thomas said, looking into the camera and tipping his hat.

The other judge, a young woman who shall remain anonymous, also thought the show should continue.

The studio audience had witnessed the scene from start to finish. Carl asked them, "What do you guys say, you want to keep going?"

According to Dione, about half the stunned audience seemed ready to call it a day. However, a small but vocal contingent of bloodthirsty spectators wanted the show to go on.

The entrepreneur whose product precipitated the emergency took the stage then to argue for continuing. She wanted her moment of fame, of course, even though her product almost killed one of the Barracudas.

Carl, knowing a ratings boost opportunity when he saw one, concurred, and Kali continued with her presentation. At that point, though, the Barracudas were not feeling much enthusiasm, according to my source, and so they all gave her a thumbs-down. She berated them to no avail and left the studio weeping and calling the Barracudas a bunch of egotistical racists (so I was told).

No doubt you heard about the episode on the news that night. Hamilton did indeed die after sniffing the mysterious perfume. However, there was a defibrillator on the set, as well as a production assistant who knew how to use it. Hamilton was breathing on his own when the paramedics arrived, and his doctors anticipate he will make a full recovery. Apparently, he was allergic to something in the perfume.

My sister thought it was quite hilarious that Kali claimed her perfume would send users to heaven. She said Hamilton went to heaven, all right, just perhaps not the way he imagined.

This story is probably entertaining to you, and under other circumstances, I might have found it mildly hilarious myself. However, partway through the screening, I became aware of a phenomenon I can only describe as a flurry of wings beating at my head and shoulders. I felt as if I were under assault by a colony of invisible bats. Or ravens, perhaps. I could not quite see them. However, I could smell them and I could feel them. I was not in a trance. They were definitely real.

My sister appeared to hear and see nothing. She gave no indication that she was aware of the beating wings, so I stayed silent. The amulet on the cord around my neck heated to such a degree that I found a mark on my skin when I returned home. My neck was bruised and in a couple places, the creatures had drawn blood. My sister barely noticed. I was under attack, Blog Readers, by an unknown enemy in my sister's house. I think if I had not been wearing that amulet, I might have been badly maimed or killed.

—Yours in exile, Delphina

ﻌ

"Oh, no, tonight is a business meeting," Lena groaned as she and Pythia walked together to the door of the church.

"I've noticed fewer members attend on business meeting nights," Pythia said.

"Ick, business," Lena teased and bumped Pythia's shoulder with hers.

Pythia followed Lena through the maze of underground hallways to the A.A. meeting room. *How does she always know where to go?*

A handful of people sat spread out among the chairs, which were arranged in rows, as usual. George alone sat near the front, studying material in his meeting binder.

"I don't see your friend Arnie," Lena said. "He doesn't come to every meeting, though, I don't think. What was that thing he gave you?"

"A talisman to ward off evil spirits."

Lena stared at her. "Whoa. That's cool. Does it work?"

"It appears to be working."

"I'm going to sit up front where I can see and hear better," Lena said. "Oh, before I forget, you want to work a few nights a week at the Arcade? Mario wants to hire someone part-time. I thought you could use the money. Think about it and let me know later, okay?"

The attendees' shares waxed more thoughtful than usual. That sometimes happened with a small crowd. People had time to develop their stories beyond their familiar rote shares. One member's reminiscing set off emotional memories in another. Shares dug deep into childhood wounds and teenage peccadillos. Tears began to flow.

Pythia closed her eyes and let her mind drift to her visit to Divina's house.

After the viewing of the Business Barracudas episode, Divina had led Pythia around the perimeter of the pool to a small patio table under a white trellis laden with wisteria. The rest of the guests chose chairs and chaises spread along the deck on the house side of the pool, watching the two sisters from behind dark sunglasses. Debra perched on a hard-back chair, wearing a natty uniform of white cotton slacks and a navy blue jacket with white sneakers. She poked the screen of a tablet she held on her lap.

Divina gazed at her guests with apparent satisfaction. "You want something to drink, my sister?"

"No, thank you. Tell me, Dione, why did you come back?"

"Is that my name?" Divina looked into her glass, now empty, and waved it at Debra, who leaped out of her chair and ran into the house.

"I do not know you anymore," Pythia said.

"What makes you think you ever knew me?"

"What is your purpose here?" Pythia said, feeling the amulet pulsing against her skin.

Divina sniffed in her direction, frowning. Then she flicked back her hair. "Purpose? I want what I've always wanted."

"And what is that, my sister?"

Divina shrugged. "Wealth. Fame. Power. A big house and a fancy car. World domination. I don't know. Is that blood on your neck?"

Debra appeared in the patio door carrying two glasses of ice and a bottle of something on a small white tray. She'd tied a red and white scarf around her neck, which fluttered as she hurried around the pool.

"Here you go, Ms. Dee," Debra said, out of breath. *All she needs is a yachting cap.* "Is this okay?"

"Thank you, Debra," Divina said. Debra unloaded the glasses and bottle onto the table with a flourish. Pythia saw the label on the bottle. Ouzo. Debra trotted away, smacking the tray twice against her thigh. "She's a treasure," Divina said. "I can't believe you let her go."

"She goes where she will," Pythia said. "Why come to Los Angeles, my sister? You were in New York for a long time, and doing quite well, I understand. Why come out west?"

"My . . . call it intuition . . . told me it was time to look you up."

"Time to look me up? That sounds like part of a plan."

Divina opened the bottle and poured clear liquid into both glasses of ice. The liquid turned a milky white. "What about you, my relentlessly self-righteous sister? What is it you want?"

Pythia looked at the hazy blue sky. A slight breeze stirred. Purple wisteria blossoms floated down from the trellis onto the table. She felt like weeping.

Before she could dredge up an answer, the teenaged son of one of the guests cannonballed into the pool, splashing water everywhere.

Saved from having to answer, Pythia said her goodbyes and made her exit, feeling lucky to have escaped in one piece.

George's voice interrupted Pythia's reverie. "It's now time for the Seventh Tradition. We have no dues or fees. Please give as generously as you can. This meeting room costs $150 a month."

Members grumbled as they passed a basket, which gradually filled with paper money and some coins. Pythia put in her customary $5.00, even though she was running low on cash.

"Now it's time for our business meeting," George said. "Our treasurer is not here tonight. I'm sad to report, he may not be back for a while. He called me this morning to say he went out last night and spent the group's cash on a few rounds for friends. Then they went to the track. When he gets out of the hospital he'll be in rehab for thirty days. All that to say, our cash is gone and so is the money in our bank account."

George closed his eyes and sat in a meditative pose. The group sat in stunned silence. After a few minutes, heads began to nod.

"Cunning disease," someone said in a quiet voice.

"Baffling and powerful," another concurred.

"Fatal progressive illness," intoned another member.

George opened his eyes and began counting the money in the basket. "I'd like to invite you to pray that our former trusted servant will regain his sobriety soon and return the money. We are not a punishing group. All we can do is pray. In the meantime, we need a new treasurer."

"I'd like to nominate Pythia," Charlotte said.

Pythia shrank into her seat as all eyes turned to her.

"Is that a good idea? She's not even an alcoholic," an unseen contributor said.

"She's a member if she says she is," Lena reminded the group.

George said, "Pythia, what say you?"

Pythia shook her head. "Thank you. Please forgive me, I must respectfully decline the honor. I am not certain that I can currently be trusted."

September 25, 2015

I went hiking alone this week. My hiking partner L had a commitment to take her mother for a cognitive evaluation. I offered to accompany her but she declined. There is little I could have done but lend emotional support. Dementia, like alcoholism, is a progressive and fatal illness for which there is no cure.

Not wanting to revisit the scene of the cow stampede, I hiked this week in Griffith Park. September weather in Los Angeles reminds me of harvest time in Delphi. During harvest, all the acolytes, young and old, roamed the terraced hillside vineyards, carrying wicker baskets, dodging bees and picking and eating lush purple grapes. We were not involved in the crushing of the grapes—that task was left to experts. However, our task was important. Some of us were more diligent at harvesting than others. Dione, lazy at the best of times, was often nowhere to be found during grape harvest.

Writing about my sister makes me unexpectedly weary. I suddenly feel compelled to take a nap. I am embarrassed to admit I may be afflicted by a popular modern mental malady. I believe I am depressed.

I am having trouble finding any meaning or purpose in life. I feel especially foolish, given my good fortune. After all, my beloved sister returned—from the dead, from my perspective. A miracle! I prayed to Apollo for such a gift but never actually had faith my prayer would be answered. After she returned, I thought my life would be perfect.

Far from being perfect, I find my life burdened with a bewildering multitude of new troubles.

You might be saying, Delphina has finally lost her mind. In my defense, I am not pulling my stories out of thin air just to elicit your sympathy. Since my sister has returned, my business failed and my identity was stolen. In addition, I think I may have been attacked by a pack of phantom bats or sharp-beaked birds. To add insult to injury, I am starting a part-time waitress job on Saturday. What am I to make of this strange turn of events? I must remember, no one is forcing me to take this job. I am not a victim. I am a volunteer.

Maybe this litany of woes is common to a typical modern American life. Please set me straight, if that is so. However, you should know, a friend gave me a talisman to help me ward off evil. I believe if not for that protection, my eyes would have been pecked out of my head. I ask you, is this not evidence that something troubling is going on?

Am I right to be worried? I await your comments.

—Yours in exile, Delphina

Chapter 15

"You'll be covering just these five tables." Mario, the manager of the Wild West Arcade scanned his arm in an arc. "Lena will cover the rest. If you get stuck, ask her what to do."

Pythia nodded. She remembered this room from her prior gig as the fortune-teller. Tonight another fortune-teller was sitting in the alcove. She glanced at the clock on the wall. The doors would be opening in ten minutes.

"Uniform looks good," Mario said. "Make sure your apron stays clean. If it gets dirty, grab a clean one from the break room. Don't let the kids steal your hat."

Pythia smiled as Lena entered, tying an apron around her waist. She patted Pythia on the arm. "Don't worry, Mario. I'll help her out. We got this."

"I know. It's going to be a great night." He walked over to the fortune-teller, bent down, and gave the woman a kiss on the lips. *Ah. His wife.* He flicked the light on above the booth, illuminating a woman with dark curly hair wearing an off-the-shoulder white lace blouse and a flowered skirt.

"You look fabulous," Lena said. "Royal blue is definitely your color. You've lost some weight?"

"I do not know. I have paid little attention," Pythia said.

"Well, I love what you did with your hair. It looks so natural," Lena said.

Before Pythia could reply, a crowd of people rushed into the room to find seats at the tables and booths. Pythia touched the amulet hanging on its cord around her neck under her Wild West Arcade polo shirt and murmured a prayer to Apollo that everything would go well on her first night on the job. She checked her apron pocket for her order booklet and pencil. She settled her cowboy hat on her head and greeted her first table.

Her many years of restaurant experience gave her confidence. Soon she rediscovered the satisfaction of serving patrons. She developed a rhythm. The evening flew by. She was surprised when the last customers had been thanked and ushered out the door. She wiped down the tabletops and filled salt and pepper shakers while Lena vacuumed the carpet. In a few minutes, the room was in shape for the next day.

In the break room, Pythia and Lena exchanged smiles.

"You really have done this before," Lena said. "How are your feet? Hey, before I forget, remember, we'll both be working Halloween. We can dress in costume, yay! No cowboy hats, just for one night. I have a great costume idea, but you'll have to wait and see."

Pythia enjoyed the cooler temperatures and blue skies as she drove to the radio station for the October show. With no business to manage, no clients to coach, her time was her own. She was free to come and go as she pleased. The job at the Arcade was only three nights a week—Thursday, Friday, and Saturday—and didn't start until 5:00 p.m. She had a lot of free time now and a little spending money. She arrived early, hoping to see Arnie.

Her heart lifted as she got off the elevator and saw Arnie in the DJ booth. He saw her at the same moment and beckoned her inside.

He wore his usual uniform: gaudy Hawaiian shirt, loose blue jeans, and well-worn sneakers. His beard seemed less gray and more gold today. His eyes seemed deeper blue. *Maybe it is just the fluorescent lights.*

"Have a seat, Pythia. How are you doing today? Help me pick some music from that stack of records and CDs."

Pythia sat in a shabby visitor chair and shuffled through the albums, perusing the worn covers one by one.

"Quite a variety," she observed. "Classical, rap, rock, country, and . . . spoken word? What is that?"

"Poetry. Old time bardsmith stuff. I throw that on once in a while to blow their minds. People call in and yell at me. They either love it or they hate it."

"You have eclectic tastes."

"Around here, I'm the god of music," Arnie grinned.

Pythia looked at him, but he was preparing a record for the turntable and didn't see her surprise. He cleaned the vinyl with a cloth and set the record in place. As the current song was fading, he pressed a lever on the machine and the needle descended into position. A new song began to play. He reached over to a deck of CD players and popped out the CD that had just finished playing.

"Say, Pythia, are you wearing that thing I gave you?"

"Yes, thank you, I am." Pythia tapped her chest. "Did you find out any more about it? What is it for?"

"All I know is it came out of an ancient forge in Greece so it must be good, right?" He grinned at her. "Do you notice any difference?"

"Difference?" she asked, frowning.

"You know what I mean."

Lena rapped a knuckle on the glass and waved at them, mostly at Pythia.

"I do feel different," Pythia said. "More clear. Less foggy."

Arnie nodded with evident satisfaction. "Please don't take it off, Pythia."

Arnie stood up and put out his hand. She took it. He helped her to her feet. For a moment, she was lost in his blue gaze. He leaned in and kissed her cheek. She felt herself sway as a surge of energy ran up her spine. *What is this?*

"You'd better get going. It's the Mystics hour."

Pythia hurried across the hall. The Mystics were already assembled.

"Old guys make the best lovers," Sylvia teased.

Pythia took her seat, cheeks burning, as the Mystics laughed.

Lena put on her headset. "Fair warning, ladies. The topic for today's show is doubt."

"Ah, Lena," Moon said.

"Doubt? Did I hear you right?" Mary said.

"Yep. Sorry. Doubt, uncertainty."

"This should be interesting," Sylvia said, shuffling her tarot cards.

"I doubt it," Moon said, and everyone groaned.

Lena opened the show. "Our first caller is Jackie. Jackie, go ahead, you're on the air. Do you have a question about doubt? The Mystics are standing by."

"Hi, ladies. I recently got divorced. My friends tell me I need to start dating again, but I'm have a lot of self-doubt. Does that fit the topic? Can you offer some suggestions?"

"Mystics, what do we have to help Jackie?"

"Jackie, when is your birthday?" Mary asked. Jackie responded, and Mary proceeded to calculate Jackie's astrological status.

Sylvia held up a card. "Jackie, I just drew a tarot card to represent your situation. What came up was the Moon, but reversed. This confirms to me that you are feeling some anxiety and fear over your current situation. It would make sense. We aren't trained therapists but I think it's common knowledge that divorce is very unsettling, maybe one of the most traumatic events a person can experience."

"I'm not sad about the divorce," Jackie laughed. "I'm glad to be rid of him. I just wonder if I'm ready to date."

Moon held up a hexagram she'd drawn on a sheet of paper. "Jackie, the hexagram that came up for your question was 40, which stands for liberation. I'm inclined to believe you might be happier if you remain single."

Mary leaned into her microphone. "Jackie, I show your moon in Sagittarius. That sign relates to freedom and independence. I concur with Moon."

"We have a lot of moons going on today," Lena laughed. "Pythia, do you see anything for Jackie?"

Pythia saw things in Jackie's future she would not mention. She pulled the mic closer. "Jackie, life is short. Uncertainty is our natural state. We do not know how much time we have left. I encourage you to explore the experiences on your— what do you call it? Your bucket list." *And do it soon.*

"Wow. Okay, thanks, you guys," Jackie said and hung up.

Pythia looked at the other Mystics and shook her head. Everyone drooped a bit.

"Best of luck to you, Jackie. Be well. It's a good reminder to all of us to enjoy life while we can. Let's hear our next caller," Lena said. "We have Andrew on the line. Andrew, do you have a question about doubt for our Mystics?"

"Hello, Mystics. I'm calling in from Anaheim. I've been told by, well, by everyone, that I can't make decisions. I'm constantly in a state of doubt. I end up pretty much sleeping all the time. Maybe I'm drinking a little too much, too. What does this mean, and what can I do about it?"

"Andrew, while the Mystics get busy, let me ask you, are you afraid you might make a mistake? Is that why you hesitate to make a decision?"

"Yeah, sometimes," said Andrew. "Like, my girlfriend asked me if I plan to go to college. I'm like, I don't know, should I? I am not sure I want to. But maybe I should."

"When is your birthday, Andrew?" Mary asked.

"October 15, 1997," Andrew said. "I'm turning eighteen in a couple weeks."

"Happy birthday! Libra! Your Zodiac sign is part of your story. Indecisiveness is baked into Libras. Not to worry, though. Certain times of the year are better than others for you, when it comes to making big decisions like college and such. "

"Andrew, today your card is the Two of Swords, which is the indecision card," Sylvia said.

"Oh, man," said Andrew. "It sounds like there's no hope for me."

Lena turned on her sponsor voice. "Andrew, I've learned that if I can't make a decision, it means I don't know who I am. In other words, I have some internal conflict that needs to be explored before I will feel ready to make a decision. In your case, you are young. Nobody expects an eighteen-year-old to have it all figured out."

"My mother does," Andrew said.

"When I left home and got away from family for a while, I was able to see things more clearly," Lena said. "Maybe that will happen for you. Pythia, any insight to offer Andrew?"

Pythia sighed. *He's so young, barely a man. What can an ancient Oracle say to someone who has not yet lived?*

"Doubt, uncertainty, indecision—these are the hallmarks of the human condition. Whatever path you choose, you will learn some interesting things about yourself and about life. Flip a coin, it does not matter. Go make something happen. Do not wait for life to happen to you."

"Carpe diem!" Andrew shouted. "Right on! I think I'll take a road trip to Mexico! Thanks, Mystics."

෨

"You look amazing," Lena said, admiring Pythia's costume in the break room at the Wild West Arcade.

"You also, Lena," Pythia said. They stood and smiled at each other. Lena had tucked her hair under a creamy white top hat. She wore a slim-fitting off-white pantsuit, complete with satin vest and long-tailed jacket. She carried a white wand and wore white sneakers.

Pythia wore what she usually wore when forced to dress for Halloween: an authentic Greek peplos with a shawl, both of pale gray linen. Instead of sandals, she wore sneakers, a concession to the job. The rest was as genuine as she could make it in the twenty-first century. The peplos was long and voluminous, pinned at the shoulders with modern-day fibulae to keep it from falling off. She had wrapped and tied a scarf at her waist, hidden by the drape of the peplos. The shawl draped over one shoulder and around her torso. For modesty, a dark linen headscarf covered her neck and shoulders.

For verisimilitude, she had spent an afternoon making a crown of sweet-smelling lavender and rosemary, which she slipped over the scarf to keep it in place. *Do I look like an Oracle now? Or rather, what moderns think an Oracle should look like?*

The amulet was tucked deep in her apron pocket, wrapped in a handkerchief. She didn't want to take a chance that a curious child might grab for it.

"Hey, look at this!" Lena took off her hat and pulled out a stuffed white rabbit.

Pythia laughed. "I have nothing so entertaining."

Lena glanced at the clock on the wall. "Anna is here already," she said, pointing at the fortune-teller booth. "What do you think of the decorations?"

Ghosts, goblins, spiders, and mummies hung from the ceiling and walls. White spider webs big enough to trap a child were tended by enormous hairy black spiders. The staff had covered all the lights in red translucent film, bathing the tables in a creepy red glow. A soundtrack of screams and moans played at a low volume through the speakers.

"This is terrifying," Pythia said. "What if the children start crying?"

"Let the parents handle it! Don't you love that fog thing?"

In a hidden corner, a fog machine belched out streams of fake fog that swirled around the floor, softening the edges of the room and making it seem bigger than it was.

The door swung open to admit the first costumed family.

"It's show time!" Lena said.

In a few minutes Lena and Pythia were busy handing out menus, taking orders, and bringing drinks to parents and children. Almost everyone was in costume. The older kids gobbled their food so they could play the games in the other rooms of the Arcade. Pythia received a couple compliments on her costume, but Lena reaped the larger share. Children and parents applauded when she pulled the stuffed rabbit from her hat. The evening passed quickly. Pythia's only challenge was making sure she didn't trip on the hem of her garment, which had a tendency to sag.

One hour before midnight, the parents and children were mostly gone. Pythia was starting to relax when she felt a shift in the energy of the Arcade. A wave of anxiety swept through her. She looked around, alarmed. Two small kids began to wail. Parents frowned in confusion. Nothing looked different, yet patrons sensed something had changed.

Parents quickly rounded up kids, grabbed their checks, and headed for the exit. Only the fortune-teller remained in her alcove. Lena stopped clearing a table and looked at Pythia. *Lena feels something, too. What is happening? Apollo, be with us.*

Pythia set down a tray of empty glasses and clutched her head. It felt like a hammer was bashing her skull. The pounding intensified. *I know this feeling. It is as if a hundred murderous black crows were battering my brain. Here she comes.*

She turned toward the entrance, hands raised in a warding gesture. She was not surprised to see her sister, Divina Dee, standing in the doorway dressed in a pale gray linen peplos and shawl, a mirror image of her own. Behind her was an entourage of a dozen people, dressed in colorful costumes and smelling of ouzo. Pythia recognized Glen—even though he was dressed in a red devil costume, his dark skin was hard to miss. Others wore masks. She recognized no one else.

Mario edged around the group and hustled over to Pythia. "They've booked the room until closing. See what you can do. Drinks and dessert only. Kitchen is closed, okay?" He hurried over to his wife. After a quick exchange, Anna turned off her neon light, grabbed her purse, and followed Mario out of the room.

Pythia took a deep breath and approached Divina with hands extended, palms open. "Welcome, my sister." *She has invaded my territory now. Why do I feel unsafe? She is my sister!*

Divina gave Pythia a distant kiss. She smelled like lavender and something else less pleasant Pythia had smelled before around her sister. She could see nothing untoward in the dim light of the restaurant, but everything now seemed precarious.

Pythia turned to Lena. "Lena, may I present my sister, Divina Dee? My sister, this is my friend, Lena Tollefson."

"So pleased to meet you!" Lena said, shaking Divina's hand with unfeigned awe.

"Did I not see you that day at Malibu?" Divina said.

"The day of the stampede, you mean?" Lena laughed. "Yes, I was there."

"With your mother, if I'm not mistaken. Wasn't she one of the old crones protesting the site of my hotel project?"

Lena cocked her head to one side and thinned her lips. "Let's get these tables cleared so you all can sit down, shall we?"

"Excellent idea," Divina said, smiling.

The group scattered around the room looking at the movie posters and monsters hanging on the walls while Pythia and Lena cleared the tables. Pythia took deep breaths and followed Lena's lead, stomach churning. They butted three four-tops together in the center of the room and put silverware, napkins, and menus in front of each chair.

Divina moved a chair to one end of the table and sat in it. Someone dressed like a mummy placed another chair at the other end of the table, but that chair remained empty, even though all other chairs were filled.

"Pythia, can you bring me some water?" someone dressed like a Holstein cow said.

Pythia peered at the guest. "Debra? Is that you?"

Debra lifted up a black and white mask of a cow's nose and ears to expose her irritated face. "She made me dress up like a cow," Debra whispered, slapping the pink udder and teats attached to her stomach. "I would have preferred something a little less, I don't know, stupid?"

"I'll have a glass of ouzo, waitress," someone called, waving at Pythia.

Pythia and Lena spent a few minutes bringing water and taking drink orders. Lena entered the orders into the computer. A few minutes later the bar server brought the drinks on a tray and distributed them with Lena's help. Pythia worked one side of the table, ready to take dessert orders, and Lena worked the other.

"Chocolate mousse, please," said a person draped in a sheet perforated with jagged eyeholes.

"I'll have the Graveyard Special with no caramel sauce," said a princess in a glittering gown with a shiny half mask decorated with molting turquoise feathers.

Glen waved a pint-sized pitchfork and grinned. "Hi, Pythia. Happy Halloween! Let me have a piece of apple pie, please. With vanilla ice cream."

"And for you, my sister?" Pythia paused next to Divina, pencil poised.

"Why are you doing this, Pythia?"

"Doing what, my sister?"

"Working at this crap job. Serving."

Pythia frowned. "I am sorry you do not approve."

"This is bogus. We need to figure out your future, Pythia," Divina said.

"What would you like to order, my sister?"

Divina looked annoyed. She smacked the dessert menu onto the table, making the goblin to her right jump in alarm. "Pythia, get off your high horse and listen for once. Success doesn't just happen. Winning takes work. We have to make plans." Divina's guests fell silent, and then started mumbling to each other, trying not to listen.

Pythia stopped pretending to care about taking orders. She put her hands on her hips. "My sister, I have no idea what you are talking about. Your words are as muddy as a stream fouled by a herd of goats. You will need to be more specific if you want my cooperation. First of all, who is this mysterious 'we' you refer to? Second, plans to win what? We are not at war."

Divina stood up, making calming motions with her hands.

Pythia did not back down. "And third, why, oh why, after almost three thousand years of letting me believe you were dead, do you suddenly care about my future? What is my future to you?"

Instead of responding, Divina cast a glance toward the other end of the table. *As if she is seeking guidance.*

Pythia whirled and stared at the empty chair. *Is there a slight shimmering there, or is it just a trick of the lights and the fog machine?*

"What is this?" Pythia turned back to Divina. "Is someone else here?"

Divina caught Pythia's arm with one hand. "No, don't be silly. We'll talk of this next week, at the planning session for the

Christmas show." She leaned in and offered Pythia a weak embrace. "I want you to be the guest of honor. How fun will that be! We'll do a holiday makeover on you." She released Pythia's arm and sat down in her chair. "Bring me another glass of ouzo, if you don't mind. And some more ice water."

Pythia backed away and almost tripped. Like a plug had been pulled, the strength had drained from her arms and legs. Nausea boiled up in her stomach. The fog floating around the corners looked gray, as if a veil had been pulled over her eyes. On autopilot, she said, "As you wish, my sister."

In the hallway, Pythia met Lena returning with a tray of desserts. Lena paused and stared at her with concern in her eyes. "You look like crap. Are you okay?"

Pythia shook her head. "Something is going on I do not understand. I think . . . I do not know what to think. My brain is in a fog." *Oh, no, Apollo save me.*

She patted her apron pocket. Frantic, she dug through all her pockets. The amulet was gone. Her heart stuttered with dismay. "Oh, no, it is not here, Lena. My amulet, my protection, it is gone. Arnie is going to be so angry." *No wonder the currents of my insight are a chaotic mess. I have lost my protection. Apollo, forgive me!*

"It's only a few minutes to closing. We'll make it. May God grant us the serenity. We'll suit up, show up, and get it done."

Pythia hurried to the kitchen. *I wish my sister would go back to New York. No, wait, what am I thinking? She is my beloved sister! Apollo, grant me clarity! My mind is in a muddle.*

Non-Halloween music was blaring in the dining room when Pythia returned with the orders. The sheeted ghost was kneeling in front of the sound system cabinet, fooling with some knobs and levers. Pythia delivered desserts and drinks, trying to focus on the task and ignore her quaking stomach.

She glanced at Divina. Her sister seemed to be assessing her from behind her glass of ouzo. *Is she waiting for me to collapse? To explode in a cloud of blood and guts? What is happening here? Why do I feel as if my sister means me harm?*

Feeling close to vomiting, she retreated to the vestibule by the doors to the restroom and leaned against the wall. *I am doomed. I am lost. Apollo, forgive me, I have failed you.*

She heard footsteps and stood back to let the person pass. A figure in a long black robe and a long-nosed white-faced mask with grinning red lips stopped and grabbed her arm.

She shook her arm free. "Let go of me."

"Delphina, no fear. It is I, Rodney Blass from the Church of Apollo."

Pythia peered into the eyes of the mask. "Rodney? Who are you supposed to be?"

"Mephistopheles, I guess. I don't know. I thought about going as Apollo but I thought that might be sacrilegious. Plus I like to save my gold robe for services. It's not a costume, you know. Anyway, are you okay?"

"No, I am not. I am missing my, my protective device."

"Ah, your mystical talisman."

"Yes, that thing. I cannot think clearly without it. Something is blocking my mind. I am lost in a fog. That thing helps me think. Oh, my Lord Apollo save me! It must have fallen from my pocket."

"No, Delphina, someone took it from your pocket." The long nose on his mask bumped the wall as Rodney looked over his shoulder. "I saw her."

"It was my sister?"

Rodney nodded. "When she pretended to hug you."

"What are you doing here, Rodney? Some of these people are dangerous."

"I know. I'm undercover." Rodney lifted the mask to grin at her. His teeth looked crooked and yellow in the overhead light.

"Undercover? What does that mean? For whom?"

"Apollo, of course."

November 1, 2015

Blog Readers, I have lost my protective amulet, brazenly stolen by someone I love and cannot trust.

Since I lost the amulet, my visions, when they come at all, have been flat and lacking in substance and color, the way looking at a faded photograph of a sunset is not a substitute for seeing the sunset with your own eyes. The images in my visions are gray and grainy, like poor reproductions. People in my visions are silent and still. They just stare at me, as if I could do something to help them but I am not.

Perhaps I am just feeling the aftereffects of Halloween, an odd American holiday I have never understand. I think, however, it is because I have lost my protective device, the thing I mentioned in my last post.

It was a magical amulet, a talisman of sorts. Without it, I feel as though I am walking blind-folded on a thin rope stretched over a deep canyon. I cannot see the bottom of the abyss. Are there dangerous rocks? Is there a pool of deep water? I peer into the darkness but my eyes are blind. I am listening with all my might but I hear nothing, not the wind through trees, not the trickle of a spring, not even a raging torrent. Nothing. I inhale, and I smell nothing. I confess, I am thirsty for the stench of tar and methane.

It is as if my most important senses have been dulled by something—or someone. That talisman blocked their efforts to keep me muddled and unsure. Now that it is gone, I am back in the miasma of uncertainty, worse than ever.

What do they fear? What could I possibly do to harm them?

Perhaps it is not about me at all.

Perhaps it is what I represent.

I believe I am a pawn in a game I do not understand or control. I am suspecting this game has been played for millennia. I do not yet know all the players.

I believe my sister is also a pawn.

I do not want to fall into the abyss.

Blog Readers, perhaps all is not lost. The strange thing is, I am discovering I am not alone. I have allies.

More will be revealed.

—Yours in exile, Delphina

Chapter 16

Early Monday morning, Pythia trudged to the basement and felt her way to the stool in the dark. The simple act of lighting candles seemed impossible. She hadn't slept well. The line between waking and sleeping had blurred, leaving her groggy and confused.

Will this even work? Apollo, help me. She inhaled the mélange of basement odors. After years of sniffing earth fumes, she could identify the individual notes of decaying concrete, white mildew, and black mold, each a unique and disgusting addition to the noxious perfume of methane, tar, and sulfur.

Now with dulled senses, the methane and sulfur smelled like a distant memory. She inhaled until she felt dizzy. She rode memory down into a dark murky roiling center, somewhere south of her shriveled uterus. It took a long time. The vision, when it came, started in her toes and swallowed her bone by bone.

She opened her eyes to a familiar scene. She sat in her usual chair in the back row of the A.A. meeting room in the church basement. Her mind balked. *How did I get here? Is there a tunnel connecting L.A. basements? How did I not know this? I could have saved myself so much time and trouble by just using the tunnel.*

Wait, what am I saying?

George came into the room through the front doorway, carrying the blue meeting binder. He looked dapper in a navy blue suit and brown wingtips.

"Greetings, Pythia. It's time to start the meeting. Would you like to lead tonight?"

"I have never led before. I do not know what to do."

George smiled. "You just read out of the notebook. It's not too hard. I think you can do it. You believe in a higher power, don't you?"

"Of course. I believe in my Lord God Apollo with all my heart."

"That'll do," George said. "Come on up here."

Pythia got out of her seat and ascended the steps to the lectern. George handed her the binder and took his seat in the front row.

She opened the binder. The first page was blank. She turned to the second page, and then the third.

"There must be some mistake, George. All the pages are blank."

When she looked up, the seats were filled with people waiting for her start.

"What am I supposed to do?" Pythia asked George. A few people clapped.

"Make up something, I suppose," George shrugged. "Isn't that what we normally do?" The group erupted with hoots and laughter.

"But what will happen if I just make up something?" Pythia said when the noise had subsided. The group clapped and nodded.

"You never know," someone said, and everyone laughed.

"That is the entire problem," Pythia said. "I am supposed to know!"

The group applauded with gusto.

"You do not understand. I am an Oracle! I am supposed to know the future. People are depending on me. The leaders of nations need guidance before they go into battle. Farmers need to know when to plant and harvest. "

George smiled. "It's okay not to know, Pythia." The group nodded and smiled. A few clapped.

Pythia took a deep breath. *What happened to my faith? It used to be so easy to believe.*

She looked at the familiar faces. "Hi, Pythia!" they shouted before she had a chance to speak.

She smiled and relaxed. "Hi. My name is Pythia, and I am an addict."

The group nodded and clapped.

She saw Lena in the front row wearing her favorite green fedora. Charlotte and Patty sat together in the second row, nodding encouragement. Blake was in the back, giving her a thumbs-up. She recognized other faces, people she'd seen every Tuesday evening since she started coming to this group a decade ago.

Some have been here from the beginning, longer than I have. There is Crazy Polly, wearing her roller skates. There is that other man, what is his name, the one who always talks about his mother. There is Norm, the one who does not believe in anything. I see Brandi and her partner Candace, there is the woman who cries all the time, that is the man who cannot stay sober. Wait, who is that tall woman with the black hair? I do not remember seeing her before.

The woman in black rose to her feet. *Oh, no, not her again.*

"Sit down, you poorly dressed excuse for a quasi-human being," the woman said, pointing a black wand at Pythia.

With that thought, Pythia was kicked out of the meeting room and back into her body.

"My mother has agreed to move in with me." Lena put her head in her hands.

"How do you feel about it?" Pythia asked, sipping hot coffee from a tall clear glass mug.

Lena and Pythia watched the weather through big rain-streaked windows as they waited for their bagels at a table in

Nagel's Bagels in Westwood. The November Mystics show started at 10:00 a.m. They had plenty of time.

After a beautiful October, fall had finally arrived. Rain pelted the windows. Pedestrians in thousand-dollar raincoats dodged puddles and careening SUVs and cursed when their designer umbrellas turned inside out.

"Not great, to be honest. I'm taking a two-week training on how to do stuff like give her a shower without letting her fall. Taking her blood pressure. Working with the insurance company. Tracking her meds. It's unbelievably complicated and hard. The people who do this work for a living are absolute saints."

"I wish my second sight was working better. I would perhaps be able to give you an idea of what is coming."

Lena shrugged. "I know what's coming. The question is, how long is it going to take? And how painful is it going to be?"

Their bagels arrived. The server poured more coffee. Pythia inhaled the steam, searching for the aroma. *Real life smells wonderful. Even weak American coffee smells like heaven.*

"Are you going to ask your sister about your amulet?"

Pythia contemplated her plate. "I do not think so. She seems to want to make a career in television here in Los Angeles. I promised her I would do everything I could to support her efforts. It is my living amends to her."

Lena frowned. "Yeah, I still don't see what amends you owe her, seems to me she owes you, bigtime, but whatever. I respect your Ninth Step work. It's important we do our best to clean up our side of the street, no matter what the other person has done."

"She invited me to her house to talk about the Christmas special."

"That's the makeover show, right? Boy, I don't know. Sounds fishy to me. I thought Divina Dee was so cool when I found out she was your sister. I was so excited to meet her. Then she made that comment about my mother being one of the protesters. A *crone*, for God's sake. That just ticked me off. She has a mean streak, doesn't she?"

"In some ways your mother reminds me of my sister."

"What! How's that?"

"Your mother has a disease that is essentially destroying her brain. She is losing her free will and autonomy."

Lena sighed. "Yes, you are correct. She has no choice, though. What's your sister's excuse?"

"I believe my sister has also lost her free will and autonomy. However, unlike your mother, she has a choice. She has voluntarily relinquished her will to someone else, a . . . what we would call a higher power substitute."

"Assuming she doesn't have dementia, do you think she will figure it out?"

"One can always hope."

"Look at the clock! Time to get going."

They paid for their food and went outside to their cars. Soon they were pulling into the parking structure.

Pythia parked in her usual parking space. Lena followed and pulled into the next spot.

"Is this where you always park? There are spots closer to the elevator."

"I park here so I can find my car again," Pythia said. "When I am underground, I lose my sense of direction. From here I can still see daylight. I know where I am. That is why I am often late to the meeting. Did you know that? I spend a lot of time lost in that church basement."

Lena laughed. "No, I didn't know that. You are such an interesting creature."

"What is our topic for today?" Pythia asked as they entered the parking elevator. They waved at Brian as they walked through the lobby to the main elevators.

"You can't tell?" Lena teased.

"My gift of insight has failed me since I lost the amulet Arnie gave me."

"Speak of your hero," Lena said. Arnie was waiting for them as they got off the elevator.

Arnie took Pythia's hands for a moment. "Are you okay?"

"I am so sorry, Arnie. I lost the amulet."

"You didn't lose it Pythia," Arnie said as they walked along the hall. "It was stolen. I should have known she would fight back."

"You mean my sister?"

He shook his head. "Never mind. You have an important show to do today, I hear. Oops, gotta go, my song is ending. Catch you gals later." He went into the radio station office across the hall.

"He also is a very interesting creature," Lena said, shaking her head as they went into the Mystics sound booth. "You two seem made for each other."

Pythia smiled. "We are friends, Lena. Nothing more. I feel safe with Arnie. I do not think of him as a lover. Just a very good friend."

"Right, you keep telling yourself that."

Sylvia and Mary arrived, followed shortly by Moon. The Mystics took their places, and Lena opened the show.

"Hello, everyone in Mystics land! I hope you had an excellently mystical Halloween. We certainly did! Last month our topic was doubt. Today we are tackling the ultimate topic. Today we'll be talking about God."

Moon said, "Oh, no!" Sylvia groaned. Mary laughed. Pythia put her head in her hands.

Lena grinned. "That groaning sound you hear means our Mystics are ready! Remember, we explore our topics in the spirit of entertainment, fun, and education. We use our mystical tools and approaches to shed light on callers' questions, all in the spirit of fun. Let's take our first caller. We have Denise on the line. Go ahead, Denise, do you have a question about God for the Mystics?"

"You are without a doubt either the bravest, or possibly the stupidest, people I have ever heard on the radio." Denise said. Her voice indicated a middle-aged person with some life experience.

"Uh, gee, thanks, I guess," Lena laughed. "Do you have a question?"

"Well, the obvious question is, does God exist, and I doubt if your tools are going to be able to answer that one. So, let's see. How about this? If there is a God—and I'm not saying I believe there is—what can God do for me?"

"When is your birthday, Denise?" Mary asked, pulling out her star charts.

"Believe it or not, December 25, 1952."

"Ah, Capricorn, born under the Christmas star," Mary said. "Some of my Christian friends would say that was a special day."

"To them I would say hogwash," Denise said.

"Well, I identify more as a pagan than a Christian, myself," Mary admitted, earning some interested glances from the other Mystics. "So I look for areas of alignment that make sense for me. But this reading is for you, so let me pull up your chart here and see if God—or something like God—is in your celestial universe."

"While Mary works on that, let's see what our other Mystics have come up with. Sylvia, are you seeing anything helpful in the tarot?"

"You know, ancient Christians would have stoned you all to death," Denise said. "Just thought I'd mention it."

"Thank you, Denise, for that cheerful bit of trivia!" Lena said. "Aren't we glad we live in the twenty-first century?"

"Not particularly," Denise said. The Mystics rolled their eyes at each other.

Moon leaned into the microphone. "Denise, after throwing the I-Ching coins, I came up with Hexagram 48, the sign of insight. The enlightened person learns the truth and shares her insight with others. If she fails to share the truth, misfortune could occur."

"So, what, am I enlightened or not if I believe in God?" Denise said.

Sylvia held up a tarot card. "Denise, your tarot card for the question is the upright Devil card. Usually the Devil card relates to living in a material world, seeking power, control, and domination, that sort of thing. We should remember that a mystical experience doesn't have to be a religious experience. For instance, I find God in nature."

"Oh, how sweet," Denise said. "I find nature in nature."

Lena grimaced and waved her hands to keep it moving. She pointed at Pythia.

Pythia sat up and pressed the mic button. "Denise, you asked what can God do for you? What makes you think God's job is to do something for you?"

"What? Isn't that what people say God is for, to bring us peace, good health, money, our heart's desire?"

"If you seek only to get but not to give, then the answer to your question is nothing. God can do nothing for you."

"Hooboy," said Lena, flapping her hands. "Let's remember we are here to enjoy our mystical tools and have fun."

"No, I want to hear what Pythia thinks," Moon said.

Pythia felt a weak ripple of insight bubbling up. She held her head and forged ahead. "Denise, your daughter is dying. Her most fervent prayer is that you come to believe in something, even if you do not call it 'God.' She is frightened that you will be alone with no support after she is gone. She loves you and she thinks if you embrace God, you will feel better."

The Mystics stared at Pythia. There was a long silence.

"Denise?" Lena said. "Are you still there?"

"I want to scream right now," Denise said. "I'm a rational, well-educated woman. I believe in science. I use facts and evidence to make decisions. I am sick at heart and furious that modern medicine is failing to save my only child. I am disgusted and terrified that my only recourse is to surrender my rational mind to a figment, a concept, a panacea. The whole thing defies logic and makes me sick."

"And yet we have been doing just that since the beginning of human existence," Pythia said. "There is no shame in believing. It is just another kind of knowing."

"I hate you. I hate you all. I despise your stupid god," said Denise and hung up the phone.

"She didn't question how Pythia knew," Moon said.

"We wish only the best for Denise and her daughter," Lena said.

After taking a break for some station announcements, during which the Mystics stared at their hands, Lena took a few more callers. Each time, the Mystics floundered with their tools and answers.

At the end of the show, Lena said, "I had no idea this topic would be so difficult. I apologize to our listeners. We did our best, but we clearly know nothing about God. At least, no more than you, and in some cases, probably less. We all struggle with the same question: What is going to happen next? The not knowing is what drives some of us to seek comfort in something greater than ourselves. Whatever you call it, I hope you find your own source of comfort as you wrestle with your own great unknowns. That is all for this edition of the Mystics Roundtable. Next month, I've already decided, our topic will be hope! See you in December!"

࿇

"Come into the kitchen, Pythia." Divina held the door open. Pythia followed her sister into the kitchen, where Tina bent over a cutting board, chopping red and yellow bell peppers in a loose sweatshirt and baggy pants. *No more Greek costume—is the honeymoon over?* Tina looked up once and nodded at Pythia with no expression.

Divina perched on a tall carved wooden stool at the counter. "Do these stools remind you of someplace?"

Pythia raised her face to the sunshine coming in the skylights and closed her eyes.

"Hey, what's up with you?" Divina said.

"I do not feel well, my sister. Since Halloween, I have not been myself."

"Sorry to hear that," Divina said. "How about some tea? Tina, would you put on the water to boil?"

Tina laid down the knife and filled an electric kettle. She opened a cupboard. "What kind do you want?"

"Pythia used to love pomegranates."

Pythia shuddered. "Nothing for me, thank you."

"I invited you over so we could talk about the special, if you feel up to it."

"Certainly, my sister. I will do my best to be what you need me to be." Tina set two teabags in mugs on the counter. Pythia smelled pomegranates and felt her stomach clench.

"As you have heard, it's a makeover show."

"What does that mean, 'makeover'?"

Divina shrugged. "We do a few makeovers every year. My producer finds them. All women, naturally. Men don't need making over. We find subjects everywhere. On the street, at the grocery store. We look for the most frumpy and unstylish, of course."

"Of course," Pythia said.

"Not that you are frumpy and unstylish!" Divina laughed. "Oops. You know what I mean."

"Making a swan out of an ugly duckling."

The electric kettle snapped. Tina poured boiling water into the two mugs. Pythia watched the teabags expand and sink in the hot water. Steam curled into the air.

"Right! My sister, you don't really need a makeover. Not now. When I first saw you, I hardly recognized you. Now, you seem younger. What has changed you lately? Is it Apollo?"

Pythia shook her head. The stench of pomegranate was nauseating. *Lord God Apollo, grant me strength.*

"How is the banking problem going?" Divina asked. "Has your identity been returned? Do you know who you are now?" She giggled and pushed a steaming mug of tea toward Pythia.

Pythia pushed the mug away. "My sister, do you ever pray?"

"Pray? What, like get on my knees, that sort of thing?"

"Pray as we did in the Temple."

"Prayer is spiritual masturbation."

"We used to pray to Apollo," Pythia said.

"That tarnished antique! Pythia, here, have some tea. You used to like pomegranates, as I recall."

"You are avoiding my question."

"What was the question?" Divina slurped from her mug. "Hot!"

"I surmise the answer is no, you no longer pray."

"Pythia, get a clue. I never prayed. Even when we were children, I never believed in Apollo. I know you did. I believed you when you said he appeared to you. No, I mean, I believe *you* believed you saw Apollo."

"What do you mean?"

"Apollo never appeared to me, Pythia. I never saw your god."

Pythia stared at her sister. "But you were an Oracle! How could you have served in the temple if Apollo did not lend you his power?"

Divina watched Tina tear lettuce into small bits and toss them in a large white salad bowl. "Well, I'm not saying he did, and I'm not saying he didn't. All I'm saying is, I never saw him. I can read people sometimes, Pythia, just like you can, and with a little ingenuity, I can sometimes predict what is going to happen."

"Ingenuity?" Pythia echoed, trying to keep her stomach from rebelling all over the table.

"Well, what do you think I pay Glen for? He's my eyes and ears on the ground. That man knows everyone. Anytime a celebrity marriage is going belly up, whenever a company is going bust, or launching a new product, he's got his army of informants sniffing out the information. It's not hard to put two and two together and make a prediction."

"But—all this time, all these years, how did you survive, if not for Apollo?"

"Well . . ."

"Are we cursed to live forever?" Pythia whispered.

"Oh, now, don't get melodramatic and weepy. Is it really so bad sacrificing a virgin or two once in a while, for the sake of immortality?"

Pythia gaped at her sister in horror. "Sacrificing—?"

"Sure, no one misses a junior secretary or an intern every now and then, right Tina?" Divina said, examining her nails.

Pythia recoiled. Then she saw Divina's sly smirk. "Wait, you are not telling me the truth."

"Oh, please, as if that would ever work. You should see your face, Sister," Divina laughed.

"Then how? How is it we still live after so many centuries?"

"Oh, this is getting boring. Let's put her out of her misery."

At the sound of a new voice, Pythia spun around on her stool to face the threat. A gorgeous woman of indeterminate age stood in the kitchen doorway. Her long black hair was split by a wide streak of pure white.

Pythia leaped to her feet. Divina grinned over the mug. Tina threw down the knife and disappeared out the glass doors to the pool.

"The witch of my vision," Pythia said. "Who are you?"

"Hello, Pythia," the woman said in a melodious voice. She snapped her fingers and a black wand appeared in her hand. She pointed it at the wall. A black crow materialized out of nothing and hopped onto the kitchen counter. It began to peck at a dish of shelled sunflower seeds. "Oh, come on, you moronic dolt. Don't you recognize me? Think! Gorgeous older gal, always wears black, has fantastic taste in shoes, hates Apollo, hates Zeus even more . . ."

"Hera!"

The woman smiled, showing sharp white teeth. "That wasn't so hard, was it?" She leaned back against the counter and crossed shapely legs, admiring her designer footwear. The crow fluttered into a bowl of just-washed carrots in the sink and began preening its feathers.

Pythia turned back to Divina. "You were consecrated to Apollo!"

"Relax, Sis. Sit down, you'll bust a gut."

Pythia backed away, mind whirling. *My Lord Apollo, help me!*

"Pythia, you poor innocent," Hera said. "I would pity you if I didn't despise you so much." She pirouetted toward the doorway, black sundress swirling around her knees. "Well, that was fun, big reveal and all, but now I must be going. I have some more Oracles to terrorize." She cackled. "Just kidding. You-know-who is near! I can't pinpoint his location, but I can feel his energy, and it's upsetting. I like my calm little beach town. Reminds me of Argos."

Hera posed for a moment, baring her teeth at Pythia in a shark-like grin. With a graceful flick of her wrist, she vanished. The crow disappeared as well, leaving black feathers in the sink.

Pythia sank onto the stool and put her head in her hands, gasping for air. She felt weak and faint, similar to the nausea she felt in the park when Divina first appeared. She fought off her dizziness and pointed her finger at Divina.

"That was Hera I was feeling that day I fainted!" she said. "I thought somehow you caused me to lose consciousness, but it was Hera! And at the Arcade at Halloween—she was there, in that chair. How long has she been your mistress?"

"We're more like partners, really."

Pythia raised her head to stare at Divina. "You were never such a fool."

Divina looked uncomfortable for a moment, and then she shrugged. "We have mutual interests. She helps me out with a little prescience once in a while, and I help her with her little schemes."

"And in return, you are immortal."

"Damn near, as good as," Divina nodded. She sipped from her mug. "That stuff is rancid, isn't it? Ick." She pushed away the tea and grinned at Pythia. "My dear sister, as usual, you are overlooking the obvious. If Hera's sponsorship is keeping me youthful, what about you?"

"What about me? I would never worship Hera!"

"Pythia, unlike me, you always were a fool. And you seem to have grown more foolish with age. Come on, think. Who is sponsoring you, Pythia? Who is the source of your youth?"

Pythia felt as if she'd been punched in the stomach. The air rushed out of her lungs. She leaped to her feet, heart pounding.

"My Lord Apollo!" she cried, raising her hands in the air. "My Lord Apollo lives!"

November 14, 2015

I feel like such a fool, Blog Readers. Since my sister has reentered my life, I am reeling with one revelation after another. I have no time to assimilate, to regroup, to make sense of anything. I confess, I am lost.

It has been brought to my attention that my long life is a direct result of the intervention and beneficence of my Lord God Apollo. Now that Dione has pointed it out to me, I am chagrined I did not see it sooner. How could I have been so blind? I pray daily for forgiveness to my god, but I do not know if he hears me. Is it possible he is held in stasis, unable to communicate with me, despite my pleas and prayers? For if he is held in stasis, then I am surely consigned to an eternity of confusion, locked in this endless half-life. If he cannot free me, I fear I am lost forever.

Without the talisman, I can see little with my special sense. I am blind. As blind as a human, as blind as all of you. I want to be of service, but my predictions are erratic at best. It breaks my heart to know I might be doing more harm than good. I cannot even reliably predict the small, personal, immediate things, things that used to be so obvious to me. I am learning to stay silent. So much heartache and sorrow. Train wrecks, building collapses, mass shootings . . . I can see nothing. Nothing! I, who was once the most powerful Oracle in Greece. My arrogant wings have truly been clipped.

My sponsor reminds me to pray for knowledge of Higher Power's will for me and the power to carry it out. I seem to be able to pray only for relief from my misery.

My sister and I are taking a little break. I promised I would help her with the special holiday event she is producing, but after that, I hope she will go back to New York. My heart breaks. I pray daily to my Lord God Apollo for rescue.

—Yours in exile, Delphina

The commenters were swift and ruthless. RunningWild42 wrote, "Delphina, you need professional help, now. Go to the hospital, commit yourself to the psych ward on a 72-hour hold. I am a mental health professional. Please listen to me. You are a danger to yourself and others. Please take this seriously." LivingInADream69 commented, "Girl, you insane. U need a detox. I know a place on South La Brea might let you in." Reality101 wrote, "Twelve Step programs don't work, Delphina. They just perpetuate the cycle of self-obsession and self-blame. You need a round of NLP and NVC. If that doesn't work, try electroshock. That did the trick for me."

∞

After the revelation that Apollo lived, Pythia had been unable to sleep. She waited in her apartment for a sign. As the hours crept by without any communication from her beloved god, her excitement began to fade and anxiety took over. *Why should he deign to appear to me now? In my selfishness, I lost all faith.*

In desperation, in the middle of the night, she grabbed a flashlight and descended to the basement. She gazed at the portrait of Apollo. No connection, no spark. Nothing.

She sat on her four-legged stool and raised her hands in the Oracle's stance. "Apollo, my Lord, my God, I am here! I believe in you. Please come to me!"

Her cries echoed off the concrete walls. She could not make herself fall into a vision, no matter how deeply she inhaled the fumes. Exhausted and dizzy from hyperventilating, she returned to her apartment and sat by the window, watching the sky lighten in the east.

At 6:00 a.m. she remembered the Early Bird A.A. meeting. The group met every morning in a modern multistory annex to a Catholic Church in Marina Del Rey. Pythia had attended twice since June and found the group welcoming, despite her confusion about her status as an alcoholic.

Lena would say, when in doubt, go to a meeting. Soon she was dressed and driving south toward Marina Del Rey.

She sighed deeply and felt herself relax a little as she parked her car in the lot. The wind off the ocean carried the scent of late autumn storms and seaweed. *I once dug holes in the wet sand with a stick I found on a narrow rocky beach. I ran through waves, screaming with joy as the cold water covered my feet. I helped my father load driftwood into our donkey's saddle bags. I remember.*

Today Pythia had arrived early because parking was scarce for latecomers. To her chagrin, she found the doors to the annex locked. She peered in the window.

"Good morning! Are you here for the meeting?"

Pythia turned to see an older woman with weathered skin smiling at her. She wore a long flowered skirt, a white cotton spandex tank top, and dozens of colorful beaded necklaces and bracelets. The woman selected a key from a keyring, stepped past Pythia, and opened the annex door.

"I'm Janine. I'm the November key holder."

"Good morning. I am Pythia. I am here for the Early Bird A.A. meeting."

"It's down the hall on the right." Janine smelled strongly of patchouli, tea tree oil, and marijuana.

"I have attended a couple of times," Pythia said as they walked along the hallway. "This is a wonderful location."

"There are tons of meetings here. I've been to all of them at least once," Janine said. "That there is Clutterers Anonymous. They meet tonight at seven. There's Overeaters, for the big gals, you know. That one there is Debtors Anonymous. They meet Tuesdays at six. Small group, great program. Can't seem to stick with it, for some reason. There's the A.R.T.S. meeting, you been to that one?"

"What is A.R.T.S.?" Pythia asked.

"Artists Recovering through the Twelve Steps," Janine said. "I'm a jewelry artist. I make these things." She fluttered her hands, making her bracelets chatter.

"They are lovely. Do you sell them anywhere?"

"Well, not really," Janine said. "Word of mouth, mainly. I can't seem to stay sober long enough to really get the thing going."

"I know what you mean." *Sobriety seems to be a missing ingredient in my endeavors too.*

"Plus, my boyfriend is an addict. Hey, you want to help me make the coffee?"

Ten minutes later, Pythia found herself carrying two large carafes of freshly made coffee from the annex kitchenette into the meeting room across the hall from the A.A. meeting room. Both meeting rooms teemed with people.

"Set them down right there, would you? Can you get cups out of that box?"

Pythia found paper cups, sugar packets, a half-full jar of powdered creamer, and some wooden stirrers in a cardboard box on a nearby shelf. She arranged the items on the coffee table. Soon people were milling around, grabbing cups, jostling for a place in line in front of the carafes.

"Hey, Pithy, save me a seat over there, would you?" Janine pointed to two chairs in the row of seats by the window.

Pythia sat in a chair. Janine joined her. Across the hall, the A.A. group started chanting the Serenity Prayer. All along the hallway, other groups could be heard murmuring the same prayer. Someone near the door got up and closed it.

"Hi, I'm Suzanne," the secretary said. "Welcome to the Early Bird Al-Anon meeting."

November 22, 2015

Everything begins and ends with family. That is my astute observation for the day, Blog Readers. I am fresh out of insight, literally. With the loss of my talisman, I see virtually nothing of the future. With that part of me dormant, I am now starting to sense the vendetta that underpins recent events. This vendetta is even more ancient than I.

As I said, it begins with family.

Dione and I came of age in Delphi without parents, without healthy role models to show us how to be compassionate, kind, contributing citizens. We were both haughty and proud, each in her own way. I was arrogant and prideful in my lofty position as Oracle. Dione was jealous and came to believe her only path to happiness lay in destroying my popularity.

Between two ordinary sisters, it would have been a spat.

However, I was a favorite Oracle of the great god Apollo, illegitimate son of Zeus. And no one hated Apollo more than Zeus' wife Hera. It did not take long for Hera to figure out she could make Apollo's life miserable by destroying me, his favorite Oracle. She recruited Dione for the job.

As far as I know, Hera is still married to Zeus. I do not have a lot of evidence, just a couple of visions of Zeus and Hera. I do not ascribe a lot of credence to the veracity of my visions—they often do not reveal actual truth. Instead, they offer me ambiguous hints of what was and what might be.

I used to be adept at interpreting the images and translating them into predictions that leaders found valuable and actionable. Since my childhood illness, that talent was greatly reduced, as I have described to you before. Since the loss of the talisman, my talent is virtually nil.

Therefore, I can only assume that Hera remains married to Zeus, her philandering husband. In today's vernacular, we would diagnose him as a compulsive sex addict. I should not take his moral inventory. However, as long as I am pointing fingers, I would diagnose Hera as a candidate for some kind of relationship program, I am going to guess Al-Anon. She probably has some kind of personality disorder as well. When it comes to her husband, she has lost all sight of reason, in my opinion.

Even when I was a child, Hera was famous for being petty and vindictive. People claimed she was one of the most beautiful women in the world. I do not know about that. I have no sense of the standards one would use to make such a judgment. I heard she has always been obsessed with her appearance, and current events seem to bear that out.

Now I know who was ordering all that anti-aging face cream.

Hera's anger at Zeus was common knowledge. The priestesses used to share stories of Hera's efforts to retaliate against Zeus by tormenting his illegitimate children. I have now come to believe she is still waging that war of revenge. She is definitely a bitter, resentful, controlling, untreated Al-Anon.

Again, my opinion.

I pity Hera. I've seen enough to know she has not had an easy life. Zeus overpowered her, raped her, and then bullied her into marrying him. In this modern era, if he were a man, he would be in prison.

You do not put gods in prison, though. Not that god, anyway. He is the one who imprisons other gods. I felt his lightning bolt in one of my visions. That thing is terrifying.

Back to the topic. Family. My sister was a ripe target, waiting to be plucked. As my sister, Dione had value as a weapon. Given her resentment toward me, Dione was an easy pawn to put onto the field. I do not know how it unfolded, but I can imagine Apollo, once he realized that Hera was out to destroy him, chose me as the logical counter-pawn.

Dione and I never had a chance.

—Yours in exile, Delphina

On Friday, Pythia's cell phone rang.

"Pythia, it's Debra," said a familiar voice. "Listen, I have some information for you."

"Where are you? You sound like you are standing in traffic."

"I am! I'm at Gelsen's, picking up lunch. I had to get out of there. Clementine is driving me crazy. Every five minutes, she wants a new towel. Or a pineapple juice. Pythia, can we meet? I have something to give you."

"Of course. Do you want to come to the apartment?"

"No, we have to do this in secret. They are probably watching you. Where's a place your sister and her insane groupies would never think to look for us?"

An hour later, Debra and Pythia walked into the Senior Sanchez Adult Daycare Center in Hollywood. At Debra's insistence, they had taken separate cars, driven by roundabout routes, and parked in back in the employees' parking lot.

Debra paid the day fee, $5.00 each. "How did you find this place?" she asked as they found two vacant seats at a table. The table's other two occupants, Dotty and her friend Marge, both older women with bluish-white hair, sunken cheeks, and bright watery eyes, were setting out Bingo chips and cards.

"Lena. She's started bringing her mother here sometimes." She stared at the pile of chips next to her Bingo card. "I have never played Bingo before. What are all these numbers?"

"It's easy, you just listen for the numbers and put your markers on the card. If you get markers all in a row, you shout 'Bingo.'"

"I'll help her," said Dotty, rolling her dentures around in her mouth. "Here, honey, put a chip on the Free spot." Dotty and her friend Marge were playing five cards apiece.

The sunlit room contained ten round tables, all of which were occupied with Bingo players. Most were women, but a few men were scattered among the crowd, slurping coffee and preening for the women.

Two older women sat on plastic chairs at a long table at the side of the room. The one with pink hair and an animated chin wattle turned the handle on a wire cage full of colorful objects. Her companion, a tall pale woman with thinning gray hair, pulled a small oblong object out of the cage. She examined it carefully and shouted "Bee-three!" into a battery-powered microphone.

Debra moved a marker onto the 3 in the B column on her Bingo card and rubbed her hands with excitement. "Isn't this fun? I haven't played Bingo since I was a kid."

"It certainly seems to be a competitive sport," Pythia said. "Do you feel ready to tell me the purpose of our meeting?"

Debra looked embarrassed. "Of course, sorry, I got carried away. It just feels so good to get out of that crazy house. Hey, you remember when Divina Dee asked me to look into those emails you got?"

"The ones related to my stolen identity?"

Debra dug into her purse and pulled out a sheaf of computer printouts. "Yeah. I took a cyber security class last month, and I used some of the tools from the class to find the IP address of the computer that sent those emails."

"What is an IP address?" Pythia asked.

"Eye-twenty-five," shouted the gray-haired woman into her microphone.

"It shows where the computer is. Pythia, the computer that sent those emails to you? It was in Divina Dee's office!"

Pythia stared at Debra in confusion. "You mean, someone in my sister's employ stole my identity?"

Debra pointed to one of the printouts. "It's all right here. You can take these to the bank."

"Enn-Fourteen!"

Dotty tapped the table. "Come on, girls, you aren't paying attention. Put a chip on it!"

Pythia moved a marker onto the square. "It was not you, I presume. You had your chance to be me and wisely declined."

"I'm pretty sure it wasn't Glen or Tina."

"Then I think I know who it was."

"Who?"

"Oh-forty-seven!" blared the microphone.

"My sister has an associate who always wears black."

"Ms. Hera, you mean? Oh, no, it couldn't be her. She can't even use a cell phone, much less a computer."

"She might not know modern technology, but she knows how to wreak havoc. She has had many years of practice."

"I must say, she makes me a bit nervous. I don't like the way she looks at me."

"You should stay away from her, Debra. She is a dangerous person."

"She doesn't come around much, and she ignores me like I'm a bug. She dresses like a goddess, though."

Pythia rolled her eyes. "Thank you for these, Debra." She folded the papers into her purse.

"One more thing. You can't tell anyone I told you this. I saw your thing. That weird piece of jewelry? I know it's yours. I saw Divina Dee take it out of your pocket at the Arcade."

"Where is it?"

"I'm sorry to say, in a drawer in your sister's office. I wasn't sure I could steal it back without getting caught."

"Thank you, Debra. You did the right thing by telling me. I hope you will not get into trouble."

"I'll try to get it for you before the Christmas show."

"Please do not place yourself in danger."

"I don't care. I'm leaving at the end of December. I've learned a lot and Divina Dee is cool, even though she's a thief and a total bitch, but I've decided to start my own marketing firm."

Pythia smiled a genuine smile.

"Gee-two!"

"Bingo!" Dotty shouted, raising her fists in the air.

"Oh, you always win," Marge said. She looked around as people started rising from their seats. "Dang it, there's the bus. Time to go back to the hellhole."

"We'll come back tomorrow, Marge," Dotty said, patting Marge's shoulder. She turned to Pythia and Debra and said, "We come every day but she forgets, poor dear." She twirled a gnarled finger around her temple and mouthed the word "dementia."

Chapter 17

"I don't like speaking in front of groups," said the speaker at the A.A. meeting. "I would rather hide out in the back of the room, listening or pretending to listen, and pretending like none of this means anything to me."

The speaker was perhaps a woman, but perhaps not. Pythia couldn't tell. The person's name was Chris. Chris wore loose black jeans and a baggy t-shirt over a bulky figure, hiding any curves that might be present. A thick mane of green and blue hair covered the top of Chris' head. The sides were shaved to the scalp.

"I started drinking when I was in elementary school. I never fit in, I didn't have any friends. Kids used to bully me. I drank my grandfather's beer because he was a drunk and couldn't keep track of how much he had."

Members of the group nodded.

"Life sucked. I drank to take the edge off." Chris leaned sideways on the lectern, avoiding eye contact with the group. "At first I could handle it. I was young and resilient. After high school I had to get a job and my drinking started interfering with my work. I was in healthcare. Someone died because I was drunk on the job. I was fired. I went to jail for a while."

Pythia heard the unspoken sadness and fear in Chris' voice.

"For a long time, I thought the only way I could access God was by drinking."

"Right on," said someone in a soft voice. Pythia put her head in her hands. *Do I believe the only way to find Apollo is to inhale methane gas? What if my addiction is actually blocking me from finding him?*

The lectern creaked as Chris leaned on it. "I don't know how to trust God if I'm not drinking. If I consciously surrender my drinking to the care of something greater than me, I feel like I'm jumping off a cliff. I feel like I'm going to die."

Chris picked at the side of the lectern. "Then I remember, hey, I'm going die anyway, whether I choose to surrender or not!"

The group chuckled and heads nodded.

"The truth is that I'm going to die. Someday. It doesn't matter what I believe, or what I trust or don't trust, I'm going to die. I'm sad about that sometimes, but then I think, hey, I don't want to live forever. Then I think, hey, what can I do today to help the man who is still sick?

"Or woman," Chris added. "Or whatever. We're all on the firing line of life. I pray I can show up with grace."

Chris clomped down the steps and sat down to polite applause.

In the sharing that followed, the theme seemed to be the importance of showing up for recovery, no matter what. After the meeting closed with a prayer circle, Pythia sat again in her chair, feeling ill and off balance. Since she had lost the amulet, she often felt a low-grade nausea. Sometimes it seemed the invisible bats or birds circled her head, just out of reach, trying to peck out her eyes. She often heard the hiss of tires on pavement coming toward her, indoors, where there could not possibly be any traffic. *I am constantly on edge, expecting disaster. Is this what it feels like to be a normal human, constantly besieged by anxiety? Talk about the firing line of life!*

"What are you doing?" Lena stood in front of her. "Are you okay? You haven't been yourself since Halloween. That thing that Arnie gave you, it really was a thing, wasn't it?"

Pythia nodded.

"Dammit. Your sister is a real piece of work." Lena grabbed her hand and pulled her to her feet. Through their physical connection, Pythia caught a glimpse of her friend sitting on a chair next to her tub as Madame B took a bath. *I am not the only one suffering with family troubles.*

"We will get through this, Lena," Pythia reassured her friend. "Remember our Roundtable theme this month was hope. I believe our faith is being tested."

"Argh. I could do without it." They started walking through the basement maze to the exit. "Are you going to do her show? It's coming up soon, isn't it?"

"A few days before Christmas. I am not able to discern much insight as to what will happen. However, I am hoping it will go smoothly."

"Meaning what, she'll turn you into a gorgeous super-model?"

"Meaning no one will die."

"Welcome to Psychic to the Stars. I'm Kat Cameron, the director. This is Jimmy James, the head cameraman."

Pythia stood inside the door of the sound stage, staring at the young woman, knowing the only way out was forward but wanting desperately to go back to her car, to drive home, to drive away from Los Angeles, to forget she ever had a sister.

The day had finally arrived. Worry sapped her willpower. *Uncertainty has carved a permanent nest in my bones. I am blind.* Even though she was filled with dread, she also felt relief that it would soon be over. *Apollo, wherever you are, I pray you be with me. I am here because I made a commitment to myself to be a good sister, whether she deserves me or not. But I have little hope that I will survive this makeover.*

Jimmy patted her arm and walked away grinning. Kat did not seem to notice Pythia's discomfort. She waved at a young man hovering nearby.

"This is Steve, our intern. Steve, get her set up. Pythia, I'll see you later!" The young woman bounded away, long hair flying. Steve shook long black curls off his face, facial piercings glistening in the overhead fluorescent lighting. "Did you find a place to park? It's a long walk to the sound stage, isn't it? Let me give you the grand tour!"

He led Pythia along a hallway with no ceiling. Doors lined either side, marked with names she didn't recognize. "These are some of the dressing rooms. You don't have one, sorry. There's hair and makeup. There's the green room."

"Why is it green?"

"I don't know, it's not green, that's just what they call it," Steve said. "Let's get you into wardrobe. Come on through here."

He led Pythia into an open space filled with garment racks of clothing. At one end were shelves full of shoes. She saw hats, gloves, belts, shawls, purses, ties, and underwear neatly folded in clear plastic bins. Two small dressing rooms made of thin white fiberboard stood on spindly legs next to a rack of hot pink leggings and over-sized white blouses. *Divina Dee's costumes.*

"Adina! She's here!" Steve called. He paused to check his appearance in a full-length mirror and fussed with the starched collar on his tailored white shirt.

A elfin woman hopped out from between two racks of clothes. She was wearing yellow silk pants so thin they were transparent, silver plastic shoes, and a long pink t-shirt with a big-eyed cartoon character printed on the front. "Here I am!" she said in a high breathy voice. "Is this the sister?"

"Yeah. Her name is Pith . . . Pish? What is it?"

"Pythia," said Pythia.

"Ah, Pythia, in honor of the original Python," Adina said, nodding. She danced a circle around Pythia, eyeing her body, humming a tuneless melody. "You allergic to synthetics?"

Adina grabbed some garments off a rack and led Pythia into one of the dressing rooms. "First, strapless bra and slip."

"Do I really need to change my undergarments?" Pythia asked.

"Fewer lines to show up on the camera. Are you shy? I'll wait out here. Pull this on, right? And then the dress. It wraps, right? Hooks on the sides, ties in front."

Pythia sighed and complied with Adina's instructions. The beige strapless bra and slip were combined to create one foundation garment, a step-in arrangement with two hooks in back, not as difficult to put on as it looked.

Resigned to her fate, she hung her own clothes on a hook, put on the first layer, and slipped her arms into the slinky pale blue dress. She wrapped one side over the other in front. It crossed just above the bra and hooked at both sides at the waist. A false belt tied at the waist and hung partway down her thigh. *This dress looks as if it were made to come off in a hurry.*

Adina flung open the wooden door and led Pythia over to the mirror. Steve sat on a plaid loveseat checking his phone. Adina said, "Voila! I present you to . . . yourself!"

Pythia risked a glance in the mirror and saw an unfamiliar thin dark-haired woman wearing a clingy pale blue dress that almost covered her knees. *Is that me? I look frumpy and exhausted.*

"Mission accomplished!" Adina clapped her hands.

Pythia didn't have the energy to comment. The brain fog seemed to be getting worse. *Hera is around here somewhere. Why will that silly goddess not find someone else to terrorize?*

"Yoo hoo, Pith, time for hair and makeup!" Steve leaped off the couch and clapped his hands. Pythia thanked Adina and followed Steve out of the wardrobe area back into the hall.

"Thirty minutes!" shouted Kat as she ran by, bumping Pythia. "Sorry! Wow, you look perfect!" she yelled over her shoulder.

Steve led her into the make-up booth, another room with four walls, a door, and no ceiling. He pointed at a swivel chair bolted to the floor. Pythia sat. In front of her was a large mirror framed by glowing light bulbs. "Karen, she's here!" he yodeled and sat in the other swivel chair, scrolling through his phone.

"Coming!" A woman with long hair and perfect makeup came into the booth. She was tall, dark-skinned, and clad in a chartreuse tailored wool business jacket and slacks. Her hair was pulled up into a curly lump on top of her head.

"Hi, Pythia. I'm Karen Scottsdale. I'll be doing your makeup and hair today." She grabbed a square of vinyl from a hook and draped it over Pythia's shoulders, pressing it closed at the back of the neck with sticky tape. She stood behind Pythia and peered at their combined reflection in the mirror. "Light blue, huh? Not your color." She tucked a stray curl into place in the lump on her own head. "All right, let's turn you into someone who needs to be made over."

Fifteen minutes later, Karen had patted Pythia's face with a gray foundation and topped the layer with a yellowish powder.

Steve looked up once or twice. When Karen had finished and stepped back to assess her work, Steve said, "Great job, Karen. She looks like hell!"

"Thank you," said Karen, pleased at the compliment. "Now let's see what I can do to ruin your hair."

In a few more minutes, Karen removed the protective cape and said, "You are now ready for your makeover, Pythia. I'll see you on the set pretty soon."

Pythia stared at her reflection. *I now look as sick as I feel.*

Steve snapped his fingers. "Let's go, Pith."

Pythia followed Steve out into the hallway. She saw Debra coming toward her with a concerned look on her face.

"God, you look like crap, Pythia. Are you feeling okay?"

Steve chortled. "Karen is a true artist."

Debra came closer and edged Steve out of the way. "Get lost for a minute, Steve." He tossed his head and disappeared around a corner.

Debra leaned toward Pythia and whispered, "Pythia, I have it."

"What? What do you have?"

"Coming through!" The two PAs, Ralph and Sid, shoved past Pythia and Debra, carrying two pink beanbag chairs.

"Pythia, here!" Debra held out something small. Pythia opened her hand. Debra dropped the amulet onto her palm.

In an instant, Pythia felt power flow into her like a flash flood rushing through a dry wash after a monsoon rain, like maple syrup dripping over a stack of warm pancakes, like the heat of the summer sun at Delphi. She gasped and enfolded the amulet in her hand. *Oh, my Lord God Apollo!*

"I couldn't find the cord that went with it," Debra said.

Pythia tucked the amulet into the strapless bra against her skin. The amulet pulsed with glorious energy. She took some deep breaths. Her stomach started to settle. She flexed her insight. The fog in her brain began to lift.

"You okay? What is that thing, anyway?"

Pythia grinned. "My secret power." On impulse, she gave Debra a quick hug. "Thank you, Debra. You have saved me. I feel much better now."

"You still look like crap," Debra said. Then she giggled and smacked her forehead. "Oh, yeah, hey. It's a makeover show. Duh!"

Steve returned, scowled at Debra, and hustled Pythia onto the set. She scanned the area, looking for Hera or Divina but saw neither. She recognized Delores, sitting in the front row of the audience bleachers fiddling with her camera.

Kat bounded onto the stage.

"These won't work," Kat shouted, pointing at the bean bag chairs. "What the hell are you guys thinking? Think Oracles, idiots. Didn't you read *The Iliad and the Odyssey?* Bring the stools!"

Ralph and Sid lugged the bean bag chairs off the stage, almost knocking over Adina who was coming through the doorway to the off-set area. Behind her came Divina Dee, the star of the show. Divina stood looking at the stage with her hands on her hips. She wore tight black jeans and a loose white shirt.

Ralph and Sid returned with two simple tall wooden stools.

"Put them there and there," Kat ordered. "What do you think, Divina? That going to work for you?" She turned back to the PAs. "Hey, where the hell are the fake rocks? Where's the fake crack? Come on, you guys!"

Divina grinned at Pythia. "Welcome to my world, my sister. Wow, they did a number on you, didn't they? You look like shit."

Pythia shrugged and smiled.

Divina leaned in a little closer and sniffed. "What have you got going on there, Sister?" she mused, frowning.

Ralph and Sid carried enormous fake boulders onto the stage and placed them by the two stools. Next they carried in a long narrow piece of wood that had been cut in a jagged shape and painted to resemble a crack in the floor. They laid it across the stage between the stools.

"Ten minutes, everyone!" Kat shouted. "Debra, let in the audience."

A minute later, a hundred people entered the sound stage and rushed to fill the bleachers, pushing and muttering, trying to get positions near the center aisle, side aisle, or in the front row. Debra wrangled them, checking off names on her clipboard and educating them on proper behavior during the show. Jimmy lurked behind his camera.

Divina looked at the set as if she'd never seen it before. She shook her head and chuckled. "Idiots. Stupid sheep. Look at them competing for the best seats."

"Where would you like me to sit, my sister?" Pythia said.

"You there, me here. I'm going to introduce you, just like we rehearsed, okay? We'll do the makeover part first. That will take two segments, with commercials in between, right? You don't have to say anything until we get to the audience participation part. They'll ask questions and you just say whatever comes to mind."

"I understand, my sister."

Divina pointed at the fake jagged crack on the floor between them and sniggered. "At least this one we can't fall into."

"One minute, people," Kat shouted.

The lights dimmed. A strong spotlight illuminated Divina and Pythia sitting on the two stools.

Steve handed Divina a microphone and backed away. Adina approached Pythia, holding up a tiny black microphone.

"I need to clip this to the neckline," Adina said. She clipped the mic in place. "Let me just smooth out these wrinkles." Her fingers began to rummage inside the neckline of Pythia's dress.

Shocked, Pythia moved her arm to push away Adina's roving fingers. Adina growled but backed off. *Apollo help me, she knows about the amulet!*

Adina whispered into her communication device.

"Three, two," Kat said, pointing at Divina.

Music played over a sound system. Jimmy moved the large camera on wheels in front of the stage. The audience murmured and mumbled with anticipation.

Pythia knew a red light over the camera lens indicated it was filming. She felt Divina sit up straight on her stool and lean toward the camera. *Amazing how her on-screen persona emerges when a red light glows.*

With her trademark energy, Divina opened the show. The audience applauded on cue. Pythia gazed into the spotlight. She did not turn around as a video played on the enormous screen behind the stage. She was busy focusing on the power of the amulet, hoping to build a protective barrier in her mind.

The introduction was short. After a commercial break, during which Divina stared in bemused silence at the floor, the show resumed. The lights dimmed and the sole spotlight came up. Pythia squinted against the bright light. Divina stood up and addressed the camera in a serious tone.

"We welcome you to a special makeover edition of Psychic to the Stars. This is the Pythia. My sister was famous in Greece for telling the future. Kings and queens came from everywhere around the ancient world to hear the prophecies of the great Pythia." *What is she doing? This was not in the script.*

Divina motioned to Pythia to stand up.

"We are going to transform my sister into the Oracle she once was. The frumpy bland creature you see before you will become the most powerful Oracle in the world. Then she will answer your questions and predict your future! Watch! First, the hair and makeup!"

Karen the makeup artist entered with measured steps as if she were in an Ethiopian bridal procession. She wore a long sleeveless gray gown and carried a tray of haircare items. Her bronze skin glowed in the spotlight.

"Hold still," Karen muttered at Pythia. Eerie flute music played as she quickly styled Pythia's hair and placed a crown of leaves and flowers on her head. Delores leaned in close with a camera perched on her shoulder.

Karen powdered Pythia's face, added some smoky eye shadow, and cheek blush. She applied foul-tasting lipstick with quick sure strokes. After a slow bow to Pythia, she backed away with her tray of beauty products. Pythia stared at Delores' camera, seeing a stranger reflected in the lens.

"Next, we remake the Oracle's robes!" Divina said into the mic. "Watch as we transform my sister into the Pythia, most feared and dreaded Oracle in all of ancient Greece."

Divina motioned to two staff members dressed in long gray robes. Their faces were masks of shiny white greasepaint. They stepped onto the stage holding a lightweight paper screen between them, blocking the audience's view of Pythia from her neckline to the floor. Adina crept behind it, out of view of the camera. She carried a pile of cloth over one arm.

"Shoes, quick!" Adina hissed. The flute music continued.

Pythia slipped her feet out of her shoes and stood barefoot on the stage. She saw her sister standing nearby but could not locate Delores. A crew member hustled the shoes away, hidden by the screen.

Adina jerked on the belt at Pythia's waist and pulled the dress backward, leaving Pythia standing in just the silk slip. Adina scuttled offstage with the dress. Delores popped up in front of her with the camera. Even though she knew only her head was visible above the screen, Pythia flinched.

"Pythia, stand fast. You are about to be restored to your former glory," Divina intoned into the mic. *Meaning, stop it and play your part.* The music began building to a crescendo.

Pythia held still as another assistant wrapped a length of wispy white linen around her torso and quickly added a leather strap contraption that no one in ancient Greece would ever have worn. The linen draped to the floor, leaving her shoulders bare and the leather straps crossed over her breasts. *Now I understand why Adina wanted a strapless bra and slip.*

Divina moved in front of the camera, facing the audience. "When we return, you will be astounded at this makeover of a three-thousand-year-old Oracle. Stay tuned."

When the red light went off, Divina bounded back onto the stage. "Pythia, sorry I didn't warn you. We thought it would be better if your reaction was natural."

"Of course, my sister. I understand. My apologies."

"Two minutes to air," Kat shouted. Crew members rushed around the set.

Karen returned with a powderpuff and dabbed at Divina's nose. The two assistants holding the screen complained about their arms. Pythia stood barefoot, trying not to look beyond the stage at the audience waiting in the bleachers. The amulet pulsed with heat against her skin. *Something is coming. I cannot see what it is, but I can feel it. The train in the tunnel. The bull in the lobby. The rider in the storm.*

"We are live in three, two," Kat said and pointed at Divina. The light on Jimmy's camera glowed red.

Divina moved up close to the camera. "We're back with our makeover of my sister, Pythia, a three-thousand-year Oracle. When we had to take a break, we were just about to reveal her to you. As you remember, we gave her new makeup and a new hairstyle. Now we are going to show you our made-over Oracle. Assistants, you may remove the screen!"

The assistants moved off stage, taking the screen with them. The applause sign went on. The audience applauded to a swell of music.

"Behold, the Pythia!" Divina said in a deep voice.

A harsh spotlight came up on Pythia. She recoiled.

"Be seated on your stool, Oracle," Divina commanded. "Assume the position! Where is our first supplicant?"

Pythia frowned at her sister. *Is she serious?*

Divina motioned with her head. Pythia sat on the stool. It wobbled slightly. *If this will make her happy, I will comply. It is a small thing to dress in a costume and pretend.*

Pythia raised her arms at shoulder height in front of her, ducked her head, and cupped her palms downward.

Divina moved behind her. Pythia felt a hand groping at her shoulder, reaching into her tunic.

"Where is it, Pythia?" Divina muttered into her neck. "Give me that thing."

Pythia shook her head. "I love you, my sister, but this is not acceptable," she said and grabbed her sister's hand.

The connection was instantaneous.

Pythia slipped into a flashback like slipping down a hill of mud into a freezing pond. One moment she was sitting on a wobbly stool under harsh lights, the next moment she was lying in her draped bed in Apollo's temple, clutching her belly in agony. *No, send me back! Apollo, help me, the pain.*

"Where am I?" she groaned, squinting her eyes. "Dione? Who . . . Namia, is that you?"

The young servant grabbed Pythia's arm. "Wake up, Pythia. Soldiers are in the temple. What would Apollo have us do?"

Pythia rolled from side to side with the pain. Her lower belly felt like she'd been stabbed through with a sword. "Dione, where is Dione?" She tasted pomegranates. *The wine.*

"We need you to pray to Apollo for us. You must intervene on our behalf. Tell us our future, Pythia. Will we live or die?"

"Where is my sister?"

"She's gone, Pythia. She has abandoned us, and soldiers are sacking the temple. Get up and tell us what to do."

"Go find my sister and tell her I am dying and she must save me."

"She did this to you, Oracle," Namia said. "You'll find no succor there." *Pomegranate wine had stained Dione's robe.*

"You lie. Oh, my Lord Apollo, the pain!"

"Oracle, do your duty. Tell us our future. Guide us to safety!"

"Find my sister, you wretched girl."

"Useless whore. The soldiers are outside. We are going."

Namia fumbled at the girdle around Pythia's waist. "What are you doing?" Pythia gasped.

"You will have no need of this, and the jewels may save my life. Farewell, Oracle." Namia fled through the bed drapes.

Screams echoed across the hall, cut short. She recognized the voices of other servants. Pythia parted the linen drapes and crawled out of her bed onto the floor. A few steps further, she found a body lying inert across the marble steps.

"Ami, Ami, help me." She shook the woman's hip.

"Greetings, little Oracle," the woman grinned. "A little too much wine, I fear." She fell back, senseless.

Pythia's limbs felt heavy and slow. The stabbing pain in her gut sapped her strength. Her mind was fogged, her foresight leaden. As she reached for her insight to read the future, she felt her power split and tear apart. Her insight receded behind a dark veil and shrank to a nub. The gushing fount that had always appeared at her command shredded into tatters. Something bad was coming but she knew no more than any mortal who smelled blood, breathed smoke, and heard screams.

She felt rather than saw someone large coming up behind her. A heavy hand grabbed the back of her tunic, lifted her, and dangled her in the air. Feet kicking, she tried to scream but could only whimper.

"Hello, little fox," growled a voice in her ear.

"Dione, help me!"

"She will not come, Oracle."

"Galenos, is that you?" Pythia squirmed. She smelled wine on his breath. "You are drunk. I am ill. Let me go."

"Speak, little Oracle. Tell me, will I win the competition tomorrow?"

"You have lost your mind, Galenos. Who told you to do this?"

The soldier leered at her. "Your sister, that is who! You've lost your powers, have you not, little Oracle? What good are you now?"

"This is madness. She would never hurt me. Dione, where are you, save me!" Pythia kicked weakly as another soldier ran past them, laughing and hoisting a spear into the air. In his other arm, he carried a basket overflowing with gold and silver baubles.

"Apollo's day is done, Oracle. Make way for new gods."

Pythia vomited on the marble floor.

Galenos released her tunic. She dropped in a boneless heap. "Stay out of the way if you want to live." Galenos followed his comrade.

A slow paralysis claimed her limbs. Pythia settled in her vomit, gasping shallow breaths, and waited for death. Two of her fellow acolytes crossed the hall. She recognized Cleosa and Rose, two junior servants in the temple. They scuffed closer in their jute sandals.

"Oh, look, here's the Pythia." Cleosa stood over her with bright eyes and a malicious leer on her round face. Both young servants wore jewelry not theirs to wear.

"She looks in a bad way," Rose said, poking Pythia with her toe. Pythia moaned.

"So sad," said Cleosa. She waved at a group of passing soldiers. "Look. Here lies the Pythia."

The soldiers approached. They stood with the acolytes in a circle around Pythia and contemplated her plight as they passed a goatskin of wine.

"Is she dying?" asked someone wearing dusty leather sandals. Pythia could no longer raise her head.

"Should we have a little fun with her?" asked a man with a bloody toe.

"Well, I do not know. If it as she says, this is the Pythia, then perhaps it would not be a good idea."

"You can have a little fun with me," said Rose.

"How can this be the Pythia?" his friend argued. "Would she not have foreseen this and avoided it? Nah, this must be a serving wench who drank too much wine."

"I tell you, this is the Pythia!" Cleosa insisted.

"Well, I will have no part of her. She is lying in her own filth. Let us take someone willing. This one is worthless."

Pythia heard shouting in the hall.

"Apollo's men are coming!"

Cleosa bent down near Pythia's face.

"You are no longer the most powerful Oracle in Greece, Pythia. Your sister has destroyed you with a poison. We are going now to her temple."

"Dione," Pythia whispered on a thin breath.

"You will die soon, Oracle."

"Cleosa, come on!" cried Rose.

Sandals scuffed away. Pythia was alone. She rested, focusing on her breathing, feeling a numb heaviness settle where her oracular sense used to be. She waited, resigned. At last the pain in her gut was receding and with it her worldly cares. Death might not be so bad. *I have died before, have I not? Is this real? Or am I in a trance? Was I not in a television studio . . . With my sister . . . ? Yes, in a place called California.*

The scent of lavender wafted near her nose. A gentle hand touched her shoulder, although she saw no one.

"Dione," she sighed with relief.

"No, my Oracle. Your sister has betrayed you at the behest of my enemy. Dione is dead to you now. Sleep. Let these sad memories fade. There will be time for all things, including a reckoning. For now, rest, my beloved Oracle. Be at peace."

Pythia sank into deep darkness.

. . . And emerged from the darkness three thousand or so years later, give or take a few centuries, in a TV studio in Hollywood, California. In front of the avid uncaring eyes of a randomly chosen studio audience, and in front of her sister, her beloved sister who had poisoned her almost to death, Pythia emerged into the light, and with it came her memory.

Like the clearest vision at the peak of her power, Pythia remembered the pain and fear of that terrible day. She recalled the soldiers laughing and gloating, drunk on the temple wine, desecrating the altars, defiling the Oracles. She remembered Namia's fear and the taunts of her fellow acolytes. Worst of all, she recalled the taste of the poisoned pomegranate wine, which she drank unknowing as Dione looked on. She understood now the strange combination of resentment, fear, and regret on Dione's face.

Pythia leaped off the stool and faced her sister. Divina stood back in alarm.

"Pythia, what—?"

"Why did you not just tell me?"

"Tell you what? You don't like that powder color? That's okay, we have lots of others." Divina smirked at the audience and put her hand on Pythia's arm.

Pythia shook her off. "I trusted you, Dione. I was your sister. I would have willingly died for you. You had only to ask."

"Oh." Divina looked around the set, frowning.

"You poisoned me. You tried to kill me."

"Do we have to do this now? Gods, Pythia, can't this wait?" Divina waved at Debra, who was standing frozen next to Kat. "Where is Hera? Tell her I—"

"You abandoned me to them, Dione. To the soldiers who sacked the temple. Your servants laughed at me as I lay dying on the floor."

"Oh, don't be so melodramatic. Clearly, you lived."

Divina turned to the audience members, who were watching spellbound. "My sister and I are fighting over a little thing that happened a long time ago."

"You almost killed me, Dione. Your own sister!"

"Let's go to a commercial break now while we soothe my sister's histrionics and see if we can get on with our fortune-telling."

As soon as the director motioned all clear and the red light was off, Divina turned to Debra and screamed, "Find that goddamn witch Hera before I feed you to the wild wolves of Mt. Parnassus!"

Debra dropped her clipboard and ran in the direction of the green rooms, yelling, "Ms. Hera!" Ralph and Sid scrambled after her.

Karen backed up, shaking her head. "I can't work under these conditions. My agent will be in touch." She picked up her makeup kit and marched off the set.

Kat was gesturing at Divina from behind the main camera. "One minute to air," she warned.

"Well, hell," Divina Dee said, standing with her hands on her hips. "Pythia, you self-righteous prig, why couldn't you have waited just a little longer? Maybe like two more years. Two years would have been good. I could have settled here, become a mover and a shaker, built a West coast following. We could have eased into it slowly."

"Eased into what, my sister? Eased into my remembering that you stole my gift and tried to kill me?"

"Ten seconds to air!" shouted Kat.

"Pythia, we don't have time for this. Sit on the damn stool until the show is done. Then we can fight."

Pythia thinned her lips but climbed onto the stool.

"And three, two . . ." Jimmy pointed at Divina. She turned toward the camera. The red light over the camera appeared.

"Welcome back to the Psychic to the Stars, where we were in the process of discussing the future with an actual Oracle, my sister, Pythia. After her makeover, Pythia went into a psychic trance, as you could see. That was bizarre, huh? Pythia, would you like to tell us what you saw in your vision?"

Pythia looked at Divina in silence.

Divina growled. "Pythia, all these good folks and all the people watching at home are wondering what tomorrow holds. They live their lives in fear of the future. Can you give them some assurance?"

"My sister, everyone knows what their future holds. There is no great mystery knowable only by Oracles."

"While Pythia sorts herself out, let's take some questions from our studio audience," Divina said, hopping off the stage and ascending the steps into the bleachers. She grabbed a mic from a production assistant and thrust it into the red face of a large white woman. "Hi, welcome to the show. Isn't this exciting? What do you want to know about your future, Ma'am? Ask the Pythia your question."

"Will my husband cheat on me?"

Pythia rolled her eyes. "Yes, most likely."

Delores moved in for a close-up. "But you aren't sure?" asked the woman.

"He is already cheating on you. Her name is Brenda. If you are asking this question, it is because you already know the answer and are unwilling to face the truth."

The woman fell into her seat, mouth hanging open. Delores paused in front of her to see what else she would do. The woman held up a fist, and Delores backed off.

"Ooh, harsh, Pythia," Divina snickered. She paused next to a sandy-haired man in a plaid shirt and blue jeans. "You sir, what is your question for the Oracle?"

"Uh, yes, can you tell me, who will be the next president?"

"Not the person you plan to vote for," Pythia said.

"But—"

"Hey, sorry, dude, you can't argue with an Oracle," Divina said, moving further up the aisle, leaving the man sputtering. Delores trailed in her wreckage, camera rolling.

A tall black woman grabbed the microphone from Divina's hand and stood up, towering over the TV host.

"I want to know when systemic racism will be erased in this country!"

"Never," Pythia said. "It will never go away."

"Say, Pythia, give them some hope, will you?" Divina laughed, taking the mic back from the furious open-mouthed woman. "We need to hear some good news, right?" She addressed the entire audience. "It can't all be bad."

"I just want to know what will happen next," cried a pudgy pale woman in a magenta dress. "I can't stand not knowing!"

The audience muttered in agreement. Divina hopped up and down in place, ecstatic, dreadlocks quivering. Kat gave Divina a thumbs-up. Delores swung her camera around to capture the energy in the bleachers. People were on their feet.

"Yeah, tell us the future!" someone yelled.

"Come on, you can't keep it from us."

"Tell us, tell us! Tell us what is going to happen!"

Pythia scanned the bleachers for a long moment, then slowly rose to her feet. She raised her arms in the classic pose of the ancient Oracle she once was. Her hands were claws, rigid with tension. She closed her eyes and threw her head back. She waited, and after a few long tense moments, the audience fell silent, anxious and unnerved.

Pythia called upon her voice, the voice she once used to make proclamations to the ancient world's mightiest leaders, that they might win their wars and save their kingdoms.

"I am Apollo's Oracle. I have seen the future. I withhold nothing. It is the same for all of you. You are all going to die."

Pythia lowered her arms and resumed her seat on the stool.

After a shocked silence, the audience gasped and mumbled in protest.

"What! You're insane!"

"Crazy bitch oughta be locked up."

"Yeah, lock her up!"

"You're nuts," the woman in magenta said, outraged. "Where do you get off? Roy, tell her!"

Her husband gave her a disgusted look and stood up.

"Well, Sylvia, in your case, she's right!" he said and pulled a gun from his waistband and raised it in the air. "I am fed up with all your bullshit yammering day in and day out! All you do is talk smack about my family, never a good word to say! And I'm really sick and tired of your godawful meatloaf!"

At the sight of the gun, the audience members in the vicinity of the couple began screaming and scrambling over seats to escape, stepping on the shoulders and laps of people who were slower to move.

In short order, the area around the man and his wife had cleared, and people jammed in a pile at the exits. A couple brave souls had their phones out to record the melee. Delores zoomed in for close-ups.

The woman in magenta stayed seated. She put her head in her hands. "Roy, stop it, you are embarrassing me."

Her husband turned toward her, gun wilting. Two security guards in black Psychic to the Stars t-shirts rushed the man and tackled him. All three fell over the backs of seats in a grunting heap. The gun went off once with a muffled pop.

Two other security guards hustled over to Divina, lifted her off her feet despite her protests, and carried her onto the stage away from the bleachers.

As the security guards marched Roy toward the exit, he said, "I'm sorry, I didn't know it was loaded! Sylvia, I'm sorry!"

"Put me down! Was anyone hurt?" Divina said, dusting off her black jeans. She motioned to her guards to back off and looked around the studio.

Steve looked down at a large splotch of pink paint on his white shirt. "Goddammit! I've been shot!"

Jimmy hunkered behind his camera, still filming. He had an unlit cigarette between his grinning lips.

Kat yelled, "Great job, guys!" She pointed to the smiling producers in the glassed-in viewing booth at the back of the bleachers.

Debra had retrieved her clipboard. She approached the stage. "The press is outside, Ms. Dee," she said. "And I can't find Ms. Hera."

Divina waved her hand. "She doesn't matter. Pythia stole the show! Awesome! Somebody let the press in!"

The doors burst open and a small mob of journalists flooded in, trailing their camera operators and sound crews. Pythia recognized some famous local newscasters. They rushed at Divina, waving microphones.

"How did they get here so fast?" Steve asked, staring at globs of pink paint on his fingers.

"Because I called them!"

Everyone turned to see Hera strolling across the stage, as if she had materialized from thin air. Her personal hair stylist followed close behind, a mini-version of Hera, dressed in black from head to toe, waving a comb. She paused for a moment to allow the man to sweep her black hair back in dramatic fashion. The white streak glowed. Then she elbowed him aside. Her black skirt swirled around her calves as she posed with one hand in the air.

"You are welcome!" she smiled, showing sharp white teeth. A black wand appeared in her hand. "Look, new Vinzendos," she announced, turning her foot to the side to display a glittering black pump. She pointed the wand around the room as if she were deciding which person to destroy. The wand landed on Steve the intern.

"Don't think I'm not grateful," Divina began.

"What is this doing here? I thought I . . ." said Steve, twisting open a large green bottle that looked like it might hold perfume. He reared back. The stench of asphalt, tar, diesel fumes, road grime, methane, and sulfur poured out into the air with a wallop.

"Oh, gross!" Steve said, holding the bottle at arm's length in disgust. He rounded on Hera. "You said this was Givenchy."

Hera threw her head back and cackled.

The staff ran off the stage, pinching their noses. The members of the press began to cough and gag.

"Oh, no," said Divina, turning toward Pythia.

No use holding my breath. The last thing Pythia saw before her trance slammed her into darkness was Hera's laughing face.

&

Chaotic images unrolled at blinding speed, too fast to comprehend, like a sped-up movie, a thousand frames per second. Pythia lost all sensation in her body. She felt as if she were flying through darkness, feet disconnected from the earth, as images flowed past her and receded behind.

Talk about powerlessness. Apollo, help! I fear this might hurt. The future was riding her against her will. No, make that multiple futures, clawing at the inside of her skull. Bile rose in her throat. She choked, tasting gasoline, and spat a prediction at random: "There will be an earthquake in San Francisco in 2026," she groaned.

Someone bumped her, then grabbed her hand and squeezed hard. *Could that be Apollo? Am I saved?* Her eyes would not open, no matter how she strained to see.

She held onto the hand as if it were an anchor in a storm. Then the grip tightened beyond the point of pain. She tried and failed to shake free. Her eyes seemed glued shut. *Why can I not see?*

A voice proclaimed, "Climate change will create an army of climate refugees, who will move inland and take over entire cities. Seattle will fall to Spokane." *I know that voice. Better than I know my own.*

Pythia twisted her hand, gagging on methane gas. Another image usurped her brain. She barked, "The simplicity movement will gain momentum and then fade away in 2020!"

She felt sweet hot breath on her cheek. Dione intoned, "Pandemic! A terrible virus will kill millions around the world!"

In desperation, Pythia began to squeeze Dione's hand as hard as she could. "U.S. citizens will storm the U.S. capitol!"

"At the instigation of a U.S. president!" Dione declared.

"The color of 2025 will be lavender puce!" Pythia yelped.

"Bellbottoms will return but they will be called sweepers!" Dione proclaimed and giggled.

Pythia used her free hand to grab a hank of Dione's long dreadlocks. "A volcano will erupt in Malaysia," Pythia said. "No, wait. Indonesia. No, wait. It is both! It will rain pumice and ash for days. Let go!"

Dione released her hand but managed to poke Pythia in the eye. Grunting, Pythia yanked hard on a handful of spongy hair.

"Ow, Hurricane Seymour will devastate Miami. Ow, stop it, Pythia!"

Pythia felt Dione's hand rummaging in her own hair. Pythia opened her eyes and realized she was back in her body in the TV studio, one hand wrapped in Divina's dreadlocks. She let go as Divina ripped the crown of flowers off Pythia's head.

Divina's eyes opened. She let go of the crown and said, "Oops."

"Well, that was entertaining."

The sisters turned, breathing hard, and recoiled in surprise.

During their trance, Hera had used the interlude to make a costume change. She wore a different black dress and designer heels. However, she appeared to be ten feet tall, and somehow during the commotion, she had grown a set of black feathered wings. Her new wings fluttered as her floating hair scraped the lighting canisters hanging above the stage.

"Whoa, are those wings?" Debra said in awe just as Hera swept a wing and knocked Debra into the camera pit.

Pythia advanced on Hera. "Hera, this is not your place or time."

"Oh, yes?" Hera sneered. "Little broken Oracle, who are you to tell me, a goddess of Mt. Olympus, whether this is my place and time? You pathetic pawn of a pathetic god!"

Hera pointed her black wand at Pythia. Pythia had just enough time to think *Where did she get shoes that big?* before she found herself on the floor next to Debra.

"Hey, that's my sister, you decrepit hag!" Divina yelled and launched herself at Hera. With another flash of her wand, Hera swept Divina into the base of Jimmy's camera.

Jimmy helped Divina to her feet. Divina helped Pythia up.

"You okay?" Divina asked Pythia. They both helped Debra stand up. They all staggered to the front row of the bleachers and collapsed into seats.

"Ms. Dee, can you tell us what is going on?" asked a wide-eyed woman carrying a microphone decorated with the logo of a local TV station.

Divina looked worn out. A paper clip, a bottle cap, and a small plastic cup were embedded in her hair. When she didn't respond, Pythia pointed at the stage. "The show continues."

December 23, 2015

Blog Readers, you may have heard, the television show was a catastrophe. Later, some grips blamed the air conditioning. Others said a skylight blew out. Some credited ley lines.

The director said it looked as if two whirlwinds came through the roof and started twisting around each other on the stage. One whirlwind was black, the other gold, and together they stirred up quite a breeze. Sheets of paper, napkins, empty plastic cups and bottles, a couple crows, and my crown of flowers—it all lifted off the ground and began to swirl around the sound stage.

Poor Steve the intern got caught and hurled off to the side. He was all right, though, just a bit winded. Debra seemed to be in shock, unaware that she had a broken wrist.

I sat next to my sister, and we watched the last two gods on the earth (as far as I know) battle for supremacy on a Hollywood sound stage.

"You hurt my hand," Dione complained.

"I am sorry, my sister," I apologized. "But in all fairness, you did try to kill me."

"That was a long time ago, Pythia. Can't we just forget it?"

I had to ponder that one, Blog Readers. Could I accept the idea of forgiving my sister, even though she poisoned me? I thought I could feel my heart soften a little.

"Maybe," I said. We ducked as a flurry of plastic bottles flew past our heads.

"I was envious, Pythia. Everyone loved you. You had all the power and strength. I was nothing. I hated you for having all that power."

"You were a pawn of Hera, Dione, just as I was a pawn of Apollo."

"I was such a fool. I thought it was my idea but it was Hera's all along. She made the poison and showed me how much to put in the wine."

"But you spilled some."

"How did you know that?"

"I saw the stains on your robe. And I know you, Dione. You are my sister. Everyone kept saying you poisoned me but I refused to believe them. In fact, I rejected Apollo when he told me of your betrayal."

"Well, you were wrong. I did try to poison you. It was pure luck that you lived. What happened to your shoes?"

"I know you, Dione. You did not want me to die. Hera did, but you did not. And it was not luck. Apollo found me at the end. He saved me, but he told me what you had done. I refused to believe him. I wandered the earth for millennia believing you were dead and that Apollo had abandoned me, when in truth, I had abandoned him. Now that I think about it, I am not sure he knew about Hera. He always had a blind spot for family."

"That wretched Apollo!"

"Well, he is still quite a warrior," I said, nodding toward the battle raging on the stage.

"Hera is no slouch."

"No, but they are both too old to keep this up for long."

The noise echoing on the sound stage was deafening. The twisters circled each other, occasionally bumping and overlapping. However, the two entities seemed to be losing speed, although neither one had slowed enough to be visible in their human forms. I could hear them muttering, though. Laboring breaths were audible under the patter of debris raining around the sound stage.

The two stools spun into the rafters above the backstage area. The fake wood crack went airborne and smacked the wall next to the viewing room, causing several producers to duck under their chairs.

Dione sighed. "That bitch Hera played me over and over, then and now."

"She controls the threads of your life."

"Not anymore. I'd rather die than hurt you again."

We ended up holding hands. Gently, of course, because our bones are old and brittle.

What happened back in Delphi was this, according to Dione, who I admit might not be telling me the entire truth. Hera had always hated Apollo because of a family thing that happened a long time ago. You might have heard the story. It is rather famous. If you ever had to read classic Greek literature in secondary school, you will recognize the tale.

Essentially, Hera's husband was fooling around, and Apollo was one of the outcomes. There were other gods and goddess involved, but all that was long before my time, and it is still none of my business. Suffice it to say, Hera has carried a lot of animosity toward Apollo for the sins of his father. By the time Dione and I were consecrated to Apollo's temple, Hera had figured out a strategy to bring Apollo down.

Hera got her hooks into Dione when my sister was quite young, almost as soon as we arrived at Delphi. Hera had been waiting for a certain type of acolyte, and when Dione showed up, she knew she had found her pawn. Dione, the ambitious poor farmer's daughter, was susceptible to the promise of riches and fame.

When I was at the height of my power, they hatched a plan. Dione pretended to foresee disaster, warning of an impending attack on the temple. In fact, she and Hera were the instigators of the attack. Dione's plan was to put me out of commission for a while. She planned to depart before the problem became acute.

Hera's plan was to put me out forever. She helped Dione prepare a poison in a bowl of pomegranate wine. Dione made sure I drank most of it and then left me, thinking I would eventually recover but be ruined as an Oracle. Under cover of darkness, and under Hera's protection, she took her handmaidens and departed to start her own temple in another part of Greece.

Since the day in the TV studio, I have regained more of my memories. I recall Apollo trying to warn me not to trust Dione. After the sack of the temple, Apollo tried to tell me what had happened, that Dione gave me poison. I refused to believe. I spurned my Lord Apollo. I ran away and lived in the margins of society like an animal. I had lost my senses. Nobody knew I was the Pythia. I remember walking hundreds of miles across Greece, looking for Dione, my beloved sister. Hera kept me from finding her. Apollo followed me and protected me.

The battle on the sound stage between Hera and Apollo was not one of the greats, as battles between gods go. I am certain neither would admit it, but I am guessing they are long past their prime. I could not see them clearly—they were fighting in a haze of color and sound. We saw flares of yellow and white fire ricochet off the swirling figures and burst into sparks on the floor. We could hear them grunting at each other as they lobbed their fizzling little fireballs and energy missiles.

My beloved Apollo's voice betrayed his irritation. He sounded weary and winded. "You old bitch, why don't you let it go?"

"You are an embarrassment." Hera spun a dark missile where I assumed Apollo's head would be, if he were to take solid form.

The fireball halted suddenly and fizzled out, although I could see no hands catching it. "Embarrassment to whom? To you? So my father cheated on you. Get over it!"

"You and your sister should not have been born!"

Apollo radiated a wall of golden light toward Hera. "Well, you are persistent, Hera, I have to give you that. All these years! Why don't you go get some Botox or something. Get a massage. A mani-pedi. Let it go!"

She warded off the light with a sweep of a hazy black wing. "And leave you to muck around here on Earth by yourself? Not a chance."

"Hera, we are too old for this."

Even before the two beings finally shuddered to a stop, they were wheezing and stumbling. At last, there they stood, two ten-foot tall entities quivering on a sound stage littered with paper cups and plates, tissues, pizza boxes, and pages torn from Steve's latest script.

Hera's hair was disheveled, her dress was ripped up one side, and her wings were tattered. She was furious. I had seen that look of rage before, when she was frozen in mid-lunge on a copper throne in a hotel banquet room. Mainly, I believe she was angry that her designer shoes got scuffed in the fracas. She kept checking her footwear.

The good news is, I finally laid eyes on my beautiful Lord God Apollo. Not quite as golden and smooth as I remembered but still a welcome sight for my lonely eyes. His curls were somewhat singed. His tunic seemed to be smoldering. I cared naught. I was ecstatic. What a sight to behold after almost three thousand years in exile. I waited for him to notice me, but he seemed exhausted and perhaps not in the mood for an old acolyte who had been less than faithful.

I was tapped out myself, to be honest. Hera's violence left us all with bruises. In any case, it was enough to know he existed. Apollo lives! I have seen him with my own eyes. Even as I write this, my heart swells with joy.

Within a few seconds, both he and Hera melted into mist, leaving a few small fires and many shocked witnesses. I am not sure who won the battle, but for now, they both seem to have retreated. My sister says she has not heard from Hera, and I believe she speaks the truth.

By the way, the story of the sack of the temple and the rape of the Oracles—the way you might have heard it told isn't quite the truth. Even though I lay dying, I could see what was happening. Some soldiers got drunk and stole some things. It happens. Some Oracles were ravished in the chaos, but none who did not want to be. Over the centuries, poets wrote about the incident, and it got a lot of bad press.

Meanwhile, I pray Apollo will reach out to me. No matter what comes, I am content to know he exists.

—Yours in exile no longer, Delphina

Pythia tuned into the local news the day after the battle of the gods, curious to see how the reporters would spin their stories. The local television news anchors were unusually reticent about discussing the phenomenon they witnessed that day on the Psychic to the Stars set. For some reason, their cameras caught only blurry pops of sound and color.

Despite Jimmy's valiant efforts to film the battle, the Psychic to the Stars cameras did not do any better. Eye witness accounts of journalists were subdued, focusing mainly on Roy, as if they had collectively agreed to downplay their experiences.

"Wow, what a show, Grace!" said the blonde anchor of the Daily Breeze lifestyle cable network out of Burbank, California. "Divina Dee's show Psychic to the Stars was interrupted briefly by a man pulling a gun on the studio audience!"

"That's right, Camilla," said her co-anchor. "Roy Burpee was booked into the county jail after the incident. During his arraignment, he said he didn't plan to hurt anyone. It was only a paint gun. He said he just wanted his wife to cook steak once in a while."

Chapter 18

On Christmas Eve, with Louise's permission, Pythia invited the tenants of the office building to a brunch meeting. Louise had laid out a simple buffet of scrambled eggs, bacon, roasted potatoes, and toast. Frank and Helen sat across from Pythia, looking anxiously at their food. Louise topped off their coffees and sat down in front of her own plate of eggs and bacon.

"Thank you, Louise, for giving us a lovely place to meet," Pythia said. "I have some announcements—and a proposal."

The tenants sat in silence, staring at their plates. The food smelled delicious but no one seemed to feel like eating. Pythia could see the tension in their postures.

"First, as you all know, I have closed my coaching business. It was not doing well for a long time, and after Debra left, there seemed to be no point in keeping it going."

"We're sorry to see it close, Pythia," Frank said.

Pythia nodded. "Second, our building is old and needs renovations."

"We knew it would eventually," Frank said. Helen nodded, poking at her eggs with worry lines on her forehead.

"Third, I have been doing a great deal of thinking. I do not want to reopen my coaching business, or any business, but I do not want to sell this building and destroy our homes."

"Oh, my God, Pythia, please don't sell," Helen said. "Where would we go?"

"We can't afford to buy the building from you outright, Pythia," Frank said. "Maybe we could work out some sort of payment plan?"

Louise stared at her plate, looking grim.

Pythia smiled. "Please, my friends, there is another way. In the spirit of the giving season, I have a proposal. I have talked to my advisor and given this a lot of thought." *My spiritual advisor, that is. Lena gave it her blessing.* Pythia felt genuine joy as she said, "I would like to make you all joint owners in a new venture. A building co-op."

The tenants stared at her.

"How would that work, exactly?" Frank said.

Louise said, "Frank and Helen would like to expand into your old office space."

"That's true. What about you, Louise?" Helen said. "Would you want to take over Stacy's studio?"

All eyes turned to Pythia.

"In this co-op, we would all be joint owners. Four owners, equal shares. We propose ideas and we vote."

"Will you draw up a proposal?" Frank said, starting to grin.

"I will. In the meantime, I would like to suggest we name our co-op in honor of Stacy and call it The Goat Block. Let's meet next week and talk some more."

Christmas Eve at the Wild West Arcade kept Pythia and Lena busy from opening to closing.

"You'd think they would want to be at home, tucked in bed, waiting for Santa," Lena said, as they took a short break from hustling desserts for weary parents and excited kids. "I know you say you aren't a Christian, but don't you love this season? It's so festive!"

Pythia smiled. "How are things going with your mother?"

"I am so happy we found the Senior Sanchez center. My mother loves that place. They've got her doing arts and crafts.

She even played Bingo. I couldn't believe it. The hoity-toity Madame B, playing Bingo."

"I had no idea how competitive a sport Bingo is," Pythia said. "I am glad your mother is adapting. How are you doing?"

"Surprisingly well, actually. I think I finally surrendered to the idea that I'm not my mother's higher power!" Lena rolled her eyes. "It's so humbling. Once I let go, I realized that I need to enjoy the life we have together, as it is, without regretting the past or trying to get her to change."

Pythia nodded. "She is lucky to have you."

"I'm lucky to have her," Lena said, massaging a foot. "What about you? It sounds like that TV thing was a total fiasco. Are you ever going to tell me what happened?"

"You saw the news. A man pulled a paint gun. It was exciting for a few minutes. Then it seems there was some kind of problem with the air conditioning system. Papers and trash started flying all over the place. It was a huge mess."

"I hope they air it someday, as a blooper or something." Lena took off her white cowboy hat and inspected it for crumbs and stains. Kids sometimes threw pizza and cookies.

"My sister told me the show was cancelled, so I do not think we will ever see it."

"You didn't get your makeover!"

"My sister said she would take me shopping. We have plans to meet at the Santa Monica Mall the day after Christmas. She is going to give me a new look."

"I can't wait to see that. You've lost weight. You look great. Now is the time." Lena massaged the other foot. "God, my feet hurt. Say, have you got the stolen identity thing resolved yet?"

"I think so. The bank has released my accounts, so I have access to my funds. They still do not know who the thief was."

"But you do."

"Yes, thanks to Debra's sleuthing, I am pretty sure I know who it was. Someone who used to work with my sister. That person is gone now."

"Your sister should compensate you for all the trouble her employee put you through."

"I would not call the mischief maker an employee. More like an advisor."

"Mischief maker! What a quaint way to put it. That person was a thief! I hope they get what is coming to them. What goes around comes around. Karma is a bitch."

"Happy Christmas, Lena, my friend," Pythia smiled. She settled her white cowboy hat firmly in place and stood up.

"And merry ho ho to you too!" Lena said, slipping her sneakers back on. "Let's get more sugar into these rugrats so their parents will have a Christmas to remember!"

"It's time for your makeover, my sister. Long overdue." Divina pointed to Pythia's worn beige linen jacket.

They sat at a small round table in the foyer area of Macy's at the enormous three-story enclosed Santa Monica Mall. The place was packed with after-holiday shoppers swarming in search of markdowns. "You need some new duds."

Pythia smiled into her coffee. "Of course, my sister. As you wish." *She is still as annoying as ever, but I am so glad she is back.*

"How do you feel about a onesy? I could see you in a black leather catsuit."

"Are you sad that your show was cancelled?" Pythia asked.

"No, I was tired of it anyway." Divina tore open a sugar packet and emptied it into her coffee. "I was thinking about pitching a property investment reality show. To a different network, of course. The Psychics Network isn't too happy with us right now. We totally trashed their set."

"In exchange for making me over into a twenty-first century fashion plate, would you like me to teach you how to drive?"

Divina looked alarmed. "No, thanks, I'm happy to let Arnie keep driving." She took a bite of chocolate croissant and grinned with chocolate-smeared teeth. "Can you imagine me driving that limo?"

"Speaking of trouble, do you hear anything from she who shall remain nameless?" Pythia asked.

"Crazy-ass Hera?" Divina laughed when Pythia made shushing motions. "Relax, I haven't seen or heard anything. She's a two-bit washed-up has-been. She's probably gone back to Mt. Olympus to lick her wounds, by that I mean get her nails and hair done and spend some quality time by the pool admiring her designer shower sandals. I imagine Apollo is doing something similar. They can continue their fight there. I'm glad to be shut of them both."

"As you say," Pythia said. *I am not so sure.* "Although Apollo is not the type to cut and run. I would not have said Hera was either."

"Do you still have that amulet your friend gave you?"

"The one you stole from me?" Pythia smiled. "I gave it back to my friend. I do not think I need it anymore, do you?" She reached out her hand. Hands clasped, they smiled at each other. *Does she know my friend is her part-time chauffeur?*

"Yeah, I don't think I want to kill you anymore." Divina wiped her fingers with a paper napkin and leaped to her feet. "Come on, Sis. Let's start in the shoe department."

Soon they were strolling among the displays in women's shoes. Pythia watched with fond affection as Divina wandered. *Thank you, Apollo, for bringing back my sister.*

"These would be so cute on you!" Divina said, holding up a royal blue spike heel shoe.

"They would go nicely with my Wild West Arcade uniform," Pythia smiled.

Divina put the shoe back on the rack. "Are you going to keep working there? You know you can always come work for me at the property development company."

"I know, and I appreciate that, my sister. For now, I am content."

"All those kids!" Divina shuddered. "I don't know how you stand it."

Pythia sniffed the air. "Do you smell something odd?"

Divina inhaled. "No, what? I don't smell anything."

"I smell trouble, Sister," Pythia said, looking around. She saw several customers browsing the shoe displays but none who seemed suspicious. "Something is coming."

"All I smell is leather and shoe polish. Relax. Look at these flats, these would suit your laid-back California style. Great, here's a salesperson." Divina held up the display shoe to the tall, dark haired woman approaching them. "Excuse me, Miss, do you have these in a size . . . what are you, Pythia? Eight?"

The air around the salesperson seemed to be shimmering. Pythia's stomach was doing flip-flops. "My sister, prepare for battle," Pythia said.

The salesperson shook back her mane of black hair. "Yes, listen to your sister, stupid fake Oracle," she said, morphing into Hera. "Those shoes are so last season. I require your services, Oracle of Delphi. Not you, the real one. It will just take a few minutes. Then you losers can get back to shopping the bargain racks."

"Hey, you can't just barge in here and interrupt our shopping excursion," Divina said, scowling. "Haven't you heard? Your day is done. Begone!"

Hera showed her sharp white teeth. "I'll decide when my day is done, you miserable maggot."

"Hey, I served you for almost three thousand years!" Divina protested. "This is the thanks I get?"

"You were expecting perhaps a pension? A 401K? An itty-bitty retirement fund? Take this severance package as a token of my esteem!" A wand materialized in her hand. "Two-bit washed-up has-been indeed. Pension *this.*" She waved the wand, and Divina flew toward the ceiling as if she'd been shot from a cannon.

Divina cried, "Pythia!" before she evaporated into nothing.

Pythia contemplated the future. Not much was coming clear. *I am not afraid. If this is the day we die, so be it.* Pythia put her hands on her hips. "What is on your mind, Hera?"

"You ridiculous human, I despise that I have to admit this, but I need you. You used to be the most powerful Oracle in the ancient world."

"Yes, I was, until you persuaded my sister to poison me."

"Boo hoo. You survived, obviously, and you've managed to stay alive all these years. You must have some power. Tell me what I want to know, Oracle, and I'll refrain from killing you."

"Hera, I am sorry, I simply no longer have the ability to see clearly into the future. Sometimes I can see small things, but often I see nothing at all."

"Miserable human, what do I have to do to convince you I am not joking?"

"What did you do to my sister, Hera?"

"I threw her into another dimension."

Pythia pulled against Hera's grip. "Surely you realize you will not get my cooperation if you have hurt my sister."

"Relax, she's in housewares. Stop stalling. If you don't reveal to me the answers to my questions, I swear I will kill you and turn your sister into a rabbit."

"Okay, that seems like an odd choice but lately I am trying to respect creativity in all its myriad forms." Pythia pulled to no avail. Hera's grip was iron.

"Oracle, I must know my future."

"Hera, the future is an array of infinite possibilities. Nobody knows the future, not even me, not even when I was at the height of my power. The best we can do is catch is a glimpse of possibilities.

"You have the stink of Apollo on you," Hera spat, shaking Pythia until her teeth rattled. "Stop wasting time. Tell me what I need to know."

"Ouch, all right, I will try, Hera, but I cannot promise anything. I really am telling you the truth.

"Now, Oracle, or else."

"All right. Come, we must do this properly. I need some things. We have to go upstairs to the food court."

"Don't think you can escape from me, little Oracle."

"I would not dream of it, Hera. Please, just come this way. Here is the escalator. Okay, here we go, step."

Pythia led Hera onto the escalator. Hera leaned close and put her lips next to Pythia's ear. "You *will* comply, Oracle, or I *will* kill you."

Pythia rolled her eyes. "Hera, people would like you better if you a little less rude. Watch your step, you crazy old goddess."

At the top of the escalator, Pythia looked around. The food court was a chaotic mass of humanity. Most of the tables were occupied by frazzled parents and screaming children intent on eating large amounts of unhealthy food as fast as possible.

"What now, Oracle?" growled Hera.

Pythia scanned the food vendors. Pizza, Chow Mein, burritos, salad . . . soon she saw what she sought. "There. That one. Do you have any money on you?"

"Money? No, I don't have any money. For what would I need money?"

"I need you to go over to that ice cream place and buy a canister of whipped cream. I would do it, but you are the supplicant. It will not work if I do it."

"Oracle. I am a goddess. Behold." Hera waved her black wand and a canister of whipped cream appeared in her hand. "What do you plan to do with this?"

Pythia approached a man in a red baseball cap sitting alone at a pub-style table. "Excuse me, may I borrow this chair for a minute? I will bring it right back."

"Certainly, doll," the man said, looking up from his comic book. He caught sight of Hera and his face lit up. "Whoa, who's your gorgeous friend?"

"You can ask her yourself in just a minute," Pythia said. She dragged the tall chair to a clear area away from other diners. Hitching up her skirt, she settled onto the chair with her sandals tucked behind the bottom rung. "All right. Give me that thing."

Hera handed her the can of whipped cream. Pythia took off the lid and dispenser and held the can upright. She pressed the nozzle and inhaled the nitrous oxide gas that began to escape.

"Uh, hey, dollface . . . ?" the man said, waving his comic book.

"Be silent, or I will destroy you," Hera said. The air around her had begun to shimmer. Children stared as her hair began to lift and float around her head.

"Hey, don't have a cow, darlin'," the man said. "Wow, I like your style."

Pythia giggled. She couldn't help it. *Don't have a cow. Cows are Hera's symbol.*

She continued to inhale the gas. *Before I lose control completely, I had better get on with this. How does it go, again? Oh, yes.*

Pythia tossed the can on the floor and adopted the traditional Oracle pose, arms outstretched in front of her at head height, fingers taut, palms slightly cupped to capture images that might emerge. She raised her voice, trying not to laugh, and spoke the words.

"Hear me. I am the Pythia, former Oracle of Delphi, acolyte of the Lord God Apollo, once the most powerful Oracle in Greece."

"Oracle, speak not of Apollo!" Hera growled.

Nearby parents grabbed their astonished children, pizzas slices and burgers suspended mid-bite, and moved back. Other diners remained seated, looking on with interest.

"Silence!" Pythia commanded. "Petitioner! What is your question?"

Hera winced and looked around with embarrassment. She'd drawn a bit of a crowd. She grimaced and took a deep breath. Finally, she cleared her throat. "Oracle," she muttered, "I come before you as a supplicant according to the customs of our ancient tradition."

"Speak up, Petitioner. I cannot hear you," Pythia said, giggling.

Hera growled. "I *said*, according to the customs of our ancient tradition, Oracle, I beseech you to look into my future and tell me the truth." She paused and took a deep breath. "Oracle, my question is this: Does he still love me?"

December 27, 2015

Blog Readers, this may be my final blogpost. I am thrilled to report, my prayers have been answered. I have been reunited with my Lord God Apollo. I am in a strange state of ecstasy and shock. I can hardly type.

Let me tell you what happened.

I met my sister at the mall yesterday. Hera showed up while we were shopping for shoes. You remember Hera, wife of Zeus, stepmother of Apollo? I knew she would not just go away after the battle with Apollo at the television show, but I was hoping she would calm down a bit, perhaps find her way back to Mt. Olympus and rest for a while. Sadly for us mortals, goddesses—and gods—but in this case, one particularly codependent goddess with a personality disorder—typically hold grudges. Hera would not let it go.

She found us in the shoe department and demanded I reveal her future! I tried to tell her my gift was anemic at best. Despite being the cause of my depleted state, she threatened me and caused my sister to dematerialize.

So I agreed to do a reading for her, of course. What could I do? I wanted her to receive the answer she sought and then go away. I thought she would ask me about world domination, would she always be beautiful, would she be invited to Fashion Week, would she be queen forever, that sort of thing. Of course, I was prepared to tell her, no, I am sorry, you will be the queen of nothing, because, you know, global warming. No more Fashion Week because—no more climate! I was definitely not expecting the question she asked.

She asked her question (no need to invade her privacy by repeating it here) and at that point, Blog Readers, the lights went out in the food court.

I thought perhaps Dione had managed to create a diversion.

I should have realized what was happening, but I admit, after almost three thousand years, my mind has slowed somewhat. I did not catch on until I saw sparks start to fly around Hera. In my defense, I was higher than Mt. Parnassus on nitrous oxide, laughing uncontrollably.

Of course, it was Apollo, swooping in like an avenging warrior. He stood easily twelve feet tall, as golden and glowing as brightly as I had ever seen him. At the television show battle with Hera, he had seemed old and tired. I admit, I felt concern for his well-being. That battle left him wounded and weary.

Not this time!

At the mall, he was as beautiful as I remembered. Except for a longish golden beard, everything about him was the same. Same flashing eyes and full lips, same smooth golden skin. He wore a short tunic, which displayed muscular thighs (but never anything more, somehow), and his enormous feet were bare.

He floated down, or flew down from a skylight, or something. I was not in the best shape and thus missed some details, to be honest. He might have materialized from thin air, the way Hera does. The tears streaming from my eyes blurred my vision somewhat.

Hera saw him coming and expanded her size to match his, sending tables and chairs flying as she prepared to fight.

Apollo didn't give her a chance to get started with the fireball thing. He flew at Hera and grabbed her arms.

"Hera, this is it. Last chance. You've had your three wishes and then some. This will not stand."

That voice! After so many centuries, I cannot tell you how wonderful it was to hear that strong confident voice once again. I felt my soul open.

"You pathetic cretin, you're just like your father!" Hera screeched, struggling to break his grip. She is very strong. I got the feeling he could have crushed her bones, but he held her like she was a baby bird, with care. "Let me go!"

"Hera. Hera," he said in a soothing voice. "Stop this. Please."

"You treat me like I'm nothing! I who used to be the most beautiful, the most powerful queen in all the land!" she sobbed.

"I know, and you still are, Hera. But this has got to stop."

"I will destroy you! You should never have been born." She squirmed in his grasp, wailing. "Where are you getting your power?"

"I'll give you one guess," Apollo said.

"No, no, it can't be," Hera wept. "Why can't he fight me himself? Why does he hide behind his bastard offspring? Let him confront me!"

"Hera. Hera. Mom."

Hera stopped struggling and stared at Apollo. "What did you call me?"

"Mom. You're my stepmother, aren't you? Come on, Hera, we're family." Apollo enfolded Hera in his powerful embrace. At last, I thought, an end to the vendetta. Finally, we can all relax.

I was rocking on my chair, trying to hold in my laughter and keep from falling. Suddenly I felt warm hands propping me up. Dione had returned.

"I found you a purse," Dione whispered and opened a Macy's bag to show me a beautiful royal blue leather shoulder bag. "What the hell is going on? Whoa, is that Apollo?"

I nodded, giggling.

"Wow, what a stud. Hey, what's wrong with you? Are you drunk?"

I pointed to the whipped cream canister on the floor, laughing too hard to speak. I leaned against Dione, gasping and holding my stomach as we watched the final scene unfold.

Apollo patted Hera's back. "He misses you, Hera," he said. "He loves you still."

I could see Hera wanted to believe. Then I could see her face harden. She was probably remembering a certain incident in a cave. She put her head back, took a huge breath, and let loose a gut-wrenching anguished howl that sent diners scrambling.

"Too late!" she screamed. She got one hand loose and jabbed a black claw toward Apollo's eyes. He jerked his head back just in time.

Apollo snapped his fingers at Dione. "Alright, that does it. Give me that bag, would you?"

I believe it was the first time Dione had actually been addressed by the god she supposedly served all those years ago, so it is not surprising she was a bit slow off the mark.

"Come on, Dione, make yourself useful." Apollo pointed at my new blue bag.

"You aren't getting this bag, golden dude!" Dione said. "This is for Pythia." She grabbed a stained paper sack off a nearby table. The sack reeked of greasy hamburger and French fries. "Here, use this." She handed it to the god Apollo.

Somehow he stuffed Hera into that bag. I do not know how he did it, Blog Readers, but as I said, I was not fully functional at the time.

In fact, I do not remember much of what happened after that. I had intended to prostrate myself before him, as a good acolyte would, and beg his forgiveness for forsaking him, but instead, I ended up on the floor, holding my aching belly as I rolled with laughter. I was barely aware of strong arms lifting me like I weighed nothing. I smelled heather and sweet wheat grass and sunshine. I smelled home.

I guess he carried me out to Dione's limousine, which was parked outside the food court in the VIP parking zone, and that is how my sister and I found out Arnie was actually Apollo.

Chapter 19

"Thank you for meeting me today," Pythia stammered. She sat across from Arnie at Niko's coffee shop, hardly able to think. She felt her vision going black.

"It's my pleasure, Pythia," Arnie smiled. "Relax. Seriously, Pythia, breathe!"

Pythia gasped and felt her heart settle a little. "It is hard to know how to think of you now," she said. She stared into her coffee cup, afraid to meet Arnie's eyes. The eyes she'd come to know as Arnie's were superimposed over the eyes of the god she'd worshiped, sought, hated, and loved for almost three thousand years.

Arnie slurped his brew with gusto and nodded with appreciation to Niko, who gave him a thumbs-up and a big grin. "He makes the best coffee. I wonder if I could get him to open a franchise on Mt. Olympus?"

"Should I kneel whenever I see you? Should I call you My Lord? I do not know what to do. Tell me what you desire."

Arnie set his cup on the saucer and contemplated Pythia with kind eyes.

"Most faithful of Oracles. Dearest of friends. After almost three thousand years, you've earned the right to make your own choice. Treat me as you wish. I do not require any special obeisance from you or from anyone. However, do me a favor, please don't kneel. People will think you need medical attention. How would we explain?"

Pythia laughed and wiped away a tear. "I wondered why I always felt so safe with you."

"I've been with you everywhere, Pythia—as much as I could, anyway, given your sister and Hera. You were my voice, my most beloved Oracle. I would never abandon you."

"I thought you were dead." Pythia studied a framed photo of a Greek ruin hanging on the wall above the table.

"Sorrow and pride conspired to build a strong fortress in your mind. Time etched your heart with despair. Even so, you never gave up."

"I almost did, My Lord. I renounced you and renounced my soul. I chased you even as I kept you at arm's length. I did not want to admit my powerlessness. I lost my self. And then my sister returned! What a mess that turned out to be."

"Hera was the instigator. Your sister was merely a human pawn."

"Was I not a human pawn as well?"

Apollo grinned and shrugged. "Maybe. At first. You have to understand, those were different days. Different rules."

They sipped coffee in silence. Condensation misted the window. Arnie's orange pickup was parked behind her Honda Insight across Washington Blvd. Tires swished on wet pavement, which glistened briefly as sun peeked between gray clouds.

Pythia sighed. "What happens now?"

"What do you desire, Pythia?"

Pythia shrugged. "What I have always desired. To serve. To be useful."

"You've had a life of service," Arnie said.

Pythia nodded. "I am exhausted, truth be told," she said.

Arnie looked at her over the rim of his coffee cup. "You could come home with me. Leave this earth."

"Die, you mean." *What would it be like to cease to exist?*

"Yes, if you want to put it that way. I think of it as living forever."

"But not on this earth."

"No." *What about Lena? And the Mystics? What about my tenants? Could I abandon my friends?*

"What if I want to stay?"

Arnie nodded. "Then you would live out your mortal lifespan like any mortal, growing old, until the final death claims you."

"What comes after the final death?"

"I can't say, Pythia."

"Do you know? Or you just cannot tell me?"

Pythia studied Arnie's face and saw only love and concern as he said, "I don't know, my Oracle. Truly, I am a minor Olympian at best. Can you not see what comes after death? Your foresight was always better than mine."

Being reminded of her gift opened up vistas Pythia had not seen before. She started to see some intriguing paths. "What becomes of Dione?"

"Hera has agreed to make the same offer: Retire to Mt. Olympus and live forever there or stay on earth and live out her mortal lifespan."

"What has Dione chosen?" *Can I imagine living without her, now that I have found her?*

"You'll have to ask your sister."

Pythia sighed. "And what about you, my Lord Apollo? If I stay here on earth, will you be here with me?"

Arnie looked at the photo on the wall. "Only in your heart and your memory, Pythia. My agreement with Hera is that she and I both retire to Heaven. We will no longer interfere in the doings of mortal men."

"Oh, dear," Pythia smiled. "What about the Church of Apollo? Rodney will be devastated.

"He'll always be a fan," Arnie grinned. "After I set that statue glowing, he'll never look at another god."

After a long moment, Pythia said, "And me, will I find a new god?"

Arnie smiled. "Pythia, you should know by now, the world of humans is full of gods. And goddesses. Take your pick, try one out. Choose several. Make up one of your own. Or choose none, it doesn't matter."

Pythia's heart swelled. "How could any other god measure up to you?" she said.

For a moment, Arnie seemed to expand in his chair. "My Oracle, I was once a beloved and powerful son of Zeus." A faint golden light began to shine around his head. Then he sat back and the light faded. Arnie sighed. "Now it's a new age. My power has waned, and my time on Earth is done."

"Apollo, tell me, is there no meaning or purpose to life?"

Arnie lifted his shoulders. "Just what you give it, Pythia. Day to day, you create your own meaning and purpose."

Pythia scowled into her coffee cup. "It was easier when I had you to blame for everything."

Arnie grinned and reached across the table to enfold her hands in his. "You can still blame me if it makes you feel better. But I think you know that isn't the answer."

Pythia basked in his touch and felt a measure of serenity displacing her anxiety. After a long peaceful moment, he released her hands, smiling. She smiled back.

"Dione is still furious that you were her driver."

"I'm going to miss driving that car," Arnie said. "But seriously, you've always been strong, Pythia. Don't you realize? Your strength is in your desire to help others. The Oracle's power was strong in you from the beginning because you used it to serve. Even after Hera tried to extinguish your gift, you still used what was left to try to make people's lives better. You were my last Oracle, and without a doubt, my best."

Pythia's coffee was down to the dregs. "I will miss you. Will I ever see you again?"

"If there is a Heaven."

"You do not know?"

"Pythia, cut me some slack. I know it might be hard for an Oracle to accept this idea, but it's possible some things we aren't meant to know ahead of our time. Sometimes we have to wait and find out."

"As if we were mortal."

"Yes, my beloved Oracle. As if we were mortal."

A few minutes later, they bade farewell to Niko and walked out to their cars.

Pythia said, "There is something I have wondered."

Arnie paused by her car. "What is that, my friend?"

"I have wondered how Rodney knew I was your Oracle. He somehow knew I was posting as Delphina. He knew me at the Church. He came to the Arcade to warn me about my sister. Is it possible he is a natural Oracle himself?"

"Possible, but unlikely," Arnie grinned. "I sent him an email."

January 10, 2016

Happy new year, my faithful Blog Readers. Here is a question for you: What do you want in a higher power? Have you ever asked yourself that question? While I try to decide if I want to live or die, I took some time today to make a list.

To be worthy of my reverence, I expect certain characteristics in a higher power—namely, unconditional love, trustworthiness, compassion, optimism, competence, and the usual omniscience and omnipotence. In addition, if possible, I would prefer a higher power who can hold an interesting conversation, who shows up on time, who can deliver a joke (but not at anyone else's expense, including my own), and who has a self-expressive fashion sense. By that I mean, please, no long pastel robes or boring wool suits.

Ultimately, a higher power has to pass the same two-question test we give to family and close friends, whether we realize we are doing it or not. There are only two questions worth asking:

Can I trust you?

And will you love me?

I await your comments with anticipation.

—Yours with love, Delphina, Oracle of the Lord God Apollo

~

"I still can't wrap my head around the fact that Arnie is Apollo. My chauffeur!" Divina shook her head in disbelief. She poured a dollop of ketchup on her hash browns. "I should be furious. All this time, he had eyes inside the operation! That sneak."

Norm's was nearly empty on a weekday morning. If any other diners recognized Divina Dee, Pythia hoped they were politely waiting until Divina had finished her breakfast. *Fame is fleeting.* Maybe Divina Dee's celebrity status had faded since the TV show was cancelled.

"He fooled me, too. I knew Arnie as the DJ at the radio station," Pythia said. "Then on the day you made yourself known to me at the park, I found out he was driving your fancy car. I thought nothing of it until he gave me the amulet for protection. He never told me it was to protect me from Hera. I had no idea he was Apollo."

"That thing was so weird." Divina twirled her fork in the ketchup. "Do you still have it?"

"No, I gave it back so he could return it to its maker."

"Hera told me Hephaestus forged it. She said he's an old fat dude who lies around listening to records. Can you believe it? Actual vinyl records. These gods and goddesses are such relics."

Pythia pondered her hash browns. "Arnie mentioned his friend had excellent taste in music. That must have been Hephaestus. Arnie traded some of his best collectibles to borrow that amulet. It is odd imagining them listening to records on Mt. Olympus."

"Hera was pissed that she couldn't figure out how to use it. You should have seen her, bashing around in my kitchen. She left crow shit everywhere."

"My luck. Do you want my bacon?"

Divina scooped up Pythia's bacon with her fingers. "Speaking of the old cow, I had coffee with her a few days ago. She's on probation or something."

"Did she get back together with Zeus?" Pythia poured maple syrup on a short stack of pancakes.

"Don't know. We met at a Denny's in Sherman Oaks. I think we were supervised by a goddess. I didn't recognize her, it might have been Artemis."

"Apollo's sister? How do you know it was Artemis?"

"She looked like a tough biker chick. A really cute tough biker chick."

They ate in silence for a few minutes.

Pythia set down her fork. "As you no doubt have heard, I met with Apollo."

"Yeah, Hera said. Did he give you the offer?" Divina refilled their coffee cups.

"The offer as I understand it is to retire to Mt. Olympus and live there forever or stay on earth and live out my mortal life-span."

Divina nodded. "That is what Hera told me as well. Did you decide?"

Pythia gazed at her sister. "If I chose Heaven, my sister, it would be because that is where you are."

Divina cocked her head. "Not because of Apollo? Your lord and master? The old goat, does he still own you?"

"My sister, wherever you are, that is home for me."

"Even after what I did to you? Even after Hera tried to kill you?"

"My sister, you are my heart and soul. If you had asked, I would have died willingly in your arms to make you happy. You had only to ask."

Divina shook her head in amazement. "You are really the stupidest creature ever made by the gods."

"Stay or go, my darling sister. Your choice. I will gladly let you choose my fate."

Divina grinned. "Very well. You asked for it, you crazy Oracle."

"Happy new year, everyone!" Lena said as the Mystics arrived for the first show of 2016. "What a crazy year, huh? I imagine 2016 will be even more interesting. Today our topic will be new year's resolutions. What else, right? Before we start the show, let's share our own resolutions."

Pythia sat in her seat by the wall thinking about the nature of change. She sensed her body was changing. She felt different. Her second sight seemed to be intact, but her body felt odd, or maybe she was inhabiting it in a new way. Her skin tingled. *I can feel my hair growing out of my head. I sense my fingernails changing. My cells are dividing. My neurons are firing. I am aware that I am made of flesh, blood, and bone. Apollo has rendered me human.*

"Pythia, you start." Lena interrupted her personal inventory. "What is your resolution for 2016?"

"I would say this year I hope to enjoy and appreciate good health, family, and friends. In addition, I plan to reflect on a new concept for me: the idea that each day could be my last."

Sylvia clapped her hands. "That's a morbid yet strangely wonderful intention, Pythia. What about you and that DJ across the hall? Got any plans?"

"I saw they have a new DJ," Mary said.

"Yes, Arnie told me he is retiring," Pythia said. "Last week was his final show. He has moved to Costa Rica. We will keep in touch, I think."

"Oh, good! I hope you don't let him get away. You two make a cute couple," Sylvia said. "I have a resolution to report. Doug and I are hoping to start a family! I'm a little too old for birthing a baby, but we decided we are not too old for parenthood. We are going to adopt!"

"Fabulous!" Lena said. "A little glitter baby! Mary, how about you?"

Mary looked a little embarrassed. "Nothing exciting, not compared to starting a family, anyway. I'm going to quit this soul-sucking teaching job you know I've hated for a long time and start writing cozy mysteries. I've always wanted to be a writer. I'm going to focus on giving astrology readings and writing."

"Yay, no more grading papers," Lena laughed. "Moon, do you want to share your new year's intention?"

"Well, I want you guys to be the first to hear it from me, and this is not for our radio audience. I have decided to come out. You guys, I am a lesbian. I'm gay! Queer. Whatever people call it these days. I have a girlfriend. Her name is Maria. There. I said it. I hope this won't change my friendship with you guys, but if it does, so be it."

"Thank you for your courage, Moon!" Lena said, clasping her hands over her heart. "We love you! I'll speak for myself, I love you, and I'm so glad you love us enough to let us know about this part of your life. Thank you!"

"Oh, and Riley is graduating from high school. A little late, but better late than never. You are all invited to his graduation ceremony and party!"

"Wonderful. Thank you, everyone!" Lena beamed at the Mystics.

"What about you, Lena?" Pythia asked.

Lena sagged a little, then took a deep audible breath. "My intention is to give my mother the best quality of life I can and to enjoy her and love her now, as she is, for as long as she lives. I hope we have lots of time left together, but the doctors say her dementia is progressing fast. We are taking each day as it comes. Meanwhile, I'm learning the subtle nuances of Bingo!"

The Mystics laughed and applauded in appreciation.

Lena wiped her eyes. "Happy new year, Mystics! I love you all. Are you ready? Let's start the show!"

For the first time since coming to the A.A. meeting, Pythia sat in the front row next to Lena. When it was sharing time, Lena nudged Pythia and motioned with her head. "Now or never, my friend," she said. "Well, not never. There's always next week. Still, no time like the present. Best to come clean. You can do this."

Pythia ascended to the podium, heart pounding, and stood at the lectern. She surveyed the group, noting some surprised faces. She took a deep breath.

"My name is Pythia, and I am an addict."

"Hi, Pythia!" the group responded.

"Some of you know that I have been coming to this meeting for quite a few years. I have never shared before. I have not had the courage to admit to you what I am. I am an Oracle. What I am is not really important. What it means is that I am addicted to breathing geothermal gas fumes that emanate from the earth."

The group was silent as members furrowed skeptical brows. They all had lots of experience sipping alcohol from bottles, cans, and glasses of every sort. Some had imbibed shaving lotion, cough syrup, and rubbing alcohol. They were struggling to imagine what huffing geothermal gas fumes from the ground would look and feel like.

"I know it is a bit hard to picture. I have been working the Steps on this problem, and I believe I understand what I am powerless over. I am powerless over the gas—it can be in the form of tar, asphalt, gasoline, diesel, sulfur, helium, nitrous oxide—just about any type of gas that comes out of the ground or out of a can or bottle. I know it sounds insane.

"You might believe I do not belong at an A.A. meeting, and I would respect your belief. I supposed I could try to find some other substance-abuse program. However, this is an open meeting, and I need what only you offer—a spiritual solution to a life-threatening compulsion. We may not be addicted to the same substance, but nobody outside these rooms understands compulsion and addiction like we do. There is no place on the planet where I can go for relief, except here."

Pythia glanced at Lena. Lena gave her a big smile and put her hand over her heart.

"I am sorry for being such a slow learner. My compulsion is definitely baffling and powerful, and my drug of choice is unusual, to say the least.

A voice muttered, "Is it odd, or is it God?"

"Bill, shush," someone said. "Let the lady talk."

"You shush," said Bill in an irritated voice.

Some people snickered. Pythia smiled. "I have had this compulsion to breathe in geothermal gas almost my entire life, and I am much older than I look. Breathing this stuff has caused me to suffer mind-altering hallucinations, leading to many problems. My life has definitely been made unmanageable because of this compulsion."

Pythia scanned the audience. *Is Apollo here? I do not see him. Does he know I am finally telling the truth?*

"The main purpose of my addiction has been to give me a false sense of power over uncertainty. I have been terrified of the unknown future, and with the drug, I can see things sometimes before they happen. Knowing what is coming is highly addictive. Living with uncertainty is utterly terrifying.

"I know I must accept that life is uncertain, and I believe that accepting life's uncertainty is an invitation to embrace the spiritual way of life promised in the Twelve Steps. I am grateful for what I have learned here, and if it is acceptable to the group, I would like to keep coming back."

Pythia resumed her seat to a round of good-natured applause and a few whistles.

Lena grabbed her hand and gave it a squeeze. Through that contact, Pythia was able to see that soon Lena would be cast as a regular on a popular television show. She would have the money to hire a caregiver for her mother. At last, her friend's dream of making a real living as an actor would come true. *At last, it has happened—the blessed intersection of talent, persistence, and luck . . . mostly luck. The secret to success really is to not give up.*

Chapter 20

Pythia stood in the basement of her office building watching three workers in white denim overalls scrape the concrete walls with wire brushes. They had set up brilliant lights on tripods, illuminating every crack in the floor and walls. The basement seemed much smaller when every corner was visible.

Bob, the contractor, took off his baseball cap and wiped sweat from his forehead with the back of a dirty hand. "We'll scrape and patch. Then we'll put on another layer of concrete and seal it. That should prevent any leaks."

Pythia nodded.

One of the workers yelled from the alcove. "Hey, what should we do with this table and stuff? There's an old painting here."

"Oh, that is mine," Pythia said, rescuing the painting and the clay bowl of pebbles. "The table and the candles can go into the dumpster."

"The stool too?"

"Yes, the stool can go."

"What about all those old file boxes by the stairs?"

"Those can go as well."

"Yeah, I'm sure all that paper is moldy as hell. I can't believe anyone spent time down here. The mold alone is enough to cause major health problems," Bob said. "And all the methane coming up through the floor, wow. When we are done, you should not smell a thing down here."

"Thank you," Pythia said. "That is my hope."

"You are lucky this place didn't catch fire," Bob said. "This whole block would have blown sky high."

"I am indeed fortunate."

Pythia left the workers to their work and carried the painting upstairs to her newly remodeled apartment. With Debra's input, she had chosen a pale green and yellow palette. The small apartment had been transformed into a serene and relaxing oasis. A small white table under a window served as an altar. She placed the offering bowl on the table and leaned the painting against the freshly painted wall as the backdrop. She gazed with love on the handsome face. Tall ceramic vases of fresh lavender and rosemary scented the air.

January 31, 2016

Happy new year, faithful Blog Readers. You may remember, I was considering the idea of abandoning this blog. I thought perhaps once I was reunited with my Lord God Apollo, I would not feel the need to document my search for my lost faith. However, I have made the decision not to accompany him to Mt. Olympus. Are you surprised, after all my histrionics? I am sad, but I believe I have made the correct decision. I was not ready to give up my human life. Like any human, I want to see how my story ends.

I expect my life going forward will consist of mundane trivial occurrences, much like your own. Excuse me. I mean, as mundane as any human life, because that is now what I can anticipate—a human life, with a human lifespan and eventual final death. I hope death does not come soon, for I am rather enjoying the experience of feeling fully human; however, I cannot foresee my own demise.

In the interim—meaning until my death arrives, I've decided to continue blogging. I may not have much to write about in the future, but it sounds as if some of you would be disappointed if I stopped. Thank you for your support.

Some of you have wondered what I will do now that I've closed my business. I appreciate your concern. I am not sure yet. The future offers so many possibilities. Any path I choose looks interesting. For now, I plan to continue my part-time serving job and do some spiritual consulting at local fairs with my friends. I think I might have an affinity for predicting paint colors and baby name trends. I am open to suggestions.

Some of you have expressed skepticism that I will be able to stop inhaling methane gas. To be honest, Blog Readers, I am not certain how I feel about giving up my addiction. Will I miss my visits to the basement? It is a little like an alcoholic who thinks she is free from temptation simply because she no longer stocks her pantry with gin. I can find noxious methane inhalants everywhere in the twenty-first century. This modern age does not lack for petroleum distillates and solvents. If I wanted to get high, all I would have to do is trade my electric automobile for a car that requires me to pump gasoline.

I suppose this is why at the A.A. meeting, they say "keep coming back."

Some of you will be happy to hear I am beginning to socialize. I have been part of a group of women for some time but I have tended to keep my emotional distance, considering my difficult-to-explain position as an ancient Oracle. My sponsor L has encouraged me to work at building friendships. With that aim in mind, I attended a ceremony to mark a young man's high school graduation. Having never attended high school, or any school for that matter (other than as an acolyte in Apollo's temple), I was unaware of the magnitude of such a milestone. Attending the ceremony was eye-opening. I felt renewed and refreshed to see so many hopeful futures. The young graduate was the son of one of my friends; it was heartwarming to see how proud she was of his accomplishment. I had a brief moment of prescience during the ceremony and saw the young man would soon be attending our A.A. meeting. It is never too late, or too soon, to stop trying to self-destruct.

Blog Readers, as always, a new year brings opportunities and challenges. In the spirit of the season, let me offer you some guidance to ease your way into the new year.

GrandMaster25, I predict you will have an energetic and satisfying experience this year serving as a precinct volunteer. Please leave your gun at home.

Sheryl69, do not give up on the Cubs. This will be your year to celebrate.

Rosie666, your sister is waiting for your call, and she does not have a lot of time left. Please call her as soon as you can.

Here is a special note to GodsChosen: Thank you for the invitation to the Church of Apollo. I attended a service there last year, if you remember, which I found helpful and enlightening. I wish you and your mother a safe trip to Oregon. I predict you will find a warm welcome among fellow believers in the Portland neighborhood called Montavilla. Thank you for everything.

Here is an update on my property situation. My tenants and I have signed documents to create a co-operative venture. Thus, I now have three co-owners of my office building. We have started renovations, as I mentioned. We have memorialized our friend S by sponsoring the installation of a special bench at the La Brea Tar Pits park. Please stop by and enjoy the bench to honor her memory if you are in the area.

In other news, my former assistant has opened her own marketing firm. I knew she would (and not because I am an Oracle). She always wanted to be self-employed. I am glad that she seized her opportunity. Breaking her wrist at the final Psychic to the Stars TV show episode (which I understand will most likely never air on TV) apparently showed her that she was not meant to work for others. That is what she said, anyway. I was happy to sign her plaster cast as I wished her luck in her new venture. I traded her some coaching for some decorating advice. With her help, I finally remodeled my apartment.

I have been spending a lot of time with my sister, Dione. We are working on establishing a new basis for our sisterhood and a solid foundation for our friendship. She did my colors for me, whatever that means. Apparently I am a winter, and we need to go shopping. She spends a lot of time shopping.

She told me she received a postcard from Hera, ostensibly from Miami. I told her I received a postcard from Arnie, supposedly from Costa Rica. We assume they are both enjoying their retirements in Heaven at Mt. Olympus. I miss my friend Arnie and wish him well. I have a renewed spiritual commitment to my Lord God Apollo, and I am considering adding some other higher powers to my pantheon of gods. Now that I am human, I need all the spiritual help I can get. I think I will start on a memoir. That should keep me occupied for a while.

Happy new year to all. I await your comments.

—Yours in recovery, Delphina

"We have a very special guest for our March episode of Mystics Roundtable." Lena's voice vibrated with excitement. "We are so pleased to welcome the former Psychic to the Stars, Divina Dee, to our humble radio show. Welcome, Ms. Dee, we are so thrilled to have you here!"

Divina and Pythia sat shoulder to shoulder in front of one microphone. Pythia sat back in her chair to make room as Divina leaned forward. "Thank you, Lena. Great to see you again. Please call me Divina! I'm excited to be here."

"We are going to do something a little different for today's show. Usually we propose a topic and the listeners ask questions. Today we are going to turn that around. Our topic for today is a question. We want to hear your answers today. Our question is, what is the purpose of living?"

Sylvia groaned. "Oh, Lena!"

Mary laughed. Moon applauded.

"I know, right?" Lena laughed. "Just a small inconsequential question about the meaning and purpose of life. Our Mystics will apply their tools to confirm and understand your answers. I hope this works! Let's see if we get any callers." Lena poked the computer screen. "Yes, looks like we have our first caller. Barry, go ahead, you are on the air."

"Hi, Mystics. I'm calling from my bachelor pad in La Cañada Flintridge. Great topic. Interesting question. I'm a philosophy professor at UCLA. I often ask my students this question. It's quite comical to see them dance around it without actually formulating a response."

"Right," said Lena. "It's not an easy thing to pin down, is it? What would your answer be?"

"My students usually choose one of two responses. On one side, they say the purpose of life is to care about others—to give them the merciful benefit of the doubt. The other camp says the purpose of life is to do the right thing, no matter who gets hurt when applying justice. They never seem to agree on what that so-called right thing is. As you can imagine, our discussions are quite lively."

Mary turned on her microphone. "Barry, when is your birthday?"

"October 10. I won't tell you the year because my students might find out I'm older than they think."

Pythia leaned against her sister's shoulder and sighed with contentment.

"Libra. Right," said Mary. "Represented by the scales. A tendency to linger long over decisions? Does that sound like you?"

Barry laughed. "I don't put a lot of credence in your mystical tools. I'm a practical fellow, for a philosopher."

"So, to get back to the topic, what do you think the purpose of living is, Barry?" Lena said.

"I'd like to think the purpose of life is to have fun," Barry said.

"I'm hearing a 'but' in there, Barry," said Lena.

"It's a 'however', actually. *However*, I wish my students behaved as if the purpose of life were to learn."

Mary laughed. "As a fellow teacher, I can relate!"

Moon held up a piece of paper. "Barry, today the coins presented me with Hexagram 23, which means mountain above, earth below, leading to deterioration. The advised course is to be generous to those in need."

Barry sighed. "In need of what? I have a group of artists in my Intro to Philosophy class. I'm certain they believe the purpose of life is to make art, and someone should pay them to do that. The business majors, on the other hand, probably believe the purpose of life is to make money so they can buy whatever they want."

Sylvia held up the Justice card. "Barry, the tarot card I drew for you today makes sense, given your Zodiac sign. It's the card of Justice."

"Whoa, I'm a philosopher, not a judge," Barry said.

"The Justice card stands for balance and harmony," Sylvia said. "Would that lead you to believe the purpose of life is justice and fairness?"

"Perhaps, if I thought your mystical tools held any value," Barry laughed. "No offense, ladies! I might not be the best caller to answer your question. Maybe you need someone with a more mundane outlook. However, it is the essential question of human existence, so I dialed in, thinking we could solve it together."

"Spoken like a true scholar," Lena said. "Let's ask our guest Mystic, Divina, for her insight."

Divina sat up to the mic. "A few short months ago, I would have said the purpose of living is to get my hands on everything I can, as fast as I can, no matter what. Somewhere along the way, during my long life, I lost sight of other things that make life worth living."

"Things like what, Divina?" Moon asked.

"Well, family, for one," Divina said. The Mystics nodded.

"What do you think, Barry?" Lena asked. "Could family be the purpose for living?"

"Maybe in a tribal sense. We would all probably agree, we need our tribal connections to keep the species alive. On a personal level, as a recently divorced person, I'd say no. Really, I think you could say I'm more of a nihilist than anything else. For those who don't know what that is, a nihilist believes there is no purpose or meaning to existence."

"That sounds like a lonely philosophy, Barry," Lena said.

"Not really. I'm happy not believing in anything. Other than my wife leaving me and my kids avoiding me and my students giving me bad evaluations, I'm really quite happy."

The Mystics looked at each other with raised eyebrows.

"I'm kidding," Barry said. "Actually, my life sucks."

"We are sorry to hear that, Barry," Lena said. "We haven't heard from all our Mystics yet. Let's ask Pythia, our Seer Without Peer, to share her thoughts."

Pythia sat forward, putting her arm around Divina and pulling her close. "Barry, after almost three thousand years, I think I can claim wisdom based on experience as the foundation of my belief. It is not sexy and it is currently not very popular, but every now and then, groups of humans remember this fact and act in accordance with the common good. It is simple. The purpose of living . . . is giving."

Divina looked at her sideways. "Oh, brother."

Pythia laughed. "What, my sister? You do not believe me?"

"We've been fighting over this question since we were children," Divina said.

"My position has not changed," Pythia said.

"And you are still such a sap!" Divina said with affection.

"Divina, when is your birthday?" Mary asked.

"I don't know, really. Pythia, do you know my birthday?"

"No, not precisely. My best guess is around 820. B-C-E, that is."

"What? I don't understand," Mary said.

"Oh, never mind. It doesn't matter. Old, we are really, really old." Divina laughed. "Hey, have we lost Barry?"

"No, I'm still here," Barry said. "I'm enjoying your conversation. Lena, are you free to meet me for coffee one day this week?"

"We'll have to see what the future holds, Barry," Lena laughed. "Any final predictions for Barry, or for any of us, Pythia, our beloved Seer?"

Pythia leaned against her sister. "My advice is to hang onto your hats, as the saying goes. I predict 2016 is going to be a year to remember."

Acknowledgments

First, apologies to all Greek scholars everywhere. Odds are, this isn't your kind of book, but if you do happen to read it, I fear you will cringe at the liberties I've taken with Greek history and culture. I took what I found useful and ignored the rest, which is not the scholarly method but it works for the fiction writer. I admit to twisting facts and myths to fit my story. I recommend you just go with it.

Second, all the characters in this story are fictitious. Some of the places exist, or used to exist, but don't go looking for Pythia's coaching office on Wilshire Blvd. Do go visit the La Brea Tar Pits, though. Maybe you will have some interesting visions of your own.

Finally, I offer thanks to my friends and family for their encouragement of my writing life. I don't know where it is going, but I'm enjoying the journey.

Tucson, Arizona
2021

Crossline Press is an imprint of Carol M. Booton, Ph.D. Yes, I am self-published author and owner of an independent small press. I designed this book using Microsoft Word. The font is Garamond. Email me at carol@carolbooton.com if you have questions. Please consider leaving a review on Amazon.

Dedicated to Mom, Meme, Eddie, and Karen.